GOLDEN
NOTES

SAMUEL
JOECKEL

For Tory

PART ONE

"They are all of one mind, their hearts are set upon song and their spirit is free from care. He is happy whom the Muses love. For though a man has sorrow and grief in his soul, yet when the servant of the Muses sings, at once he forgets his dark thoughts and remembers not his troubles. Such is the holy gift of the Muses to men."

—Hesiod, *Theogeny*

"You don't become a rock star unless you've got something missing somewhere, that is obvious to me."

—Bono

1980-1981

ONE

January 1980

B Y THE TIME Cali Sky Braithwaite was fourteen years old, rock and roll was in its mid-twenties. For years, it honored its blues roots. But then some blended it with folk, others injected it with psychedelia, a few with glam, some with opera, and still others with country. Rock and roll had successfully negotiated numerous intersections and crossroads. But by the end of the 1970s those intersections and crossroads multiplied so quickly that rock and roll no longer seemed to be a musical monolith. The classification, "Rock and Roll," could no longer contain subdivisions. The spawn had devoured the mother.

The end of the decade encountered a new intersection with the demise of a rock and roll giant. In 1979 Led Zeppelin released their final album of new material, *In Through the Out Door*. The band would break up the following year with the death of drummer John Bonham. The heavy use of synthesizers on this album, especially on tracks like "In the Evening" and "All of My Love," helped paved the way for New Wave, which turned a corner in rock and roll history by placing at its musical center an instrument other than a distorted electric guitar. And of course, Punk reared its pissed-off head during the latter half of the 1970s, flipping the musical bird to everything and everyone from the hippie movement and Pink Floyd to guitar solos and the Queen of England—all within the span of a song that generally did not last more than two minutes.

These new movements in music crawled from the sludge of pubs and clubs in London, New York City, and San Francisco. But nowhere did the buzz spread so palpably as it did in southern California. Numerous record companies based their operations in Hollywood. World-famous venues, where any act that wanted to make it big simply *had* to play, lined Sunset Strip. Famous musicians found the Golden State cool and funky enough to call it home. The place was a part of rock-and-roll lore: bands like Zeppelin, the Doors, and the Mamas and the Papas wrote songs about it.

The Beach Boys immortalized California beach culture. An LA radio station called KROQ spread across the airwaves new songs from cutting-edge bands, unknown groups who would not be unknown for long.

In the winter of 1980 Cali Sky knew little of these phenomena. Despite living near the epicenter of the buzz, she had quietly developed her prodigious musical talent in isolation from the flourishing music scene that was spilling out into the very streets of her own neighborhood.

Five years earlier, the Braithwaite family had settled into one of the unassuming housing developments absorbed into the expanse of seamless civilization that is the lower-rent valley of Orange County, a vast network of houses, highways and strip malls. They had moved into a small home too far to the east to catch the ocean-breeze presence of the Pacific, too far to the west to sense the boundary-closing security of the San Gabriel Mountains. Standing in their front yard, the uninitiated would have no idea that the world's largest ocean lies just beyond the horizon in one direction and a 10,000-foot mountain looms just beyond the smog in the other.

At the age of eight, however, Cali Sky's universe could be measured in feet. Their new house was an unexplored world. And so she was the first to burst through the front door on move-in day, her thick black hair, unkempt as usual, swaying stiffly against her back. Wide eyed and curious, too excited to simply walk, she ran, jumped, pounced, sprang and skipped around the house, humming an erratic melody. She paused, however, when she entered the bedroom that she took to be her own.

The sound of her last hummed note echoed in the small room. Though empty, the space bore signs of the previous owners: spot-stained carpeting, scuffed walls, and nicked baseboards. The morning sun filtered through a dirty window. Cali Sky bounded in and as she surveyed the room, something caught her eye. The house was not empty. Propped in the corner of the tiny closet stood an acoustic guitar. The body of the instrument was light brown. Its pick guard was pine green and tear shaped, giving the impression that the guitar was weeping from its sound hole. Cali Sky approached slowly and cautiously. She stopped at the threshold of the closet and became acutely aware that she was alone. Her parents were still outside, laying out a strategy for the soon-to-arrive moving crew. Their voices sounded distant and dreamlike.

When she stepped into the closet, she found that the guitar was nearly as tall as she was. She reached out her hand and fingered the edge of the guitar body, tracing its gradual curves and feeling its smooth surface. Then she brushed her right thumb across the low E string. Although the contact between flesh and instrument was slight, Cali Sky could hear reverberation in the room from that deep, single note. She smiled. And as it traveled up her face, the smile became most expressive in the eyes, revealing in their blueness not only the joy of surprise, but the promise of possibilities and the thrill of mischief.

Despite her young age, Cali Sky was already a skilled piano player. In fact, her piano teacher called her a prodigy. "I have never seen such natural ability in a child," he had informed her parents, Philip and Joan. "Just look at her fingers. These are the fingers of a musician."

Her parents did not know what to make of this gift. Neither one played an instrument. But they did possess in their house an heirloom, passed down through Philip's family for a couple generations: a mahogany Clarendon upright piano. Philip was told that the piano was made sometime around 1910. It was an instrument of fine craftsmanship. For decades, the piano lay silent until a three-year-old Cali Sky began to bang on the keys. Within a few years, she could make the piano sing.

She loved the piano, but she wanted more. Whenever she asked her parents for a guitar, the answer was always the same: "No. Play the piano. Focus on one instrument." She pleaded. She wept. She even reasoned as well as an eight-year-old could manage. All of her emotional and logical appeals crashed into the same brick wall: "No. Play the piano. Focus on one instrument."

When the Braithwaite family moved into that small house in Orange County, California, Philip and Joan finally let Cali Sky have a guitar. Not because they were worn down by her heart-wrenching hysterics. Not because they were convinced by her preadolescent logic. They let her have a guitar because when they moved into the house, they made the startling discovery that one mysteriously stood propped against the wall in the closet of her bedroom.

Over the course of five years her parents' concessions multiplied.

With each Christmas and birthday, they contributed to her store of instruments, all used, which included another acoustic guitar (this one with an electric pick-up), an electric guitar, an electric bass, two amps, and a wah-wah pedal. They also converted their tiny utility room into a makeshift studio. It was for her friend Brodie's benefit that Cali Sky sat in the studio one Saturday morning, electric guitar on her lap, lowered volume on the amplifier, upon which sat a tape recorder/player. Brodie had heard a song played on KROQ called "Bloodstains." That very day, he added the band's name—Agent Orange—to the doodled art of other band names that adorned his Pee Chee folder. The all-American athletes depicted on the iconic folder seemed oblivious to the menacing names surrounding them. Agent Orange found a tantalizing home near the ankles of the short-skirted female tennis player, fittingly positioned alongside the Sex Pistols and DK, which the teenage cognoscenti knew to be shorthand for the California punk band, the Dead Kennedys. Brodie was popular. Other students at his school dug his surfer-punk haircut, sun-dried curls appearing to be weighted down by sand and ocean salt, his haphazardly layered long-sleeve/short-sleeve shirt combo, his long OP shorts, lace-less Vans, and of course, his identity-proclaiming Pee Chee graffiti. When they got a load of him, they knew they were in the presence of a personality that, run through the inscrutable algorithms of high school popularity, would generate the unmistakable quality of cool.

Brodie had managed to get a bootlegged copy of "Bloodstains" on cassette and had given it to Cali Sky, asking her to teach it to him. She pressed play and listened intently to the hard-driving, opening riff. She cocked her head, bringing her ear closer to the tape player. The sound quality was poor. Nevertheless, after just a few measures, she transcribed the riff into tablature. She was putting the finishing touches on the guitar-solo tab when she heard her dad's voice on the other side of the closed door.

"Cali Sky. I'm taking Cami hiking. Do you want to come?"

She set the guitar down, switched off the amp, and joined her dad in the kitchen, where she helped him make sandwiches for a picnic lunch. Five-year-old Cami bounded into the room, bounced off her dad, tugged on the folds of his beat-up jeans, and began barking commands.

"I want extra jelly on mine! I want extra jelly on mine!"

"Okay. Okay. Not so loud—your mom is asleep.... Cali Sky, will you make Cami's sandwich while I get the drinks?"

Cali Sky pulled out two slices of bread with her left hand, fingertips calloused by guitar strings. She found herself spreading peanut butter in time with the tempo of "Bloodstains" when she felt Cami's moist hand slapping against her leg.

"Cali Sky! I want extra jelly on mine!"

"I know, Cami."

As the orange Ford Bronco settled northbound onto the Newport freeway, Philip asked Cali Sky about the song she was listening to—and then playing—in the studio.

"It's just a song Brodie wants to learn."

Her response was met only by road noise and the sound of Cami humming and mumbling in the backseat. Philip offered a faint smile through his beard and nodded his head. Cali Sky decided to push back a bit against her father's mild reaction.

"It's a song called 'Bloodstains.'" Another subtle smile, this time even fainter. "He heard it on KROQ.... Can we turn it on?"

"No, let's just enjoy the silence for a while."

The Bronco now sped down the Orange Freeway, smog stretching in the distance across the Inland Empire. A half hour later they turned onto Euclid Street, which sliced through suburbia all the way to San Antonio Heights and the San Gabriel Mountains.

"Dad, what did you listen to when you were my age?" Cali Sky had asked this question before. But she wanted to push back some more, test her dad's indomitable tranquility.

"Oh, I listened to what was popular at the time, lots of my dad's music. When he wasn't around, I listened to Elvis."

"He didn't like Elvis?"

"Not at all."

"What about later?" Cali Sky pressed, "like when you were in college?"

"All sorts of stuff. You know, the stuff you can listen to today on the radio."

"The Beatles?"

"Yeah."

"The Rolling Stones?"

"Yeah."

"Led Zeppelin?"

"Yeah." The smile began to peek out of the beard more prominently.

"The Grateful Dead?"

"Yeah."

"Jimi Hendrix?"

"Yeah."

"The Doors?"

"Yeah."

Before she could continue, the smile waned, reconstituted itself as a smirk, and he said, "How do you know all these bands?"

Cali Sky knew she did not have to answer the question. She knew it was shorthand, her father's way of saying, "Okay. That's enough." To remove all doubt and to dispel the tension created by the lingering question, he added with earnest gentleness, "Well, let's not worry about this now. Let's just enjoy the present."

She nodded.

Sometimes Cali Sky played mind tricks on herself, tricks that tweaked her sense of the present. What if she could forget who she was, step outside of time, and look at individual moments of her life? What would she then think about herself? What would she then think would happen next? For instance, once when Cali Sky was learning to shave her legs, she cut the skin near her ankle and bled profusely. The bleeding would not stop. She wondered what she would conclude from her hypothetical perspective of timeless oblivion if she glimpsed that one moment, not knowing what happened before or what would happen after? If all she saw from her perspective-less perspective was unstaunched blood? Or what would she think if she looked down upon herself playing a song called "Bloodstains"?

As they pulled onto a dirt road heading in the direction of Cucamonga Peak, Philip opened the windows. Cali Sky heard the sound of the tires spinning on dirt and gravel. The jolt of rocks passed instantaneously from tire to rim to shock absorber to frame to seat. Giggling hysterically, Cami ricocheted from one end of the bench seat to the other, bouncing on her butt, back, side, and even her head. Philip laughed. As they neared a pass, the road smoothed. The sudden quietness brought to Cali Sky's attention their isolation. When they got out of the truck, Cali Sky's ears rang. The quiet made her feel deaf. It took a while for her ears to adjust to the sound levels: the far-off calls of birds, the drone of insects, but most of all the variety of wind sounds, at times percussive when they met the resistance of rock formations, at other times placid when they rippled through manzanita bushes. Cali Sky closed her eyes and listened to the song. Unlike those she heard on the radio, or those given to her by Brodie, or those her dad did not want to talk about, this one she could not figure out. They set off down a trail that meandered through an oak forest.

Ten minutes into their hike Cami began to complain. "Daddy, bugs are crawling on me!" They stopped and Philip brushed a gnat off of the white flesh of Cami's little knee. He took off the backpack, unzipped it and pulled out the small thermos filled with cold water. He took a small drink, helped Cami take a sip, then passed the thermos to Cali Sky. As she tilted it towards her mouth and felt the ice settle against her lips, Cami said, "Daddy, I want some Gatorade now!"

Cali Sky looked at her dad: unflappable as always, despite Cami's complaints and commands. She watched as he scanned the ridgeline, squinting. For as long as she could remember, her dad had had bad vision, especially in his left eye. She could sense his contentment, here in the elevated hinterlands, above the reach of routine, responsibility, parking lots and punk rock, all of which coalesced into an abstraction that, in his world-weary conversations with Cali Sky, he would identify as "sin." "We live in a fallen world, Cali Sky." This was his lament, though never spoken with bitterness.

After their short water break, Philip asked Cali Sky to wear the backpack so that he could carry Cami on his shoulders. And so they pressed on, the trail now becoming steeper. When they reached the first switchback Cali Sky caught a full glimpse of her dad and sister, facing her direction after they negotiated the U-turn in the trail. Philip smiled; he looked sweaty and tired, but happy, squinting through his bad left eye. Cami was mumbling something over and over. With the third repetition Cali Sky discerned the words: "Jesus walks on water, Jesus walks on water, Jesus walks on water." Cami no doubt picked out this phrase from one of the Bible stories that her parents read her.

The mumbled phrase became a full-blown chorus in Cali Sky's head. She wrapped some guitar chords around it and added piano phrasings to give it texture. She made it more complex by altering the time signature. And how about a solo? She tried out a few, for both piano and guitar, and settled upon one that she felt would work best with a harpsichord setting on a keyboard, with staccato notes. The song played in her head. The next thing she knew, the Bronco was well out of sight, sweat was running into her eyes, and she had fallen behind.

Cali Sky first sensed the affinities between music and the rhythms of nature at the condo of her piano teacher, Mr. Nussbaum. He had a stiff German demeanor that called for formality and distance. He was in his 60s but looked as if he were in his 80s, with his deeply lined face, thin white hair, and hunchbacked walk.

The entryway of his condo was dark and foreboding, but opened past the hall into a kitchen/dining room area fresh with natural light from a sliding-glass door. Along a wall next to this door stood the piano. Mr. Nussbaum rarely played himself, especially after a couple of months once Cali Sky got the hang of it. Instead, he sat in a wooden chair nearby, listened to Cali Sky play, offered corrections and suggestions, and stared wistfully out the windows of the sliding-glass door.

At first Cali Sky found this distracting: She was tempted to stop playing and look outside to see what drew Mr. Nussbaum's rapt attention. After a while, however, she realized that the scenery never changed. On the other side of Mr. Nussbaum's sliding-glass windows was a small atrium. A single ficus tree stood in the center, rooted in rich soil filling an enormous pot. A hummingbird feeder hung from a low-lying branch. Scattered on the concrete ground was birdseed, which Mr. Nussbaum occasionally replenished mid-lesson. While playing scales, Cali Sky would hear the creaking of the wooden chair, usually accompanied by a grunt. Then came the sound of the sliding door being pulled open slowly and quietly. While Mr. Nussbaum spread the seed, Cali Sky might hear a comment or word of instruction from the atrium: "Good!".... "Now the Mixolydian scale....." "Let that note linger a bit more." All spoken with a slight German accent.

During these moments, if she had a chance, she looked up briefly from the piano into the atrium: the old man, the tree, the birds, occasionally a hummingbird flitting around the feeder. The image lingered in her mind's eye after she returned her attention to the piano. The image then became formatively involved in the act of concentration, the dynamic of keystrokes and emitted notes, ultimately being absorbed into the music itself.

When the trail leveled off, the geography changed radically, from sharp edges of rocky, unforgiving terrain to the soft colors of a green mountain meadow dotted with wildflowers. Surmounting the switch-backed rockslide and entering the meadow, Cali Sky felt a decline in temperature and a rising wind. No longer ascending, she exerted less energy. The sweat dried cool on her skin.

In the distance, Cali Sky saw Cami bobbing on the shoulders of her dad. They had entered the heart of the meadow, dwarfed by sky and mountain. Wild grass rippled in the wind. Tree branches swayed with a dream-like languor. Glancing to the side, Cali Sky caught sight of a structure, standing at the perimeter of the meadow, near the base of a small cliff. She stopped. She had never seen this structure before, despite crossing this meadow a number of times with her dad. She soon discovered why. If she took two steps forward, trees obscured her line of sight, making it virtually impossible to spot the structure. If she took two steps backward, her vision was likewise impeded. She had glanced in the right direction at the exact right time.

She squinted, bending down slightly to get an unobstructed view through the trees. A small cabin. She could make it out now. Forlorn and dilapidated. No door. Windows long since smashed. What appeared to be a rusted tin roof. It looked like it might have stood there for at least a hundred years. She could not look away. As this vision cast its spell, Cali Sky heard a faint voice, a voice that reached her ears from a distance, buffeted by the wind. It was high-pitched and ethereal, coming in and out of hearing range with the gusts.

It slowly dawned on Cali Sky that the sound came from her sister. But that did not break the spell as the otherworldly voice repeated its far-off cry: "Cali Sky. Cali Sky. Cali Sky."

In 1965 Philip Braithwaite had his first experience with acid. He and a like-minded adventurer were at a small ranch in Topanga Canyon. When the LSD first kicked in, things went wrong. Gazing at a field with horses in a corral, Philip saw a world that turned monochrome: black sky, black hills. Streaks of white offered a hint of visual definition. Things really went wrong when he turned his attention to the horses. The streaks of white became their bones: He saw the horses as ghastly skeletal creatures. Now horrified, he beheld a doomsday world. He was in the grip of the hippie's worst bummer: the bad trip, a freak out. He began to panic. His fellow adventurer, named Lester, was in a different place altogether, but somehow managed to become aware of Philip's terror. So he led him into the mess hall. A few knowing bystanders came to Philip's assistance.

"Lie down here, man. You need to ride it out. Like, relax. Don't fight it. Take a deep breath."

Now on his back Philip stared upwards. He saw in color again. This pleased him. But before he could appreciate this turn of events, the ceiling evaporated. Just de-materialized. In its place he saw light and clouds. He became aware that some important event was imminent. And so it was. *Everything* became light and cloud. In the rising tide of his trip, he knew what this was: a spiritualized world. He braced himself for an epiphany.

He felt the approach of something, something exuding energy and life. It was feminine and beautiful. Then his heart was rent open by the presence of a smile, radiating love upon him. He reached out his arms with pained desire. But then he held back, withdrawing his arms ever so slightly. Aware of his hesitation, the presence slowly, but still lovingly, faded away, drawing into its departure the light and cloud. His trip was winding down. Before disappearing completely, the female presence burned into his consciousness a name. He found himself breathing the words over and over for what seemed like a year: "Cali Sky. Cali Sky. Cali Sky."

"Cali Sky. Cali Sky. Cali Sky." Cami's voice hung above the meadow. Cali Sky continued to stare at the cabin, letting her sister's words wash over her. The three syllables became an invocation, summoning the elements and the hidden cabin into a myth that Cali Sky felt she had enacted a thousand years earlier. With a sudden jolt, as when switching on an amp, a thrill of anticipation ignited her senses. All at once everything took on heightened significance: mountains, rocks, meadow grass. They all became more than themselves, pulsating with life.

She experienced all of this at the edges of cognition. The experience was too large to understand; it squeezed everything else out of her mind, giving her neither time nor space to analyze and comprehend. Most of all, she felt a longing, triggered primarily by the image of the hidden cabin and its mysterious past. A longing to free herself from the containment of her own body. To soar like her sister's lifted voice and participate in the spiritualized rhythms of Mountain and Sky. The longing was overpowering, almost sickening. She did not understand. As the vision evaporated and the spell subsided she wondered if the longing might be the desire to live in a song.

When Cali Sky turned thirteen, Philip finally managed to tell her where her name came from. He told it to her shame-faced, a painfully narrated story sprinkled with the phrasings of his recycled lament, like "sin" and "fallen world." But Cali Sky was more awed than embarrassed. It was a side of her dad that she did not fathom. In fact, from that moment on, Cali Sky insisted on being called by both her first and middle name. Previously, she was simply known as Cali to family, friends and teachers. Most obliged, though she did not escape some ribbing. One particularly savvy classmate once asked her after class, "What, were your parents some sort of fucking hippies?"

Later during the ride home, Cali Sky decided to direct the conversation toward him. "How about you, Dad?" she asked, "Back when you were a hippie, did you know that civil engineering was in your future?" She did not mean for it to come across as an insult, but it sounded a bit that way.

"No," Philip smiled. "When I graduated from college, I needed the first job I could get, and took it." He scratched his beard and shifted in his seat. "Before that," he began, his voice sounding strained, "I wanted to be a writer."

"A writer!" Cali Sky had no idea.

"Yeah," he laughed, blushing. "I wanted to be a writer."

"Well, did you ever write anything?" she asked.

"Not… really. I kept a diary, though," he added. "Hundreds of pages. It's somewhere in the house, I think."

"Can I read it?

"No. Definitely not. Maybe when you're older."

"I wanna be a cheetah!" Cami did not like to be left out of conversations for long.

"What?" Philip asked, looking at Cali Sky and smiling.

"When I grow up I wanna be a cheetah!"

When they pulled into the driveway Cali Sky noticed Brodie's weather-beaten skateboard near the front door, a faded skull-and-crossbones graphic imprinted on its deck. Inside, he sat at the kitchen table with Joan, sipping a bottle of soda. They appeared to be deep in personal conversation, as if they were discussing aspirations or their love lives. This was Brodie's way: He assumed an intimacy with nearly everyone he met. He called Mrs. Braithwaite Joan; he called Mr. Braithwaite Phillip. He could nearly get away with calling even his teachers by their first names.

"Hey, you little punk!" he called out affectionately as Cami bounded into the room. Her eyes lit up when she saw him and his shag hair.

"Brodie, a bug bit me!"

"Where?"

When Cami pointed to her knee Brodie lifted her off the floor, held her upside down by her ankles, and kissed the small red mark. She laughed hysterically.

"How was the hike?" Joan asked behind a tired grin as Philip and Cali Sky walked in to the kitchen.

"Great. Just beautiful," answered Philip. He opened a cabinet door and pulled out a bottle of Bayer Aspirin. "My back's sore, though. I carried Cami most of the way."

Philip eased himself into a chair as Cami settled in Brodie's lap.

"How about you, Cali Sky? Did you have a good time?" asked Joan.

Cali Sky thought about her vision of the cabin, the distant

sound of her name in the air, and the mountains towering around her. The very memory re-triggered the desire, filling up her consciousness, then spilling over, expanding her capacity to feel.

"It was fun," she replied. "We hiked to the meadow."

She felt restless. She needed music.

"Come on, Brodie. I'll show you the song."

Brodie plopped Cami into Philip's lap. "You stay here, you little punk. I need to be *alone* with your sister." Brodie winked.

Cami giggled. Philip frowned. Joan smirked. Cali Sky rolled her eyes. But all the reactions leveled off in the disarming intimacy that Brodie left in his wake.

Inside the studio Cali Sky sat down with a Telecaster on her lap. Brodie stuck a tape in the stereo and pressed play. The sounds of The Clash's *London Calling* traveled through the small, feeble speakers; "Train in Vain," the hidden track, added to the album at the last minute, came on mid-song, all treble on the cheap player. The album had dropped just a few months earlier, panned for its eclectic style by some British critics, who accused the band of selling out to the American mainstream.

Nothing seemed mainstream about Cali Sky and Brodie, however, as they sat down to play a song by an American punk band while a different song, by a British punk band, played through the speakers of a cheap stereo. "Bloodstains" was not hard to play, though, once Cali Sky showed Brodie the chord progression. Teaching Brodie the solo, however, would have to come later.

The year before, Brodie knocked at her door one day after school. Cali Sky mainly kept to herself and said little in class. She was not ostracized. She was aloof. Word spread around school that she could play anything on piano and guitar, including the songs by the edgy bands around which the countercultural school cliques staked their identities. Consequently Cali Sky sat at the Skater/

Surfer/Punker table at lunch. It was there that she caught the attention of Brodie one day.

He was intrigued. He noticed her unkempt black hair. The blue eyes. The indifferently worn, old clothes. From one angle, Brodie thought she looked plain. But from a different angle, she looked unlike any other girl he had ever seen—definitely unlike the garishly pretty girls he "scammed" with after school at the far end of the football field. Her large eyes and rosy cheeks gave her face an expressiveness that made her look older. She appeared wise and sure of herself. *Doesn't care what anyone else thinks of her*, thought Brodie, feeling the infatuation shaping his thoughts. When Cali Sky opened her front door, Brodie stood there with skateboard in hand and a confident grin on his face.

"Hey, how's it going?" he said in his best California-native-surfer voice. He exuded that sense of intimacy, which is to say he acted naturally.

"Hi." Cali Sky was surprised to see him at her front door, but disguised it well. Her facial expression said, "Yeah, you're here. I'm here. We're here. What you say next probably won't surprise me either."

"What's going on?" Brodie asked, still grinning confidently, grooving on the tension of the situation, into which he stepped with mastery and control, spinning the awkwardness into flirtation.

"Just practicing guitar," replied Cali Sky.

"Really!" Brodie's eyes got big. She paved the way for his next line. "'Cuz I heard you were, like, an awesome guitar player!"

Cali Sky's smile brightened her face, giving it warmth and, to Brodie's eyes, unexpected beauty. She had not played much in front of other people.

"Yeah, I can play." A bit of arrogance to match Brodie's.

"Right on!" Brodie's fourteen-year-old hormones started to

kick in. He was becoming aroused. "Well, I knocked on your door this fine afternoon to ask if you could, like, maybe teach me some of your skills." Silence and a confident grin.

"You wanna learn guitar?"

"Hell yeah!" Brodie quickly peeked over Cali Sky's shoulder, looking for a parent.

"Well," she teased with a confident grin of her own as they entered the small room that she referred to as her studio, "these are guitars."

"Right on!"

She taught him how to play an A chord, sitting directly across from him as he fumbled with the fingering.

"Like this?" he asked.

She pushed one of his fingers over slightly, into the tight formation of the A. "There."

He strummed the chord, looking amazed. As the chord carried from the strings and then began to fade, without warning, Brodie, perhaps instigated by his own amazement, slowly leaned over the guitar to kiss Cali Sky. When he was within an inch of her face, Cali Sky burst into laughter. For the first time in young Brodie's life he was turned down by a girl. She observed the good looks, the charisma, the California cool, but with detachment, with the aloofness that came to mark her growing reputation.

"What..." The word came awkwardly from Brodie's mouth, sounding ambiguous: Was it a question or a statement?

"How about a D?" she asked.

"Huh?" In his amazed mind Brodie was still on the verge of a kiss. What the hell happened?

"A D chord. Play a D chord."

Brodie's fingers slowly found their way to their destination. He strummed the chord uncleanly, a sound signifying failure and confusion. They looked each other in the eyes. Two powerful personalities came face to face, but powerful in much different ways. With any other girl in this situation Brodie may very well have abandoned his dreams of becoming a musician, metaphorically slipping them into his Pee Chee folder where they would die the death of neglect alongside his math homework and detention referrals. But in the brief moment of that exchanged glance, Brodie felt the potential turn toward ruined dreams and a failed relationship dissipate. Her smirk revealed the mutual awareness that she had just rejected him—flatly and unceremoniously. But her eyes, which dominated the expression on her face, sent a different message. Something like, "Who gives a shit? Let's play music."

Brodie played aggressively, faithful to the Agent Orange original. His bangs dropped over his eyes as he watched his fingers on the fret board, his head bobbing slightly. Cali Sky saw how well Brodie played the role of surfer punk, pounding out a song that, spun over and over on KROQ, was defining a subculture. Like Brodie, she felt empowered playing it. With a musician's knowledge she understood the component parts of a song—each chord change and note—the awareness of which differentiated the cool kids from the uncool kids, those in the know from the shuffling masses and nameless faces who formed the blasé backdrop around school. "You don't even know Agent Orange." Among Brodie and his set, that dismissal was devastating and final.

That night after dinner Cali Sky sat on her bed strumming her acoustic guitar. In the next room Philip was trying to put Cami to bed. He had already kissed Cali Sky goodnight and said a bedtime prayer with her. Cali Sky could hear Philip in Cami's room, paraphrasing a Bible story in a soft, bedtime voice.

"...and then, after John baptized Jesus in the Jordan River, a dove flew down from the sky and a voice came from heaven, saying, 'This is my son, with whom I am well pleased.'"

"Did that *really* happen?" Cami interrogated in a loud voice, one that upset the tranquil mood of the bedtime ritual.

"Yes, that really happened. When Jesus was baptized in the Jordan River, God was happy….Just like he was happy when you were baptized."

"Did he say anything when *I* was baptized?"

"Well, not with any words we could hear with our ears. But I know that he was happy. He chose you to be his daughter and so loves you just like he loves Jesus."

"But…"

"Cami, no more questions now," Philip interrupted in a gentle voice. "It's way past your bedtime. Time to sleep. Let's say your prayers."

The bedtime ritual reached its most quiet and solemn phase, so Cali Sky stopped strumming and simply fingered notes on the fret board. In the hushed atmosphere of the house, she played without using her right hand.

Ten minutes later, Cami was still awake. Cali Sky could hear her sing-song voice, repeating a few words like "river" and "dove." Then Cami called out her name.

"Cali Sky. Cali Sky. Cali Sky."

"Shh. Go to sleep, Cami," Cali Sky responded in a loud whisper.

"Cali Sky, tell me a story."

"No. Go to sleep."

"Pleeeeeaase."

Cali Sky rose from her bed, propped the guitar against the wall in her closet, and entered Cami's room. She kneeled at the bed. Cami sat up excitedly.

"Lay back down, Cami."

"Okay."

"One story. That's it, Cami."

"Okay."

Cali Sky could think of no new story to tell. She had already told Cami all the classic tales she knew, repeated from Cami's books and Disney movies. Surrounded by silence, Cali Sky felt the weight of Cami's expectant stare. Still no story. She closed her eyes. Her mind wandered, then went blank.

From deep within the ever-metamorphosing patterns of light and shade that flickered and fluxed behind her closed eyes, Cali Sky caught sight of a vision. It came into sharper focus instantaneously, almost as soon as she was aware of its presence. Although it was not a story, Cali Sky relayed this vision to Cami.

"Once upon a time there was a beautiful valley. There were trees, rocks, springs, and waterfalls in the valley. All around it were green hills. In the middle of the valley was a meadow with a river going right through it."

"Like the Jordan River?"

"Uh, yeah. And next to the river, in the meadow, was a small house. A cabin. And in the cabin lived a young girl."

"Was the girl me?"

"No."

"You?"

"No, Cami, just a girl. She loved her cabin. The weather was always nice so she kept her windows open. And when she looked out of her windows, she could see the trees and rocks and springs and waterfalls. She could hear birds singing. It was all so beautiful that she would cry with joy.

"She liked to walk around her valley and explore. She followed the river from one side of the valley to the other. She sat by the waterfall and felt the misty air on her face. She climbed the rocks and lay down on the grass.

"One day as she looked out of her cabin window at the green hills, she saw something she had not noticed before. It hung from the top of the window. She stood up to look at it. She did not know what is was, only that it was a strange and magical object. But still she could not figure out what it was. When she got closer…."

Cali Sky opened her eyes and looked at Cami. She was asleep. So Cali Sky ended the story. Her vision was incomplete.

TWO

May 1980

THE DAY CAME when Cali Sky stopped taking piano lessons with Mr. Nussbaum. It happened like this.

Cali Sky sat behind the piano warming up as Mr. Nussbaum slouched in his wooden chair, staring, as usual, out of his sliding-glass door window into the atrium, where the birds pecked at seed. Cali Sky could hear chirping in between the notes she played. Out of the corner of her eye she saw the quick movements of birds alighting and hopping. The Saturday afternoon ritual followed its normal course. Then came the creaking of the wooden chair. Mr. Nussbaum rose. But instead of attending to his humble aviary he approached the piano, reached over the keys with the slow and feeble movement of old age, and placed on the music rack some sheet music. Cali Sky stopped playing and looked up. It was a composition she did not recognize by a composer she never heard of.

Mr. Nussbaum finally caught his breath and said, "Cali Sky, I would like for you to play this." He then gingerly shuffled his feet to change direction and slowly made his way to the sliding-glass door. Cali Sky studied the sheet. It was a complex Baroque score overwrought with ascending and cascading notes. As her eyes followed the musical symbols—the note lengths, the accidentals, the articulation marks—she heard the music in her head.

Mr. Nussbaum slid open the door. He took one step outside. Before he had taken the second Cali Sky called out, "I have it."

"Eh?"

"I have it. I mean, I'm ready to play it."

Pride spread across Mr. Nussbaum's face as he glanced back at her. "Well, go on."

So Cali Sky began. She played fluently. Her hands and fingers danced on the keyboard, fingers small and delicate—musician's fingers—yet moving confidently, creating strong sounds. She did not look fourteen, more like twenty-three. Concentration gave her face that look of wisdom, her blue eyes now incandescent. Her body occasionally rocked back and forth, the frizzy black hair, in a ponytail, moving only slightly. Sound filled the condo. In the atrium the birds continued to ascend and descend.

A few minutes later Cali Sky finished. She felt like she had conquered the score with technical mastery. The last note lingered in the small space. Mr. Nussbaum waited until it dissipated. Silence returned. He gazed out the slider window. Cali Sky sat patiently at the bench, her cheeks now flushed a bit, though serenity had washed over her face. She turned her head and looked out at the birds.

Mr. Nussbaum then said in a voice barely above a whisper, "Well done, my dear. Well done." He sat down in his wooden chair and, for the first time, asked Cali Sky to turn around, to sit with her back to the piano and face him.

"Cali Sky, you do not need me anymore." He spoke slowly, sounding tired but pleased. "I cannot teach you anything more that you cannot learn on your own." He looked out of the window again, then returned his attention to Cali Sky, who had come to understand and appreciate the strange ways of Mr. Nussbaum—the preoccupation with his birds, the long silences between statements, and the brusque delivery of sentences. She felt herself settling in to her well-worn persona: the quietly arrogant musical prodigy.

She was not prepared, however, for what he said next: "But you too often play with no emotion…like a…a robot." Her persona faltered. She wanted to reply, "What? What are you talking about?"

He continued, "You need feeling…. passion….. Music has to do with the heart….. You need to play piano with emotion….. This I cannot teach you." During the six years that Cali Sky took piano lessons, Mr. Nussbaum offered critiques. But they were always minor, specific, and easily corrected: "That should have been a quarter note, not a half note" or "Play that as a four-note chord, not a three-note chord." For the first time Mr. Nussbaum critiqued Cali Sky in a way that seemed to her fundamental and devastating. Her first coherent thought was defensive: "I play with emotion!" The defensiveness was quickly replaced with uncertainty: "Don't I play with emotion?" She then wondered hopelessly, "If not, how do I?"

"A few months ago," she suddenly announced, "I was…I was in the mountains. Something happened to me. I was in this meadow. It was beautiful. All of a sudden I felt this strong longing… or a strong desire to play music, but I didn't have an instrument." She laughed. Mr. Nussbaum smiled. The tension eased. "But it was more than that. I felt like I wanted to fly or something…. I can't explain. I…I don't know…I guess I don't understand what happened to me."

"The Blue Flower," Mr. Nussbaum muttered.

"The what?"

"In my country we talk of the Blue Flower. Or at least some of us do—the older ones, the wiser ones." His German accent became thicker than Cali Sky had ever heard it. "It is behind your strong emotion…your passion. It is what you, what we, long for. When we are in the forest. When we play music. Even when we are in love. Whenever we find beauty. It is…it is the source of our desires."

"So…do you think this is what happened to me?"

He smiled. "The Blue Flower tugs at our souls. When you find it, the spirit wants to escape from the body. But it cannot be explained. Only felt."

"Maybe that's what happened to me."

"Maybe it is, my dear."

Mr. Nussbaum looked out again at the birds in the atrium. "Maybe you *have* found passion, the strongest passion there is. But you must understand, Cali Sky. No one can grasp the Blue Flower. It is always beyond reach…. Still, its beauty burns our hearts…. For this reason, for *this* reason, we play piano."

During the drive home Cali Sky told her dad what Mr. Nussbaum said about piano lessons—that he had nothing more to teach her. Philip's eyes got big.

"Really? He said that?"

Cali Sky sat back in her seat, slipped off her flip-flops, and put her bare feet on the dashboard. Next to her heel she could see imprinted teeth marks in the dashboard's edge, the result of one of Cami's tantrums. She had taken her anger out one day on the nearest object she could bite. Somehow she managed to get her mouth around the curvature of the plastic.

"Yeah, he still wants me to come over, though, and play for him."

"Wow, I really am proud of you…. In fact, to celebrate…why don't you turn the radio on?"

Cali Sky smiled and sat up. She leaned over and turned the radio dial to KROQ. As she did so, she felt a thrill of the forbidden. Rarely did her dad indulge her like this. When the static cleared, Oingo Boingo's "Only a Lad" came on. Cali Sky turned it up a bit.

"Your Aunt Nancy is at our house. I brought her over this morning," Philip said as the first chorus winded down.

"How is she?" asked Cali Sky.

Philip shrugged. "Well, she's okay. I mean, as we know, as we knew would happen, she is getting steadily worse."

Ten years earlier Philip's sister Nancy was diagnosed with multiple sclerosis. Five years later she had difficulty using her left hand and she dragged her left foot when she walked. Now her left hand was nearly useless and she was barely able to walk, even with the use of a walker. She was by far the youngest resident in the nursing home. She played Scrabble with some of the other residents, read voraciously, watched some game shows and wandered—or wheeled—around the nursing home's outdoor grounds.

"We'll keep praying for her," Philip continued, "Pray for a miracle."

Cali Sky sat back and placed her bare feet back on the dash. They remained silent for a while.

"Dad, what do you love?"

"What?" Philip heard the question, but it was not the type that Cali Sky asked.

"What do you love? I mean, besides me and mom and Cami and all that. And, besides God. What do you love?"

"What do I love? Well, I think you just hit most of them. I love God first, since he's the source of all love. I love you…."

"I know, Dad," Cali Sky interrupted, impatience in her voice, "Besides all that. What *else* do you love?"

"Well…I love…mountains. Yeah, I love mountains. I love being in the mountains."

Finally, Cali Sky thought. She continued, "Do you ever feel strong emotions in the mountains? A strong….passion?"

"Um, yeah, sure. I mean, the mountains are God's handi-work. They are evidence of God's existence. *That* makes me feel strong emotion."

Cali Sky turned her head and looked out the passenger-side window. Philip got the sense that this moment was passing him by and that she was searching.

"Did I ever tell you about the time I hiked part of the Alps when I was living in Europe?'

"No, I don't think you did." His time in Europe was a part of the past that he did not usually discuss.

"Well," he began, "a friend of mine and I were in Austria. We decided we wanted to hike some of the Alps. So we drove to a trailhead near the Austria/Germany border. We had back-packs, but limited supplies inside. Off we went." Philip spoke with increasing animation. "We saw a peak in the distance we wanted to reach, but we underestimated the distance. We hiked and hiked. But by late afternoon the peak still seemed far off. We knew we had to turn back because night was coming. Well, a few hours later and we couldn't see a hundred yards in front of us. We were exhausted. It was summer, but at nighttime at that elevation it still got pretty cold. So we made a sort of camp. I don't think I have ever been colder than I was that night."

Philip was now absorbed in his own story. Cali Sky listened attentively. "By morning, we thought we were going to freeze. We set off at first light and climbed a pass not more than five hun-dred yards from our campsite. When we reached the top, we felt so stupid. Because there, not more than a ten-minutes' hike away, was our car."

Cali Sky chuckled.

"So we spent," Philip continued, "a miserable, cold night only a short walk from our car. We were so close, and we didn't even know it." His reverie ended. Almost at once Cali Sky noticed that her father reassumed his world-weary pose, his everyday demeanor. "I suppose that night was like my life in a way. God was always there for me, arms wide open, not far away. But I wandered around in the cold, in the dark. I made a lot of mistakes before I ran back into his arms."

The mood in the truck became somber. It felt like church to her. Philip sensed it too. He felt like the moment was once again vanishing away.

"But the ordeal did not end there!" he said in an upbeat tone. "By the time we got back to the car, my hands were so cold that I could barely move my fingers. I couldn't hold the key to unlock the door. So there we were, finally back at the car, and we couldn't get inside. It took me about five minutes of rubbing my hands together and smacking them against my legs before they thawed out enough for me to unlock the door!"

By now they had reached the house. Outside the front door they saw Brodie's skateboard. Next to it was Aunt Nancy's wheelchair. By the time he put the Bronco into park Philip felt like he made the most of the moment. Cali Sky never turned away from the window, giving nothing away.

Joan and Cami sat at the kitchen table coloring.

"Look! Look!" Cami shouted as she saw Philip and Cali Sky enter the room.

"Wow, very nice, Cami," Philip said, placing a hand on his wife's shoulder and bending over to admire Cami's picture.

"Look, Cali Sky!" Cami shouted again.

Cali Sky walked over, less enthusiastically than her dad. "Good, Cami. You colored Jesus purple."

"It's my favorite color!"

Cali Sky bent down to look at the page of Cami's Bible coloring book more closely. It was a picture of Jesus feeding the 5,000. Cami had colored the multiplied loaves and fish black, going outside the lines, so that you couldn't even see them, or figure out what they were. The disciples could have been distributing anything to the multitudes underneath the wildly scribbled black coloring. Purple Jesus stood back, set apart, admiring it all.

Cali Sky heard music coming from the studio. She exited the room and peeked around the corner. Brodie was playing the new Ramones album, *End of the Century*, on the cheap cassette player. He must have helped Aunt Nancy into a chair, for she sat near the entrance to the studio, her walker by the piano, listening to the music and talking with Brodie. Cali Sky stood there for a while, eavesdropping, watching Brodie, watching Aunt Nancy.

Finally she entered the room and said, "Hi Aunt Nancy."

"Cali Sky, how are you?" Aunt Nancy had short hair, black with a touch of gray. She wore loose-fitting polyester clothing. Cali Sky bent down to hug her aunt and as she did, she could smell the faint aroma of the nursing home, the scent of Lysol and urine.

Brodie sat near the cassette player, a fanzine called *Slash* in his hands. It was the April 1980 issue, with a cover that included an illustration of Johnny Rotten. Like everyone else, Aunt Nancy was enveloped by Brodie's widely spread net of intimacy.

"Brodie was telling me about some of the new local punk bands," Aunt Nancy said, gesturing toward his copy of *Slash*. She cast a net of intimacy of her own—motivated, not like Brodie, by charisma and confidence, but by circumstances. Aunt Nancy welcomed the opportunity to talk with anyone about nearly anything.

"Well, any you like, Aunt Nancy?" Cali Sky asked, smiling.

"Yes. Yes," replied Aunt Nancy, straight-faced, dead serious, "There was one. What were they called?" She paused in reflection, searching her mind. "Oh yeah. The Damned."

Brodie laughed. Emboldened by her aunt's sarcasm, Cali Sky dug into Brodie a bit. "Your hair is getting a bit long, isn't it?" It was a recurring joke, one that Brodie heard a lot at school. Long hair meant hippie, which figured squarely within the range of punk rock's contempt and aggression. At what point does one's hair become long enough to qualify one as a hippie? Brodie flirted with that undefined line of demarcation.

Cali Sky and Brodie picked up guitars and played for Aunt Nancy. Brodie insisted that they play some songs by The Damned. They also played some of their own creations, which then became improvisations. Cali Sky always in control, Brodie trying to keep up. Once, Brodie had to stop when he found himself playing in a key that Cali Sky had long abandoned. He sighed, put his hands back in position, and said, "Let's try something else."

Cali Sky stopped playing. "Okay, what?"

Brodie: "How about Joy Division?" So they broke into a rendition of "Love Will Tear Us Apart." Brodie played rhythm on an acoustic, Cali Sky led on an electric, adapting the riff played on keyboard in the original and improvising some of her own solos. Brodie sang. After the first chorus Cali Sky glanced up and saw strong emotion in her aunt's face—part melancholy, part appreciation. That expression motivated Cali Sky to play with even more passion. And so, apparently, did Brodie. He struggled with some of the low notes, but the delivery of his unsteady voice carried unpolished emotion. Brodie and Cali Sky smiled with satisfaction. Aunt Nancy appeared to be restraining tears.

She broke the strange silence: "That was really moving. Tell me something about that song... and about the band."

Cali Sky and Brodie looked at each other.

Brodie answered, "The lead singer of the band—his name is Ian Curtis—he killed himself a few days ago." It was the suicide that ironically immortalized Curtis. He became a legend, but he was not unique. He was in a line of figures—some historical, some mythical, many a bit of both—stretching back to the dawn of time, all of whom sprang from an archetype: the tortured artist, destroyed by the pain and suffering that was also his inspiration.

Aunt Nancy seemed unfazed. No "How awful!" or "So tragic!" But she was curious so she asked, "Are most of his songs like the one you played?"

"Yeah, pretty much," replied Brodie, "really sad songs.... He had asthma and would have seizures on stage."

"Asthma? I think you mean epilepsy," Aunt Nancy corrected.

Everyone laughed, Brodie sheepishly but with characteristic charm.

Aunt Nancy asked, "So what do you think that song means. What's the title? Love will tear us apart. What does that mean?"

Brodie spoke first: "I think it's like love makes you do some crazy stuff that hurts other people. Like you might get all jealous or something."

Aunt Nancy gave no sign that she agreed or disagreed. She just listened.

"Yeah," Cali Sky chimed in. "But I also think that we want to protect the ones we love, but sometimes the opposite happens, you know?"

Just then, Philip approached. "Sounds like some deep conversation in here." He scratched his beard nervously, sensing that he was intruding.

Aunt Nancy said, "They were just telling me about this singer who committed suicide."

"How awful!" Philip exclaimed. "That's tragic."

"And they just played one of his songs—I mean, one of his band's songs," she said.

Philip asked about the name of the band. When he was told, he lamented, "That's sad. A band called Joy Division. But no joy."

"But I think that's the point," she replied, "Maybe the name is ironic, Philip."

"But a band all about despair? That's just sad. It doesn't have to be that way. 'Whatever is true, whatever is noble, whatever is right, whatever is pure, whatever is lovely—think about such things.'"

He spoke the words in his Bible voice with a solemn intonation. Cali Sky was feeling uncomfortable. She did not like it when her dad recited Bible passages—or talked about religion—in front of her friends.

Aunt Nancy answered, "Well, in the real world, real people struggle with things like pain and despair."

"I know, I know, Nancy. And God helps us through those struggles. So we don't have to despair." Philip said it gently and lovingly, conspicuously so. Cali Sky played a riff on her guitar, trying to derail the embarrassing conversation.

"True enough, no need to argue," Aunt Nancy replied, though without much commitment. She added, "Love will *not* tear us apart." Philip and Aunt Nancy smiled. Brodie's laughter seemed unnecessarily loud, like he was drunk or stoned.

"Well, anyway," Philip said once the air was cleared, "we're grilling hamburgers tonight. Brodie, would you like to stay for dinner?"

"Yeah! That'd be great.... Can I help?"

With Brodie in the kitchen, Cali Sky and Aunt Nancy were left alone in the studio. An air of conspiracy descended on the room.

"Your dad tries too hard to say the right thing—to the point where the thing he's saying is not even right anymore," said Aunt Nancy.

Cali Sky nodded.

Aunt Nancy continued, "That's why what you said about the band and their song title was so true."

"Really? I didn't explain myself very well."

"You did well enough."

"Yeah." Cali Sky sounded depressed as "Love Will Tear Us Apart" echoed in her brain.

Later that night after Brodie skated off into the overcast night and Philip returned from the nursing home where he dropped off Aunt Nancy, Cali Sky stood in front of the bathroom sink brushing her teeth. Joan peeked her head around the corner.

"Sweetheart, Cami wants you to tell her a bedtime story. Could you do that?"

Cali Sky rolled her eyes but answered, "Okay."

"Also, we are going to the late service tomorrow. Your dad's gonna get donuts in the morning. Then we're gonna pick up Aunt Nancy and take her with us to church. Okay?"

"Okay."

"Oh, and one more thing. You *did* study and practice the organ music didn't you? You are playing tomorrow. And you're supposed to accompany Michelle on piano. Remember?"

"I forgot. I'm sorry," Cali Sky said apologetically. "But it's alright. I'll go over the music right now."

"Cali Sky." Joan pronounced the name with anger and disappointment, the last syllable sustained and marked by a descended pitch. "But don't you need to practice it too?"

"No, it'll be alright. I can give it a run through before the service begins."

"Okay. If you say so. I think Dad left the sheet music in the living room armoire. You can go over it after you tell Cami a story."

Joan stood behind her daughter, held her by the shoulders,

bent down and kissed her on the top of the head. She brushed Cali Sky's hair with her fingers.

Cami was making fart sounds with her mouth when Cali Sky entered her bedroom.

"Cali Sky, listen to this!" Cami stuck her tongue out through pursed lips and took a deep breath, poised to produce a grand-finale flatulence noise.

"Don't do it, Cami," Cali Sky warned, "or I won't tell you a story."

Cami's face contorted. She exhaled anti-climactically.

Cali Sky kneeled at Cami's bed. "Okay, I'll tell you a story…. Let's see…."

"Cali Sky, why is your hair always so messy?"

"Be quiet, Cami! Do you want me to tell you a story or not?"

"Yes."

"Once upon a time," Cali Sky began, "there was this big, ugly monster…"

"No," Cami interrupted, "Not a scary story!"

"It had long, ugly hair," Cali Sky continued.

"Cali Skyyyyy!" Cami yelled.

"Shhh! Okay, okay. I won't tell you that story." Cali Sky thought for a while. "It's hard, Cami. I just run out of stories to tell."

Cami stared at the ceiling for a while and said, "Tell me about the princess in the cabin. With the river and the trees."

"The what?" Then Cali Sky remembered the story she began months earlier. Her vision. "She wasn't a princess. She was just a girl."

"Yeah, tell me that story," Cami insisted.

Cali Sky shifted her weight on her knees, bowed her head, and closed her eyes. Then she began:

"Once upon a time there was a beautiful green meadow. In the center of the meadow was a cabin, and inside the cabin there lived a girl. Right next to the cabin there was a river that ran from one end of the meadow to the other. The girl loved her home and the meadow. She liked to walk along the river. Sometimes the river became a waterfall, and she would sit on a rock and stare at it, watching the mist and the spray. She liked to run around the trees, touching the trunk of each one as she passed.

One day she sat in her cabin looking out of the open window at the tallest tree in the valley. The leaves way high up moved in the breeze. Then she saw something in the window that she hadn't noticed before. It hung down from the windowsill. At first she couldn't figure out what it was. Then when she looked closer, she saw that it was an instrument, a musical instrument. Like organ pipes, only you blow through them. She could not understand how they got in her window. Then, all of a sudden, it began to play music. All by itself. The most beautiful music you've ever heard, golden note after golden note. The music was so beautiful that the girl began to cry...."

Cali Sky opened her eyes and looked at Cami. She was asleep.

Following her mom's instructions, Cali Sky found the sheet music for the morning services in the living room armoire. She took them to the studio, walking barefoot and catlike. Nightlights—testaments to Cami's fear of the dark—guided her way through the hallway and the living room. Her parents were settling into bed. She looked over the sheets, studying each measure carefully. The house was quiet. She nestled the acoustic onto her lap and played quietly. She tried to adapt the hymn scores to guitar. She loved jazz phrases that made use of octaves so she played some of those. After that, she tried to write a folk song. Her dad once played a Bob Dylan album on the Bronco's eight track on the way to the beach. She was becoming sleepy, drowsiness dulling her creativity.

As she passed through the kitchen on her way to the living

room she glanced at the clock hung above the table. Both hands were nearly vertical. She heard the ticking of the clock with striking clarity.

The living room was dimly lit by a night light plugged into an outlet about a foot above the floor. The location of the light exaggerated shadows. Darkness gathered in the corners and edges of the room. Cali Sky opened the armoire drawer and returned the sheet music to its place. On the bottom shelf she saw her dad's old record player, untouched for years. She had discovered it as a child after they first moved into the house and used it as an imaginary fortress. She had put toy figures and cars on the turntable, battlements from which to fend off imaginary villains. When she was older she asked her dad if they could play a record. He asked why she would want to use an obsolete record player when they had cassettes and eight tracks. End of discussion.

Now she stared at the details of its foreign parts. She lifted the needle and noticed dust on the upward facing surfaces. Her own body blocked the light so she moved slightly to the side. Doing so enabled her to study the intricacies of the device. She gently spun the turntable and focused her sight on one spot at the circumference of the circle, following the slow revolution. She became a bit dizzy, her field of vision already disoriented by shadow and light.

When she removed her finger from the turntable and refocused her eyes, she caught sight of something that startled her, something beyond the record player. It was located in the deepest recesses of the armoire, tucked away behind a dozen or so large scented candles and the flaps of a cardboard box used to hold old Christmas cards. The only reason Cali Sky spotted it was that the nightlight shone directly on it and she was perfectly situated to see through the clutter. When it first appeared she drew back sharply. Once she recovered she irresistibly moved back to her original position and looked again. And there it was.

It was a face. Its nose was yellow. The rest of the face, as well as the hair, was orange-red. It was a man staring directly at her, expressionless. Cali Sky inched closer, trying to figure out what exactly she was looking at. A picture of some sort. An image, but imprinted on what? Then it dawned on her: a record, the front cover, album art. She turned her head and peeked behind her. All was quiet. It was now after midnight. She carefully removed the scented candles and laid them down horizontally on the carpet. She tugged the box of Christmas cards and slid it toward her, easing it onto the floor and pushing it out of the way. Next to the box she discovered what appeared to be half of a rock, about the size of a grapefruit half. On the uncut side was the spherical shape and brown roughness of ordinary rock. The other side, the side that had been cut, revealed translucent crystals glittering beneath the surface. Cali Sky stared at the strange rock for a moment, then placed it alongside the Christmas box.

Her view was now unimpeded. She lay on her stomach, staring in fascination. Her thrill of discovery was tinged with a sense of guilt. She was not intended to see this. Her dad's old record collection. There must have been fifty of them. *But why did he hide them like this?* she thought. *Why wouldn't he let me listen to these, being who I am?* She wondered who should feel the guilt, she or her dad.

She reached deep into the armoire and pulled out the record with the man's face on the front cover. She sat cross-legged and held it with both hands. There was not one man but three in the picture. She did not know this now but she would learn in the coming days that the three men were Jack Bruce, Ginger Baker, and Eric Clapton. Bruce was the one with the yellow nose and orange-red face and hair. She had, in fact, on her lap Cream's 1967 album, *Disraeli Gears*. The day-glow colors and psychedelic designs on the cover marked its place in history, a monument to the 60s. With the care of a votary performing some pagan ritual, she set the album on the carpet off to the side, front cover up. She reached back into the armoire and pulled out the next record. The band on the cover of this one she immediately recognized: the Rolling Stones. It was the American version of their 1966 album, *Aftermath*. Images of the quintet, which then included Brian Jones, appeared blurred as if they were in motion or were being transfigured. Cali Sky set the record alongside *Disraeli Gears* and reached into the armoire for another. She immediately recognized this image as well, but it was not of the band members but of what would become a rock-and-roll icon: a dirigible going down in flames, crashing to the ground. This was Led Zeppelin's first album, released in 1969. She turned the record over and there they were—Bonham, Plant, Page, and Jones. She placed the album next to the others on the carpet.

Twenty minutes later, a good-sized swath of the living room was covered with records, all of the album art creating a rock-and-roll mosaic. Cali Sky stood up to get a larger perspective. Music history lay stretched across the floor. She admired the whole for a few seconds. Then she focused on some of the individual albums: the Byrds' *Mr. Tambourine Man*; the Jeff Beck Group's *Truth*; the American version of *Are You Experienced?* by the Jimi Hendrix Experience; and the only album from the first "super group," Blind Faith.

The now venerated names and titles beckoned to her. Vistas of the past opened in her imagination, tantalizing her, like the mystery of her father's youth, with the stories that, she was sure, lurked behind each band, album and song. She felt like she had discovered the genesis of rock and roll. The musical foundations of nearly everything she played on guitar lay at her feet.

Then without warning, she felt the tug at her soul, the extrasensory heart-piercing desire that both fascinated and ached. It was the same sensation she experienced in the meadow when she caught sight of the abandoned cabin as her name hung in the air. This time, however, the experience was more objective and even impersonal, as if she were disembodied, like a sentient particle of light observing the objects of its own illumination. Yet the experience was equally wild and uncontrollable, as if the light particle was hurtling unavoidably and spectacularly toward darkness. She felt the shortness of breath, accompanied by the dawning sense of awe and profundity. Most of all, she felt, from the depths of her identity, the reaching beyond herself.

It was over almost as soon as it began, within a few seconds. It left her unsettled, agitated and charged with desire. But once again the desire was vague and directionless. She knew of only one outlet for this sensation: music. Playing guitar. Playing piano. She thought about Mr. Nussbaum and the Blue Flower.

She returned the records to their hidden place in the corner of the armoire, abstract notions of mystery, secrets and darkness revolving, as if on a turntable, in her tired mind.

That night she dreamed she was hiking. The trail was brightened by nightlights. Somehow she knew it was midnight. She was ascending a steep ridge, winding back and forth up a long, rocky switchback. At the top of the ridge she could see the edges of a massive dark cloud, which in the night sky looked like a blank, a ball of nothingness. Every now and then blindingly bright bolts of lightning flashed from the cloud, transforming night to day in the instant they appeared. With each flash, Cali Sky looked up, but always too late. The light was gone before she could attend to its source. She knew she had to reach that cloud. It was her appointed destination for some reason.

She saw someone else hiking in front of her. She could tell by the gait that it was her dad. When he negotiated the u-turn of the switchback and turned toward her direction, she could see him from the front. She saw that he had the face of Jack Bruce, his entire head orange-red in color with the exception of his nose, which was yellow. His appearance did not surprise her; she looked upon his transformed face with calm acceptance. When she herself made the u-turn, she looked down the trail. She could see someone else mounting the switch-backed ridge. It was a woman, but she couldn't make out who at first. As they passed going in opposite directions, Cali Sky looked almost straight down at the figure. It was Aunt Nancy. No walker. No wheelchair. Hiking up the trail with determination on her face. Unlike the spectacle of her father with his surreal face, the vision of a walking Aunt Nancy shocked Cali Sky. The jolt of the shock awakened her from sleep.

Cali Sky could hear her family in the kitchen. It sounded like Cami was squealing, evidently clamoring for the donuts that Philip brought back from the bakery. The morning sun made her room appear smaller than it did the previous night when she was still reeling from her experience with the records in the living room. She trudged into the bathroom. It was a mess. Apparently in her haste to nab the best donuts, Cami dropped the hand towel into the bathtub, dripped water all over the counter, and missed the toilet on two counts: pee on the seat and used toilet paper draped across the floor. Cali Sky sighed and grudgingly tidied the room.

She then made her tired way into the kitchen and paused at the entryway. Cami sat at the kitchen table, alone, with her back to Cali Sky. Their parents were in their bedroom getting ready for church. Cami was frantically licking the frosting off of a donut. Cali Sky watched as she re-deposited it into the box, pulled out another and began the process once more of removing frosting with her tongue. Cali Sky stepped forward, anger now mounting.

"Cami!" Cali Sky stopped her sister mid lick.

"Hi," Cami said in a tone of surprise and defeat. Guilt marked her face, with just a hint of shame. She quickly threw the donut back in the box and covered her face with her hands.

As she approached Cali Sky looked into the box of donuts. Cami had licked the frosting off of every single one. The donut tops glistened with saliva. Cali Sky's anger turned to fury. She was livid.

"Goddamn it, Cami!"

At that very moment, Philip and Joan entered the room. Cali Sky heard them at her back, sensed her father's shock during the horrible pause that lingered after her shrieked profanity. She braced herself.

"Cali Sky!" Philip yelled. Turning around, she saw fury on his face as her own subsided. In seeming slow motion she saw him march directly at her. He reached up and grabbed her shoulders. They looked at each other face to face.

He yelled, "Don't ever take the Lord's name in vain. Ever. Do you understand?"

She became aware of her sister and mom looking on. She wished she could disappear. She nodded petulantly, lips pursed and Philip released his grip. She felt tears welling in her eyes and wanted to scream back at him. Instead she ran out of the kitchen and into her bedroom, slamming the door behind her.

From the top drawer of her desk she removed her yearbook from last year. She flipped through the pages until she got to the spread on jazz band. She found her name: "Cali Braithwaite, Guitar." She glanced at her picture and grimaced when she saw the thick, frizzy hair. She once again felt herself slipping into self-pity. So she pulled a piece of paper and a pencil from the drawer.

She began doodling, letting her mind wander. She traced lines around the many words scattered on the page. She remembered that she and Brodie used this piece of paper the week before as a lyric sheet when they were trying to write a song. She flipped the piece of paper over and realized that Aunt Nancy must have been there that day when they were composing. She had recited a poem, which Cali Sky then transcribed onto the lyric sheet. Cali Sky remembered that she did this to be polite, to make Aunt Nancy feel like she was involved. Cali Sky had spoken a word or painted an image that triggered Aunt Nancy's memory, which was stocked with lines of poetry from her hours of reading at the nursing home. Cali Sky sat patiently and Brodie looked on in awe, slack-jawed, as Aunt Nancy recited the lines. While she did so, she stared intently at Cali Sky, as if no one else or nothing else was in the room. She smiled compassionately as she concluded, clearly moved. Cali Sky then announced, somewhat disingenuously, "Let me write that down. Maybe we can use some of that." So Aunt Nancy recited them again, this time more slowly, spelling out some of the words. The lines were thus recorded in Cali Sky's handwriting:

"So let me be thy choir, and make a moan
Upon the midnight hours;
Thy voice, thy lute, thy pipe, thy incense sweet
From swinged censer teeming:
Thy shrine, thy grove, thy oracle, thy heat
Of pale-mouthed prophet dreaming."

The first time Aunt Nancy recited it, Cali Sky understood none of it. The second time, she understood little of it. It sounded like Aunt Nancy was directing the words to her, that Aunt Nancy would somehow be her choir, be her voice and lute, be her shrine and grove.

"So what does it mean?" Brodie asked.

Aunt Nancy answered, "It's a poem about bad timing. About being born at the wrong time, at the wrong moment.... You see, there was this girl in Greek mythology who was deified—became a goddess—at the very end of the reign of the gods. At that time, men stopped worshipping the gods. So this poor young goddess never got what she deserved. She was never really loved by anyone. Everyone turned their back on her. Except one person. One person remained faithful to her. One person still sings songs to her, builds a temple for her, and worships her at midnight in the forest."

Cali Sky remembered Aunt Nancy's words. She thought about being born at the wrong time. She thought about what it would have been like to grow up in the sixties. To listen to those records she discovered when they first came out. To go to a Cream concert, to watch Jimi Hendrix play guitar.

About fifteen minutes later Cali Sky heard a knock on her door followed by her mom's voice: "Cali Sky, can I come in?"

"Okay."

Joan was dressed for church: a long black dress with a pink belt that offered more than a hint of her thin figure. Her black hair was frizzy like Cali Sky's, but shorter and thus curlier. She had on high heels. She took two slow steps forward and held out a bag for Cali Sky. "Here, these are for you. Your dad went back to the donut store."

"Thank you."

"We need to get you ready for church. You sit here on your chair and eat your donuts. I'll do your hair." Cali Sky nodded and sat down, not before her ever-affectionate mom gave her a kiss on the cheek.

"You know," Joan said as she braided Cali Sky's hair, "Your dad feels really bad about yelling at you. He lost his temper." Cali Sky nodded again after taking a bite of a chocolate glazed.

"He'd do anything for you."

Another nod. Joan was always so gentle with Cali Sky's hair, even when detangling the knots and rats' nests.

"You do realize that, right?"

"Yeah. I guess."

"You guess?"

Cali Sky shrugged.

"Let me tell you a story," Joan said. "After your father and I first met each other, we were swimming up at Castaic Lake. It was so beautiful that day. Not a cloud in the sky. The sun sparkling off the water. A hot summer day. And we were having a great time. It was like we were in our own little world. Swimming. Laughing. Talking. Until these...these real assholes came." She whispered the word "assholes" as if sharing a secret with Cali Sky, then paused, uncertain whether to continue.

"Yeah," Cali Sky said, "so what happened next?"

"They started hassling your dad and saying nasty things to me. Your dad stood right up to them. Pushed them back. Protecting me. They ganged up on him and punched him. It all happened so quickly—like they invaded our little private world. And that's why your dad can't see very well out of his left eye." Pain and regret spread across Joan's face. "Oh, I felt so sorry for him. Lying there bloody on the sand. I knew then that he had such a big heart. He'd do anything to protect me. And to protect you."

"Yeah, I know," Cali Sky said as she wiped her hands with a napkin. "But why did those guys hit dad? And say nasty things to you?"

The question appeared to frazzle Joan a bit. "Oh, mainly because of the way we looked, I guess."

"How did you look?"

"Like hippies. Your dad had long hair. They heard our music."

Before her mom exited her room Cali Sky said, "Mom, I need to tell you something." The room seemed suddenly quiet, not unlike the silence earlier in the kitchen after the words "Goddamn it" escaped from Cali Sky's mouth. But this time she was in control of the pause, wielding it like a caesura in a piano phrase. She had a story of her own to relate. "Last night, when I was putting away the music sheets in the armoire, I found...something."

"What?"

"Dad's old record collection."

"Really? He tucked it away back there?"

"Yeah..... I'd really like to listen to them. Do you...think I should ask him?"

Joan said nothing for a while, looking out of Cali Sky's dirty window.

Then she answered, "Sure. Why not?" Cali Sky felt warmed by her mom's encouraging smile as well as the gleam in her eye.

Cali Sky liked playing the organ at church. It was one of the rare moments when she performed in front of a group of people. Cornerstone Community Church provided her with a friendly audience. As usual, butterflies churned in her stomach before the service as the early arrivals—mostly old people—found their way into the pews. But once she began to play, the nerves and anxiety disappeared.

After the sermon she walked over to the piano, followed by Michelle, the solo vocalist. Though in her late twenties, Michelle possessed a frumpy and plain appearance that made her look older. She clutched the microphone and smiled at the congregation. Cali Sky played a short intro, then Michelle began singing. They had practiced together for an hour or so earlier in the week. Cali Sky had focused on her parts, made a few changes and eventually agreed with Michelle that they were ready.

Now, however, Cali Sky was distracted by Michelle's voice. She thought to herself, *She sounds terrible!* It was a sudden realization, as if she were hearing the voice for the first time. In her eagerness to please, Michelle sang notes too sharp, overcorrected and slipped into flat notes. Her pitch was unsteady and sloppy. The upper ranges of the melody forced her to sing falsetto, which served only to make her sound like a caterwauling child. Cali Sky cringed. She felt embarrassed for Michelle, but also ashamed herself since she was a part of what she realized with sudden clarity this performance had become: a debacle. She added some runs in the phrasing, attempting to salvage the song with musical sleights of hand. *Finally*, Cali Sky thought to herself as Michelle sang her last part. She played the outro with a flourish, again trying to compensate for the Michelle's shortcomings.

After the song, the congregation applauded. But Cali Sky barely heard it. She was preoccupied with her own conflicting emotions: first disgust with the musical abomination, then shock that she experienced this disgust so viscerally, and finally guilt over her disgust, which had slowly transformed into a dislike of Michelle herself. She had to double her concentration as she played the final hymn.

As the congregation filtered out of the church, groups consisting of three to five people, usually families, approached Cali Sky. They shook her hand and, as they did every Sunday when she played, fawned over her talent. She was known there as the prodigy, the one God blessed with amazing talent. She smiled and said "thank you." She assured them that she still practiced every day. "No," she replied to the oft-repeated question, "I don't like one better than the other. I like the piano and the guitar the same."

Outside she spotted Michelle in the center of a small crowd. As she approached she heard the perfunctory praise, always expected after a vocal performance at Cornerstone: "Beautiful song, Michelle, just beautiful." "So uplifting!" "Great job, Michelle!" As she passed, Cali Sky felt an overwhelming temptation to speak the truth, to shatter the illusions that most of them had about both the untalented vocalist and the sweet Braithwaite girl, and to unleash the charred words that lay smoldering in her breast: "You sucked!"

"Hi Cali Sky," said her dad, approaching from the other direction. As always his squint favored his left eye.

"Hi Dad," she replied.

"Mom is taking Aunt Nancy back to the nursing home. Will you ride with me?"

"Okay."

As he pulled the orange Bronco out of the church parking lot, he wasted no time: "Cali Sky, I'm sorry. I shouldn't have yelled at you like that earlier this morning. I was wrong."

"That's okay," she answered, feeling uplifted by the cleaning of slates. "I'm sorry too. I know I shouldn't have said that."

"I know you do, Cali Sky. But I want to make sure you know why you should not take the Lord's name in vain, why it's wrong…. His is the name above all other names. The alpha and omega. To use his name so…crudely and trivially is disrespectful."

"I know, Dad. I understand."

"Good." He looked at her compassionately. "But I really do feel bad about what I did earlier. My anger got the best of me."

"That's okay," she asserted appreciatively. "I accept your apology."

"Good."

After making a left turn, he said, "Great job playing this morning! You sounded great! Of course, I knew you would."

"Thanks…. What did you think of Michelle's singing?" Cali Sky could not disguise the disdain in her voice. Philip ignored it.

"Uh, she was okay, I guess. I think Pastor Kevin is just happy to have someone volunteer to sing."

They were nearing home, past the strip malls and gas stations. A heavy marine layer thickened the atmosphere, making everything seem closed in. It felt vaguely to Cali Sky like a sort of insulation, warming the spirit in the cab of the Bronco. Reconciliation left her feeling unburdened. She still felt a lingering trace of uneasiness, but she had forgotten its source. Then an orange, red and yellow face appeared in her mind's eye. She remembered now. As they pulled into the driveway Cali Sky realized the time had come.

Feeling her heart pounding in her chest she blurted out, "Dad, last night when I was putting the sheet music back in the armoire I found your old record collection." She added before the pause became long enough for a response, "I didn't mean to. I just happened to look in the back…and…I saw them."

Philip said nothing. At first his face was blank. This revelation appeared to catch him completely off guard. Then, as comprehension dawned on his face he seemed to struggle with his own feelings.

Appearing a bit stunned, he managed to say, "I…had forgotten I put them there." His mumbled utterance was aimless, leaving Cali Sky with no question to answer or declaration to comment on. She sat up in her seat as Philip turned off the Bronco's engine.

"Well," Philip began, "It was nice of you to tell me you found them. I mean, that was really considerate of you…. It shows your character." Philip smiled suddenly as he turned to her. Then the smile faded.

"Did you look through them?" he asked.

"Just a little."

He appeared to steady himself, then posed a firm question: "And I suppose you would like to look through them all?"

She nodded.

"And I suppose you would like to listen to them?"

She nodded again.

With ambiguous gestures and body language, suggesting

uncertainty, pain, hope, and resignation all at once, Philip nodded back at his daughter and whispered, "Okay."

Every day the following week Cali Sky returned immediately home from school to listen to her dad's old records. She listened for hours at a time, staring at the album art as the record spun on the turntable. Cali Sky's musical world was unmade. Then reassembled with each riff, chord progression, guitar solo, rim shot and bass line. She marveled at some of the song structures. After a while, she noticed patterns, utilized by likeminded songwriters who influenced each other. She reveled in the power and emotion of some songs, which resonated throughout her entire body. She admired the various attitudes of others: from anguished and angry to affirming and even devout. And the crackling from the needle on vinyl transported her back in time.

The following Saturday she was once again in the living room, spinning records and studying album covers. It was an uncharacteristically rainy southern California day. The gutters became small, muddy streams. Cali Sky felt cozy in the cocoon of the living room, the atmosphere outside once again compressed, this time by a passing cold front.

Philip had brought Aunt Nancy over from the nursing home. He then took Cami to a birthday party. Cali Sky lay sprawled on the living room floor, records scattered around her. Aunt Nancy sat in her wheelchair at the edge of the border where the entryway linoleum met living-room carpeting, not far from Cali Sky. Joan occasionally passed by and smiled at them both. Every now and then, she paused to listen to a song. Once, as the Electric Prunes' "Too Much to Dream Last Night" spun on the turntable, she halted near Aunt Nancy's wheelchair and stood frozen.

"Wow," she muttered. Cali Sky and Aunt Nancy looked up at her. She wore an expression that Cali Sky had never seen before, one that did not belong to the life she now lived. The expression looked out of place in their house.

"Wow," she muttered again. Cali Sky felt amused but also disconcerted. *Who was this stranger?* she wondered.

Joan snapped out of her reverie and turned to her sister-in-law: "Nancy, do you remember this song?"

"Sure," Aunt Nancy replied, "but evidently not like you do."

"Summertime in Hollywood. And the beach. Up and down the coast. Hermosa Beach, Huntington Beach, Laguna Beach. It must have been…what…1967. The Summer of Love!"

Joan sat down next to her daughter and listened to a few more songs on the album, reminiscing a bit, but mainly listening in silence. She sat behind Cali Sky, cross legged, and braided her hair. Then at once, Joan kissed her daughter warmly on the cheek, rose and walked out of the room.

For nearly the next three hours, Cali Sky and Aunt Nancy sat almost motionless, listening to albums and exchanging a few words every so often. After Cali Sky fetched Aunt Nancy a glass of water with a straw, she put on the Beatles' White Album. She was intrigued by the diversity of songs, from pure rock and roll to blues to folk to psychedelia to dance hall. When "Mother Nature's Son" began, she felt her mood adapt to the sonic landscape. McCartney's plaintive voice, accompanied by an acoustic guitar, carried her to the meadow in the mountains.

Earlier they had listened to the *Rubber Soul* album. Cali Sky heard now the musical maturation of the Beatles. She asked Aunt Nancy, "Why do you think they called themselves the Beatles?"

"I think they were trying to be clever. I guess they liked the pun, the wordplay."

Cali Sky did not understand. What pun? What wordplay? Then it dawned on her: *Oh, beetles and Beatles. Bugs spelled with a B-E-A-T, instead of a B-E-E-T. That's the pun.* She felt relieved that she did not ask her aunt about the wordplay. It seemed so obvious now. How could she be so stupid not to notice it before?

Aunt Nancy asked, "How do you like their name?"

"I don't know. I guess I really didn't ever think about what it meant."

"Yeah. I think that's because they are so big, so popular. Their reputation precedes them, you know? They've been so successful that people don't even think about their name anymore." Cali Sky had never considered this. *It's like they have become bigger than their name.*

Aunt Nancy noticed the look of concentration on Cali Sky's face and said, "Let me ask you this. Try to imagine that you were there when they decided to call themselves the Beatles, before they became popular. What would you think of the name then?"

Cali Sky considered the question. She tried to forget everything she knew about the Beatles and just think about their name. The Beatles. The Beatles. The Beatles. She analyzed the word until it stopped making sense, until it looked foreign and weird. She started to lose focus. Then remembered that Aunt Nancy asked her a question.

"I don't know. I guess it would sound kind of silly," Cali Sky finally answered.

"Yes," Aunt Nancy erupted with a laugh, "I think so too. The Beatles. How...cheesy! But because they made records like this one"—she gestured toward the record player—"we don't think their name sounds cheesy at all. The Beatles became...the Beatles!" She spoke the first iteration of the name as if she took a large swig of curdled milk; she pronounced the second with reverential awe, as if she were Yahweh identifying himself as "I am" from the burning bush.

Cali Sky laughed. What her aunt said seemed right. She catalogued in her head the names of legendary rock-and-roll bands:

the Who, Cream, the Yardbirds, Led Zeppelin, the Rolling Stones, the Byrds, the Kinks. At their genesis these names may have seemed odd and unlikely, but now, whenever they were spoken, they rolled off the tongue like incantations or magic spells. Cali Sky looked around: Albums circled her like a talismanic ring.

By Tuesday Cali Sky had still not picked up a guitar or set a finger on the piano keyboard. She worked her way through her dad's collection until, on Tuesday afternoon, she listened to the last record in the stack. On Wednesday after school, she selected a few of her favorites and began transcribing the music. Once the notation was complete, she played them—practicing the songs until her performance was clean and tight. She then closed the studio doors, set the cassette player on a chair in front of her and recorded the songs she played. If she made a mistake, however slight, she started over again. The process was methodical and painstakingly slow.

By midnight on Thursday she had worked her way through three albums. On Friday after school she approached Brodie, who stood at his opened locker, flirting with a passing girl.

"Brodie," she announced, "I'm ready to do it."

Brodie turned his attention to Cali Sky, connected her ambiguous words with her expressive eyes, and felt a spasm of lust.

"Really?" he replied suggestively.

She read his expression and laughed at his mis-interpretation.

"No, you horn dog," she exclaimed, "I'm ready to start a band."

THREE

S UMMERTIME STRETCHED INTO long days and late nights. Cali Sky worked part-time at the church helping the music director. She gave guitar lessons once a week to a boy in the neighborhood whose father wanted him to be a rock star. "Can you teach him 'Free Bird'?" That was the first thing the exuberant father ever said to her. And after he deposited the would-be guitar god at the Braithwaite house, Cali Sky struggled to keep the bored boy's attention on the guitar and his clumsy fingers out of his nose. She spent time with her aunt, listening to records and talking, usually slanting subjects—in true Aunt Nancy fashion—toward humor and sarcasm. Most days, because of her open schedule, her parents made her look after Cami.

Much of her time was spent playing guitar and piano. Brodie came over every day. They wrote some songs and played covers, coming up with creative arrangements that gave the songs they knew so well a fresh sound. Their attempts to start a band proved unsuccessful. They put up a flier at a local skate shop. The four kids who called Brodie were disappointments: one said he played drums but didn't have a kit; another played drums and even owned a kit, but had it taken away when his mom found a bag of weed in his pocket; one promising guitar player backed out when he discovered that the person placing the ad was Brodie, who evidently put a move on his girlfriend; and a second guitar player decided at the last moment to join another band.

One day Cali Sky sat behind the Clarendon, readying herself to play a song, running through some of its phrases as if introducing the piano to what lay ahead. Brodie sat on the other side of the wall, in the studio, electric guitar poised in his lap. Cali Sky saw Cami and hesitated. She nearly shooed her away, as she normally did when Cami entered the studio. But she let Cami be.

Cali Sky counted off the song and, together with Brodie, eased into the intro of The Stranglers' "No More Heroes." They both loved to play it, one of those songs with a good guitar/piano combination, even though the original made use of a synthesizer. But Cali Sky could adapt. She led the musical phrases up and down the scale, squeezing notes into each busy measure. Brodie played rhythm and sang. He had no idea who Leon Trotsky and Sancho Panza were, but he memorized their names as the lyrics dictated. He sang it like he meant it. Until they got to the first chorus, which he flubbed. Cali Sky circled back and helped him re-enter the song. Musically she was always patient with Brodie, and he was always accepting of her patience, part of the circularity that grounded their relationship. When he finally made it into the chorus he held on for dear life: He was astounded how quickly Cali Sky played, amazed that she could move her fingers that rapidly. He did not notice that Cami left the studio, fingers plugging her ears.

"There's something else I've been wanting to try," Cali Sky

said when the song ended and Brodie was catching his breath. "Follow me."

They entered the living room and Cali Sky pulled out the record player. Cami rejoined them. "Are you gonna play a record? Can I listen?" she asked.

"Okay," Cali Sky replied, a response which seemed to surprise both Cami and Brodie.

Cali Sky thumbed through the records, selected one in the middle of the stack, placed the vinyl disc on the turntable, and gently set the needle on a middle track. A D chord exploded from the speakers, weighted with an accompanying bass as well as the pop of a snare drum and the crash of cymbals.

"I thought maybe we could play this," Cali Sky said quickly before the vocals entered. "It's a song by Cream called 'Tales of Brave Ulysses.'" Brodie looked dubious, raising his eyebrows and rolling his eyes. Cali Sky knew his reaction without even looking at him. She understood what he was thinking: far-out hippie lyrics, guitar solos, parents' music, the establishment.

"So what do you think, Cami?" asked Cali Sky at the conclusion of the song, "Do you think Brodie and I can play that?"

"*You* can, but Brodie can't."

Ten minutes later Cali Sky was contorting the song, tweaking it even further into the surreal. Down the guitar neck she harnessed the notes, then let them sink into the slow vibrato effect of the wah-wah pedal. Cami always giggled when Cali Sky used it. It made music sound like a toy. Brodie only just heard the song, still trying, reluctantly, to get inside it. So he played it literally and unimaginatively. The words caught Cami's attention. With their mythical imagery, they almost sounded to her like a bedtime story. The imagery seized Brodie's attention for entirely different reasons, reasons purely male and purely adolescent: quivering mermaids, Aphrodite poised on a seashell and a girl's body dancing in the surf. Either way both Cami and Brodie were left spellbound by Cali Sky's performance.

Her cheeks were flush. Cami stared briefly at her, then bolted from the room. Brodie glanced at Cali Sky's face, but avoided eye contact. Although she had stopped playing almost a minute earlier, Brodie felt like she still emitted music. He imagined touching her, kissing her. Then wrenched himself out of his fantasy by announcing in an enthusiastic whisper, "That was fucking great!"

Cali Sky hurled at him a look of reproach. But her parents, and more importantly her dad, were out of earshot. A gradual transition then blossomed on her face, from righteous anger to devious joy, scattering the intimation of music in every direction. Face uplifted she fixed her eyes on Brodie. "Yeah," she responded in an unhesitating voice, "it was."

She began to experiment with the wah-wah pedal, Brodie still looking on like a genuflecting choir boy. She knew the sounds would summon Cami back into the room. Sure enough, not long thereafter, she came bounding into the studio. "Make it laugh!" she demanded. Cali Sky created guitar laughter. "Make it cry!" Cali Sky created guitar weeping. Cami's demands rose up like feverish prayers.

Brodie offered his own supplication, his throbbing mind and imagination still lingering on girls dancing on the beach. "Make it…" he began, but hesitated, looked at Cami, stopped and quickly added, "never mind."

"Make it what?" asked Cami.

"Yeah, make it what?" asked Cali Sky, a gleam in her eye. Brodie broke out into his sheepish look. Cali Sky reveled in his discomfort.

"Uh, make it tell me to shut up," he mumbled. Cami laughed. Cali Sky gave it a shot, while Brodie's mind lingered for a few more moments on the pornographic possibilities of guitar sounds.

For the next few minutes, flipping various effects switches on her amp and maximizing the potential of her wah-wah pedal Cali Sky created a sonic universe populated by invisible people laughing, crying, screaming and even having conversations. There were invisible dogs barking and invisible cows mooing. The wind blew and thunder rumbled. Two armies clashed on a battlefield, the shrill whistling of bombs culminating in massive explosions, the fate of thousands resting on Cali Sky and her guitar. Brodie acted out some of the drama, gazing up in mock terror at the descending bombs and hurling himself to the floor with each imaginary impact. The spectacle sent Cami into hysterics.

Feigning injury Brodie rose to his feet and limped toward the door. "Gotta go," he stammered laboriously, fake agony etched on his face, "gotta...find....a....hospital."

"Bye!" said Cali Sky, handling her guitar like a rifle and taking aim at Brodie. He rushed out the door.

Twenty minutes later Cali Sky was still in the studio when he rushed back in. This time the emotion painted on his face was genuine.

"Hey," he began breathlessly, "I just got off the phone with John Lanza. He and his brother want to start a band with us."

"Who? What?"

"John Lanza. His brother's name is Jim. They go to Sutter." Attending a different middle school would explain why Cali Sky never heard of them. "Their bass player is Gary Heaton. Well, he *was* their bass player. He left to play drums for another band."

"Okay," said Cali Sky, cutting to the chase, "so Gary left the band. They need a bass player and, what, another guitar player?"

"Yeah."

The silence was open and wide, then funneled into significance, ultimately becoming the straitjacket of a dilemma. The opportunity: two musicians needed, one on bass, one on guitar.

Two applicants: Cali Sky, a divinely gifted guitar player who also happens to be a competent bass player, and Brodie, a barely competent guitar player who plays bass like a kindergartener connecting dots with a dull crayon. The bass stood there lonely in the corner of the studio, looking sad and pathetic like the last boy chosen on a kickball team during recess. Cali Sky and Brodie both played it occasionally, when they felt a certain song or jam needed a deep anchor. They enjoyed it at first, giving them entrée into the music from a completely different angle. But after a short while the sexy guitar beckoned, and playing its thick-stringed, long-necked ugly cousin was a bit like brushing your teeth.

"So when are you going to learn bass?" Cali Sky smiled. Brodie looked deflated.

"You need to become one quick," Cali Sky continued, "Start by picking up that bass over there and playing a song with me. Why don't we try 'Tales of Brave Ulysses' again?"

Brodie rolled his eyes. "Fine." He slung the hefty instrument around his neck. "Where's the D on this thing again?"

They pulled up to a small house not far off the Santa Ana Freeway. Philip once drove Cali Sky and Cami through this neighborhood on their way up Red Hill Avenue to the higher elevations, where the CEOs from Irvine and the occasional actor from Hollywood burrowed into their orange-groved palatial estates on the side of the mountain, high above the Tustin commoners. Philip had labored to drive the orange Bronco inconspicuously among the opulence in search of an open space from which he could offer his children a panoramic view of the fireworks show at Disneyland.

This time, they stuck to the lowlands. The house had a crescent driveway slicing through a yard more dirt than grass. It looked tired and worn, like it would be content to slide down the hill, merge onto the Costa Mesa Freeway, and drift toward the ocean, plunging into Newport Harbor. Philip killed the Bronco's grizzly motor and opened his door. The sound of drums boomed from inside the house. The muffled snare and bass drum triggered for Philip a flashback: Sunset Strip, late at night, Whisky a Go Go, a foggy night. Or was that fog in his brain?

Brodie had to time his knocks, pounding the door in between drum beats and cymbal crashes. He and Cali Sky laughed because they found it amusing. Philip laughed because he was nervous. Finally a wispy middle-aged woman opened the door. She was short and thin. Her smile was careworn and fragile. Her straw hair was disheveled. *The kind of person who has given up on appearances, pressed by hardship to stop caring*, Philip thought. *This is what a parent who has a kid in a band looks like.*

"Hi. You must be Cali Sky and Brodie. And you are Brodie's dad?"

"No," Philip answered, "Cali Sky's dad. Philip."

"My name is Barbara. Barbara Lanza. Please come in."

Soft spoken and mild mannered, she came across as gentle and benevolent, the sort of person anxious six-year-olds would want to hug before their first day of school. Philip felt more comfortable. Brodie meanwhile led Cali Sky down a darkened hallway that smelled like French fries and teenage funk. Cali Sky's guitar case bumped lightly against the yellowed walls as she followed Brodie nervously, struggling with his amp in the other hand. She watched as he opened the farthest door.

"What the hell, man? Your drums are loud!" he called into the room. Cali Sky could tell by the ingratiating tone of his voice that he was smiling, casting wide his net of intimacy.

"They're drums, you hippie! What do you expect?" came a voice from inside the room.

"Cut your hair, you poser!" came another, softer voice somewhere else in the room.

"Kiss my ass," hissed Brodie in return, using his conspiratorial parents-in-the-vicinity voice. He and his bass guitar pivoted into the room, with his amp, swinging from his arm, bringing up the rear.

Cali Sky followed, guiding her guitar through the doorway. She looked up and surveyed the room. A boy sat behind a black drum kit set up in the corner. Another boy sat on an orange plastic classroom chair next to the drums. A guitar and amp, quiet but threatening, stood ready behind him. Coke cans and fast-food trash lay scattered around the room. A homemade Social Distortion poster hung above the drum kit. It depicted a skeleton sipping from a martini glass. John, who played guitar, once told Brodie that he met Mike Ness, lead singer of Social Distortion, at an In-N-Out Burger somewhere on Sepulveda Avenue in LA. The room was windowless, lit by a single high-voltage light bulb hanging from the ceiling. Cali Sky had the sensation of being underground.

"This is Cali Sky," Brodie said, leaving the room to fetch her amp. That was the extent of his introduction, as if he were merely reminding them of who she was, for in Brodie's close-knit, intimate universe it was unfathomable that people like them did not all know each other already.

"I'm John. I play guitar." He rose and moved toward his instrument.

"Hey," replied Cali Sky as she gently set down her guitar.

"I'm Jim. I play drums," Jim said from the drum stool.

"Obviously, you dip shit," John scoffed at his brother.

Cali Sky laughed. She felt more comfortable. Brodie returned with her amp.

John agreed to tune his guitar to Cali Sky's, since hers was already in tune with Brodie's bass.

"Alright," John said to Cali Sky, "Give me an E."

While she picked the low E Jim rose from his drum stool, turned his body sideways, and tried to form an E with his arms and head. "An E!" he declared. Brodie laughed.

"Shut up, Jim," whined John, who seemed perpetually exasperated with his brother. Cali Sky got the impression that Jim made that joke more than a few times.

"Does that sound close to you?" John asked as he plucked the E after a slight rotation of the tuning key.

"I think just a bit sharper," replied Cali Sky after she compared her note to his.

Jim meanwhile began a soft drum roll on his snare.

"Shut up!" John snapped, "Let us tune our guitars!" He worked his way down the strings, concentration knitted on his face. Once he had finished he and Cali Sky played a few chords together, to be sure they were in tune. A restless Jim began tapping on his snare again.

"Shut the fuck up! Stop playing!" John snapped again, losing both patience and concentration. Brodie laughed. Cali Sky pretended to ignore the bickering.

"Okay," John announced suddenly and irritably, "That's good enough." He looked at Brodie, Jim and Cali Sky, in that order. "What do you want to play?"

Silence. Cali Sky and Brodie were hesitant to propose a song, Cali Sky because she felt like she was on John and Jim's territory, Brodie because he did not know how to play any songs on bass.

John and Cali Sky looked at each other guardedly. Tension. They had the intention of forming a band, of working together to create music, of being on the same team. But in that moment it felt to Cali Sky more like a competition, to see how she stacked up against this other guitar player, to prove to John and Jim that she was what many others already knew her to be: a prodigy.

"How about 'Another State of Mind'?" John finally proposed. A Social Distortion song, one that played on KROQ, a bootlegged single. Cali Sky had never heard the song, but knew she could play it anyway. Brodie had heard the song many times, but nevertheless knew he could not play it at all.

John took Cali Sky through it. She was surprised, perhaps pleasantly surprised, when he was not able to identify by name some of the chords he played. Especially since all the chords of the song were power chords, simple fifths. John *literally* showed her how to play it, demonstrated it chord by chord. Cali Sky then had to translate the song to bass for the benefit of Brodie. Finally, after everyone was brought up to speed—agonizing minutes for the ever-restless Jim—they readied themselves.

Jim began the song, hitting the ride cymbal in sixteenth time. The tempo was fast. Then John and Cali Sky entered, joined shortly thereafter by Brodie. She played her parts, but the song did not give her much room to roam, and since she had never heard it before, she did not want to go too far off course. She played some chords further up the neck, threw in some runs in between changes, but mainly felt stifled. She also was forced on a few occasions to assist Brodie, who got his notes a bit confused. They both missed the ending, which came abruptly and which John never signaled. Cali Sky covered her mistake, sliding the added chord down the neck to give it a sense of closure. Brodie just stopped playing unceremoniously.

"Alright," said John at the conclusion. "That was good."

Good for you, thought Cali Sky. The song showcased the talents of the Lanza brothers. Jim reached down from his drum stool to take a swig from a Coke can. Brodie relaxed his fingers, trying to appear nonchalant.

"How about we try something we all know?" offered Cali Sky. It was the most she had spoken at one time since she arrived.

"Okay," answered John. He proposed some other songs, mostly esoteric punk songs. Finally to Brodie and Cali Sky's surprise, he asked, "How about 'Smoke on the Water'?" The classic garage-band jam. But also anathema to punk sensibilities.

"Are you serious?" asked Brodie.

"Yeah," replied John. Then to Jim, "Can you play it?"

"Does Dolly Parton sleep on her back?"

John rolled his eyes. Brodie laughed.

Like everyone else Cali Sky knew the song, not only from the radio but from her dad's record collection. He owned a copy of Deep Purple's *Machine Head* album. She had listened to it a couple of times.

She risked it and asked John, "Do you have the song on tape?"

To Brodie's further astonishment John replied, "Yeah." His reply was not in the least bit defensive. To Brodie, such an admission was tantamount to admitting that you used to sleep in your parents' bed.

"Well," Cali Sky asked again, "why don't we listen to it once first, just to remember the parts?"

John looked at Jim. Jim shrugged. John answered, "Okay."

John dug up the tape from his collection and for the next five minutes they listened to the song. After the first verse Jim asked, "What the hell is he singing about?"

"Shut up, Jim," barked John. He pressed stop before the song ended.

They briefly discussed how to arrange it. Cali Sky figured out the chord progression, correcting John, who then became silent, deferring to Cali Sky's instructions. She spoke confidently. She demonstrated some of the arrangements. For the first time John focused his attention on Cali Sky while she played. She fingered notes both quickly and cleanly—no mistakes. While she waited for everyone else to return to their instruments John looked on as she absentmindedly played some riffs, miles away from Deep Purple, that came from nowhere, like her fingers were operating independently of the rest of her body. The riff made her electric sound like a Spanish guitar, low notes bubbling deep underground, slowly rising to the surface and finally rocketing from the earth like a geyser.

"Do you mind if I play solo and you rhythm?" asked Cali Sky. John hesitated. "Um, okay."

"Everyone ready?" she asked. Nods all around.

She began the riff that made Deep Purple famous. As she neared the end of the second measure she looked at Jim and John, and nodded. John joined in on the chord progression, Jim worked the high hat. Brodie entered at the beginning of the next measure. John sang, only because he was standing closest to the mic. Not including the chorus he knew about four words of the lyrics. He made up the rest, often just yelling nonsensical words.

Halfway through the song Cali Sky got everyone's attention and nodded once again: They were approaching the guitar solo. Brodie knew what to expect, he had been listening to Cali Sky play guitar for eight months. Not John and Jim. After she began the solo John took a step back, a bit staggered. Jim, who rarely looked up from his drums, could not resist: He watched her. Unlike John, Cali Sky cued everyone as they neared the end. She synced with Jim and slowed the last half measure down. They brought "Smoke on the Water" to a gradual halt. Everyone exchanged glances but Cali Sky. Everyone smiled but Cali Sky.

"That was great!" cried Jim, producing a short torrent of idiotic laughter. John nodded.

"Didn't I say she was incredible?" Brodie enthused.

Cali Sky was kneeling, her back to the band, fiddling with her amp settings. This was the first time she played with a complete band. This was, was supposed to be, a real rock-and-roll experience. What she had dreamed about. What rescued records scattered on a living room floor had promised at midnight. Where her sickening desire on a mountainside pointed. She felt let down, like a promise was broken. The enchantment fled, chased away by hard, cold material realities: empty McDonald's cups, an overtaxed light bulb, brotherly bickering, fucked-up notes and shitty acoustics. Cali Sky confronted the seismic chasm—dark, deep, unbridgeable—between their version and Deep Purple's original.

But it was more than that. She heard some lines from Aunt Nancy's poem flickering angrily in her head:

"So let me be thy choir, and make a moan

Upon the midnight hours."

The summons was unheeded. Where is that choir? What produces that moan? Who is worthy of dwelling in those midnight hours?

"And," Brodie continued, "she's just as good on keyboards as she is on guitar." He let that sink in for a moment. John took another step back. Jim waited for Cali Sky to rise and face the band. She remained kneeling.

"Well," John put in, "maybe we can find some. I can probably borrow some keyboards from someone."

"Gary's new band has a keyboardist. Maybe we could borrow his?" offered Jim.

"Fuck Gary," John hissed. "He betrayed us. I wouldn't borrow shit from him." He looked at his brother and shook his head, "What are you thinking, Jim?"

Cali Sky rose suddenly, faced the band and announced, "How about 'Gloria'?"

Befuddlement spread across the room.

"You know," she continued. "'Gloria.' The Them song. It's only three chords. It would be easy for us to play it."

Lingering befuddlement. They had never heard of Them. She ran through the three chords and sang the chorus once. Then they all immediately recognized it, like most, having heard it somewhere, sometime on the radio but not knowing where it came from. The song is like sonic sex. It builds and builds and makes you wonder if the chorus is ever going to come. Like so many rock songs "Gloria" could be about a girl or God, about salvation or damnation, about death or screwing.

Which is why Brodie, John and Jim could barely play the simple three-chord song when Cali Sky led them through it, belting out the lyrics and ripping through solos. Glancing up at the long, messy, dark hair, the passionate face, words burning from her soul, and the sometimes finessed, sometimes throttled guitar, John felt intimidated. He took another step back and thought of a painting he once saw in a history textbook of a woman being burned at the stake, wild hair and enraptured face. But what struck John about the painting was that the woman seemed to face the flames, and death, with defiance.

Jim lacked the capacity for such meditations. He merely thought, *Cool. She's singing about a girl.* Once again however he managed to sync with Cali Sky: As they approached each climactic chorus he gradually opened the high hat, heightening the sense of anticipation. As instructed beforehand, John sang the chorus with Cali Sky. Once, their cheeks touched. Later that night when John masturbated he thought only of that one moment, his mind feverish with images of flying hair and an impassioned face threatened by the licking tongue of fire.

"How about The No Men?" proposed Jim after they played the song. "Get it? One girl and three boys? No Men?"

"Shut up, Jim."

"What about The Nobodies?" Brodie offered.

"Umm."

"How about No Shit?"

"Shut up, Jim."

"Nowhere," said Cali Sky.

"That's pretty good," commented John after a pause. "I could introduce us at gigs and say, 'We're Nowhere.'"

"Or, we could say, 'This band is going Nowhere.'"

"Shut the fuck up, Jim."

Everyone knew that Grandpa's breath smelled but no one admitted it to Cami.

"It does! It really does!" Cami whined.

"That's enough," threatened Joan feebly and unconvincingly as she powdered the hamburger patties with seasoning salt.

Aunt Nancy, seated in her wheelchair, shrugged.

"Seriously, though," Cali Sky reasoned, "who likes to be around them?"

Aunt Nancy smirked. Cami looked at Joan. Joan disguised her silence by industriously racing from one end of the kitchen counter to the other, superfluously stirring the macaroni salad. Cami walked quietly and slowly to her mom and clung to her leg. She rubbed her face on Joan's upper thigh, at the base of her shorts. Joan set down the spoon and ran her fingers through Cami's hair.

"Anything I can do, Joan?" asked Aunt Nancy. "I mean, from my wheelchair?" Aunt Nancy looked malnourished and weak, as if holding up her head required focused effort.

"No, I think everything is ready," Joan answered.

The back door opened, letting in the sound of a short and startling popping noise. Philip closed the door behind him.

"I hear those firecrackers every five minutes," he said as he entered the kitchen. "Just hope nothing catches on fire, as dry as it is." Cami burrowed her head between Joan's legs. Joan flashed Philip an imploring look that said, *Be careful what you say in front of Cami.*

"The grill is lit," Philip added quickly. "I'll start the burgers once Grandpa and Grandma arrive."

"Noooo," came the muffled cry from the vicinity of Joan's crotch. Philip caught another flash of the look and winced.

"Cami," exclaimed Aunt Nancy, coming to the rescue, "do you wanna play a game with me?" Cami peeked up at her aunt, weighing a response. "How about Candy Land?"

As Philip helped Joan make final preparations for the Fourth of July barbecue, Cami, Aunt Nancy and Cali Sky followed the Rainbow Trail to Candy Castle. Aunt Nancy genuinely loved board games, all board games. At the nursing home she played Scrabble with the resident in the next room for hours at a time, deliberating each move for ten minutes, dissatisfied with any word score totaling less than twenty-five points. Cali Sky's participation was less enthusiastic. Cami had just entered the shortcut at Gum Drop Mountain when the doorbell rang.

Grandpa wore polyester slacks. Nobody could remember the last time he wore shorts. Dangling from his hand was a six pack of Old Milwaukee. Grandma wore dress pants and a staid blouse. She cradled in her arms a bowl of fruit salad. As usual she salted the cantaloupe. Both stood in the kitchen doorway, smiling. A chorus of "Hi's," "Hello's," and "How are you's?" filled the clichéd space of social decorum. Grandpa struggled with the beer.

"Here Dad," Philip offered, "let me help you."

Slightly hunchbacked, Grandma walked methodically, like a mechanical contraption, toward the wheelchair, following an imaginary path illuminated by tunnel vision. "Nancy, how do you feel, dear?" Grandma affected a look of well-wrought pathos.

"Great, Mom. Ready for the marathon," joked Aunt Nancy from her emaciated mouth. As Grandma frowned, missing, as usual, the sarcasm, Cali Sky stood nearby, ready to dispense the perfunctory hug and greeting. It took Grandma a few seconds to notice Cali Sky standing at her side: Aunt Nancy's witticism had distracted her, sidetracking her literalizing mind.

"Cali! There you are! Give your grandma a hug." Cali Sky smelled perfume and moth balls.

Once the occasion for greeting Cali Sky had elapsed, Grandma hefted her slowly gathered attention to Cami.

"Cami, you come from behind Aunt Nancy's wheelchair and give your grandma a hug." Cami remained motionless, peering over Aunt Nancy's shoulder. Cali Sky braced herself for a stand-off. Aunt Nancy uttered a noncommittal "Cami." Grandma's face darkened in slow motion and evolved into a scowl.

"Cami," she barked, "you *stop* that." Simultaneous with the hiss of the word "stop," Grandma slapped her hands together sloppily in a clap of reproach. Cali Sky had seen the gesture before. With effort she stifled a mocking smile.

"Mom," interrupted Aunt Nancy gently. "You're going to scare her…. Cami, please come here." Cami timorously tiptoed out of hiding. Aunt Nancy looked in her eyes, smiled and said, "Give Grandma a hug, and then we can finish our game!"

"But she smells like Grandpa." Cami's voice was small, intended only for Aunt Nancy's ears, but it spread audibly to everyone in the room.

Grandpa returned from the refrigerator, can of Old Milwaukee in hand. He bent down toward Cami. "Cami, you mustn't say things like that. You must respect your grandparents. Don't you know what happened in the Bible, to the children who made fun of Elisha because he was old?"

Cami shook her head. Aunt Nancy interjected, "Dad, don't! Come on!"

"Do you know?" pressed Grandpa.

Cami shook her head.

"Dad!" Aunt Nancy called out again.

He ignored her: "God sent a bear to eat those children."

Joan whisked Cami away before the image became concrete, distracting her with a small sample of the freshly baked apple pie.

"Dad!" Aunt Nancy felt defeated, powerless to confront a parent who had cared for her for two long years, who had taken her back into his home after a thick-skinned neurologist looked her in the eyes and announced, "It's multiple sclerosis."

Undaunted, Grandpa rose, turned to his wife and spoke in his own version of a small voice: "They really do spoil these children." Unlike Cami's, Grandpa's voice was insincerely confidential. Like Cami's it went unheard by no one in the room.

Philip too resorted to distraction: "Dad, the Dodgers game is starting soon. Why don't we listen to it on the radio?"

Cali Sky spent the next thirty minutes in the studio, quietly playing the acoustic guitar. She could overhear voices scattered around the house:

Grandma: "Joan, you always do such a nice job making everything look so nice."

Aunt Nancy: "Ah, you're lost in Lollipop Woods."

Vin Scully from the backyard radio: "It's time for Dodgers baseball!"

Cami: "No."

Some fake woman on TV: "Lipton's Cinnamon makes me feel slightly devilish."

Joan: "Cami, rules are rules."

Grandpa: "Steve Garvey. Now that guy has some forearms."

Joan: "That table is so beat up."

Philip: (Laughter)

Cami: "I don't like this game."

Grandma: "The Petersons always have such nice things."

Vin Scully: "A high fly ball to right field. Reggie Smith is there to make the catch."

Cali Sky tried to play, but felt distracted. *I'm in a band.* She remembered, again, for the thousandth time. The refrain gave her a sense of relief. She always knew it would happen, but when, when, when. When was now. She embraced the oncoming epiphany, the flash of self-understanding, and let it scatter and resituate all of the other refrains that shaped her: *I have weird hair, My aunt is disabled, I am a musician—no, I am a great musician—no, I am—as my own piano teacher said—a "prodigy," my parents love me and they love God and keep secrets, my sister is weird—and I like it, people look at me like they can't figure me out—and I love it. I am in a band.* She imagined terminating a conversation with a normal person, an average person, a non-musician, by saying, "I'm in a band. You wouldn't understand."

The acoustic seemed stubborn and lazy, so she set it down. She pressed play on the cheap cassette deck. Brodie had recorded a bootlegged single from a band Cali Sky had never heard of: U2. During the second band rehearsal with John and Jim she had asked Brodie about the name.

He said, "It means, you too can join the band."

John responded, "No it doesn't, you dumbass. U2 was a spy plane."

"Why would they name their band after a spy plane?" asked Jim.

"Because it's cool, dipshit."

The sound of a guitar with strong echo effects bounced from the small speakers. The song was called "A Day Without Me." Cali Sky heard that U2's singer, Bono, wrote the lyrics after hearing about the suicide of Ian Curtis. *A song about a singer? A song about dying?* She drifted upward into her Olympian perspective, into timelessness: *How would this day be different without me? If I were dead would Cami still hate Grandpa and Grandma? Would Dad still let Grandpa and Grandma treat him like shit?*

She snapped out of her reverie and attended to the song. It was different, certainly not American sounding. It was not obvious, like punk. It avoided the blues framework from which was constructed nearly every song she heard on her dad's records. She had heard someone, probably Brodie, use the phrase "New Wave." Was this it? She thought about how difficult it would be to play the song: Her amp could not produce those echo effects. Most of all, she had never heard a song with which she felt so immediately intimate. The voice was passionate and believable, like it flowed from the heart of some uncorrupted humanity. It stood for something. She could trust the song. She wondered for a moment if maybe she had heard it before, but remembered that was impossible. Suddenly she jumped, startled. The studio door opened. In walked Grandpa, smiling. Until the U2 song reached his ears. Then the smile became dismissive.

"You like this better than music?" he joked.

Cali Sky said nothing, trying to calm her uncharacteristically skittish nerves. She darted toward the cassette player, fumbled with the buttons and pushed stop. "Um, yeah," she mumbled.

"Really? Do you really think that song is good?" His smile softened his inquisition as he took another step forward.

"Yes, I really do." She had regained her composure, digging in, not willing, this time, to back down.

"Why? What's good about that song?"

Cali Sky was not surprised that he pushed the point and answered, "The guitar riff, the beat, the voice...."

"But the voice is awful," Grandpa interrupted. "It can't hold a candle to the singers of old. Rosemary Clooney, Nat King Cole, Frank Sinatra in his prime—those were the days. Truly talented singers."

"Rosemary Clooney, Nat King Cole and Frank Sinatra couldn't sing that song if they tried," retorted Cali Sky, pointing to the cassette player, as if the song sat inside it like a defendant in a courtroom.

"Well, I'm not sure they would want to. It's so...repetitive."

"It *has* to be repetitive," she answered with rising emotion. "Because music is gone the moment it's heard. Repetition helps us remember." Her words were pastiche, assembled inexactly from the aphorisms of Mr. Nussbaum and her own fragmented thoughts.

His smile released tension, relaxing into the comfortable self-assurance of victory. "Well, I can't say I know what you mean there. But you're a smart kid. And I know you are a good musician. The next time you visit us, I'll play you some of *my* music. Then you'll see what I mean."

Cali Sky felt the anger surge, robbing her, in a flash, of self-control. She nearly released a response that began, "I'm in a band. You wouldn't understand." But before she could let fly a reply, Grandpa added, "Oh, I almost forgot why I came in here. Dinner's ready." He shuffled out of the studio.

In the kitchen Grandma was making a fuss. Philip had finished grilling the hamburgers when Joan realized—and made the mistake of vocalizing—that she had forgotten the vegetable tray, which was supposed to be an appetizer. Grandma then announced that she and she alone, so as to lighten Joan's burden, would prepare the vegetable tray at once.

"But Mom," Aunt Nancy reasoned, "dinner's ready. It's too late for an appetizer now."

"No, it's okay. It's the least that I can do."

Joan poured herself another glass of wine. Grandpa popped

open another Old Milwaukee. Cali Sky returned to the studio and listened to the U2 song again, half-hoping that Grandpa would re-enter. Philip went outside, eased himself into a lounge chair, and let the soporific voice of Vin Scully serenade him into a nap. Grandma cut and sliced the vegetables with painstaking deliberation, gumming her dentures and humming a tune lilting with an exaggerated 1950's vibrato. Fifteen minutes later the hamburgers were cold, but the appetizer was prepared. Everyone stood around the dining room table. Everyone but Philip.

"Philip!" called Joan.

"Daddy!" called Cami.

"Food's getting cold!" complained Grandpa.

The back door opened and closed, punctuated by the popping sound of a firecracker from some distant street in the neighborhood. In walked Philip, half asleep and zombie-like, trying to shake off the nap that had seized him in the backyard. He looked disoriented and lost, scratching his beard.

Joan snickered and sarcastically steered him toward his place at the table. "There you go, Philip. Yep, this is your place." Joan looked like she was training a puppy. "Now, will you lead us in a prayer so we can eat this food?"

Philip nodded, closed his eyes, bowed his head and folded his hands. Everyone followed suit. And waited. Cali Sky cracked open an eyelid and peered at her dad. At first she thought he had fallen back asleep, while standing. Then she heard him clear his throat.

"Dear God," he began. She felt relief. *Yeah, Dad, that's the way you start.* But then he seemed to drift off again into a sleepy fog. Awkward waiting again. Joan made a noise, which sounded to Cali Sky like the beginnings of stifled laughter.

"Dear God," he repeated, apparently making another run at it. Then more silence. Joan made another noise. *No doubt about it*, thought Cali Sky, *she's starting to laugh.* Grandpa shifted his weight. Grandma gummed her dentures nervously. Philip's brain was not yet working.

"Thank you…for this food…" he mumbled incoherently. Joan laughed out loud. Philip looked up and glared at her. He tried to piece together a sentence: "to which…our bodies…to the nourishment…which it will receive." Aunt Nancy now let out a nasally guffaw that sounded like a thwarted sneeze. Sensing merriment Cami looked at Aunt Nancy and giggled. The sound of giggling dispelled the reverent mood of prayer, which now gave way to the din of ridiculousness. Grandma looked scandalized. Grandpa frowned.

Cali Sky remained expressionless. In the midst of her dad's babble and her family's hubbub, disturbing reflections thrust themselves into her mind. *Does God hear a prayer like this? Is this stupid prayer really any different than all the other prayers Dad makes—the ones that are serious and real? How does Aunt Nancy pray?* The laughter surrounding her gave the reflections a sinister shape, as if they were mocking her. The experience de-familiarized the familiar: She had the sensation of looking through something that she thought was solid. It was too late now for Philip to regain control and restore dignity to the pious moment. Laughter now flooded through the opened gates. The dam had burst.

"Oh, for the love of…" Grandpa had enough. "We thank you, God, for this food," he proclaimed with raised voice. He waited for the laughter to stop. "And please help this family…" A calculated pause. "…to be respectful…" Another calculated pause. "…and to teach their children respect." A final calculated pause. "Amen." The word shot from Grandpa's mouth with the finality of a knock-out punch.

By dessert the popping of firecrackers echoed off the houses more frequently. Philip had brought the radio inside and turned it on. During a lull in the conversation the voice of Vin Scully carried into the dining room: Jose Cruz had just hit a double, driving in the go-ahead run to put the Astros in front of the Dodgers in the top half of the fifth inning.

"Time to yank Welch," Grandpa commented.

"I don't know, Dad," countered Philip, "That kid has an ERA under three this year. He can work his way out of jams."

"No, he's too young to handle the pressure when the game is close and he falls behind in the count."

Cali Sky yawned. Aunt Nancy and Cami continued their game of Candy Land while Grandma and Joan sipped coffee.

"Speaking of yank," continued Grandpa, "how about this president of ours. Carter has got to be the worst president in history." No one, especially Philip, had any interest in engaging Grandpa in a political discussion. So Philip simply nodded, letting Grandpa release some pent-up disgust.

Grandma set her coffee cup down and followed her line of tunnel vision to Cali Sky.

"So how are you dear? You are so quiet."

Cali Sky pushed away her plate of apple-pie crumbs and vanilla-ice-cream residue. "I'm fine," she replied, nodding. "I'm doing well."

"How's your piano playing? You *do* have such a great gift. I *am* so happy for you."

"Yeah, it's going really well." Cali Sky smiled without conviction at Grandma.

"Grandpa and I are looking forward to your next concert at church."

Cali Sky stretched her fake smile.

"Look at those eyes—so beautiful," Grandma continued. "You probably have to keep the boys away. At your age, you know, boys have one-track minds." Cali Sky now felt like she wanted to disappear.

Grandpa pulled his attention away from Vin Scully and added, "Stay away from them, Cali. You know what I mean?"

"Oh come on, Mom, Dad," interjected Aunt Nancy. "You make them out to be monsters. Besides Cali Sky doesn't want to hear this."

"They *are* monsters," Grandpa insisted, "And Cali *should* hear this."

"No really," exclaimed Cali Sky, "I don't need to hear this."

Grandma's tunnel vision lost focus and she sat back, ignoring Cali Sky and looking nostalgic. "I remember when Philip was your age. He walked right up to me and your grandpa one day, and asked us permission to buy a poster of some pin-up girl. Something he saw in a record shop...."

"Mother," Philip interrupted, "please."

"...oh, that was so...shocking," Grandma continued. "Such... audacity!"

"Mother," pleaded Aunt Nancy, "please stop."

"Yeah," added Grandpa, unfazed, "that took a lot of guts." Cali Sky couldn't tell if Grandpa was disappointed or proud.

"Will you both please stop?" Joan skirted the line separating politeness and anger.

"Joan, I don't mean any harm," said Grandma, fixing the tunnel vision in her direction. "Boys will be boys—that's all I mean. Hormones run wild at their age. Besides, look how good Philip turned out: so respectable." She fell back into a nostalgic reverie. "And so brave, so...sacrificial."

She re-mobilized the tunnel vision and pointed it at Cali Sky. "When he was young your dad stood up for your mother...on more than one occasion—the way it *should* be. He once rescued her from these horrible boys, *barbarians* more like it." Grandma shifted her attention to her son: "Didn't that happen at Castaic Lake, Philip?"

Philip nodded, then quickly looked away.

Joan spoke up again, "We don't want to hear about that, okay."

Grandma submitted to Joan this time, until Cali Sky unexpectedly asked, "No, what happened at Castaic Lake?"

"It was chivalry," declared Grandma, turning back to Cali Sky, "He protected your mother and stood up to those horrible boys…"

"Yeah," interjected Grandpa. "until he got his head beat in."

"That's enough!" shouted Philip, standing. "That's enough!"

Cami was the first to break the silence that followed. She cried. The kind that begins slowly and pathetically, building volume until it becomes unstoppable and you wonder if it will ever end. She ran to Joan and buried her head in her lap. Joan wrapped her hands around her daughter's head and in a steady voice of barely controlled lividness she faced Grandpa and said, "I think you better go now." Philip remained standing, motionless. Cali Sky waited, hoping for a confrontation.

Grandpa had his left hand raised level to his head, which was facing down. Cali Sky could not decipher the body language. A gesture of remorse? Was he raising his hand to speak? He looked awkward and uncomfortable.

Grandma hurled the tunnel vision at him and scolded above Cami's wails, "Really, Chet, why must you say things like that? Now look what you have done!" When Grandpa looked up Cali Sky saw an expression of guilt, chased away by a look of annoyance that he flashed toward Grandma.

Grandma's attention plodded in the direction of Joan and Philip. "I *am* very sorry." She paused while one of Cami's cries crescendoed. "And Philip, you know that your father doesn't mean any harm. He just speaks without thinking." Joan soothed Cami, who now quieted. Grandma repeated to Philip, "You know that."

"You and Dad should still probably go." Aunt Nancy looked disgusted. *Yeah, get out*, thought Cali Sky.

"No. No. Don't go," Philip breathed calmly and compassionately. Cali Sky looked at him with disappointment. He continued, "I don't want our Fourth of July to end like that. And yes, Mother, I do know that Dad does not mean any harm. Stay. And watch the fireworks on TV later with us."

Joan rose, picked up Cami and left the room. Aunt Nancy turned the other way.

"Oh, good, dear," Grandma gushed with relief. "You *are* so understanding."

Cali Sky sneered at Grandpa, but his head remained down and he did not see her.

Late that night as Cali Sky lay in bed writing lyrics for some Nowhere songs she heard her parents arguing: ugly shouts that went through her like a jolt of electricity, increasing her pulse, making her feel nervous. She penned lyrics that painted emotional landscapes, vague and suggestive.

Cami walked sullenly into Cali Sky's doorway. "Cali Sky," she said quietly, "Can I sleep with you in your bed?" Cami looked pathetic, small and disconsolate.

"Alright. Come on."

Cami ran to the bed and jumped into the covers.

"Cali Sky, did God really send a bear to eat those kids?"

"I don't know, Cami."

"That's so mean. Why would God do that?"

"I don't know, Cami."

Cali Sky threw her lyric book to the floor, and the two sisters nestled together, falling asleep quickly and deeply.

FOUR

ARLIER IN THE summer on a slow-cooling evening some kids from Cali Sky's school had gathered at a local movie theater, nicknamed the Domes, to celebrate the birthday of a girl whose popularity bridged adolescent social divides. She dated a drummer, who represented the skater/surfer/punker contingent. Her best friend was a cheerleader who was rarely seen apart from the student body president, both of whom paraded around campus as veritable figureheads of popularity. The student body president's brother, one year her elder, was a star athlete on both the football and basketball teams at a rival school, one that had a superior athletic program and thus attracted the attention of a few college recruiting agents who had a vested interest in bringing star athletes together through the oblique petitioning of zone variances. The popular girl's birthday party thus had brought about a great convergence, an unprecedented coming together of diverse adolescent hordes, descending upon an unsuspecting movie theater to celebrate, crash, socialize, threaten, find love, hook up, get wasted, laugh, cry, see, and be seen. The Event had proved so entertaining that teenage multitudes showed up the following Friday night, and every Friday night thereafter, to do it all over again.

Cali Sky sat on the front porch of the house, while Brodie skateboarded in circles around the driveway, both waiting for Philip to chauffeur them to the Domes for one of these Events. Like most Friday night youth, Cali Sky informed her parents that kids just like to hang out there, play video games in the theater arcade, and maybe watch a movie or part of one. Like many parents of the Friday night youth, Philip was disarmed by the teenage insouciance of Cali Sky's description of The Event.

Brodie raised and turned the nose of his skateboard, pointing himself in the direction of Cali Sky. Rays of the setting September sun filtered through a thin haze that hugged the California coast. The strange, attenuated light shone directly on Cali Sky, painting her face with a golden hue. Her hair was pulled back tightly into a ponytail, tidy and neat. Her blue eyes reanimated the dying light, radiating the flush of her cheeks. She and Brodie both wore flip-flops. Brodie rode slowly past her, hands in his pockets, and turned the skateboard around with one fluid motion of his lower body, and glided slowly past her again. He circled the driveway a dozen times in this fashion, sneaking peeks at her with each pass.

"Wouldn't it be great," he said, "if Nowhere played the Domes?"

Cali Sky smiled and nodded. She adjusted her pony tail. "Yeah. I think we'll be ready for a gig soon."

"Aren't you nervous? I mean, aren't you afraid you'll mess up?" Brodie asked.

"No."

Brodie laughed. "Alright, aren't you afraid that *I'll* mess up?"

"Not really. If you mess up I'll cover up your mistake. Besides even if you make a mistake most people won't hear it."

"Why?"

"Because they're not musicians. They don't even know what a mistake sounds like." A brief hesitation, then she added, "They wouldn't understand."

Brodie stopped, placing his left foot on the driveway pavement, pushing the skateboard back and forth with his right foot.

Cali Sky looked up at him. "Do you feel different now? Now that we're in a band?"

"What do you mean?"

"Like who you are is changed. Your identity. Like when you say to someone, 'I'm in a band,' it affects the way they see you. And then it affects the way you see yourself."

"Yeah, I know what you mean. Saying 'I'm in a band' helps me bang more chicks."

Cali Sky jumped lithely to her feet and pushed Brodie off the skateboard. She rode it awkwardly around the driveway, stopping to turn the board in the right direction whenever she veered toward the dying grass.

Squinting through his left eye inside the orange Bronco Philip scratched his beard and cleared his throat, but didn't say anything. He placed both hands on the vibrating steering wheel, which tickled his forearms. He repositioned his hands, then let them slide to the bottom of the wheel. When Cali Sky requested KROQ he acquiesced with little resistance. They neared the Domes.

"You can just drop us off at that McDonald's," instructed Cali Sky. "Over there on the right."

"Are you sure?" asked Philip. "The theater is just right over there." He nodded to the left.

"No, this is fine."

They came to a slow stop in the McDonald's parking lot just

as a gaggle of five teenagers, one with a green mohawk, flicked cigarette butts into the gutter before entering.

"Okay," Philip turned to Cali Sky. "I'll pick you up right here at 11. No later! Be sure you are here at 11."

"Okay, Dad," replied Cali Sky as she exited the Bronco and raised a hand to close the door.

"And if there's a problem, be sure and call me from a pay phone!" Philip said breathlessly before the door could slam shut.

Cali Sky and Brodie walked toward the McDonald's entrance as Philip slowly drove the Bronco away. Two solar systems separating into different sides of the cosmos: the parent solar system of Philip's design, rotating around the warm glow of protected innocence, nervous love, and embattled patience, where God's in his heaven and all's wrong with the world, versus an imploding system of unsustainable volatility, populated by anthropomorphized planets personifying the most extreme emotions, planets that make Mercury look like a stoical octogenarian, hurtling along their unpredictable spheres toward a cosmic intersection immortalized in the title of a rock-and-roll song: "Teenage Wasteland."

Once the Bronco was out of sight Brodie scanned the scene. "Let's go in and wait," he told Cali Sky. "Someone we know will show up." They entered the McDonald's and found a booth at the back. As he passed, Brodie nodded to the Green Mohawk, who said, "You got any stuff to share?"

"No, I'm all out," Brodie lied.

He and Cali Sky sat down on the hard plastic booth. He got her attention and clandestinely pulled a small bag of weed from his OP shorts pocket and smiled. Across the restaurant the Green Mohawk angled left and right like a shark fin, throwing a rolled-up straw wrapper or piece of gum at the idiotically grinning statue of Ronald McDonald. Teenage laughter rolled from their table.

"Like I'm gonna share this with that asshole," Brodie said. "You know him?"

"I've seen him around."

"He's a poser—doesn't know shit about punk." Brodie slipped on his Friday-night persona: tough, cool and in the know. "He once jumped Jim at That's." "That's" was a local teenage club, short for That's Entertainment.

"Really? Why?"

"I don't know. Jim probably talked some shit to him. A few days later John went aggro on him. Beat the hell out of him. That mohawk turned from green to red."

"Really?"

"Yeah. John treats his brother like shit. But he'll stick up for him if anyone else does the same."

Cali Sky thought about her own sister, but was disturbed by setting Cami's image in the context of the Green Mohawk, revenge and violence. She thrust it from her mind. A commotion near the front doors drew their attention. In walked five more teenagers, two girls and three boys.

"Hey, it's Jeff…and Toby," Brodie said.

The Green Mohawk stopped the five as they passed his table on their way to Brodie. He and Cali Sky both watched. Jeff, a skater, gregarious and well liked at school, seemed on friendly terms with the Green Mohawk. From his facial expression, however, Cali Sky could see that the exchange made Jeff nervous. He labored to keep his smile from fading. Toby, less popular than Jeff, more of a recluse, eccentric and odd, hung back and said nothing, clearly uncomfortable.

"Oh, come on!" Cali Sky and Brodie overheard the Green Mohawk say. "Nothing? Are you sure?"

Jeff shrugged, smile still weak, and spoke as if to a friend, "Yeah. We're gonna go to 7-11 and try to score some beverages."

"Beverages," repeated the Green Mohawk. "I need more than fucking beverages!" He turned his attention to the two girls. "I see you did bring some hole, though!" He laughed as the two girls looked away and quickly followed the three boys to Brodie and Cali Sky's booth.

"That guy is such an asshole," Brodie said under his breath as Jeff sat down.

"I know," Jeff replied. "He's always trying to mooch supplies off me." He settled in to the outrageously yellow booth. "Hey Cali Sky."

"Hey Jeff."

"Nowhere." Jeff enunciated the word slowly. "So that's the name of your band? But what about this guy?" Jeff nodded at Brodie. "Can he really play bass?"

"No," replied Cali Sky. "Not really. He just stands there and tries to be cool."

Cali Sky observed the others who had now settled into seats in and around the booth. Next to her sat Christine, who was in her typing class. Christine's hair was cropped short in the style of Pat Benatar. A girl Cali Sky recognized but did not know sat next to Christine. She was dressed all in red, from her tight-fitting blouse to her red flip-flops. The boy on her right Cali Sky had never seen before. He was well tanned and clean cut, and did not seem to fit in with the group.

"So what do you all say?" Jeff asked. "Do you wanna hit the 7-11?"

Friday night Events at the Domes centered on a circular migration, performed in either clockwise or counterclockwise fashion, punctuated by five stops along the way: the Domes, the Big Dipper ice cream shop, 7-11, McDonald's and In-N-Out Burger (which naturally all the migrating teens called "In-N-Out Urge").

All five stopping points stood within a quarter-mile radius of the migration path's nucleus. Migration parties formed haphazardly, sometimes gaining, other times losing, members along the migration route.

On this particular evening Brodie's group migrated in a counterclockwise direction, stopping first at the 7-11. They walked a long arc, steering clear of the front doors, and gathered at the side of the building, near a green dumpster, away from the glaring reach of streetlights and the 7-11 sign. Cali Sky smelled spilled stale beer and rotting garbage.

"Okay," Jeff announced. "Time to take orders. Brodie, you're all set, right?"

Brodie smiled, nodded and flashed half his bag from his shorts pocket.

Jeff smiled and continued, "Toby and I are having a Colt 45 each." Jeff turned toward the well-tanned, clean-cut kid: "Ari, to make this easy, if you want something, it's got to be Colt 45."

"That's fine," Ari replied. His good looks lent his brief response confidence.

"Jeff," Christine broke in, "we are *not* drinking that nasty crap."

"Alright," assured Jeff, who savored his leadership role. "What *do* you want?"

"You know," Christine teased. "Strawberry Hill. Two bottles. The three of us will share." She gestured toward Cali Sky and the girl in red.

"Just two bottles? That's it? You all are lightweights." Jeff flirted with Christine, touching her arm and shoulder, play fighting.

"Come on, Jeff," exclaimed Toby, prying Jeff and Christine apart. "We want our beer!"

"Then give me your money…. Everyone pay up."

As Jeff turned the corner toward the well-lit 7-11 entrance the others shuffled further into the darkened recesses of the back alley. They had initiated the risky mission that they called "fishing." Jeff stood nonchalantly near the 7-11 ice freezer, waiting for the right "fish."

Fifteen minutes later a VW van pulled into the parking lot. From the driver's-side door stepped a barefoot man probably in his early 20s. *Perfect*, thought Jeff. *Probably used to do this himself.* As the barefoot man approached, Jeff noticed his sun-bleached hair. Jeff's hopes soared.

"Excuse me," Jeff called out.

The barefoot man reacted slowly, eventually locating the source of the greeting. He looked at Jeff's smiling face, but still seemed unfocused. *Perfect*, thought Jeff, *he's stoned.*

"How's it going?" drawled the barefoot man.

"Good, good. I was hoping you could do me and my friends a favor."

"Yah," he uttered through a laugh.

"Could you buy us some alcohol?"

Stoned laughter.

"We need three 40-ounce Colt 45s and two Strawberry Hills. I got forty bones here for you, which means you would make yourself a nice-sized profit."

"Whoa…. Yah, but I gotta, like, write that down somewhere… to, you know, remember it all…. You got a pen and paper?"

"Uh, no."

"Wait…I think I got some…in my van."

The barefoot man walked slowly to his vehicle and rummaged inside. Finally he crawled out and loudly announced in a slow California surfer drawl from twenty feet away as he ambled toward Jeff, "Bummer, man. I found some paper…. But no pen." When he reached Jeff he didn't stop but continued toward the 7-11 door. "I'll just go inside and ask that dude for a pen."

"No, wait!" Jeff exclaimed with rising panic. But it was too late. The barefoot man was apparently unaware that Jeff was talking to him. Jeff quickly hid behind the ice freezer, ready to run for it. Thirty seconds later he heard a bell sound as the door opened. He waited a moment, then peaked around the freezer. He saw the bare-foot man, miraculously waving a pen.

"Where'ja go, man?"

"Over here," Jeff whisper screamed.

The barefoot man looked the wrong way.

"No, over here!" Jeff waved his hand from behind the ice freezer.

"Paper...and pen!" declared the barefoot man triumphantly. He unsteadily pressed the paper to the side of the freezer with his left hand and readied the pen with his right—all within full view of the 7-11 employee. "Alright, bro..... Can I take your order?" More stoned laughter.

"Three 40-ounce Colt 45s and two bottles of Strawberry Hill," repeated Jeff, hidden behind the freezer, panic rising. A middle-aged woman walked vigilantly from her car to the 7-11 entrance, looking briefly and warily at the barefoot man.

"Here's the forty bones. You keep the change," instructed Jeff. "We'll meet you in the back alley, behind the 7-11."

"Crisp, clean bills...niiice," gushed the barefoot man, now distracted as he fingered a twenty. Jeff watched him slowly make his way back into the 7-11. As he placed one hand on the door handle however he suddenly turned and said loudly, "Back there, right? In that alley?" He pointed his unsteady finger in the general vicinity of the right direction. Jeff cursed under his breath, nodded his head and gave the barefoot man an incredulous and exaggerated thumbs-up. Once the door closed behind the bare-foot man Jeff bolted around the corner, running around the entire 7-11 to where the others waited.

"We're fucked!" Jeff cried.

Ten minutes later they were still waiting in the back alley.

"Fuck!" Jeff cried with disgust. "He better not have dashed with our money!"

"Just be ready to bolt if you see cops," admonished Brodie as he scanned escape routes.

In the distance headlights illumined the cinder-blocked wall as a car turned down the alley. They strained to see. Cali Sky felt her body tense up. The vehicle was the shape of the bus—long and rectangular. They heard the unmistakable sound of the VW motor downshifting to first.

The barefoot man rolled down his window, looked at the seven teenagers and laughed. He had a cigarette dangling from his lip. He put the van into neutral. The smell of pot smoke and mildewed clothes, as well as the sound of Ted Nugent's "Wango Tango," spilled from the van.

"Here you go, my good man," said the barefoot man in his California-surfer drawl. He handed Jeff the alcohol, cigarette still dangling from his lip.

"Thanks, bro!" said Jeff, relieved.

"Pleasure doing business with you gentlemen...and ladies," laughed the barefoot man. He put the van into first.

"Enjoy your party!" He removed the cigarette from his lip. "And remember—time flies when you're frying limes." More stoned laughter. Jeff nodded, pretending he knew what the bare-foot man meant. The bus disappeared down the alley, trailing VW exhaust and cranking Ted Nugent's wail.

The group spirit rose. Supplied with alcohol they made their way to the Lot before embarking on the migration. The Lot used to be the location of a department store called WonderWorld, which was demolished when it went out of business. The Lot remained undeveloped and unpaved, filled with dumped trash and large mounds of dirt, piled together by the wrecking crews and serving as the perfect cover for groups of teenagers to consume alcohol and smoke weed.

"I'll meet you guys there," Brodie said. "I gotta pick something up at 7-11."

"Are you fucking crazy?" exclaimed Jeff.

"What're you talking about?" Brodie replied. "No one saw me at 7-11. I gotta go back."

"See you in Juvie!" shouted Toby. It was always the worst-case scenario: get arrested and taken to Juvenile Hall, where law-breaking minors served their hour or two jail time, until furious and devastated parents bailed them out.

The group, minus Brodie, hiked deep into the heart of the Lot, into the protection of darkness, garbage piles and dirt mounds. They passed another group of teenagers who had settled into a small pit beside a particularly tall mound. Each had a large bottle in hand. Both groups eyed each other suspiciously, saying nothing. Not long thereafter they passed a couple making out, sitting side by side on an overturned shopping cart.

"Give her the hot beef injection," snickered Toby as he glanced in the couple's direction.

Ari walked next to Cali Sky. Small talk: Where do you go to school? How do you know Brodie? Cali Sky's brief, stand-offish answers led to more questions: What's the name of your band? How long have you been playing guitar? *I'm in a band.* The affirmation emboldened Cali Sky, intensifying her aloofness and confidence. Answering the barrage of questions, Cali Sky once looked into Ari's eyes and saw in him an expression of confidence all his own. She turned away quickly, now aware of her attraction to him. She learned that tennis was his passion, that he was very good at it, that he played in tournaments all over southern California. She knew nothing about tennis.

On the far side of the Lot the group stumbled upon a previous alcohol-drinking/pot-smoking settlement, clearly used by teen-agers before them. Three stray cinder blocks gave the girls some-where to sit. Empty beer bottles lay scattered around, along with an empty can of Copenhagen, and a cracked lighter. Jeff distrib-uted the drinks. Cali Sky had taken three swigs of the Strawberry Hill as it passed between the girls when she heard the approach of Brodie.

"Do you know how hard it was to find you?" he complained. He took a long drink from a can of Coke.

The girl in red looked up at him and asked, "You went back to 7-11 to buy that?"

"Yep," he answered, sharing a knowing look with Jeff. He looked back at the girl in red, noticed the way she looked at him and asked, "Do you want me to show you why?"

"Um," she looked around at the others uncertainly. "Okay."

"First you have to chug some of that Strawberry Hill." The bottle made its way back to her. The girl in red put it to her lips, flung her head back and took three huge swallows. Then handed the bottle to Cali Sky.

Brodie walked up to the girl in red, held out his hand to help her up and spoke enticingly: "Follow me." She looked around again, smiled and put her hand in his. He escorted her to the other side of a dirt mound, where they sat down together and he gave her a lesson in the fine art of transforming a Coke can into a marijuana pipe and where he kissed her for the first of many times that evening. The remaining five sat in a circle.

"Come on, Cali Sky—don't nurse it!" teased Christine. Cali Sky took one last drink and handed it back to her.

"Lightweight!" Christine called out as she tipped the bottle for another guzzle.

Toby belched loudly. "You're just an alky, Christine."

"You're just a loser, Toby," quipped Christine without hesitation.

Jeff laughed and put his arm around her. "That's why I like you. You don't take shit from no one. Plus you could probably drink Toby under the table."

"You think so?" Toby asked as he chugged the remaining fifteen ounces of his forty ounce without stopping. He tossed the empty bottle over his head; they heard the sound of shattering as it broke on a strip of jagged, fragmented pavement not far from Brodie and the girl in red.

"What the hell?" they heard Brodie shout.

Ari had meanwhile edged next to Cali Sky. She felt his presence, sensed him sidling closer.

"Did you know that John McEnroe plays guitar?" he asked her with a smile.

"Who?" she asked.

"John McEnroe. He just won Wimbledon."

"He just won what?"

Ari smiled, noticing the color in her cheeks. "Wimbledon. You know, the tennis tournament in England?"

Cali Sky shrugged and adjusted her ponytail, returning Ari's incredulous stare. He was the first to look away. He took a drink from his Colt 45, appearing flustered.

"Sorry," she said, "I just don't watch sports, don't really know anything about tennis."

"So you pretty much spend all your time playing guitar?"

"Yeah, pretty much. And piano."

"You play piano too?"

Cali Sky nodded. *I'm in a band.* The mantra re-surfaced in her consciousness. The Strawberry Hill flowing through her veins made everything look electric and significant. Suddenly she realized that Ari looked disinterested, seemingly alienated by her aloof attitude.

"So this tennis player who won this tournament..." she began, looking expectantly at Ari.

"John McEnroe...Wimbledon," he put in.

"Yeah, John McEnroe...Wimbledon. He's a guitar player?"

"Yeah."

"So, are you saying that tennis and guitar playing go together?"

"Um," Ari stammered. "Yeah, I guess so."

They smiled, looking at each other through the prism of electricity and significance.

"How about you?" began Cali Sky, "Are you a *good* tennis player?"

"Actually," he answered, turning to Cali Sky, "I'm the fourteen-year-old national champion." The words tumbled from his tongue like a mantra. Cali Sky felt his knee touch hers.

High-pitched giggling—uncontrollable and sloppy—broke out from the other side of the dirt mound. The girl in red, hidden from sight, cried out "Stop!" in a playful voice. "Stop what?" returned Brodie. Cali Sky and Ari looked toward the sound. Smoke emanated from the mound, rising and spreading, like incense from an altar. The smoke seemed excessive, beyond the capacity of Brodie's homemade Coke-can pipe. Jeff and Toby laughed.

"Jesus, Brodie! Is there a fucking forest fire back there?" yelled Toby.

Jeff doubled over, hysterical. Christine leaned over him, laughing and wrapping him in her arms.

"Come on, stoner! We're ready to go!" Toby continued.

The faint figure of Brodie, arm in arm with the girl in red, rose slowly atop the dirt mound, shrouded in smoke. He disentangled himself from her and lifted his arms in mock triumph.

Jeff could barely stand now. Cali Sky and Ari joined in the laughter as he put his arm around her. Toby picked up the discarded lighter and hurled it at Brodie, pelting him in the leg.

"What the fuck?" Brodie shouted. But by the time he and the girl in red descended the dirt mound he seemed to have forgotten all about the incident. A smile spread across his face and stuck there. He found that he couldn't stop smiling, even if he tried.

The group, now wasted in various degrees, set out through the Lot, pointed in the general vicinity of the Big Dipper to join the migration route. Brodie and the girl in red walked as one unit, the smile engraved on Brodie's face, the now-smitten girl in red clinging to Brodie's chest, looking up at his smile with a gaze of adoration. Cali Sky and Ari walked side by side, Ari listing the tournaments he played all over California, Cali Sky describing the musical style of Nowhere.

"Some punk, a little New Wave. I don't know, whatever we feel like playing," she explained. She still didn't really know what New Wave was, but it sounded impressive.

"Do you sing?" he asked.

"On some of the songs."

"Let me hear you sing!" He smiled. Cali Sky saw the charm in his playfulness.

"Yeah right, no way!"

"Come on!" he insisted as he took her hand.

"I would if I had a guitar with me." She felt quivering in her stomach as he released her hand.

Toby meanwhile lurked in the shadows, darting from one side of the slow-moving group to the other, seemingly incapable of migrating at their slow pace. Once he weaseled into the center of the pack and hawked a loud, wet loogie.

"That's disgusting," exclaimed a scowling Christine.

Toby finessed the contents of his inhaled snort, mined from

the recesses of his nasal cavity, to the back corner of his mouth. With the goo secure in this holding area he strained his tongue and announced with jubilation: "Green snow!" He then craned his face to the sky and spat the rank contents of his mouth toward the heavens. Everyone scattered in various directions as a blob of saliva and snot quickly reached its vertical apex, hung suspended in the California sky for a fraction of a second, and rained down upon the Lot.

"That's sick!" cried Christine from a distance as she checked her hair and shoulders for contamination. "What's wrong with you?"

Toby laughed and looked away. Everyone looked disgusted with the exception of Brodie, whose plastered smile, predisposing him to peace and understanding, made his expression of repulsion unconvincing: "Naaaasty!" he proclaimed with a laugh. His THC-laced brain tweaked his experience of space and time as well, for just seconds later his supposed disgust gave precipitous way to excitement as he made an announcement of his own: "My clothes are tickling me!" Everyone became silent. A car horn sounded from the Big Dipper parking lot.

Brodie looked around at the others in the group. "Are your clothes tickling you?"

Jeff lost it again, falling down into a squatting position, laughter once more seizing his body. Christine tried to raise him back up. Ari put his arm around Cali Sky, gently pulling her toward him, hoping that his gesture would become a hug, something more intimate.

He turned his head close to hers. "How do you feel? Are you buzzing at all?"

"Yeah, a little bit. How 'bout you?"

"I'm really wasted." He was poised to kiss her, but by now Christine had raised Jeff back to a standing position, Brodie's dazed mind became preoccupied with some other fascinating detail and the group resumed its migration.

In the Big Dipper parking lot they encountered a large crowd of teenagers. As if by radar they located and honed in on those in the crowd they knew, friends and acquaintances. Vacuous conversation filled the parking lot, prompted by oft-repeated questions: "When 'dju get here?" "Are you wasted?" "Who're you trying to scam with?" "Guess who likes you?"

In the midst of the chatter Cali Sky, who was the most sober in their group, spotted the Green Mohawk. He was making his way through the crowd, occasionally pushing people out of the way. He seemed to be heading toward Brodie. She grabbed Ari's hand and pulled him away from an aimless conversation, determined to get to Brodie before the Green Mohawk. Brodie and the girl in red were still wrapped around each other, talking to some friends.

"Brodie," Cali Sky interrupted, "Look!" She nodded toward the approaching Green Mohawk. Brodie seemed incapable of comprehending the situation. He smiled stupidly at Cali Sky and proclaimed to anyone within listening distance. "This girl right here," he tried to point at Cali Sky, but since she was standing two feet away he was unable to extend his arm. So he pulled her into an embrace with his right arm, still clutching the girl in red with his left. "This girl right here," he continued, "is the best guitar player...." He seemed distracted by some commotion. "...is the best guitar player...in California."

The commotion that momentarily sidetracked Brodie was the approach of the Green Mohawk, who now stood directly in front of him.

"What the fuck, man?" he yelled threateningly. "You said you were empty handed! You said you didn't have any!" He waited for Brodie to focus. "You were holding out on me!"

"What are you talking about?" replied Brodie, whose smile faded, but only slightly.

"You're high, man…and you didn't share. You *lied* to me."

Brodie stood smiling stupidly.

"Dude," he said, "take it easy…Are your clothes tickling you?"

"See! You're holding out on me!" repeated the Green Mohawk, working himself up to that point of violence when a punch could fly at any moment.

"He's not high," interjected Cali Sky. "He's drunk."

"Bullshit!" answered the Green Mohawk.

"It's true," Cali Sky replied. "We scored some alcohol at 7-11. Me, Jeff, Brodie, and a few others."

The Green Mohawk was unswayed. "Bullshit! I can tell the difference between someone who is stoned and someone who is drunk."

"No you can't," Cali Sky replied. Those gathered stared at her, taken aback by her brazenness. "Especially with Brodie. He gets stoned and drunk so much that sometimes he forgets which is which." Some in the gathered throng, which had by now doubled, laughed.

"If you don't believe her," Brodie said, still smiling, looking relaxed and very stoned, "then you can search me." He raised his hands, the gesture of the innocent man. He then lowered them and began to turn out his pockets. He pulled out the liner from the right pocket of his shorts: out came some loose change. He did the same with his left pocket: two guitar picks fluttered to the pavement. He smiled at the Green Mohawk. More laughter from the throng.

"See," continued Cali Sky, "no weed, no pipe, no matches. Just look at him. He's totally drunk." She gave Brodie a sharp push to the right shoulder and he stumbled back. More laughter.

The Green Mohawk now aimed his aggression at Cali Sky.

"I'm trying to talk to him, not you, *bitch*! Why don't you step back before I slap you?" Before the last word descended upon the throng Ari bolted from Cali Sky's side and shoved the Green Mohawk, who reeled backwards on his heels.

"Why don't you shut the fuck up!" yelled Ari.

The Green Mohawk regained his footing and launched himself toward his new adversary. He pushed Ari back, at which point the two were separated by two men, bystanders, in their thirties.

"Break it up!" one shouted. "The cops are on their way!

With those words panic spread. The Green Mohawk, Ari, Brodie and the rest of the teenage masses fled. The exodus disrupted the migration routes, scattering teenagers in every direction. Cali Sky found herself walking hand in hand with Ari, heading toward the Domes. They crossed the street, cars braking and honking to avoid the scattering teenagers. Out in the open Cali Sky felt chilled by the night air.

"You're crazy!" joked Ari, swinging Cali Sky's hand as they slowed to a walk after crossing the street. Ari slurred his speech, the effects of the Colt 45 still potent.

"*You're* the crazy one. I thought the two of you were going to fight."

"That's because I thought he was going to hit you."

"No, the tennis player and guitar player would have kicked some ass!" she replied as she turned around to see the girl in red steering Brodie across the street. Cali Sky and Ari waited for them.

"Are you alright?" Cali Sky asked.

The girl in red held Brodie tightly, clinging passionately to his chest, looking like both a mother and a lover. Brodie looked up at Cali Sky and said, slowly and deliberately, "I lost one of my picks!" His lament was offset by his smile, which through it all remained etched on his face. Jeff, Christine and Toby were nowhere to be found. Teenage crowds thinned as they rejoined the migration route from various locations. Cali Sky looked back at the Big Dipper. The parking lot was empty, not one teenage soul. No cops either.

Cali Sky felt the quiver in her stomach again as she and Ari, Brodie and the girl in red, all of whom now unmistakably formed into two couples, turned the corner into the Domes' back alley. *This is where it will happen*, she realized. Every fifty feet or so along the Domes building were little alcoves, recessed into the building, with doors to one side. These were emergency exits, one for each individual theater of the Domes.

On Friday nights these alcoves had two uses, neither one of which had anything to do with emergencies. First, they were used as assembling spots for teenage groups that wanted to watch a movie: One person in the group purchased a ticket, entered the theater and opened the emergency door ever so slightly, thereby allowing the group, assembled in the alcove, to slip in for free. Second, alcoves were secluded areas for scamming, for the teenage couple that heeded the chemical impulses of their relentless hormones, explored their blossoming and often awkward sexuality, to make out, grope, pet, feel out, and, on the rarest of occasions, round second base and head for third or, rarest of rare, wave each other on to home.

The first alcove they passed was occupied: slow movements in the dark. Cali Sky tried not to look, but out of the corner of her eye spotted two heads fused together, tilting left and right ever so slightly. The quiver in her stomach intensified, shortening her breath. She was nervous, holding Ari's hand. The second alcove was vacant. Brodie and the girl in red cut a direct line across the path of Cali Sky and Ari and into the concrete bower of bliss. The two were at it before they even settled into its protected space, ambling forward, sideways, backwards into the darkest corner, never letting go, never once interrupting their passionate kiss. The third alcove was taken. This time Cali Sky resisted the temptation to look. Her peripheral vision registered the two shadowy figures.

As they approached the fourth and final alcove Cali Sky both wanted and didn't want it to be open. She tried to be nonchalant and casual. Though drunk Ari tensed up a bit himself, walking more stiffly. The silence now between them riveted their attention upon what they both knew would happen, sharpening their awareness that there was no turning back now. And when the alcove showed itself to be empty the awareness gave Cali Sky a jolt, a tingle of excitement and nervousness that took her breath away. She adjusted her ponytail.

Inside the alcove, up close, Cali Sky noticed, even in the dim light, the few small freckles dotting Ari's dark-skinned cheekbones, the long lashes, and the brown eyes which, in the half light, seemed flecked with hazel or even yellow lines. She reached up and brushed back the hair above his left ear. She once saw a woman do that during a romantic scene in a movie. He did the same to her. Cali Sky worried momentarily about his impression of her thick, coarse hair, but remembered she had smoothed it into a tight ponytail. These thoughts, and all self-consciousness, scattered as he slowly lowered his head and kissed her softly.

The first few moments felt strangely impersonal to Cali Sky. *This is it*, she thought, *This is what the love songs are about.* Her mind raced through her dad's record collection until she placed it: *This is the early Beatles.* The kissing became more passionate, more sexual. Ari passed his hand across her back and up her neck, pressing his lips harder into hers. She responded with subtle movements intended to convey the experience of pleasure.

The outrageously loud sound of music suddenly carried down the alley and into the alcove. The song was muffled, originating from a car stereo somewhere near the side entrance of the

Domes. Closed car doors smothered the treble, stripping the song of its identity by the time it reached Cali Sky's ears, leaving only the pounding bass, which nearly vibrated her clothes as they hung from her body. *I know that bass line,* she thought to herself as Ari caressed her neck and tilted his head to the left, working the kiss from a different angle. She had trouble concentrating on the bass line. *That's got to be an expensive stereo.* Her mind wandered. She felt like she had to swallow, but did not quite know how.

Suddenly the song exploded into the alcove with clarity: Someone had opened the door of the car. Immediately she knew it, a pop song heard ubiquitously over the past year: Michael Jackson's "Rock with You." She broke off the kiss, pulling back and laughing. *Seriously?* she thought, *This song? Now?* Ari joined in her laughter, not quite knowing why. A voice from somewhere down the alley shouted, "Turn that shit off!" Hilarity seized Cali Sky, she could not stop laughing.

As if smothered by a giant pillow the song died as suddenly as it was brought to life. The car door, closed once again, locked in all the treble. The bass line, pounding alongside the kick drum, now sounded obvious to Cali Sky. *I should've known it was that Michael Jackson song all along.* Relaxed and at ease she and Ari moved closer, now more playful and comfortable. Ari's hand roamed down Cali Sky's back. He became more aggressive and exploratory. Their kisses were now wide open. She could taste the malt liquor on his tongue, in spite of the Binaca.

With a slow awareness, which Cali Sky found impossible to deny, she realized that she was becoming disinterested, that this encounter was becoming boring. The whole thing had become mechanical. She was going through the motions. He kissed her cheek, her ear and then her neck. His hand now descended down her back and beyond. She wondered how long they should continue. Ari's fingers traveled from her shoulder to her arm and then made a leap toward her breasts. She pulled back.

"No." She said it with a calm smile, a compassionate expression.

"Sorry," he replied. "I...uh...got carried away."

She leaned over and kissed him, a quick and short kiss, non-sexual and innocent. Sheepishly he wrapped her in his arms in a hug, one that lasted over a minute.

"I really like you," he whispered in her ear.

They began to totter a bit in their embrace, back and forth.

"I mean," he repeated with emphasis, "I *really* like you."

Not long after the car had carried off the Michael Jackson song they heard another commotion in the alley. They ignored it for a while until the commotion began to overflow just outside their alcove. A drunken teenager stumbled into their space, bumping into the couple.

"Sssorry!" he stammered. The front of his shirt was wet, clinging to his body. He moved away awkwardly, did a double take, looking more closely at Cali Sky, and said, "Hey...I know you!" He looked triumphant, elated. She and Ari stared at him, saying nothing. He backed away clumsily, though still smiling. Then they heard the voice of the Green Mohawk above the din in the alleyway: "Fuck you, you motherfucker!" *Brodie*, thought Cali Sky.

When she and Ari stepped out of the alcove the Fight Circle had already formed. Inside the Circle Cali Sky saw the Green Mohawk with puffed-up chest and clenched fists, on the verge of taking a swing at Brodie, who now appeared unmistakably less stoned. The girl in red stood by his side, clearly afraid, sobbing. "Please stop!" she cried pitifully. Her face was wet with drunken tears, mascara running.

Cali Sky pushed her way through the Circle, followed by Ari. She sensed the pre-fight buzz, the taut nerves, the sickening anticipation. From somewhere in the Circle she heard a female's voice: "Don't be stupid, you guys!" But the Green Mohawk was implacable. Cali Sky reached the inner ring of the Circle, the front row.

One of the Green Mohawk's friends grabbed her shoulder: "Let them fight!"

Cali Sky instantaneously rounded on him, disengaged his grip with an angry swipe of her forearm and shouted, "Fuck off!" Ari glared at him as he followed her. Someone else shouted with relish, "Kick his ass, Cali Sky!" Someone else laughed ludicrously. The Circle was ready to explode: too much tension, aggression and drunkenness. Cali Sky entered its center, stopping next to Brodie.

She faced the Green Mohawk. "What the hell? What's your problem?"

He ignored her, pacing, fists still clenched, staring at Brodie, appearing wild and unpredictable. His Green Mohawk now looked like a weapon.

"We've been through this," Cali Sky continued. "He's not high. He's drunk."

The Green Mohawk snapped. He sprung toward Cali Sky, shoving her with tremendous force. She experienced it in slow motion. Before she could process the experience she found herself reeling backwards, back into the inner Circle, where she hurtled into the front row of teenagers, knocking two of them down as she herself fell on her backside. While Ari helped her back to her feet she still did not fully comprehend what had happened. She heard shouts and screams. She felt Ari leave her side and rush toward the Green Mohawk. "No, stop!" She yelled the words feebly and rapidly.

Slow motion again. She saw Ari's trim and athletic frame advancing toward the Green Mohawk, who looked possessed, demonic. Behind the Green Mohawk she became aware of something incongruent, inconsistent with the stationary contours of the Circle. It entered her visual field as blurred motion, something long and shiny at its edges, winding back, stopping, motionless for a split second. Then a quick release. An unleashed force, swung with such velocity that it once again became blurred. Still stunned and disoriented, Cali Sky in that fraction of a second thought of a light saber before remembering that light sabers exist only in movies.

Then came a shocking crash, centered on the Green Mohawk's head. Glass exploded around his skull, cascading around his feet and spraying into the crowd. Cali Sky felt a pinprick on her shin. The Green Mohawk fell to his knees. Toby stood behind him, holding the shattered remains of what Cali Sky now recognized as a long, cylindrical light bulb.

"What the...fuck," moaned the Green Mohawk, still on his knees.

Some people in the Circle now fled. The others backed away in disbelief, hugging the walls of the alley, afraid of Toby, who still held the weapon in his hand, now transformed into a jagged, sharp glass knife. He had spectacularly released the tension that had wound up the crowd. The mood was now something else entirely. The Green Mohawk remained in the center of the alley, on his knees. Toby stood five feet away. The Circle continued to widen and thin.

"What the...*fuck*," moaned the Green Mohawk again. He was still stunned, in shock, but anger now carried in his voice. Cali Sky looked closely. Blood trickled down his head and onto his hands, which were covering his face. Toby approached, now standing directly over him, scowling.

"No...don't do it!" someone shouted. Nearly everyone in

what remained of the Circle now fled, running down the alley in both directions.

Toby took three steps back. Cali Sky watched breathlessly, feeling paralyzed. He sprung forward, kicking the Green Mohawk, directly in the ribs, with all his might. Cali Sky heard a sickening noise, a violent exhalation, then panicked gasps. The Green Mohawk was struggling to breathe, trying to suck the air. He fell to his side, then onto his back. Toby kneeled down, bringing his face close to the Green Mohawk's.

"Fuck you, you green mohawk motherfucker!"

"Cali Sky, we need to get out of here," cried Ari. She tore her attention away from Toby and the Green Mohawk, then nodded at Ari. Brodie now joined them, staring at Toby, who was running back from the dumpster, where he threw the remains of the light bulb.

"Holy shit," muttered Brodie, turning from Toby to the Green Mohawk. "Holy shit."

Toby smiled dementedly.

"You're crazy, Toby," Cali Sky exclaimed.

Toby's demented grin widened. The Green Mohawk continued to gasp for air.

"What *was* that?" continued Cali Sky. "What did you hit him with?"

"A light bulb," Toby answered. "The real long ones they use in the theater."

"Where the hell did you get it?" asked Ari.

"In the dumpster. When that asshole started shit I needed a weapon. I looked in the dumpster. And there it was! Swung it like a fucking baseball bat!"

"Come on!" cried Ari. "Let's get outta here!"

The four jogged down the alley, heading toward the In-N-Out Burger. Halfway there they slowed to a walk.

Brodie looked at Toby. "Holy shit!" The last ten minutes had reduced his vocabulary to two words. Cali Sky looked down at her shin and saw a thin trail of blood. She pulled an earring-sized piece of glass from the wound, which then began to bleed some more. A concerned Ari raced into the In-N-Out to get some napkins.

Brodie murmured another "holy shit," then looked at Cali Sky.

"How was it?" he asked her, speaking with a post-wasted tranquility.

"How was what?" she replied.

"You know."

She wondered, for a moment, if he sounded jealous. She ignored him.

Toby inserted himself into the conversation and asked Brodie, "Where's the bitch in red?"

"Huh?" responded a distracted Brodie.

"The bitch in red?"

"Uh…I don't know."

Ari returned with napkins from In-N-Out and carefully wiped the blood from Cali Sky's leg. As he did so, kneeling at her feet, Brodie gave her a knowing glance, arching his eyebrows. Cali Sky looked down at Ari, then back at Brodie. At first her face was expressionless, then assumed a look that Brodie could not read at first. When it dawned on him he did a double take. Arrogance. An image of the girl Cali Sky sang about in "Tales of Brave Ulysses" surfaced in his mind.

On their way to McDonald's Toby broke off from the migration route. They stopped before parting. Brodie slapped Toby's hand and said, "Thanks man. You probably saved me from an ass-beating back there…even though you are a crazy son of a bitch." Toby flashed another twisted grin, but as he headed into the California night, in the opposite direction of all migration routes, destined for nobody knew where, the demented smile faded into an ambivalent expression, tinged with melancholy.

Cali Sky shuddered. Ari put his arm around her as they walked to McDonald's. They encountered fewer migration parties as they traveled. In the McDonald's parking lot a group of teenagers piled into a station wagon with well-mannered efficiency, masking their buzzes from the parent behind the wheel.

"I really want to see you again," Ari said softly as he embraced Cali Sky behind the McDonald's. Brodie stood in the distance, leaning against the building. Cali Sky smiled. "I meant what I said before," he continued. "I really like you, *really* like you."

"Tennis players and guitar players!" replied Cali Sky affectionately.

By the time Ari left in search of Jeff, his ride home, it was near 10:45, enough time for a 7-11 run. Cali Sky and Brodie were both in need of some Binaca and Visine, two precautionary items useful for disguising evidence of alcohol and marijuana use—two items that also often sold out at the 7/11 on Friday nights.

"So," said Brodie, now with fresh breath and clear eyes, waiting in the McDonald's parking lot for Philip, "do you have yourself a boyfriend now?"

"No," she replied.

"Why not?" Brodie pressed.

"Why should I? Brodie, you scam with a different girl just about every week. Do *you* have a girlfriend?"

"Alright, alright—don't get all pissed off."

Cali Sky looked in the other direction, toward the Domes. "Besides, all I need is music."

At that moment the orange Bronco pulled into the parking lot. Brodie stepped carefully into the truck, working his way to the back seat with exaggerated soberness. Cali Sky plopped into the passenger seat, looking at Philip only briefly. "Hi Dad!" she piped perkily—maybe, she thought, too perkily.

"Did you have fun?" he asked.

"It was alright," she replied, reining in the perkiness a bit.

"What did you do?

"Walked around. Met up with friends. Hung out."

"That's it?"

"Yeah, Brodie and I told some people about our band."

"Anything interesting happen?"

"No, not really."

As they pulled out of McDonald's Cali Sky saw a girl, by herself, arms crossed, walking down the sidewalk. She was dressed all in red. Tears were streaming down her mascara-blackened face.

Stepping foot inside the house Cali Sky reentered the parent solar system, a sanctuary humming familiar late-night sounds—calm, soft and domestic. The myriad nightlights warmed the still house in a tranquil, secure illumination. Cami lay in Cali Sky's bed, the sheet and blanket tossed aside in a fit of restlessness.

"Cali Sky," she murmured.

"Shhh." Cali Sky pulled the sheet and blanket over her sister, who sighed, stirred, and opened her eyes.

"Cali Sky."

"What?"

"I'm scared."

"Of what?"

"The dark."

"Don't be scared." As soon as Cali Sky lay down her head began to spin. She shut her eyes tightly.

Cami shifted to her side, directly facing Cali Sky. "Tell me the story…of the princess in the meadow."

Cali Sky opened her eyes, focusing on a fixed point on the

moon-rocked ceiling, trying to slow down the room. "She's not a princess…just a girl."

"Tell it to me," Cami insisted.

Cali Sky closed her eyes again. She submitted to the spinning, allowing herself to be pulled into its vortex, entering its rotation, acclimating to the movement.

"Once upon a time there was a beautiful green meadow with a river running right through it. The meadow was filled with rocks and trees and birds singing from the branches. In the center of the meadow next to the river there was a cabin and inside the cabin there lived a girl. The girl liked to explore her meadow. She hiked up the hills and climbed the trees. She followed the river from one end of the meadow to the other. Sometimes it became a waterfall. The girl liked to sit on a rock and watch the waterfall. The spray made a rainbow.

"Inside her cabin the girl liked to look out her window. She saw the tops of trees, blowing back and forth in the wind. Far away she could see the top of the mountains. And hanging from the top of her open window there was a musical instrument. It looked like organ pipes. All of a sudden the most beautiful music the girl had ever heard came from the instrument. It was so beautiful it made her cry. Then she realized it was the wind. It was the wind that made the music, the wind blowing through the instrument, playing golden notes. The girl felt the warm wind on her face as the music filled her cabin."

Cali Sky opened her eyes. The room had slowed down. She turned her head toward Cami, who gazed directly back at her, her head pillowed by her two hands. Cali Sky smiled. "The end." She pulled up the blanket and sheets, then turned on her side.

Images from the night flickered through her brain, images that became increasingly shadowy as her body relaxed and gradually slipped into sleep: the barefoot man, Brodie's pyre, green snow, the Green Mohawk, crazy Toby and Ari. When she thought of her time with him in the alcove she re-experienced for one instant the quiver in her stomach, which tugged her nerves and yanked her back awake. The images and emotions became confused: momentary pleasure, disappointment, yellow-flecked brown eyes, malt-liquored tongue, fun and boredom. Before slipping into oblivion her sleepy memory riveted on one moment: the instant before the kiss, the thrill of anticipation, the ecstatic millisecond between desire and fulfillment. She carried that moment into unconsciousness where it blended, dreamlike, into the timelessness of a song.

FIVE

THE ROUTE TO church from the Braithwaite house criss-crossed small roads, big roads, train tracks and drainage ditches. It ascended overpasses and descended through underpasses. Atop the flat vertical surface of one such underpass, black graffitied words, unevenly spaced and sized, spelled out the words, "Let it be." City workers removed graffiti from this underpass. Crudities and vulgarities were there one week, gone the next. For years "Let it be" remained, either because clean-up crews took the message literally or because they felt that the enigmatic proverb could bolster the spirits of wearied motorists, traversing the urban California terrain on their way to work, church, pleasure and pain.

On Sunday morning hardly any traffic passed beneath "Let it be." As always Cali Sky stared at the song title, her dad seated next to her behind the wheel of the orange Bronco. She heard Paul McCartney's piano and the anthemic chorus. And in those spray-painted words she saw an affirmation of her world, imposed in all its vandalistic glory upon a passing larger world she did not understand: the world of lawyers, doctors, businessmen, secretaries, taxi drivers and garbage collectors—of engineers like her dad and curmudgeons like her grandpa. The words were written in her language. She imagined the prophet who transcribed the words. *Probably an ex-hippie*, she thought.

"Cali Sky, I want to talk to you about what Grandpa said a few months ago," Philip said uncomfortably as "Let it be" passed overhead.

"What Grandpa said?" asked Cali Sky.

"Yeah, at our fourth of July barbecue."

"Our fourth of July barbecue? Are you serious?"

"Yes."

"That was a long time ago."

"I know."

"And you want to talk about it now?"

"Yes."

"Why?"

"Because..."

"Because Mom told you to?"

"It doesn't matter why."

"Okay. Go ahead." She tried to sound nonchalant, not to mitigate her embarrassment, but his. There were times when Cali Sky felt pity for her dad, like when he came home from work looking crestfallen and overwhelmed, or when he sat alone in the kitchen reading the Bible while everyone else watched TV, or when Joan forced him to make some speech to his kids. This, Cali Sky knew, was one of those times. It was also during those times that she felt in the pit of her stomach the stirrings of disappointment in her father. A hard swallow forced the emotion back down, before it could possibly become something devastating and irretrievable.

Philip began, "Your grandpa means well, but sometimes he doesn't think before he speaks. He said..."

"Yes he does," interrupted Cali Sky.

"What?"

"He does think before he speaks. And he doesn't mean well. He's just a grumpy old man who brings everyone down."

"Cali Sky, don't say that," Philip replied, anger in his voice.

"Why do you always stick up for him? Why are you the *only* one in the family who defends him?"

Philip sighed. He spoke with belabored calmness: "For one he is your elder and you should respect him for that reason alone. He's your grandpa. Second, wisdom comes with age."

"What wisdom?" snapped Cali Sky. "His wisdom just makes everyone feel bad."

"Cali Sky," Philip reasoned, "I agree that he says hurtful things sometimes, but…but you have to overlook that and forgive him for it."

"No, I won't forgive him. I hate him." She heard the words coming out of her mouth before she made a decision to vocalize them. She experienced a sense of déjà vu: the "Goddamn" moment all over again. She braced herself, just like last time, waiting for her father's anger.

Instead he looked at her incredulously and spoke barely above a whisper, "You don't mean that."

"Yes I do."

Philip was silenced. Outside the streets were empty: Sunday morning in southern California, Sabbath on the overburdened roads and freeways, their day of rest.

Cali Sky spoke up: "So what about it? What about what Grandpa said?"

"Nothing," Philip murmured. "I don't feel like talking about it now."

Cali Sky looked out her window and said, "Mom's not going to be happy."

Philip feigned confusion. "Why?"

"Nothing. Never mind," replied Cali Sky as she shook her head.

Unlike the secular roadways the church parking lot was brimming with motorized activity. Friendly painted faces smiled as vehicles politely squeezed into tight parking spaces. Cornerstone Community Church was a casual, seeker-sensitive church. Its aim was honesty and transparency, to come across as contemporary and relevant—no religious mumbo jumbo. Services still incorporated the organ, but unlike its higher-church neighbors— the Catholics, Lutherans and Episcopalians—Cornerstone gladly made room for electric guitars. Many church members were young, in their twenties and thirties. Once, over a particularly jocular family meal, Joan referred to them as "Cornerstoners," a sobriquet which displeased Philip. But Joan would not relent and the name stuck—at least for Joan and Cali Sky. Philip grimaced whenever he heard them use the neologism, unconvinced by Joan's argument that "Cornerstoner" was a term of affection, like "Deadhead" or "hippie."

Pastor Kevin—never "Pastor Warner"—approached as Philip and Cali Sky neared the front doors of the church. He was in his late twenties and wore jeans and Birkenstocks.

Shaking Philip's hand he said, "Good morning, Philip. Where are Joan and Cami?"

"Cami has a stomachache. But they'll be here—just a little late."

Philip and Cali Sky filtered through the friendly crowd, Philip pausing every five steps to greet a smiling face.

"Hi Michelle," he called out.

"Oh, hi Philip! Hi Cali Sky!"

Cali Sky smiled back.

Philip asked, "Are you singing this morning?"

"Yeah," she answered, then added confidentially, "but I wish Cali Sky was up there with me, she's such a great musician!"

Cali Sky remembered her last concert with Michelle and forced yet another smile, resisting the impulse to shout, "Yeah, well you suck!"

Joan and Cami snuck into the pew next to Philip and Cali Sky a few minutes before the sermon. Cami appeared a bit pale as she leaned against Joan, who softly scratched her forearms and rubbed her head, gently brushing back her hair. At the front of the church Pastor Kevin roamed around the portable pulpit, stopping occasionally to consult his notes. He assumed an informal, pleasant tone: a sermon posing as a friendly conversation.

"...There are times when it's hard. Let's be honest. You know how it is. You come home after a long day, you're tired, you're wiped out, you're fried. You just want to sit on the couch, watch some TV and relax. Maybe watch the LA Rams play, now that they are back on TV." Some male cheers from the Cornerstoners. "Or maybe watch an episode of *Dallas* to try to figure out who shot J.R." A few Cornerstoners moaned. "But instead, your kids are yelling and screaming: 'Daddy (or Mommy), Bobby hit me, and Susie stuck my pencil up her nose.'" Cornerstoner laughter spreads. "Your spouse wants you to do this or that: 'Honey, when are you going to fix the fence?' or 'Dear, what are you making for dinner?' Meanwhile your next-door neighbor's dog runs loose, leaving huge, disgusting presents on your front lawn." A ripple of chuckles. "So then how do you do it? When you absolutely do not feel like it, how do you love your kids, your spouse, your neighbor? How can we love when love seems impossible? How can we love when we don't feel love?"

Pastor Kevin strolled away from the pulpit, descended the altar steps and stopped near the front-row pews, on common ground with the Cornerstoners. "The answer to those questions has to do with the nature of love. You see, love is *not* a feeling. Feelings come and go. If you build a relationship on feelings—and I mean a relationship with your spouse, kids, neighbor *or* God—if you build a relationship on feelings, then that relationship will be in trouble. Because your feelings will change. Building a relationship on feelings is like building a house on shifting sand.

"No, love is a commitment. And a commitment does not change. You build a relationship on commitment, and the relationship *will* last. Because now, now you have built a house on solid ground, on rock. God's love for us is eternal. His love is his eternal commitment to us, rain or shine, no matter the circumstances. When you love like this, when love is a commitment, then you *can* love your neighbor, even while you're picking up the mess that his dog left in your yard. And you *can* love your kids unfailingly, even when you are removing pencils from their snotty noses." The Cornerstoners laughed once more as Pastor Kevin drew his sermon to a close.

As she listened Cali Sky thought of the Blue Flower. The longing, the desire, the *feeling*. The vision of the cabin in the mountains, drawing her to her knees. The way she played music, losing awareness, the negated sense of place and time, a power entering her body, making thought impossible, transforming everything into *feeling*. Thinking about this feeling made her feel it again. Thinking about desire made her desire. The spiraling emotions rendered the concept of love-as-commitment foreign to her, like the world of non-musicians who pass through the "Let it be" underpass with blank stares.

Her thoughts became concrete. She began to daydream. She imagined herself as a rock star. She pictured herself on a stage, playing the opening notes of a song, which builds slowly, notes becoming louder, bass and drums eventually entering. A hungry audience recognizes the tune. Pandemonium ensues. The scent of the Blue Flower descends, she sees a presence sweep down upon the place. The music spreads, enveloping her and the crowd, transporting them to her world, where some laugh and some cry because the song speaks to a desire powerful enough to trigger both reactions. She is the channel, she is the instrument. The conclusion of the sermon disrupted her reverie. But she could not shake it. While the collection plate was passed images from her daydream reappeared in her mind: the darkened venue; amps surrounding the stage, bursting to life; tears and smiles on the faces of the crowd.

The daydream withered and died, however, once Michelle began her solo. As usual her voice fell into falsetto, making her sound like a child. Her pitch was unsteady, and she overcorrected flat notes, turning them sharp. As she sang she closed her eyes, emotion painted on her face, evidence of the feelings against which Pastor Kevin's sermon just warned.

Stepping outside the church Cali Sky took a deep breath. The clouds had cleared, driven off by the Santa Ana winds, which put a nip in the air. It was a California fall morning. Cali Sky felt the release of a burden, a phenomenon she experienced every Sunday after church, a phenomenon that never failed to surprise and disturb her. Joan's Celica looked tired and worn alongside the newer model cars in the church parking lot. As she and Cali Sky dropped into the torn leather seats they could hear the shocks squeak. Philip drove Cami home in the Bronco. Joan promised Cali Sky that she would take her to the music store to buy her an album.

"Mom, Dad did not tell me what he was supposed to tell me," Cali Sky announced as Joan pulled out of the church parking lot, waving to Michelle, tightly permed hair bouncing on her shoulders, as she walked to her car. "You know, about the fight."

Joan scowled. "How did you know that he was supposed to tell you about that?"

Cali Sky stared at her mom for a while before answering, "Come on, Mom. I can tell when you make Dad tell me something. Or when you try to make him tell me something."

Joan tried to look upset. But the tone of confidentiality in Cali Sky's voice was too inviting. "Well, why didn't he tell you about it?"

"Because he got mad."

"Why did he get mad?"

"Because I told him that I hate Grandpa."

Once again Joan tried unconvincingly to look upset. Cali Sky only detected surprise. Eyes widened, Joan asked, "You said that?"

"Yeah. Why not? That's how we all feel anyway—well, everyone except for Dad, I guess."

"It's more complicated than that, Cali Sky. Your dad and grandpa have a long history…that you know little about."

"Then why don't you tell me?"

"Because," answered Joan apprehensively, "I'm not the one who *should* tell you."

Cali Sky lost patience. "So *you* won't tell me but you say that Dad *should*. Well he won't tell me either."

Joan became silent. Cali Sky became more impatient: "Why is everything…hidden in our family?"

Silence followed the question, suspended inside the Celica's stale air. The shocks squealed over every bump. They pulled into the music store parking lot. Joan took a deep breath and began uncertainly as she eased the Celica to a stop, "Cali Sky, your dad just wants to protect you. And he feels he can better do that if… he doesn't tell you everything. He had a pretty rough childhood. A terrible childhood, actually. Things were…unstable for him. And when he got older…he…we both made mistakes."

Cali Sky listened but heard only the same empty words. She felt the anger surge once again, the urge to lash out, until she turned toward her mom and beheld an unexpected sight: tears welled in Joan's eyes and a painful emotion spread across her face. Cali Sky then experienced an unexpected sensation: a total reversal of feeling. Like entering the green mountain meadow after the sterile landscape of the rocky ascent, the transition from anger to compassion, resentment to love was sudden and breathtaking. It pulsed through her body like the jolt of desire.

"I don't know what to say...or do," began Joan, who surrendered to the sobs that now overcame her. "Sometimes I feel like I am cursed, like God is punishing me."

"What are you talking about, Mom?" asked Cali Sky.

Joan cried.

"Why would God punish you? Why would you be cursed?" Cali Sky persisted.

Joan continued to cry, and Cali Sky saw that her mom could not talk about it now—would not talk about it now. Cali Sky leaned back in her seat as Joan turned the ignition, killing the Celica's motor. The sound of weeping filled the car for nearly a minute.

As if starting a new conversation Cali Sky spoke calmly: "I think this is one reason why I play guitar, play piano, write songs. Chords are honest. Notes don't lie. A melody is what it is." She looked to the sky and said, "Music is the closest I'll ever get to truth, Mom."

Philip strained to see, squinting through his left eye into the distance. Down the street a cadre of teenagers was huddled together, focusing on something he knew couldn't be good. The orange Bronco's windshield was bug-stained and streaked, obscuring his vision. So he stepped out of the truck to get a better view. He heard Cali Sky rummaging through musical equipment in the back of the Bronco.

"Oh," he exclaimed, turning his attention away from the no-gooders and giving up on discovering the precise nature of their hooliganism, "Let me help you. What can I carry?"

"Here," replied Cali Sky, "take the amp. Just put it somewhere near where Jim is setting up his drums."

As Philip, amp in hand, entered the backyard of the house through the side gate, Jim walked the opposite direction and pulled his ride and crash cymbals from the car parked alongside the Bronco. As he returned to the backyard, the last beams of dusky sunlight flashed off the gold-colored instruments.

Bobby Ziegler was a new kid at school. His wealthy parents recently relocated to southern California. To help their son win friends they agreed to throw him a party in their backyard and pay a band to provide some entertainment. Since the band had never played in public before the cost was next to nothing.

A congenial Mr. Ziegler went out of his way to allay Philip's fears: "My wife and I will monitor and supervise the party carefully. We just wanted to do something to help Bobby adjust socially to a new school, new friends and a new life, really. It was very hard for him to leave his home and friends in Virginia. I hope you can understand."

"Of course," replied Philip. "And Cali Sky has really been looking forward to this."

"Good! Bobby informs me that everyone at school says that Cali Sky is sure to become a rock and roll star someday."

Philip gave Mr. Ziegler the clichéd parental expression conveying anxiety.

Before the sound check he wished goodbye to Cali Sky. "I'll be back at 11!" As hard as it was for Philip, Joan had convinced him to give Cali Sky space, to let her do her thing without the unavoidable influence that their presence would create. "Okay," replied Cali Sky who was focused on helping Brodie tune the bass and adjust amp settings. Brodie was preoccupied, his wandering eye searching the backyard for female prospects. Already a sizable group of teenagers gathered around the pool.

I'm in a band. I'm in this band. This is my band. Cali Sky had by now settled into her identity. She savored it at this moment, as she, Brodie, Jim and John set up their instruments, as the darkness of the evening spread, as the impulsive rhythms of adolescent chatter marked the Ziegler backyard as occupied territory: an emergent Teenage Wasteland. Then came the sound check: the pistol shot of Jim's snare and the experimental strums of guitar chords and bass notes rippled through the outdoor air, pushing through the wide-open atmosphere, bent by the acoustics-twisting gusts of wind.

A small clique of teenagers, weighted with deference and awe, approached John and Jim with hesitant steps, wishfully presuming an association with the duo. John simply nodded aloofly, returning the cluster to their ignominious place in the backyard corner. John and Jim had a following, acquired while gigging with their prior band. Cali Sky quickly looked away. A few moments later another clique approached, this one more socially formidable. It was led by a gangly skater who wore his scruffiness as a fashion statement.

He spoke up, "What do you say, John? So this is the new band?"

John set his guitar on its stand and nodded. "That's right. This is it."

The gangly skater turned toward the bass player: "Hell no! Brodie? What do you play, the triangle?"

Jim laughed, Brodie flashed a middle finger, smiling.

"Brodie can hold his own, man," John assured.

The gangly skater then turned to Cali Sky. "A chick! Cool!" He spoke directly to John with a suggestive expression, as if Cali Sky were not standing there and did not hear what he said or see his lewd intimation. Her face dropped; she appeared intimidated by the condescension. Looking down, she saw his checkerboard vans and hairy ankles, sensing his oppressive presence penetrating her. The sensation triggered her anger, an intense anger she last felt when Grandpa entered the studio and belittled the U2 song.

She looked the gangly skater in the eyes and said, "Get the fuck off my stage, asshole!"

Jim laughed hysterically, like a punchy toddler. Brodie's face showed admiration and deep attachment to Cali Sky. The gangly skater looked shocked and embarrassed.

"I didn't know this was your stage," he finally managed to say.

"That's my guitar. That's my amp. This is my stage," replied Cali Sky.

"Alright, alright." The gangly skater walked away. Cali Sky heard him as he disappeared into the crowd: "What a bitch!"

But she was distracted by a clicking sound coming from the opposite side of the stage. It was the sound of a camera. Cali Sky turned and saw that someone was taking her picture, focusing right on her. The confrontation with the gangly skater predisposed her to defensiveness: She felt another surge of anger pulsing through her body. But then the photographer lowered the camera and looked directly at her.

It was a girl. And she smiled. Like Cali Sky she had black hair, appearing unkempt, but much shorter. Her bangs nearly covered her eyes, while other strands of hair worked at cross purposes, some veering in one direction, others setting off in another. She looked like she just got out of bed. She wore a loose-fitting, black tank top layered over a tight-fitting white undergarment. Her pants and shoes were black. Cali Sky felt the anger dissolve and smiled back. The girl's face was powdered lightly with makeup that made her look pale and delicate. She raised her camera and took another shot while the smile remained on Cali Sky's face.

"Cali Sky," called John. "We're gonna start now."

The call to begin stirred the butterflies in Cali Sky's stomach. She made her way to John's left and lifted the guitar strap over her head. Brodie stood on John's right with an un-Brodie like appearance of anxiety. John approached the mic stand.

"Alright everybody!" his voice boomed from the amp. Those near the porch/stage pressed more closely. The farther reaches of the backyard remained unorganized and inattentive. "Alright everybody!" he repeated, this time in a tone of gathering annoyance, capitalizing on the lead singer's prerogative to occasionally incite or even berate his audience. Suddenly three jarring rim shots, followed by three cymbal crashes and three foot-pounding bass-drum beats, exploded from the back of the stage/porch: Jim's attempt to get the crowd's attention. The thundering noise startled John, nearly causing him to jump into the mic stand. He slowly turned around and gave his brother the what-the-fuck look.

"Did that get your attention?" spoke John into the mic. He nearly terminated his sentence with the word motherfuckers, but remembered in the nick of time that parents were present. "Thanks to Bobby for inviting us out," John continued. He then backed away from the mic and looked to Jim, who would begin the first song. Just as Jim began to play the opening to Social Distortion's "Another State of Mind," tapping the ride cymbal with rapid sixteenth notes, John frantically motioned for his brother's attention, yelling, with his back to the audience, "Wait! Stop! Stop!" Jim halted. John turned around, walked peevishly to the mic stand and said, "One more thing: We're Nowhere!" He turned back around, nodded to Jim, and the song got underway once again.

Within moments Cali Sky realized that the focus of the crowd was not the band. Few seemed to be paying attention. The crowd was captivated by the slam dancing that erupted near the front of the stage/porch. Bodies bounced roughly in time with the music, but seemed more intent on inflicting damage on other bodies. Soon bodies began to jump onto the stage/porch, slamming against the musicians themselves. Brodie smiled, but didn't dare look away from the bass' fret board, careful not to miss a note. Cali Sky backed away from the violence, standing beside her amp. John tried to ignore the chaos enveloping him, but when a body nearly overturned his mic stand, he raised his boot and sent the body down from the stage/porch and back into the crowd, where it was swallowed by the chain-reacting collisions of violent, throbbing movement.

Cali Sky watched Mr. Ziegler approach. Bodies knocked him off course, pushing him this way and that. Eventually he reached John and wrapped his hand around the guitar neck, muting the sound. He yelled, "Stop! Stop! Stop playing!" The song fell apart as, one by one, the musicians abandoned the song. Mr. Ziegler shouted something at John. The crowd became restless, dangerous. Cali Sky remained standing beside her amp.

John returned to his mic and said, "You guys can't slam. That's what I'm told: You can't slam. If you keep it up then we can't play." Expressions of disappointment and anger sounded forth from the midst of the bodies. Cali Sky spotted Bobby standing off to the side of the porch, looking embarrassed and miserable. "So if you want this party to have a band, then no more slam dancing."

Jim's unamplified shout reached the ears of those gathered near the porch/stage: "Peace and love! Peace and love!"

"Shut the fuck up, Jim," said an exasperated John.

Parental control now made palpable, the band recommenced. Slam dancing was kept at a minimum, thanks to the ever-patrolling Mr. Ziegler, who zeroed in on any body showing signs of inflicting damage on other bodies. He left the pogoing bodies alone. The band played some of John's originals. Cali Sky felt like she played a small role in these songs. She once had made some suggestions to improve them, but John became annoyed. "Just don't mess with John's songs," Brodie had warned her. So she stood stage left, moving slightly to the beat, pretending she meant it. She spotted Ari's suntanned face in the crowd. He smiled at her. She also caught sight of the photographer, standing off to the side, snapping shots of the band, though usually Cali Sky felt like the camera was pointed at her.

The band decided to end the first set with another cover, one arranged entirely by Cali Sky. It was U2's "I Will Follow," the first track on the album Joan bought her. Cali Sky played the opening riff, which scattered a shockwave of excitement through the crowd. After Jim entered on drums and Brodie nailed the bass line, the crowd, for the first time, began to dance—not slam dance, not pogo—but dance. Also for the first time Cali Sky felt the song she was playing. She sensed the audience's attention; her guitar was the prime mover of their experience. The photographer was now feverishly taking shots, focusing in on Cali Sky. And then she lost self-consciousness as well as any awareness of space and time. She floated around her small space on the porch/stage.

Until John began to sing. Then the enchantment was lost. She could feel her descent, her return to pedestrian realities, to the world of patrolling parents and gangly skaters. She stole a peek at John. He sang with passionate effort but her eyes were drawn to his bushy eyebrows, dominating his profile. She returned to the center of her small space on the porch/stage, feet firmly planted on the ground.

"We'll be back in fifteen minutes," John announced at the conclusion of the band's first set. He and Jim walked off the porch/stage together, met by a fawning coterie of their admirers.

Brodie looked at Cali Sky and smiled. "That was great!" he said quietly, standing close.

Cali Sky smiled back. "You played really well."

Brodie looked relieved, then elated. "Yeah?"

Cali Sky nodded.

"I'll be right back," he said. He walked off the porch/stage, heading directly toward one of the three girls who stared at him during the first set.

Cali Sky watched him disappear into the strange shadows, cast by artificial light. The pool light illuminated one side of the backyard, which was now packed with teenagers, most of whom she did not recognize. A few were staring at her. In the split second during which their eyes met, Cali Sky tried to read their expressions: Awe, uncertainty, intimidation and antagonism seemed to flit across their faces. She saw the photographer near these faces, still gazing up at Cali Sky, as if the band were still performing.

Just then Ari approached, stopped for a moment until Cali Sky gave him her full attention and hugged her.

"You were unbelievable," he exclaimed. "I loved it!" He looked neat and athletic: He possessed an attractiveness that was immediate and undeniable. Cali Sky took in his warmth, which contrasted with the cool night air. "Could we go somewhere quiet?" he asked. "Just for a moment?"

They walked past the staring faces and past the photographer. "Great set!" she said.

"Thanks." Cali Sky wanted to stop and talk with her but Ari

led her out of the backyard and to a secluded space between houses near a eucalyptus tree.

"You really were great!" he said.

"Yeah?"

"The guy standing next to me—I heard him say to someone that you were like a goddess."

"Really?"

"Yeah. You look amazing up there."

"I don't know. I got some weird looks from people."

"What do you expect? You *are* a goddess. And you're clearly the best musician up there."

They drew closer. He brought his hand up to her shoulder, then lifted it to the back of her neck.

He said, "I feel out of place here. All these skaters and punkers."

Cali Sky laughed. "You're probably the only jock here. I guess you probably get some weird looks too."

"Yeah. Mostly from the freaks."

"Hey, those freaks are my people."

"Is there a place for a tennis player among those people?"

"Only if he is a national champion," she answered with a smile.

They kissed, open mouthed, now more familiar with each other's bodies. Ten minutes later Cali Sky heard the sound of feedback. John had turned his amp on.

"Gotta go," Cali Sky said abruptly. But before she ran back to the porch/stage she said, "Ari, you and I will always get weird looks from people."

John looked annoyed as Cali Sky jumped onto the porch/stage. As she picked up her guitar John spoke into the microphone: "Brodie! Calling Brodie! I know you're around here somewhere. Please stop doing whatever you're doing—and I think we know what that is—and come up here and play the bass!"

Brodie emerged from the backyard shadows, jogging past the aquamarine light of the pool, a boyish grin on his face. John watched his approach, noticing a girl likewise emerge from the same dark corner, moving much more slowly than Brodie, but displaying a similar grin.

Someone from the outskirts of the mob of onlookers, now re-gathered in front of the porch/stage, yelled out, "How was it, Brodie?" Laughter spread across the crowd, which parted to allow Brodie through. As he pulled the bass strap over his head and settled the instrument into position, John continued the banter. Turning to Brodie, he said into the mic, "Sorry to interrupt you." Someone in the crowd shouted out, "Zip up your pants, Brodie." When Brodie fell for the joke and actually checked his fly, laughter poured from the backyard.

Cali Sky, meanwhile, seemed oblivious to the wise cracks and jocularity. She turned her amp down and played scales, trying to warm up her fingers. The photographer now stood at the base of the porch steps, directly in front of Cali Sky, snapping more pictures. As the laughter subsided Cali Sky walked back to her place and played a riff, waiting for the others in the band to get settled. She forgot however that she had turned the volume knob back up. The notes burst from her amp, startling the crowd with their suddenness. Once she began she couldn't stop. It was the Spanish-sounding riff she had played the first time she jammed with the Lanza brothers, the riff that startled John as it mined the bottom of the musical scale and rapidly ascended, notes building upon notes, to the highest range of the guitar. It sounded like a rising wind and died as quickly as it came to life. Its echoes blanketed the crowd with silence. All eyes were now on Cali Sky. She returned the stares unflinchingly. The uncanny moment was dispelled when John announced the next song. Jim counted it off and the band joined in.

They closed the second set with another cover, also arranged by Cali Sky. She stepped forward, center stage. Jim began on drums. Cali Sky adjusted the mic and said, "This is a song called 'Gloria.' You know it, even if you think you don't." Jim and Brodie then entered on guitar and bass. Cali Sky rotated the guitar to her side, she would sing the first verse without an instrument to hide behind. The photographer aimed her camera, zooming in on Cali Sky's facial expressions. John added his backing vocals to the chorus, after which Cali Sky played the sliding, syncopated high notes that cleared the musical air for the next verse. Brodie's rising confidence loosened him up, perhaps a bit too much: at times he struck affected poses, the sort that drew ridicule from certain types of boys and stirred desire in certain types of girls. Brodie and his charisma had the wherewithal to laugh off the former and indulge the latter.

As the band approached the final chorus Cali Sky stepped to the mic. Before the gig during practice John had prepped her. He had instructed, "Just say something like, 'We're Nowhere. Thanks for coming out. Good night.'" That is what she was supposed to say. When the moment came this is what she actually said: "We're Nowhere. As in, a band with three guys...and a *chick*...came out of nowhere." She waited for the next measure to begin. "As in... the most important things in life...like passion and music... come out of nowhere." She then turned to look at Jim, signaling the approach of the chorus. G-L-O-R-I-A then soared once again into the night air, sent aloft like a propitiation to the gods.

After the applause subsided Brodie, soaking up the attention and looking pleased with himself, gave Cali Sky a hug without any words. He then bathed in the adulation of the crowd, along with the occasional ribbing, before slipping off into the darkened shadows of the backyard for another tryst with the budding groupie. Jim and Cali Sky exchanged compliments. John remained aloof.

Cali Sky saw no sign of Ari. She felt little disappointment, however. On the contrary she experienced some relief. As soon as she stepped down from the porch/stage the photographer accosted her. Cali Sky studied her mussed black hair, spiking and falling in opposite directions, her dark eyeliner and black clothes.

"Oh my God, you were incredible!" The photographer's face glowed; her eyes were fixed on Cali Sky's. She raised her camera. "I hope you didn't mind. I took a lot of shots of you."

"No, that's okay," replied Cali Sky, "but why?"

The photographer looked warmly at Cali Sky, making her feel at ease. "Because you have something—a strong aura, a powerful life force."

Cali Sky waited for an expression, gesture or any sign of irony and sarcasm. But the photographer did not flinch: She appeared to mean every word. Her pale face and sparkling eyes made her look fragile in the artificial light, and the appearance of fragility sealed her sincerity.

"I'm Zoe," she said.

"Cali Sky."

"I know. Your name is so beautiful."

"Yeah, well it came to my dad during an acid trip."

"Really! How perfect! When he gave you that name he destined you for great things."

Cali Sky once again searched hard for traces of irony. Zoe remained passionately serious. Cali Sky replied, "Really? You think so?"

"Yeah!"

"Why?"

"Because your name comes from somewhere else, from beyond consciousness, from...nowhere! That's where the most important things come from, right?"

Cali Sky smiled.

Zoe continued, "I loved your version of 'Gloria.' It felt like you were channeling Patti Smith."

"Who?" asked Cali Sky.

"Patti Smith. You mean you never even heard Patti Smith's version of 'Gloria'? Oh my God, I'll have to make you a mix tape. You're channeling Patti Smith and you don't even know it!"

"Yeah, I guess so."

"Listen, what are your plans tonight? Do you wanna go with me to get something to eat? I could load your guitar and amp in my car."

"You drive? I mean, you're sixteen?"

"Yeah, my car's parked in front of the house."

"I'd love to," responded Cali Sky enthusiastically, "but my dad is picking me and Brodie—uh, the bass player—up in a few minutes."

"That's okay." Then Zoe unexpectedly gave her a hug. "Bye Cali Sky."

"Bye...Zoe."

Later that night Cami lay sleeping in Cali Sky's bed. The transition from the open air of the concert to the quiet snugness of the small bedroom was dizzying, requiring a recalibration of the senses. Cali Sky's ears rang. Once her eyes adjusted to the room, softly illuminated by the warm glow of nightlights now extended from every wall socket in the vicinity, Cali Sky saw that her sister was in a fetal position. She stirred as Cali Sky disrobed and awakened as Cali Sky crept under the covers.

"Tell me a story," she murmured. Cali Sky felt warmth radiating from Cami's body.

Cali Sky told of the girl and the cabin with the strange wind instrument hanging from the open window. But this time night cloaked the valley. A full moon was reflected in the stream where the current slowed and swelled along the gently curving grass bank. The nighttime air was cool, but the soft breeze was warm, cradling the girl's face as she gazed up at the glistening mountain peaks that surrounded her valley. The nocturnal ambiance made the trees look taller, their branches swaying, it appeared, in the empyreal regions of the stars. The girl entered her cabin, enchantingly lit by candlelight. The instrument poured forth its wind-shaped melody into the night. The girl approached the window and kneeled, resting her head on the sill, directly below the instrument. Tears welled in her eyes as the golden notes drew from her soul a heartbreaking joy and desire, irrepressible as the wind and mysterious as the moonlight.

Two weeks later Nowhere played its second gig, this time at That's Entertainment, a nightclub for the under-aged and thus the only nightclub in Orange County that did not serve alcohol. That's Entertainment bouncers were instructed to observe a zero-tolerance policy for behavior to which other clubs, given the right financial or social circumstances, might turn a blind eye: sexual favors, public urination, drug use. Local police enforcement kept a close watch on That's, and the owner knew it. His seemingly quixotic attempt to turn a profit involved the colossal task of amusing the reckless youth while simultaneously and preemptively calming parents whose insomnia-inducing fears revolved around the illicit ways their wayward offspring could amuse themselves. Moreover the clientele of the unlikely nightclub consisted to a small but dangerous degree of the sort of low-grade rogues that cops spend much of their Friday and Saturday nights chasing down.

Nowhere opened with a Cali Sky original. John only grudgingly conceded to this decision, partly because the other members of the band vociferously supported it, partly because John reluctantly understood that it was a great song. It built upon a punk framework—hard-driving beat, distorted guitars, minimalist chord progression—but was layered with nuances foreign to punk: a lead guitar line that ran through most of the song, a guitar solo (performed by Cali Sky) heralded by a change in key, and a bridge that featured ninth and inverted chords.

The young crowd predictably pogoed, working itself up into a frothy sweat. Unlike the cool California late October evening, blowing in from the frigid Pacific Ocean, everything inside That's generated heat: the stage lighting, the amps and of course the ceaseless movement of about 250 teenagers. Off came the outer-layered shirts and flannels. A few boys removed their shirts, only to be unceremoniously whisked away by two frontlines bouncers who muscled their way through the trenches with indomitable authority. Zoe stood atop a small set of stairs at the back of the venue. She was once again dressed all in black, with the exception of a beret, which was checker-boarded black and white. She rarely lowered her camera, pushing the shoot button with her right hand and adjusting the zoom lens with her left.

From her perspective, partially blinded by the stage lights, Cali Sky perceived the crowd as a multi-faced creature, moving its discrete parts incoherently, producing unintelligible noises from untraceable sources, and staring at her menacingly with a thousand eyes. Jim spoke to the creature: "Thanks for coming out. We're Nowhere." Once Cali Sky's song began, once she felt herself playing it and heard it coming from the amps, the creature became more understandable. Its movements were unified. The sounds she made from her guitar and mouth tamed its noise. And its stares, coming from a thousand different directions, stimulated and enticed her—to exhibit her passion and bare her soul. The song transformed the crowd, and since the song was hers, the crowd was transformed in her image. As her creation filled the space, everything it touched became intimate and personal, coterminous with the song and thus a part of her. She subsumed the multi-faced creature.

All of this changed however five seconds into the next song. After the applause died down and Cali Sky re-entered her conventional body with its mundane perceptions of space and time, Brodie spotted at the front of the crowd a green streak in the prickly shape of a tall hairdo. It was the Green Mohawk. The two made eye contact—prolonged and intense. The Green Mohawk scowled, then raised his right hand and extended his middle finger. As John took center stage to sing the next song, and as Jim counted it off, Brodie returned the Green Mohawk's sophomoric body language with a gesture more refined and subtle: Brodie winked—winked with a smug smile.

One second later rage contorted the Green Mohawk's face. Two seconds later Jim settled into his drumbeat, oblivious to the brewing cataclysm. Three seconds later, Cali Sky noticed aggressive movements near the opposite side of the stage. Four seconds later, John ambled toward the mic stand to begin singing the song that was abruptly terminated by the fateful events that descended upon the pivotal fifth second. The Green Mohawk slipped through a hole in the bouncer defense, climbed onto the stage, and tackled Brodie, leading with an awkward right cross. The two hurtled into Jim's drum set, toppling his crash cymbals, rolling over the tom drums and landing virtually in Jim's lap.

Jim sat dumb and amazed for a brief moment, struggling to process the strange disturbance violently disrupting his drum playing. The pointy ends of the Mohawk nearly stabbed his crotch. The neck of the supine bass guitar stretched between his legs. Brodie's bloodied upside-down face lay nearly directly beneath. Jim was immediately brought to his senses. He responded in true drummer fashion: He began to beat the Green Mohawk with his drumsticks. The Green Mohawk instinctively raised his arms to protect his battered head. Jim rose to his feet and realized that the opposite end of his sticks might wreak more damage. So he flipped his sticks around with a quick toss and resumed his attack, pummeling the Green Mohawk's head from various angles, trying to work around the outspread arms.

Meanwhile John's relative distance from the melee required less process time than his brother's. He rushed to the scrum and removed the guitar strap from around his neck. He grabbed the guitar neck with both hands and raised the instrument with the apparent intention of wielding it like a sledgehammer. But he then hesitated and set the guitar down off to the side, concluding that drumsticks are far more easily replaceable than a Fender Stratocaster. He then rained blows upon the Green Mohawk. He started with the head, but seemed to conclude that Jim had that territory covered. So he worked the midsection, sending his size 10 Vans into the ribs of the hapless Green Mohawk.

As Brodie crawled out of the way, security mobilized the entire bouncer swat team. Yellow-shirted men materialized on the stage seemingly from nowhere. They seized Jim, John, Brodie and the now barely conscious Green Mohawk and manhandled them off the stage, through the crowd, and in through a black door with a black door handle camouflaged by the surrounding black wall. Intensely bright artificial light blazed through the open door, then was summarily extinguished when the last Yellow Shirt made his way through the mysterious opening, slamming the black door behind him.

The stupefied crowd now had nothing to look at. The black door had swallowed their entertainment. One by one individuals in the crowd slowly returned their attention to the stage, where Cali Sky alone remained standing. She had in fact moved very little during the brawl. She felt the stares fall upon her. The violence had agitated the crowd. The multi-faced creature awoke.

She did what came naturally: She played a song. The first song that came to mind—no deliberation, no forethought. Not even a conscious decision. The song came from one of her dad's records: Creedence Clearwater Revival's "Bad Moon Rising." A small handful of kids in the room recognized the song from the first three chords. After the second measure of the intro, a second handful of teens could place the song. Once she began singing, that number multiplied. At first incredulous smiles appeared on faces: Is she really playing a Creedence Clearwater Revival song in That's Entertainment, musical home of punk and New Wave? Does she have the *balls* to play a song like that in a place where social pressure reduces the most charismatic and original to their knees? How *uncool* is Creedence Clearwater Revival?

Incredulous smiles then became amused smiles: This actually sounds pretty good. Besides she is playing it ironically? Isn't she?

And once the floating possibility of irony became indeterminate, once the audience could not figure out if Cali Sky perpetrated a musical joke or if she really meant what she played and sang—about dark times ahead that may or may not be the apocalypse—then the befuddled teens were left off-balance, smiling for reasons unknown. All that they understood with the least bit of clarity was that they were being entertained. Some danced. A few others sang along. Cali Sky overthrew the reigning gods of the teen temple not by storming the gates but by scattering confusion. She had once again tamed the multi-faced creature.

Absorbed in the song she seemed altogether unsurprised that she managed to finish it without interruption. Apparently the Yellow Shirts were either preoccupied with their interrogation in the mysterious room of blazing light, or they realized that Cali Sky's tune had a pacifying effect on the previously roused crowd. She concluded the song with a final D chord, acknowledged the crowd with a simple "thank you" spoken mildly into the mic—was *that* ironic?—and walked casually backstage.

She found the contrast in environments startling: from the raucous shouts and blaring amps of the concert hall to the dead silence and eerie emptiness of the green room. She sat on the worn couch, unsure what to do with herself. She brushed her hair back with both hands. She sighed and rubbed her eye. She then perceived the low hum of the crowd, now devoid of entertainment. The sound brought to her awareness recently transpired events, which she replayed in her mind: the attack of the Green Mohawk, the retaliation of the Lanza brothers, and her performance of the Creedence Clearwater Revival song. As she remembered she felt like she experienced them all over again, or at least experienced them differently—as if she were semi-conscious the first time they took place. She felt more fully present remembering the events than living the events.

She rose to explore the contents of the ancient refrigerator in the corner of the room when she heard a door open and close from an adjacent room. In walked Zoe.

"Oh my God, Cali Sky—you were terrific!" she exclaimed zealously. Her face was pale, as usual. Her fragile prettiness was at its zenith. "And you looked beautiful on stage!"

"Thanks, Zoe," replied Cali Sky, now cocooned in Zoe's embrace. "I'm glad you're here. It was really strange being in this room alone."

"I got right past the bouncers. I told them I was your sister."

"And they believed you? They look too mean to believe anything."

"But we *are* sisters, Cali Sky—spiritual sisters!"

Now familiarized with Zoe's manner, Cali Sky replied warmly, "I like the sound of that."

They sat down together on the beat-up couch.

Zoe continued, spellbound, "I was standing at the back, taking pictures. Did you see me?"

Cali Sky shook her head.

"Even though I was at the very back I could feel your presence…your musical presence. Your aura, your vibe filled the room."

Cali Sky smiled.

"I hope my camera captured some of that," added Zoe. For the first time since they met, Cali Sky saw a trace, very slight, of doubt in Zoe's eyes. That expression looked out of place on Zoe's delicate face and gave Cali Sky pain.

"I would love to see your pictures sometime," Cali Sky said hopefully.

"Of course. I've already developed the pictures from your last gig…. I love taking pictures of you."

Cali Sky sat back on the couch. Zoe's presence had completely transformed the room. They talked about the fight onstage and Cali Sky's decision to play a song solo. Then Zoe reached into her purse and pulled out a tape. "Here," she said, "this is for you. It's a mix tape. I put Patti Smith's 'Gloria' on it of course. But there are a lot of other good songs on there too. Look carefully: all female artists. Our spiritual sisters!"

Cali Sky scanned the song and artist list. Zoe's handwriting was flowing and ornate, mostly gentle curves with seemingly no sharp angles.

"Thank you so much, Zoe. I can't wait to hear it."

Later that night, back at her house, Cali Sky listened to the entire tape in the studio as the family slept. It was nearly 1 a.m. by the time the tape concluded. She pressed rewind to cue the last song. She carried the player into her bedroom and plugged it in after removing a nightlight. She prepared for bed. Before slipping into the sheets beside a deep-sleeping Cami, Cali Sky pressed the play button on the cheap stereo. The final song on the mix tape began: Kate Bush's "Breathing." Cali Sky adjusted the volume. Cami did not stir. Cali Sky drifted off to sleep to a soundscape that forever became associated with a violent attack, her solo performance and a spiritual sister.

SIX

December 1980

FORMLESS SHAPES OF dark colors advanced across a limitless horizon. The movement expressed itself as sound, the abstract sound of maybe a crashing waterfall or perhaps radio static. The volume increased as the audible shapes advanced. And the ambiguous sound very gradually assumed form, as if inching down a cosmic funnel, slowly becoming concrete as the funnel narrowed, eventually achieving aural intelligibility on the other side of the cosmic chute.

Cali Sky opened her eyes. She blinked. Dawning consciousness re-activated her ordinary cognitive process. A noise vibrated in her ears. The sound went inside her, into her neural network, and registered in her wakened mind, which finally reestablished a frame of reference grounded in the sense of self. *That is the sound,* her still sluggish mind seemed to say, *of a helicopter.* But the recognition of the sound seemed too quick for words. Perceptions now flooded her senses, conveying information pre-linguistically: dim morning light spills into her bedroom, the cassette stereo lies near her bed, from which point it played the entire second side of

Zoe's mix tape the night before and Cami slumbers in a twisted confusion of sheets and blankets, positioned on her stomach with her arms tucked under her body.

Cali Sky blinked some more. She lay on her back. The sound of the helicopter receded, replaced by another sound, this one fainter and seemingly farther off, though she knew its source was nearby, within the four walls of the house. The sound came from her parents' bedroom. They were arguing.

"Too fucking bad, Philip!" It was her mom's voice. During her parents' bedroom arguments Cali Sky could only discern her mom's words. Her dad generally kept his composure, arguing with gentleness and respect (which infuriated Joan) or, at the worst, controlled anger (which Joan found more satisfying). Either way, he rarely raised his voice. Not so Joan, whose passion occasionally ran unbridled.

"Open up, for Christ's sake!" Joan exclaimed. Cali Sky winced. Her mom broke the third commandment in Philip's presence. A false silence ensued—false because Cali Sky knew that it merely cloaked Philip's shaming reproach. Cali Sky braced herself for her mom's fiery response. She didn't have to wait long.

"Well," Joan yelled, "I guess I'm going to hell then!"

Cali Sky then heard a door slam. She sat up in bed, remaining motionless for a while. She impulsively reached into her nightstand drawer and removed her lyric notepad. She scribbled a few words onto its pages. She then got out of bed, picked up the acoustic guitar and played it softly. Cami stirred. She looked pale.

"Are you okay?" Cali Sky asked.

Cami nodded and said in a sleepy voice, "I have to go potty."

"Come on then," replied Cali Sky as she steered her lethargic sister down the cold hallway and into the bathroom.

"Why are you and Mom always arguing?" asked Cali Sky from

the passenger seat of the orange Bronco. Philip was taking her to school.

Philip sighed as he braked in the rush-hour traffic. "You don't need to know that, Cali Sky."

"Mom thinks so." Cali Sky brushed her fingers over Cami's bite marks on the front dash.

"Then ask *her*."

Cali Sky withdrew into herself. The absent sun, lost beyond the thick marine layer, heralded the dilatory approach of the California winter. Cali Sky felt chilled on this December morning. Her dad's exasperation and depression seeped into her.

Philip fidgeted. He scratched his beard. "I don't even really know why we were arguing, Cali Sky. I really don't. I guess we were arguing about a whole bunch of things."

They passed a strip mall, the lights of which seemed to glow in the compressed atmosphere formed by the low-lying billows. The blinking taillights of a bus, pulled to the side of the road to load and unload passengers, looked fuzzy in the foggy distance.

"I wrote down an idea for some song lyrics this morning," Cali Sky said about a mile later.

"Yeah, what's the song about?"

"It's about a perfect day. Well, it starts out perfect. Near a lake...in the summer. Something evil comes...and destroys it all."

Philip adjusted his hands on the steering wheel, steering the Bronco out of the far right lane to avoid a cyclist. "Evil didn't destroy it all, Cali Sky."

"It's my song, Dad."

"You know what I mean." He paused. She looked away.

"Do you really believe that?" he pressed.

"I don't know."

"You don't know?"

She shrugged.

He continued, his passion rising, "Evil doesn't destroy all. Do you understand?"

"No."

"Why?"

"Because sometimes it seems like evil does destroy everything."

Cali Sky watched some of her classmates walk across the school parking lot, looking miserable.

"You know, Cali Sky," Philip resumed calmly, "God uses evil for *his* purposes...his good and perfect purposes. Evil may make us suffer, but we become stronger through suffering. Don't you believe that?"

Cali Sky shrugged again.

"We draw closer to God, rely more upon him." He became defensive. "That is why we can even rejoice in our sufferings—like the Apostle Paul writes. Do you understand? God wins, not evil."

"Like I said, Dad, I was telling you about my song. Maybe you should write your own."

They pulled into the school parking lot. Cali Sky always associated these sorts of days—the days of fog and mist—with the anxiety of school-time mornings. Like the fog, the day had yet no shape, its future was wide-open and mysterious. Once, when she was seven or eight, Cali Sky confronted the concept of infinity. When she tried to wrap her mind around it, she felt overcome by fear, as if she were in the presence of something nefarious, something that belied the happy appearances of ordinary life.

Philip slowed the Bronco to a gradual stop in front of the school. Cali Sky jumped down onto the brightly colored yellow curb. She slung her backpack over her shoulder.

"Cali Sky," said Philip, leaning down in his seat in the Bronco so that he could look into her face. "Please don't write a song like that."

Cali Sky pulled her ponytail out from beneath the backpack

strap. She turned toward her dad, prepared to lash out in anger. But when she saw what appeared to be tears welling in his eyes, her anger dissipated. She paused, not knowing what to say.

He broke the pause with an unsteady voice: "It would break my heart."

She turned and walked toward the school entrance, joining the trickling stream of dropped-off students

Swept up into the torrent now spilling into the school's front hallway, Cali Sky looked around. The hallway witnessed the display of nearly every known human behavior: talking, shouting, whispering, gossiping, bragging, joking, laughing, weeping, kissing, hugging, petting, wrestling, threatening, spitting, nose-picking, ass-scratching, farting, and, in the hallway bathrooms, shitting and ejaculating. Social cliques and classifications blended into one as students shuffled to their destinations. The struggle for identity raged in the troubled psyches of the adolescent herd.

I'm in a band. The refrain buoyed both Cali Sky's spirits and reputation, the latter of which now rose to the surface of the sea of anonymity that engulfed her in the shape of hundreds of faces that passed by in the hall. Many of these faces met her with the now customary expressions of awe, uncertainty and intimidation. She stared back briefly, then looked nonchalantly away, permitting and even fostering the perception that she was aloof, set apart and arrogant. She walked a privileged path reserved for the jocks, the good-looking and the cool.

She passed a long row of lockers standing militaristically beneath a clock and fire bell, both of which were caged with small metal bars. Everything in sight needed to be protected from the destructive potential of teenage miscreants. The architects of WW II underground war rooms may very well have created the design for American public schools.

Cali Sky passed through a doorway and into a completely

different environment, one less sterile, more homely, one that made you feel more like a human being: Mr. Kelly's English class. The thick-ply carpeted floor, though colored a vomit yellow-brown, gave a hint of grandmotherly comfort. A large poster near the door depicted a forest and a lake foregrounded by a sage epigram from the pen of Ralph Waldo Emerson. Cali Sky took her seat near the center row.

"Hey Cali Sky," said Karen, the girl sitting in the next seat.

"Hey," replied Cali Sky with a nod.

Karen returned her attention to her backpack, pretending to arrange and rearrange her folders. Cali Sky looked at the side of Karen's face and could see the obvious make-up line, descending from her temple to her chin. On one side of the line, the white, unadorned flesh. On the other, the powdered and rouged façade.

Cali Sky gazed down at her Pee Chee folder, upon which she had written in various styles the word "Nowhere." She thought about band names: the Beatles, Joy Division, Cream, Creedence Clearwater Revival. Did "Nowhere" have it? A name that carried resonance? Could it possibly be immortal? She searched the word, looking for clues in its two syllables. She could picture it emblazoned on an album cover, adorning a concert t-shirt, spray-painted on walls, written in the stars. But the next moment it stumbled and fell into oblivion. She felt like she was trying to uncover a mystery, like the existence of God. Hope succeeded fear, fear succeeded hope as she pounded her head against a metaphysical wall. The Beatles became the Beatles only after they became the Beatles.

As the warning bell sounded students settled into their seats. Some glanced at Cali Sky and quickly looked away. Others nodded or said, "Hey." Over the past few months word had spread, some of it true, some of it false, some of it mere gossip and rumor: She was the lead guitar player of Nowhere, she was destined to be a rock star, she was stuck up, she was shy, she was beautiful, she was ugly, she was a religious weirdo, she sold her soul to the devil, she slept with everyone in the band, she slept with no one at all, she was a lesbian, she was a bitch, she was a goddess.

"Steve Adams."

"Here."

Mr. Kelly began taking roll.

"Tim Arzt."

"Here."

"Ali Bradley."

"Present."

"Cali Sky Braithwaite."

"Here."

Mr. Kelly paused, losing his place on the role sheet. The name hung in the air. No one spoke.

"Jenny Call."

"Here."

The chatter picked up as Mr. Kelly worked his way down the role, concluding with the last name, "Zuniga."

Mr. Kelly pulled his chair from behind his desk and moved it to the front of the room. He sat in it with a pile of papers in his hand, a pile which he then placed at the foot of his chair on the floor.

It was free-write day. Students had written a 250-word composition on any subject they chose. Mr. Kelly would now read some of the compositions anonymously in front of the class. He pulled one from the middle of the stack and began reading.

"'Imagine, if you will, your driving down the rode and up ahead theres a car moving in and out the lane. The break lights come on and the car slows down for no reason. Then all of the sudden the car speeds up but then slows down again. Dont you hate being behind a car like that?'"

A few students voiced agreement. Others tried to figure out who wrote it.

"'Well,'" Mr. Kelly continued reading, "'chances are if you look behind the wheel theres a woman driving that car!'"

Some boys in the class yelled approval.

"'Shes probably trying to put on her make up while driving. Shes looking at her self in the mirrur and not concentrating on driving. Woman driver's are the worst....'"

"Okay," said Mr. Kelly, grimacing, as he placed the composition on the floor beside the pile. "I think we've heard enough of that one."

The misogynistic free-write made Cali Sky think about the outdoor gig. "Cool, a chick."

Mr. Kelly said, "Time for another one." He pulled a second composition from the pile and read.

"America is facing a crisis. Immorality is on the rise. Pre-marital sex is now okay. Millions of babies are murdered through abortion. Even homosexuality is becoming acceptable.

"'The reason for this immorality is clear. People have abandoned God, they have rejected Jesus.'"

A vocal minority of the class emitted a collective groan. "Not this again. Gabriel!"

But Mr. Kelly continued. "'It is a documented fact that in 1962 when school prayer was declared unconstitutional immorality became worse. Crime rates increased. Abortion rates increased. Morally, society is going down the drain. Or, I should say, the sewer. America turned its back on God.

"'But there is a solution.'"

By now everyone in the class knew where this was going.

"'We need to return to GOD. We need JESUS. GOD says in THE BIBLE...'"

Here Mr. Kelly stopped. Some continued to roll their eyes

and moan. Most however remained silent—too uncomfortable to voice opinions either way. Gabriel sat bolt upright in his chair, glorying in his sense of persecution. For years he had been mercilessly teased. His goofy statements, socially awkward intellect, annoying habits and unfashionable clothing confirmed to everyone that he was the quintessential nerd. But he had returned to school one fall having become a Christian over the summer. He began evangelizing during lunch break; he passed out Gospel tracts after school. When the teasing commenced he spouted Bible verses. As the teasing continued he singled in on the verse that helped him make sense of the bullying, that transformed the cruelty into a crown. He looked into the eyes of his tormenter and recited Matthew 5:11: "Blessed are you when people insult you, persecute you and falsely say all kinds of evil against you because of me."

Listening to Mr. Kelly, Cali Sky considered how Gabriel's composition would please her dad. Would he want her to be like Gabriel? *Could* she be like Gabriel?

Mr. Kelly dropped Gabriel's composition on the pile and pulled another from the bottom. He read,

"John's parents didn't care. They ignored him. Once they went out to dinner. They left John at home. They said 'There's some peanut butter, jelly and bread. Make yourself a sandwhich.' But there was no bread. John dipped his fingers in the peanut butter jar. He licked the peanut butter from his fingers. That was his dinner. He had no friends. No real friends. Once some of his supposedly friends told him to meet them at the movie theater. John walked five miles to the movie theatre. They were not there. As usual he was by himself. People made fun of him. John the loner, John the loser. Why was the world so cruel? He didn't like his parents. He didn't like his classmates. He didn't like himself. He dreamed of a different life. But there was no escape. Or was there?

His parents weren't home. He knew where his dad kept the gun. His dad liked to hold it when he was drunk. John went to the hidden place. He pulled out the gun. It was heavy. He raised it. He put it in his mouth. He held his breath.

Goodbye cruel world
I'm leaving you today
Goodbye
Goodbye
Goodbye
Goodbye all you people
There's nothing you can say
To make me change
My mind
Goodbye."

The class was silent. Mr. Kelly looked pale, sad and intense. Carrie Rhodes looked searchingly around the room, studying faces, trying to identify the author. Cali Sky felt the uncanny sensation of déjà vu. *Why is this familiar?* she thought. She scanned her past, searching her memory. She sensed she was on the cusp of a discovery, but revelation eluded her. She felt dizzy as the prolonged silence hung in the classroom.

Then she realized that the free-write had the same effect on the class that her songs had on audiences. They both unsettled people, broke through something, forced a confrontation. The parallel to music brought her cascading thoughts full circle, back to the poem that concluded the free-write. She knew that poem. She heard it somewhere. Did Aunt Nancy once recite it? Then she remembered: Pink Floyd. It was a Pink Floyd song. From *The Wall* album. "Goodbye Cruel World."

Cali Sky had bought *The Wall* album on vinyl. One Saturday afternoon not long thereafter she was listening to it in the living

154

room on her dad's old record player. She lay on her back on the floor, gazing at the moon-rocked ceiling, absorbed in the dark sonic landscape. Cami walked by just as "Goodbye Blue Sky" came on. The song begins with the peaceful sound of a lilting bird, its blithe whistle suggesting spring, life and serenity. Cami stopped to listen. Then the sound of the bird's song is obscured by another sound, one emanating from a recurring Pink Floydian symbol: an airplane. Cami was now intrigued, her attention now fully on the song. The airplane sound gradually increases but the bird's song also continues. Then the impossibly innocent voice of a child carries over the two other sounds. The child says with a strong British accent, "Look mummy, there's an aeroplane up in the sky." An acoustic guitar then silences the other sounds and formally begins the song.

"Who was that?" Cami asked.

"Who was who?" Cali Sky asked back.

"That kid. The one in the song."

"I don't know."

"Did she see the airplane?"

"Yeah, I think so."

"But we only heard it, right?"

"Right."

"Someday," Cami concluded, "I want to go on an airplane."

"Me too."

Then Cami ran off. Cali Sky thought, *Why does the child in the song call attention to the sound of the plane—and not the song of the bird? But my sister did the same thing. She was more curious about the plane than the bird. Why is that?*

Mr. Kelly's class concluded awkwardly. Carrie Rhodes continued to search faces for clues. Gabriel seemed prepared to witness to the desperate author who apparently needed Jesus. But chatter was subdued. Horse play was squelched. The moral geography of the teenage world leaves little space for the sacred. The suicidal free-write however found that space. For the most part the students in Mr. Kelly's English class seemed to respect that territory.

Cali Sky headed for her locker. She needed to pick up her dreaded algebra textbook for Mrs. Schroeder's dreaded algebra class. "Goodbye Cruel World" played over and over in her head. As she neared her locker she saw Brodie. He was standing there, waiting for her. Cali Sky knew immediately that something was wrong. Brodie never waited for her at her locker. He spent his passing periods flirting and socializing. At the moment he was doing neither. She saw the look on his face—also very un-Brodie like. He wasn't smiling. His face did not even appear to be on the brink of a smile.

"Hey," said Cali Sky apprehensively as she drew near, "What are you doing?"

"Cali Sky," he began, and hesitated. She had never seen him like this. "I've got to tell you something." He stood mute.

"Okay," Cali Sky said after a pause. "What? Tell me."

"It's about the band." Another pause.

"Okay...what?"

Brodie struggled to speak.

"Tell me, Brodie. What?"

"John called me last night."

"Yeah."

"He said...that he was kicking you out of the band."

Cali Sky froze.

Remorse was in Brodie's voice: "I was gonna call you last night and tell you. But I just couldn't. I wanted to tell you in person."

Cali Sky still didn't reply. So Brodie continued, "I told him that if he kicked you out of the band, then he'd have to kick me out too.... So he did. I'm not in the band anymore either."

Finally Cali Sky spoke, "Why the hell did he kick me out?'

"He said there could only be one leader. He said you were trying to take over."

Rage poured over her. "I can't believe this! Take over?"

Brodie said, "I think he's afraid of you, Cali Sky. Seriously. He knows you're better than he is. A better guitar player. Just a better musician. He's afraid."

"The band would be better if I *did* take over."

"I agree. John's just intimidated by you."

"Well, fuck him!" she yelled as she slammed her locker. Everyone in the hall stared at the two of them.

During algebra class Cali Sky did nothing. She did not listen to Mrs. Schroeder, she did not do the assigned exercises, and she didn't write down the homework for the day. She felt a tingling sensation in the pit of her stomach, a sensation that made her feel lethargic and apathetic. Then she thought of John and experienced the rage all over again.

During lunch she sat next to Brodie. He ignored everyone else at the table. He tried to cheer her up.

"He's an asshole, Cali Sky," he said. "But don't worry. We can start another band."

But she ignored him. "I wrote the best songs for the band. I made John's shitty songs halfway decent. I arranged the covers."

"I know, I know," Brodie consoled. "But like you said, 'Fuck him.'"

Later that afternoon during jazz band class, Cali Sky got wrapped up in a song, losing self-awareness. The notes from her guitar carried her somewhere else, momentarily erasing all memory of her problems. And after the song concluded, the sense of self-forgetfulness lingered. She came back slowly. She was jolted into the present when she heard herself unconsciously repeating the identity-affirming mantra, *I'm in a band*. Then the news from the morning came crashing down on her all over again.

"Typical male insecurity. He's obviously threatened by a strong female presence. And trust me, Cali Sky—God I love your name—trust me, you are a strong female presence."

Zoe and Cali Sky sat at a small table at a bohemian-style coffee shop near the campus of the University of California-Irvine. Zoe had picked Cali Sky up from school, a transaction which had not gone unnoticed by the parent-bound students filing into the family-friendly cars in the school parking lot. They gawked at Zoe's Karmann Ghia and marveled at Zoe's spiked and mussed hair. And then they quickly looked away.

The coffee shop was university *chic*, one of Zoe's haunts. Dadaist art hung from the grimy walls. In one corner was a picture of a naked woman, sitting demurely on the edge of a bathtub, drawing water for a bath. But the water flowing from the faucet was black, and the tub was surrounded by a post-apocalyptic scene of bombed buildings reduced to rubble beneath a glowing doomsday sky. The barista, who wore an earring in his left ear, knew Zoe by name.

"Seriously," Zoe continued, "you *are* a force, a goddess. Look at these."

Zoe pulled from her bag some photos she had taken, all black and white. The first depicted Cali Sky at the outdoor gig in the Ziegler backyard, standing on the porch/stage. She sang into the mic with closed eyes. Her bangs completely covered the left side of her face. Brodie was in the blurred background. She knew that moment: she was singing "Gloria."

The second photo showed Cali Sky at the That's gig. John, Jim, Brodie and the Green Mohawk had already been removed from the stage and escorted out of the theater. Cali Sky was alone on stage. The photo captured her looking off into the far distance as she stood in front of the mic. In the bottom foreground she could see the backs of heads—people watching her perform. To the right, she could just make out the black door through which her band mates departed. It was ajar, emitting a glowing light.

Cali Sky smiled and looked up. Zoe smiled back.

"These are great, Zoe."

"You can have them; I developed another set of prints."

Zoe remained smiling. Cali Sky saw in her eyes something childlike—a naivete or innocence. But Cali Sky also saw in her face a mark of guardedness and cynicism, most dominant in her brow when she observed passersby and in the corners of her mouth when she spoke of people like John.

"Thanks," replied Cali Sky. "I think you're a great photographer. The way you took the pictures, the angle and focus and everything, you make me look like a rock star."

"You are."

"Not anymore." Cali Sky made a half-hearted effort at laughter. "Not without a band."

"Don't worry. You're destined to find another band. I can feel it. I just wish it was an all-female band."

"Do you know any girls who play instruments?" asked Cali Sky.

"No. Girls around here are all the same. Cheerleader wannabe's, student-council bullshit, Barbie-doll lookalikes. They're all fake, you know?"

The innocence in Zoe's eyes disappeared. Her statement sounded well-rehearsed, her cynicism dogmatic. She continued, "I don't hang out with many people." Cali Sky could not recall seeing Zoe hanging out with *anyone*. "But I like to hang out with you." Her smile reappeared, displacing the cynicism.

"So how'd they do it?" asked Cali Sky. "All those female bands on the mix tape you gave me: the Raincoats, the Slits?"

"Spiritual sisters!" Zoe exclaimed. "They find each other. Just like you and me!"

Cali Sky stared at Zoe's photographs of her. "I feel like this is the real me, you know?" She felt a swell of emotion, like she was about to cry.

"That *is* the real you. Don't ever forget that."

Cali Sky now felt the emotion sweep over her. Tears accompanied a torrent of words. "My piano teacher once told me that I played like a robot. With no emotion. But he was right." Cali Sky felt like she was confessing her sins. "But then I had these… intense experiences. Really strong emotions. That came from nowhere." She paused with a pained look on her face, realizing her pun too late. Then quickly continued, "And I put those emotions in my music. I tried to play with those emotions. My piano teacher called it the Blue Flower. He said all our strongest emotions come from the Blue Flower."

Now Zoe had tears in her eyes. "Oh my God that is so beautiful."

Cali Sky told her about her hike in the mountains and her late-night experience with the album covers spread across the living-room floor. About the longing sensation, the desire. Once she began talking, she found it hard to stop. She concluded by saying, "I don't know. I guess strange things happen to me. I guess maybe I'm strange."

"No," replied Zoe, "you're not strange." She reached into her large black purse, which looked more like a duffle bag, and pulled out a heavy hardbound book. Cali Sky saw by the title that it was a book of photography. Zoe flipped through the pages, searching. She opened the book wide and set it before Cali Sky.

"Look," she said.

Cali Sky saw an old photograph, yellowed by age. It was black and white. It depicted a girl with long black hair resembling her own. The flowing hair blended with the leafy background of tree branches and what appeared to be a steep hill or maybe a waterfall. She had fair features and full lips. Her attention was focused on a winged girl about a foot tall. The pixie appeared to be standing on a leaf, returning the gaze of the black-haired girl, who looked neither afraid nor astounded. Her gaze was gentle. The pixie appeared to have something in her hand, maybe a bouquet of flowers.

"This," explained Zoe, "is a famous photo from a long time ago. It was taken in England. The Cottingley Fairies. There are a few others." Zoe turned the page and showed Cali Sky more shots of girls in the presence of fairies. "When they were first printed people believed that they were real. The guy who wrote *Sherlock Holmes*—you know, the detective stories?—he studied them and even he believed they were true. Of course lots of people thought it was a hoax."

"Was it?" asked Cali Sky tentatively, realizing that she was in effect asking if fairies really do exist.

"I don't know," Zoe replied. "Probably. But I don't think that's the point. For a moment you can look at the photograph and think it's real, or imagine it's real. And then it doesn't even really matter anymore. The photograph has already made you feel something powerful."

"Anyway," she continued, "that's the sort of photography I like. Not of fairies, obviously. But the kind that makes you think there is more to reality, you know? The kind that shows you mysteries just beneath the surface."

"Mysteries just beneath the surface," echoed Cali Sky.

They sipped their coffee.

"I think you are a great photographer, Zoe. I think you're gonna make it big," said Cali Sky.

"Thanks," replied Zoe cheerfully, though Cali Sky heard doubt in her tone. "I just need to get to New York. Or London. Start my photography career there."

"You'll make it," Cali Sky said hopefully.

"I think I will. I think it's my destiny."

"It's your Blue Flower."

Cali Sky and Cami were in an airplane. But since Cali Sky had never been in an airplane before, it looked like their living room. Cami laughed while the room pitched and rolled. But something prevented Cali Sky from joining in Cami's laughter. Cami ran to the window with wobbly legs, giggling. Cali Sky followed behind apprehensively. Looking over Cami's shoulder Cali Sky could see a blue sky stretching to infinity.

"Don't get too close to the window, Cami," Cali Sky warned.

Cali Sky felt butterflies in her stomach, the kind you get when you see someone too close to the edge of a sheer cliff. Cami ran to the other side of the room. Cali Sky walked to the window and looked down. Then she remembered why she couldn't laugh: She somehow knew the plane was going to crash. Someone was going to *make* it crash. That someone was a boy. Cali Sky saw him below. Though the plane sailed thousands of feet above him, Cali Sky could somehow see him close up.

He had a gun in his mouth. He slowly pulled it out. He lifted it up high and pointed it at the plane.

"No, no, no!"

She could somehow hear the sound of the gun firing.

"No, no, no!"

She braced herself, waiting for the impact. She couldn't see where Cami was.

"No, no, no!"

Then she realized she was dreaming and thrashed herself awake. When she opened her eyes, she saw Cami staring at her.

"Oww," murmured Cami. Her face was sweaty. One strand of her hair was matted on to her wet forehead.

"What's wrong?" asked Cali Sky.

"My tummy hurts."

"Again?"

Cami nodded. At that moment Cali Sky could hear shouting. Her parents were arguing.

"So what are you saying?" It was her mom's voice.

"Just say it!" her mom continued. "Yeah, well at least I have the balls to say it, you fucking coward!"

Cali Sky felt the anxiety sweep over her.

Cami vomited. A projectile vomit, all over the bed and floor.

"Jesus, Cami!" gasped Cali Sky, instinctively stepping back, away from the spray.

"Jesus! Are you alright?"

Cami looked stunned.

"Alright," said Cali Sky, "I'll be right back. Don't move."

Cali Sky ran out of the room and headed toward the shouting. As she neared her parents' bedroom, she abruptly halted when she distinctly heard her dad call her mom a slut. Her legs suddenly went weak. Now *she* felt sick, like *she* was going to vomit. Her head spun.

"Feel better now, you...hypocrite?" her mom screamed.

Cali Sky swung open the door. Her parents turned around instantaneously. Joan first caught Cali Sky's attention. Her mom wore only a bra and panties. Her skirt was in her hands, which she used to cover herself when Cali Sky barged into the room. She then turned her attention to her dad, who wore slacks and an undershirt. He looked mortified: guilty and ashamed, as if Cali

Sky had caught him yelling "Goddamn" at the top of his lungs to the entire world. The word "slut" still hung in the air, sealing their guilt.

Before they had a chance to say anything, Cali Sky exclaimed, "Cami vomited. There's throw-up all over my bedroom."

Joan brought her hand to her forehead in a gesture of exasperation. "Oh, shit. That's just great!"

"Joan, please!" replied Philip. He looked in horror at Cali Sky. His expression had changed from guilt and shame to fear and grief. Cali Sky knew that expression well: It attended moments when he thought innocence was being taken from his children.

Joan ignored Philip. "Cali Sky," she said with clenched teeth. "Could you please start cleaning it up? I'll be there as soon as I can."

"But it's all over," protested Cali Sky.

"*Please!*" yelled Joan.

Cali Sky slammed the door behind her and walked to the kitchen where she pulled half a dozen towels from a drawer. She carried them into her bedroom. Cami lay on her side, knees pressed against her chest, surrounded by her own vomit. She faced the wall, back to Cali Sky.

She remained motionless as Cali Sky began the futile task of wiping vomit off the shag carpet with a towel. She seemed to be pushing most of it deeper into the carpeting. Still no Joan. Cali Sky's anger escalated. She moved on to the bed, wiping vomit off of the sheets and blankets surrounding Cami, who remained motionless.

Cali Sky walked to her bedroom doorway and shouted, "Could someone please help me!" She paused and listened. No sounds of arguing.

Her shouting roused Cami, who asked, "Where's Mom?"

"She's coming... I hope."

Cami looked weak and feverish. She said faintly, "I wish I didn't have this problem."

"Do you feel like you're going to throw up again?" asked Cali Sky.

"No."

By the time Joan entered the room, Cali Sky had used and soiled nearly all the kitchen towels. The guilt on Joan's face had dissipated; she now looked angry and flustered.

"Cami, are you alright?" asked Joan.

Cami didn't answer.

Joan surveyed the mess. "Cali Sky, you didn't clean it up, you just made it worse!"

"I did the best I could, Mom!" she replied as she exited the room.

Her mom yelled above her head, "Philip, bring me some wet kitchen towels! Now!"

Cali Sky gathered her backpack from the kitchen counter. Her dad entered the room and yanked the remaining towels from the towel drawer. Half of them fell to the floor. He picked them up in a fit of irritation and flung them into the sink. He turned on the tap.

Cali Sky stared at the back of his head. "Why would you call Mom a slut?"

He continued to wet the towels. He said in a timid, defeated voice, "Please don't ask me that. Please. I shouldn't have said that. Please. I'm sorry." He bundled the dripping towels into a ball and hurriedly carried them into her bedroom.

Cali Sky rushed to the phone, picked up the handset and carried it into the studio. She punched some numbers and waited anxiously.

"Is Zoe there?

"It's me. I'm so glad you answered.

"Yeah. Well, no, actually. Is there any way you could give me a ride to school this morning? I just can't be around my dad.

"Really, are you sure?

"Thanks, Zoe.

"No, don't pick me up at my house. Pick me up at the gas station on the corner. I'll walk there. I'm leaving right now.

"Thanks again.

"Bye."

She hung up the handset and returned to her room. Her parents were wiping up vomit on opposite sides of the bed, refusing to stand within five feet of each other. Cali Sky yanked some clothes from her dresser.

"Are you feeling better?" Joan asked Cami.

"Yeah."

"Can you go to school?"

"Nooooo."

Cali Sky took her clothes into the bathroom and changed. Afterwards she slung her backpack over her shoulder and announced to her parents, "Zoe is picking me up for school. I'm leaving. Bye."

"What are you talking about?" asked Philip, rushing toward the front door, which Cali Sky had now opened. "*I'm* taking you to school."

"No. Zoe's picking me up. She's already on her way."

She began walking through the door, paused, and said, "You still need to give Brodie a ride. He'll be here at 7:30."

"Cali Sky, wait…"

She slammed the door and set off across the driveway. The front door swung back open.

"Cali Sky, I said wait!" Philip yelled.

Then Cali Sky heard her mom's voice from inside the house: "Let her go, Philip! You can't control her anymore."

Philip shut the door, softly and gently.

"My parents?" The Karmann Ghia's motor whined a high pitch until Zoe shifted it into third gear. "They got a divorce when I was a baby. My dad comes around every other weekend. Buys me camera equipment, clothes, albums."

Cali Sky tried to stretch her legs around her backpack in the claustrophobic space of the passenger side. She felt achy from a lack of sleep. Zoe pushed a tape into the car's deck. Siouxsie and the Banshees' "Christine" began playing mid-song.

"What about your mom?" asked Cali Sky.

"She's pretty cool. She works a lot, which means I have the house to myself. I can do my own thing."

"My house is the opposite." Lethargy made Cali Sky feel distanced from reality, as if she watched the world go by on a two-second time delay.

"You should come and live with me and my mom!" Zoe announced suddenly. "We could turn one bedroom into a band room. Our house would be an art and music studio! Like Andy Warhol's Factory."

"What's that?" asked Cali Sky.

"The Factory? It was this huge studio in New York during the 1960s. All sorts of artists gathered there. Salvador Dali. Oh, and the Velvet Underground. They were like the house band. All these artists. Right in the middle of New York City. Andy Warhol was a total mad genius. His Factory was an oasis for artists. A totally different world!"

Zoe's description triggered in Cali Sky a memory. She wanted to share it, but didn't know where to begin. "I had a vision of a totally different world." *What the hell did that mean?* she wondered. She began again: "It's actually a story I tell my sister at bedtime. But I don't know where it came from."

"Tell it to me," said Zoe.

Cali Sky described the valley: the river, trees, waterfall, and surrounding mountains. She described the cabin and the mysterious musical instrument hanging from the open window. And she described the girl, wandering around the valley and listening to the music from the instrument.

"Oh my God that is so beautiful," Zoe said after Cali Sky finished. "I want to paint that. I *wish* I could take a picture of it."

"I've never told that story to anyone except Cami," Cali Sky said. "I guess I could probably tell my mom."

"No, don't!" replied Zoe stridently. Cali Sky was taken aback by the tone, but pleased. Zoe continued, "That story is too important. Like those photos I showed you the other day. The Cottingley Fairies. I don't show those to *anyone*. They'd just make fun of it. They wouldn't understand."

Cali Sky sensed a history of personal heartbreak undergirding Zoe's warning. Cali Sky was swayed by its vehemence.

"No, I won't," she replied, feeling at the moment like she and Zoe were protectors of a mystery. "I know my dad would think it's weird."

Zoe said, "That's because when most people get old they can't understand or appreciate the sort of stuff we talk about."

"I hope I die before I get old," proclaimed Cali Sky, wondering if Zoe caught The Who allusion.

Zoe smiled and said, "Don't trust anyone over thirty."

Cali Sky smiled back, unaware of the reference, but resonating with the idea.

After Mr. Kelly's first period English class Cali Sky walked sluggishly to her locker. An unformed song played in her head, one suggested by the whining engine of the Karmann Ghia earlier. Like the engine, the song sharply ascended and descended in pitch. Both Cali Sky's thinking and unthinking mental faculties tried to discover how the song fit together and worked out. The sound of the unformed song and the reverberation of the word "Nothing" ceased when Cali Sky saw Brodie standing by her locker. Once again, he looked un-Brodie like: serious and worried.

"What now, Brodie? They already kicked me out of the band. They can't do anything worse now."

"It's Cami. Your dad had to rush her to the hospital. I went along with him. I just now got to school. We had to wait for your mom to come before your dad could bring me here."

"But when I left she said she felt better," Cali Sky replied. Her mouth became dry.

"No. When I got there she was throwing up, but nothing was coming out. She was in a lot of pain. Her stomach. Her stomach really hurt."

The inside of Cali Sky's mouth felt like it was full of dust. She was faint.

"Cali Sky?" Brodie grabbed her by the shoulders, ignoring a passerby who called out his name.

"Is she gonna be alright?"

"I'm sure she is," answered Brodie.

A filter interposed itself upon Cali Sky's perception, a filter colored by nightmare. Everything suddenly looked unfamiliar. She felt herself adopt the timeless perspective, looking down upon herself and the discrete moment she inhabited. She felt like this had all happened before. Where and when? She searched her sense of déjà vu, looking for clues that would help her know the future. For if it had happened before, she must know how it ended, or will end. Her thoughts became too abstract and she slipped out of her reverie.

Brodie saw the emotion on her face and embraced her.

"What am I supposed to do?" Cali Sky asked.

"Just go to your next class. She'll be alright. Here, I'll help you."

Brodie walked Cali Sky to Mrs. Schroeder's Algebra class, his arm around her shoulder. Kids stared, suspecting a hook up. But when they drew closer to tease the intimately linked couple, they saw the looks on the faces of Brodie and especially Cali Sky. Something was wrong. They saw the planted flag in the otherwise ambiguous moral geography, marking off the sacred territory: Cali Sky and Brodie were having a crisis. Don't mess with them.

Brodie brought Cali Sky to her chair, other students in the class silently observing the procession.

"Don't worry," whispered Brodie. "I'll see you at lunch."

Cali Sky nodded.

The second bell rang. Cali Sky stared vacantly at the floor. Mrs. Schroeder closed the classroom door. But before she could even announce the impending quiz, Principal Watson's voice came over the classroom intercom:

"Mrs. Schroeder, could you please send Cali Sky Braithwaite to my office?"

Her name, uttered through the grainy acoustics of the intercom speakers, sounded cumbersome and complicated. It didn't sound like her name.

"Um, okay," answered Mrs. Schroeder loudly and tentatively.

Many students in Mrs. Schroeder's Algebra class had known Cali Sky for years. During that time they witnessed only the slightest displays of emotion: a half smile, a nod, a gesture of disdain. They were thus unprepared for what they witnessed at the conclusion of the brief intercom exchange: Cali Sky wept. Everyone stared. Mrs. Schroeder, a stern disciplinarian who had once exhorted the class, "Shut up or get out," now revealed a softer side that no one knew existed.

Cali Sky rose and began walking toward the door.

"Your backpack, Cali Sky," said Mrs. Schroeder tenderly.

Cali Sky stopped and returned to her desk, shoving her book into her backpack. Mrs. Schroeder superfluously assisted her. The class was hushed. They knew this sort of moment, the moment when something so terrible happens that you don't care what you do or what people think. It is always a spectacle, one of horror and fascination. It is a rare moment in the teenage script—that sacred space on the map—when crisis operates as a leveler, negating social hierarchies, reminding those on the top and bottom that shit happens to everyone.

The halls were empty. Cali Sky blinked away tears. When she stepped into the principal's office she saw the bleary image of Mr. Watson, who stood next to the door to greet her.

"Cali Sky," he said with affected authority, trying to stabilize an emotionally unstable moment, "there has been an emergency at your house. An emergency involving your sister. I am going to personally drive you home so that you can be with your family."

"Do you know if my sister is alright?" Cali Sky asked in a wavering voice.

"No, I'm afraid I don't know."

During the drive to her house Cali Sky and Mr. Watson exchanged few words. His car smelled of coffee and cologne. She felt nauseous as she gave him directions. She rarely saw her neighborhood on a weekday winter morning. An old lady she had never seen before was walking a small, curly-haired dog down the street as Mr. Watson came to a stop in front of the Braithwaite house. Grandpa and Grandma's Buick Riviera was parked in the driveway. Her parents' cars were gone.

The sight of the house brought a spasm of emotion and tears. It looked safe and familiar, dispelling the sense of disorientation she had experienced all morning. She got out of the car and wanted Mr. Watson to drive away quickly. She didn't want him or his cold authority and nauseating smells to be anywhere near her home, the place where she was vulnerable.

Her heart beat fast as she opened the front door. Grandpa sat on the couch with a blank face. Next to him, Grandma whimpered when she saw Cali Sky enter. Aunt Nancy sat in her wheelchair near the entryway. Her face was wet with tears.

"Where's Cami?" asked Cali Sky.

Grandma whimpered again. Aunt Nancy struggled to speak.

"Is she alright?" Cali Sky continued.

"Cali Sky," said Aunt Nancy softly, "Your sister died this morning." She spoke the word "died" with anger. Grandma began to wail.

"No she didn't," replied Cali Sky. "She just had a stomachache...and was throwing up. She couldn't have..."

"Her appendix burst," Aunt Nancy uttered with a sob. She swallowed hard and continued. "And then there were complications." Grandma's wails drowned out Aunt Nancy's quiet weeping.

They both stopped when they saw Cali Sky fall to her knees. Her long, unkempt hair covered her face. They saw convulsive movements but heard no sound.

"Cali Sky," cried Aunt Nancy.

The soundless convulsive movements continued.

"Cali Sky," cried Aunt Nancy again. All Aunt Nancy could see were Cali Sky's back and hair.

"Cali Sky," cried Aunt Nancy once more.

Suddenly Cali Sky rose to her hands and knees, and crawled toward the wheelchair. She put her head on the lap of Aunt Nancy, who leaned forward and wrapped Cali Sky in her arms.

Aunt Nancy now felt the convulsive movements beneath her. But she heard no sound.

Cali Sky hears wailing. A closed door and her father's desperate supplications muffle the sound. When it reaches her ears the wailing reaches an unhuman pitch. She is not startled. She does not wonder how vocal chords could possibly produce such noise. She is aware that nothing could be shocking now.

The cries seep into the walls, the ceiling, the couch, the TV. The house is transformed. Grief, Cali Sky sees, changes the shape of things. She does not know what to do. Walking, sitting, breathing become unnatural.

"Please open the door," Philip implores. Cali Sky hears in her father's voice a hopelessness that saps his plea of any conviction. Leaning awkwardly against the closed door, he turns and sees her.

"Cali Sky, I...." His voice trips over itself. The wailing continues, forcing Philip into silence. He gestures toward her: the outspread hands that betoken his relentless religious faith. Like his voice, the gesture weakens and fades.

The voice behind the door cries out, "Answer the question! Just answer the question!"

"I don't know. I don't know. Please."

Cali Sky turns away and discovers that her legs are moving her down the hall. The cool humidity of the southern California December chills her bare feet. The thick carpet feels damp. Its path directs her past her own bedroom and to the other side of the house. Her mother's wails continue. Her father begins to pray, repeating the words, "God please help us...God please help us... God please help us." Her father's voice now also seems unhuman.

She now leans against the piano, gingerly pressing her forehead against the wooden upper case and then sits down at the bench. She lightly brushes her fingers against the keys and suddenly, violently, brings them down upon a dark version of an E chord, added discordant notes giving it an unsettled sound. Delicately played, improvised riffs lead to other chords, producing a melody that shifts before it can establish itself—musical themes that are vague and abstract. The notes become a whirlwind of sound, lightening Cali Sky's grief not by softening it but by transforming it into music, which is gone, like the present, the moment it is experienced. She experiences a mode of consciousness comprised only of these discrete moments, flashing across the screen of perception like bursts of light. Cali Sky is transported outside of herself and she forgets. But only as long as the music continues.

SEVEN

Summer 1981

O N AUGUST 1ST, 1981, MTV made its debut, broadcasting what many musicologists consider to be the first music video, one bizarrely aware of its own significance, commenting with apparent self-loathing on the very musical dispensation that it itself created: the Buggles' "Video Killed the Radio Star."

Cali Sky missed the historic event because there was no TV at home. Philip had moved it into Joan's small two-bedroom apartment, next to some of Cali Sky's amps. Cali Sky, it was agreed, would live with her mom. Philip's apartment, on the other side of the Costa Mesa Freeway, was even smaller. While Joan got the TV, Philip got the king-size bed. Cali Sky guessed why: he wanted to share it with another woman.

In the months after Cami's death, it was clear that Philip and Joan could not remain married. Unanswerable questions widened the breach that came to separate them: Could we have done more to save our daughter's life? Was her death God's way of punishing us for our past? When people ask us how many children we have, how do we answer? They saw in the face of each other the dark and bottomless abyss into which these agonizing questions dropped them. Divorce—the word, like "Goddamn," was unmentionable in the Braithwaite house for most of Cali Sky's life. In 1981 it was not only mentioned but brought to life like a sleeping monster roused by the desperation of unending arguments and feeding on open wounds and unanswerable questions.

Cami's death ripped apart the moral fabric of the Braithwaite home. Philip understood he had reached a crossroads. One road led to Cornerstone, to spiritual succor in the care of a merciful God and a loving congregation. Another road led to spiritual anarchy and moral rebellion, to an attitude he had not entertained since he was in his early 20's, before his conversion. Like a good Christian, Philip chose the first path. But instead of leading him to the promised end of his faith, the road unexpectedly took a detour and led him directly into the arms of Michelle.

It happened one day in Pastor Kevin's office at Cornerstone. Philip arrived at the church one evening on a desperate impulse, frantically seeking counsel from Pastor Kevin. Pastor Kevin was not there, having just left in a rush to the hospital to comfort a parishioner with a medical emergency. Pastor Kevin had asked Michelle to answer the phone and watch over the church in his absence. Philip was grief-stricken and lonely. Michelle was empathetic and, it turns out, lonely as well. They were alone. Philip took the detour. Michelle was swept along with him.

"When you hit rock bottom," he confessed to Joan later, "you just…don't give a shit anymore." The old Philip re-surfaced moments later: "I am sorry, Joan. I really am. What I am doing is wrong…so wrong." They both wept. Philip hugged her—one last time—and Joan allowed it. They then agreed that divorce was the next step.

When Cali Sky first learned that the other woman was

Michelle, she was mortified. She thought of Michelle's big hair, her desire to please and be liked, and, most of all, her horrible voice. Nothing would stop Cali Sky now from looking into Michelle's ridiculous angelic face and shouting, "You suck!"

"It's so hard for me to tell you this," Philip had said with tears streaming down his face. His confession to Cali Sky had brought him to his knees, shame and fear crashing down upon him. *I'm fucking up my own child's life*, he thought to himself as he struggled to form the right words. "Your mom and I have agreed that we can no longer live together. It's just...too hard now...after what happened."

Cali Sky could see that he was falling apart, regressing to the emotional stability of a five-year old. But she said nothing.

He continued, "We are going to get...a divorce. We've tried, Cali Sky. We really have..." He paused to let the weeping take its course. Cali Sky showed no emotion. "And there's something else...something I have to confess. It's *so* hard for me to tell you this. But I want to be open with you now. Not like before.... I'm... I'm seeing another woman. Michelle. From church." He looked up at Cali Sky. Still no visible reaction. "I know it's wrong." He hesitated again, torture on his face. "I know it's wrong. I've already talked about all this with your mom. But Michelle and I...want to make it into something right somehow. We...at least want to try. Can you understand any of this?"

Cali Sky stared out of the dirty window of her bedroom. Philip waited for a response.

"Cali Sky," pleaded Philip, "say something. Please."

Cali Sky looked at him and said, "Fuck off." She then walked toward the door.

This confession and one-sided conversation took place on July 31st. The traumatic toll they took on Philip explained why, on the next day, the day that MTV made its debut, the house was in disarray. A shell-shocked Philip had departed in haste, precipitously abandoning the process of moving out. He had left his belongings scattered around the house.

Among them was a notebook that caught Cali Sky's attention. It said on the cover, "The Diary of Philip Braithwaite." Joan was in the bathroom, packing away her toiletries. Cali Sky picked up the notebook and sat on the floor in a corner of the living room. She opened the diary and found well-worn pages and sentences trailing endlessly from top to bottom. Her dad's handwriting cluttered every page, extending into the margins on both sides. Cali Sky sat on the floor and began reading the entries from 1965, the year before she was born.

Jan. 13, '65. "Are you a head, man?" That is the question. This cat stopped me on campus and asked me that. "Are you a head, man?" He saw my long hair and beard. He said he really knew I was, but wanted to be sure. He said some in the Straight World are wearing long hair these days. I told him I never seen that. He told me that he was at some Happening and joined in with some long hairs. They later jumped him and stole his stuff. That shocked me. Why would they pose as one of us? Neither of us could really answer that one. For the women, maybe. "Free fucks with freaks." That's what Lester came up with. That's this cat's name. Lester.

We skipped our 2 o'clock class and smoked some of his grass on the quad. Lester said he saw me and knew he needed to connect with me. "Kindred spirits" is what he said. He has a huge afro and this intense look in his eyes. I think that's because his eyes are real close together. When he stares at something it's like he's looking right through it. We laid on our backs and watched clouds overhead. He said every third cloud or so was a spirit radiating love. That's what he said he wanted to believe anyway, and wanting to believe was as good as believing. He asked me what I believe. I told him I was still trying to figure that out. I told him I wanted to explore, to find out for myself. He said he wanted to join me on that trip.

I told him about my parents and their whole conventional religion thing: the fire and brimstone, the three piece suit on Sunday mornings, all that shit. He said it sounded like my parents would fit in well at a good old fashioned burning at the stake or at a stiff cocktail party with Perry fucking Como. I told him how my dad made me walk ten paces behind him if ever we walked anywhere together, my dad said he didn't want to be seen with anyone who had hair like mine. Lester said if Jesus were around right now he'd probably be sitting right there with us, smoking grass, looking at clouds and exploring all there is to explore. I never heard anyone talk like that before.

He pulled what looked like a rock out of his pocket. He gave it to me. On the outside it looked like any ordinary rock, brown and rough. But inside were all these blue and white crystals. He said it was a geode. He found it in Utah on a road trip with a bus of heads who wanted to get back to nature. He said it was a conversation piece. People will ask me about it. Tell them what it is. Then explain how it's like a symbol of life, what you see on the surface may look ordinary. But look harder. There's something beautiful if you have the vision to see it. He said that's about the best subject for a conversation you can ever have.

I asked him where I was supposed to put it. He said in my car. I told him I didn't have a car. He said we'd have to buy one. He asked me if I had any bread. I told him not much but that I had a job at a record store near campus and that I could save up. He said that once I saved up 350 bucks to let him know. He said he'd take care of the rest.

Jan. 14, '65. For some reason, I don't know why, I might be a glutton for punishment, I was sitting on the couch with my old man watching the boob tube. It was a re-broadcast of the Hollywood Palace show. Dean Martin was holding his high ball, cracking his same old jokes. The Straight World was eating it up. Dad was laughing at least.

I was about to get up and leave when I heard Dean Martin say, I remember exactly what he said, "Now something for the youngsters." He introduced the Rolling Stones. He called them something like "long-haired wonders from England." And he had this look on his face like he was trying to take the band seriously but just couldn't, they were beneath him, they were scum. He finally gave up and just openly mocked them. He said he saw them earlier backstage picking fleas off of each other.

Dad laughed. He said, "Give it to them, Deano! I got one sitting right next to me."

I got up and walked out as the Rolling Stones began to play. Dad asked me if I liked this better than music. When I ignored him he shouted something like, "You don't want to look like these cave men, do you? Cut your hair!"

One of these days I just want to tell him to fuck off.

Jan. 17, '65. Lester and I cruised Sunset last night. Lester borrowed his parents' car. I don't know how he gets away with that. My parents barely let me get in their car, let alone drive it.

We parked near the Tiger's Tail and checked out the scene there. We walked to the Whisky. Heads and freaks filling the streets. At times I felt nervous for some reason. Don't know why. Just so many people, so chaotic. But most times I felt like I belonged. Our kind of people. Leave the Straight World behind. But Lester was still cautious. Are you a head? Are you really a head?

We went to Ciro's. Lester wanted to check out a band there.

He said they'd blow my mind. And he was right. They had a new sound. Lester said it was our music, music for our people. The place was packed.

But this is what happened before that. The band was ready to start. Except for the lead singer. He wasn't even there. The band looked around like, 'Where is our lead singer?' They all were ready with instruments in hand. Lester shouted, "I'll do it. I'll sing." Everyone around us laughed.

Finally the lead singer dropped on the scene. Literally. He came climbing down this ladder at the very back of the stage. The ladder went up to some space above the stage, an attic or something. He climbed down the ladder and picked up his guitar and the band began playing. Lester and I looked at each other like, What the hell was he doing up there? Where'd he come from? We looked at other people around us and they were asking the same thing.

Then our questions were answered. Someone else was climbing down the ladder. This time it was a girl and from where I was standing I could see that there was nothing underneath her short miniskirt. Lester slapped me on the shoulder and pointed to where she was. But he didn't need to, I was already staring. She looked unsteady as she climbed down, she was probably high. All of a sudden the crowd started yelling. Whistles and catcalls. The man standing behind me yelled, "Can I be next?"

I could tell that the band didn't know what was going on. Finally one by one they turned around and saw her descend the ladder. They smiled and laughed. The lead singer blew her a kiss. She was beautiful. Her long legs shined in the stage light. Her hair was long and black, it looked wild. When she reached the stage she didn't know where to go. She smiled at the audience as they cheered. Then she slowly walked off-stage. Lester and I were freaking out. I mean, what an exit! Lester said she was a groupie making her rounds, from club to club, looking for rock stars.

The band was great. They had a folk rock thing going on. We passed around some grass and just let the music get inside us. It was a mellow vibe. But I was still thinking of that girl.

And when we walked outside the club, there she was again! She was real skinny. Tight turtleneck sweater. Really short mini-skirt. She was talking with a couple of other gorgeous women. Total foxes. I mean, Hollywood beauties. I wanted to talk to her. Lester said no way. He said she's community goods. Been passed around, you dig? But I didn't care, I saw something in her. Lester said that all I see in her is a good screw.

I am sure as hell no rock star, but I thought, what the hell. I got out my conversation piece and walked over there. But it was too late. She got into some cat's car. But I heard her laugh. Wild, like her hair.

I told Lester that I think she's a goddess. He said that in that case I could worship her and fuck her. But he was pretty sure she's a devil.

Feb. 1, '65. Lester and I went out to this ranch in Topanga Canyon. He somehow scored 250 mics of pure Owsley. How he pulls this sort of thing off I don't know. It was windy in the canyon but still peaceful. The wind drove away the clouds, making the sky look clean. The horses were calm. Other heads set up camp around the mess hall. Some cat was talking about Vietnam. He said LBJ was sending more and more troops out there. Americans slaughtered. Vietnamese slaughtered. And for what? Some non-existent threat. He said it had to stop. We had to do something. Protest. Fight hate with love. Lester said to me, "Or expand our minds." He pulled out the Owsley.

We found a quiet, secluded place. It was my first acid trip, so Lester said to stay close to him. He showed me what to do.

At first my trip was horrible. Everything turned black and white. The horses were like skeletons. I panicked. Who wouldn't? It was like one of the nightmares I had as a child where it was the end of the world. I looked everywhere for someone to help me. But I was always alone and scared. Everything was lifeless and cold.

Lester must have heard me screaming. He was smiling but looked like a skeleton, just like the horses. I fought more panic. Because deep down I knew it was Lester, I just had to remind myself that it was him even though he looked like a skeleton.

Lester later told me that I was screaming like a little girl. I even pissed my pants, I'm ashamed to admit. Lester brought me into the mess hall. He said different scenery might redirect my trip. It worked. When I laid down, everything became color again. It was beautiful. All of a sudden, the ceiling disappeared, I saw the sky in a shade of blue I've never seen before. Clouds then appeared, I didn't know that the color white could look like that.

I knew something important was about to happen. I don't know how, I just knew. I felt calm and relaxed. I waited patiently for what came next.

I felt someone approaching. But not an approach in physical form. It wasn't like someone was walking or flying toward me. But I knew someone was coming. And I knew it was a girl, a beautiful girl, the most beautiful girl I had ever seen, except I didn't really see her. I felt her presence and just knew she was beautiful. Not just beautiful, but warm and soft and compassionate and understanding.

I also knew that she loved me. Just knew. Love flowed from her to me. I reached out to receive it. But then I hesitated. I don't know exactly why and I regret it. I held back. I guess the panic came back a little. I was afraid. She knew it too, she could sense it. So she started to fade away. I reached out again, I didn't want her to go. But it was too late, she was disappearing. But before she left, she spoke to me. I heard the words clearly. She said, "Cali Sky." I don't know why. Then she repeated them, again and again, for what seemed like hours. What does it mean?

Lester said that he heard me repeat those words as well. He didn't know what they meant either. He said that a good trip will take you beyond the material world to reveal truths that you can't even understand. He told me not to forget the words, to repeat them like a mantra.

Feb. 8, '65. Lester and I bought a van. I only contributed 250 bucks. Lester said that was good enough. He saw an ad for it and wanted to buy it then and there. It's a piece of shit, we can't get the VW motor to go faster than 50, but we don't care. It's ours! We have wheels. Freedom!

Lester picked me up in it last night. I pulled out the conversation piece and put it on the dash. We made it into a big ritual, like I was setting the crown on the queen of fucking England. The first time Lester turned a corner, the thing rolled across the dash and nearly out the window. So we had to remember to hold it every time we turned a corner. It's like the geode is our compass.

We decided to drive it to Sunset. Lester wanted to hit Pandora's Box. The traffic on the strip was at a crawl. It took us an hour just to get anywhere near Crescent Heights. The scene was outrageous. People walking everywhere, passing joints around, necking in their cars, one wasted chick flashing her tits. She had a mob of guys following her, laughing and yelling at her to do it again and again. Lester said that was a gangbang in the making.

At one point, the van stalled. The first time Lester tried to restart it, the engine wouldn't turn. I thought that was the end of our van and a waste of 250 bucks. Lester told me to rub the geode for luck before trying again. And it worked! The puny VW motor roared to life.

We crawled along Sunset and then I saw her. The girl from Ciro's. She was coming from Pandora's Box. I can't erase that sight, Joan, that is her name I later found out, walking out of the orange and pink building. She was by herself. She made walking look like dancing. She looked carefree and happy. As she walked by, Lester shouted out if she wanted a ride. She said sure. I got out and opened the sliding door for her.

She was as beautiful as I remember. Long, dark hair. Blue eyes. Her cheeks were a little red. She wore another miniskirt and her legs were out of this world. She seemed full of life. She also seemed like she couldn't focus on one thing. I just wanted to get her attention and hold it.

She asked if we had any stuff. Since we weren't moving in traffic anyway, Lester reached below his seat and pulled out a small bottle and a small towel. He poured some of the liquid into the towel. He folded the towel and handed it to Joan. He told her to sniff it, he said it was trimar. How he gets this stuff and where he gets it I don't know.

She smiled, what a smile!, and asked if it was safe. Lester asked her if she thought a couple of cool heads like us would give her something that wasn't. She still looked unsure, so Lester took the towel and sniffed it. He gave her back the towel and she sniffed it. Then it was my turn.

Within a few minutes she and Lester were laughing, like everything was funny. The trimar did not have that effect on me. But I felt good, just relaxed.

I did laugh at what happened next. Joan spotted our conversation piece and asked "What's that?" Lester and I looked at each other, and that's when I laughed. Lester said something like, "It's funny you should ask." He let me explain it to her, since it was my conversation piece and since I was the one who was really into her.

She laughed at everything I said. When I told her about how you need to look past the surface to see something important beyond, she said, "Far out." Did she really mean that? But then she said, "No, seriously man, that's beautiful." She didn't laugh when she said that. And she looked at me, really looked at me. I looked down at her lips and really wanted to kiss her.

When we finally parked, Joan said she had to go meet up with some friends. She said thanks for the ride and for the tri-mar. Before she left, I asked her for her phone number. She wrote it down on a small piece of scratch paper. She then slipped the paper into the front pocket of my pants and smiled at me and said bye.

I told Lester I was in love. He said, "You and half the cats walking down this strip. Community goods, man." I watched her walk away, those legs and that hair. I told him I was going to make her mine and mine alone. He said I couldn't tame a girl like that.

Feb. 15, '65. I called her up and asked her out. It was hard, really hard. Finally I thought the hell with it. When she answered the phone she didn't seem real into it or me. She made excuses that I knew were bullshit. It was a downer. I was ready to give up. But I couldn't. Not this time. Hell no.

So I lied. I told her I had some acid and asked if she wanted to share it with me. That turned her on. Where and when, she asked. Then of course I had to call up Lester and actually score the Ows-ley. At first he said no way, but when I told him the situation he said he'd try. And he came through.

He asked me where I was going to take her. I told him the beach. He said no fucking way. Too dangerous. He said he didn't want anyone drowning on the acid he scored. He told me his parents were going out of town. He said we could do it there.

He also gave me some advice. He told me that after we took the acid, to stare in each other's eyes. He said we needed to hold the stare for a long time. Don't look away. He said that if we did that we would be like bonded for life or something. Sounded good to me.

I picked up Joan in the van. Talk about being nervous! She asked me about the acid. I knew that was really the only reason she was there. She wasn't into me. It was a downer. But then she picked up the geode and said all sexy like, "So tell me, Philip, what is this? Is this some sort of conversation piece?" We both laughed.

But that was just the beginning. We did what Lester suggested. We stared into each other's eyes. At first it was hard not to look away. I was intimidated. I learned that it is really hard to stare into the eyes of a beautiful woman who you think might be a goddess. Then the acid kicked in.

It was like sex, except we never touched. I saw something come out of her eyes. I think it might have been her soul. Then I saw something come out of my own eyes. My soul. And in that few inches between our faces our souls intertwined. Our souls had sex.

July 20, '65. Haven't written in this diary for a long time. Lester and I spent the last five months in Europe. I dropped out of school, at least for a semester. One semester won't kill me. I needed to get away from my parents. Lester had been wanting to go for a long time. So we said the hell with it. He bought my plane ticket. Somehow he gets that sort of bread from his parents.

We lived in London most of the time. We stayed in a hostel for about a month. It was a shithole but we had to make our bread last. We met this cat named Ian who had a flat in Notting Hill.

Set up a whole commune there. So we stayed there the rest of the time. Lots of heads in our neighborhood. We'd walk to Portobello Road, buy some Spanish wine, some bread and cheese from France, maybe some Ethiopian stew, and just go from flat to flat, like a party circuit, heads spread out all over the borough.

Carnaby Street was the real scene, though. It's like everyone who's anyone goes there. We saw Paul McCartney and George Harrison there, at least we think we saw them. I never saw so many miniskirts, it's like every girl wore one. Lester said he was going to come back with a blanket, lay down in the middle of the street, and just admire the view.

One day we went to Camden to check out the market there. We ended up wandering around and getting lost and wound up at the Islington tube station. We saw that someone had spray painted on the wall, "Clapton is God." We couldn't believe it. We had just gone to a John Mayall and the Bluesbreakers gig a few weeks earlier at a pub in Putney. From what we saw and heard, Clapton might very well be God. We started to see "Clapton is God" graffiti all around London. Lester said he saw Clapton on Carnaby Street.

I wouldn't know. I was back at Ian's flat, drunk and miserable. I really missed Joan. I couldn't stop thinking about her. I swear I heard her call my name once when I was lying on the grass in Holland Park when I was in between sleep and waking.

I called her once, but she wasn't there. I wondered what she was doing, that's when I panicked and started to feel miserable. I wondered how many guys she had slept with. How many rock stars? For all I knew, she slept with the entire Rolling Stones, they toured America while we were away. And for all I knew, the Bluesbreakers played the Whisky and she slept with Clapton too.

We saw a Bob Dylan show when we were in London. He played the Royal Albert Hall in the beginning of May. We heard that he was staying at the Savoy Hotel. Lester wanted to go there to try to meet him. Lester and 100 other people. Lester said he wanted to ask Dylan what the meaning of life was. He thinks Dylan might be some sort of prophet. I pulled out a London newspaper that called Dylan an "anarchist." An anarchist because he criticizes without offering any answers. All questions and no solutions. Lester said the meaning of life was not an answer or a solution. When I asked him what it was, he said the hell if he knew, that's what he wanted to ask Dylan. I told him that if he asked Dylan about the meaning of life, he'd probably just play a song. And then walk away.

We actually did see Dylan outside of his hotel. For about five seconds. Lester shouted out his question but I don't think Dylan heard him. Dylan carried in one hand an oversized inflatable light bulb, the sort of thing you win at a carnival game. I said maybe he has an idea. Lester said he carries enlightenment with him.

The show was great, though the Royal Albert Hall freaked Lester out. He just doesn't like old buildings. Dylan actually did look like a prophet alone on that stage, just him, his guitar, his harmonica, and the spotlight. In between songs he said something I won't forget. One reason I won't forget is that Lester wrote the words on the wall of Ian's flat, alongside all the other graffiti on Ian's walls. Dylan said, and Lester wrote, "I'll let you in my dream if I can be in your dream." That became Lester's mantra. I told him maybe it had something to do with the meaning of life.

I lost my virginity after the show. It was all horrible. Embarrassing. Fucking disaster. I didn't tell anyone what happened, not even Lester. Stop reading now if you stole my diary.

I met her after the show, right outside the theater. We were both feeling good after Dylan's performance. We walked across the street to Kensington Gardens. I held her hand. She kissed me. We walked along the Serpentine. She said why don't we find a secluded place. I said why not? It was freezing so we didn't undress completely. We didn't do it for long, I couldn't hold it back. Afterwards, I cried. Like a fucking baby. I don't know why. I just cried. Maybe I do know why. Deep down part of me thought it was wrong. That I shouldn't have done it. I went to Europe to escape my parents, but it turns out I brought their religion and morality with me.

One day we loaded our backpacks and traveled around Europe. Amsterdam was a blur. Lester and I cruised the Red Light district and sought "entertainment" in one of those fine establishments. It blew my mind, beautiful women on display in the windows. Come in and fuck me! After the disaster at the Dylan show I didn't want to pay to screw some chick, but Lester said, come on, how often do you visit the Red Light district in Amsterdam? He said that he would even pay for it.

In the end I compromised. A blowjob. I tried to choose a girl who looked like Joan. Lester knew what I was up to and helped me choose. Then he said, "Now just lay back, close your eyes and pretend you are a rock n' roll star." Thanks a lot, Lester.

She took me back to a room with a red light bulb hanging from the ceiling. I felt like I was in hell. I dug it at first. The girl was sexy as hell. Beautiful black hair. But then the red lights got to me, like they got into my brain or something. It happened again, the attack of my parents' religion and morality. I got soft and couldn't finish. The girl laughed, but not in a teasing sort of way. Maybe she was embarrassed like me. She tried really hard. But it was no use. I just couldn't do it. I gave up.

Lester and I smoked so much grass in Amsterdam that we became tired all the time. It was like everything was a dream. One morning, or was it an afternoon, Lester said, the hell with this. We got to get out of here. Get up into the mountains and clear our heads.

So we took a train to Austria. We stopped first in Vienna, which was not the sort of scene we were after. Lester said we needed more mobility so he rented a car. We then drove to Salzburg. We drove past lakes with colors of blue I've never seen before. The mountain air was fresh, I felt like it was purifying my soul. Washing away bad memories.

We decided we wanted to hike up into the Alps. We didn't really know where the hell we were but we passed some enormous mountains. When we saw a trailhead we pulled over. We agreed that those mountains were part of the Alps and that we were going to hike to the top. Even though we had meagre supplies in our packs.

Off we went and four hours later we were miles from civilization. My spirit felt free, I felt so far away from the ugly scenes in the city and so far away from my parents' bullshit. I told Lester that this was the closest I had come to the meaning of life.

But then it got dark. We underestimated the distance to the mountain peak. We weren't even close. We looked back. Where the hell were we? We were not even sure which direction the car was in.

So we turned back. We followed the trail mile after mile. It got darker and darker. Eventually we couldn't see where we were going. So we made a makeshift camp. Some camp, no tent, no sleeping bags. And no fire. We're from southern California, how the hell should we know how to build a fire?

That night I thought I was going to freeze, especially right before dawn. That's when it seemed to be the coldest. As soon as we saw the smallest sunlight we got up and tried to shake off the cold.

We set off again and followed the trail up a small rise. When we got to the top, we could not believe it. There was the parking lot. There was our car. Lester and I looked at each other and just laughed. I told him that we were fucking idiots. He said no, he thought that the meaning of life was connected somehow to what happened, like it was a symbol or parable or some sort of sign from the gods. I told him that may be true but that we still were fucking idiots.

July 25, '65

I called Joan. It took me five days but I finally screwed up enough courage to call her. I told her about Europe, living in London, about my adventures and misadventures. I told her about the Dylan gig, she dug that. I then asked her out and she said yes! It was that easy!

I took her to Philip's Supper Club in Huntington sort of as a gag. You know, like I owned the place. But it was an expensive gag. The maître de gave us probably the worst table in the restaurant once he saw my hair and beard. If it were Lester, he would have raised hell. But I let it go. I was with Joan!

She seemed different. Before my Europe trip it was like she couldn't focus on one thing. Now she seemed like she was all there, like fully present in my space. When she looked into my eyes I wanted to relive our acid trip together, I wanted our souls to link up again.

When I asked her what she had been up to, she said she got arrested for possession. She was at some party. The cops crashed it. She said she was naked at the time, completely naked. She said it with no embarrassment, like she was telling me the time of day. She said the cops asked her where her clothes were. She said she didn't know. So she went into the bathroom and pulled the rug from the floor. She wrapped herself in the rug. One of the cops then took her outside to his police car. When no one was looking, the cop felt her up. She said she started to scream, so the cop handcuffed her, completely naked. He pushed her into the backseat but by now people were around, so he covered her in a blanket that he got from the trunk of the car.

Her parents sprung her from jail. She said that was the last straw. One more fuck up and they were going to kick her out of the house. She said she has a record now. But then again so do most of her friends.

She really opened up to me. I'm not sure why. She even told me about her childhood. She told me that when she was a kid some boys lived across the street. They had instruments in their garage, like a couple of guitars and a drum, not a drum set, just a drum. She used to listen to them play songs, or at least try to play songs. Elvis, some Johnny Cash. She said that even at that age the sound of the music just did something to her. It made her feel good.

Part of me wanted to ask her, "So is that why you want to fuck every singer who plays a gig on Sunset?" If I had she probably would have said with a straight face, "Yes." No shame, no embarrassment. Lester told me again just to stay away from her, don't have sex with her, he said. If you do, then you'll really be hooked. Of course my parents would kill both me and her if they found out we were together. They'd call her a Jezebel, the whore of Babylon.

But I can't resist. I still see something in her. She's connected to my meaning of life.

Aug. 18, '65.

I spent the last week in the hospital. Lester said something like this was going to happen. He said stay away from her, he called her a witch. He says I'm caught in her spell.

She and I went to Castaic Lake. Just the two of us. I wanted to be with her away from the Strip, the clubs and the bands. I knew then that she would be really with me, fully present. She said she had never even been to a lake. I said it would be beautiful and that I'd pack us a picnic. I joked that it would just be the three of us, her, me, and Mother Nature. Finally she agreed.

At first it was perfect. A beautiful summer day. We swam, we talked, we ate lunch. She was really with me. Once, we got close in the water, wrestling and hugging. She liked to feel my beard. She wore a white and red bikini. I had to think about baseball a lot, just to avoid embarrassment of what my swimming trunks could not conceal. Not that she would be embarrassed by any of that.

After lunch we stood near the van. I played some music on the radio. She danced around. Then I joined her. She moving around in her sexy bikini. Me moving around next to her, watching her and trying to hide the bulge in my swimming trunks by picturing a Sandy Koufax fastball.

That's when these three cats walked up to us. I thought they were heads. They had long hair. I was wrong. Dead fucking wrong. They were the kind of assholes Lester warned me about. Fucking wolves in sheep's clothing. To make matters worse, they were all drunk.

One of them knew Joan. No need to ask why. He said he wanted some more. Joan said no. When he grabbed her I told him to split. He pushed me away, then grabbed Joan again. He tried to pull off her bikini top. The other two helped him. It was ugly, a sight I wish I could just erase from memory.

I had to fight back. I ran over there and punched one of them as hard as I could. I remember I hit him on the side of the head. I don't remember anything after that. Joan said they hit me over the head with beer bottles a couple times.

I woke up in the hospital. They said I had a pretty bad concussion. For one week I had to stay there, lying in that damn bed watching TV or reading a book. Every now and then they'd take me in a wheelchair to some exam room where they'd run all these tests. They attached these wires to my brain and made me watch a TV screen with static and fuzz for an hour. They said they were monitoring my brain waves.

They told me the vision in my left eye will never be fully restored. Right now, I can barely see out of it, everything is dark. They said it will improve, but they don't know how much.

I have never been so down in my life. Sitting in that hospital bed. Having nightmares about what happened. Wondering if I'll ever be able to see out of my left eye again. And thinking about the meaning of life. I feel desperate, like I got to figure it out. I need some answers.

My parents visited me in the hospital every day. Once I even cried in front of them. Just broke down. I hadn't done that since I was about five. They reassured me, even my dad, though he later asked me why I couldn't handle three guys if they were drunk. Once my mom even prayed for me. Aloud, by my bedside. That made me cry even more.

Joan visited me once. Just once. She said she felt terrible about what happened. But she was distant, like she was somewhere else. She couldn't even sit still, she kept pacing around my bed as I tried to follow her with my one good eye. I lost my patience and told her to sit down and sit still. I told her she owed me that much. When she sat down I was shocked to see that she was crying.

Every time Lester visited me he asked if I learned my lesson. Stay away, he said. I already told you once, twice, a hundred times. He said this was only the beginning. If I didn't stay away from her, he said, she would fuck up my life.

Feb. 5, '66
I have neglected this journal again. Had no desire to write in it, no reason. Until now. She came to my house yesterday. To my

house! I think that as soon as my parents opened the front door and saw her, they knew who she was. And they were surprisingly nice to her. Of course one look at her and you could tell that she had been crying. I'm sure they felt sorry for her. Sorry for her and for me. She looked desperate, probably like I looked back when I was in the hospital.

I soon learned why. She's pregnant. She finds out she's pregnant and she comes to me. A lot of fucking nerve! She gets my head pounded in, I lose vision in one eye, and she comes to me for help.

I asked her who the father was. She said she didn't know. I guessed it was some rock and roll star, one of the many she slept with over the past year or two. She's going to have a kid and doesn't even know who the father is, other than that he probably played a gig sometime in the last year or so somewhere on Sunset Strip.

So what am I going to do? I know she wants me to marry her. She doesn't come out and say that, but I know that's what she wants. She wants to have the child, she wants me to be the father. She says she's going to change. Says she's going to stop sleeping around, says she'll be a good mother.

So what am I going to do? Despite everything that's happened, I do love her. I can't help it.

A father? I'm not ready to be a father. Lester says I'm crazy even to consider this. But I told him maybe this is connected with my meaning of life. I even prayed about it last night.

I think Joan and I could make it work if we got our lives together. If we built a family on a solid foundation. Religion? I don't know. Maybe. I talked to Joan about all this. She agreed. She even said that she felt guilty about her past. This was the first time I have ever heard her say anything like this. She even said she was ashamed. She too wants to find a foundation, something that can give her life some stability. I've seen a new side of Joan. And it makes me love her even more.

Feb. 15, '66

I confessed all my doubts to Joan last night. I laid it all on the line. I told her that I could not imagine myself as a husband and father. Not yet anyway. She said she understood. She agreed that it was a huge step, that I would have to make a huge sacrifice. She kissed me tenderly.

When she left I told her I needed more time to think about it. This time I kissed her. I admitted to her that if I was going to marry someone, I would want it to be her. And that if the baby was a girl, I already had a name picked out.

PART TWO

*"The third type of possession and madness is possession by
the Muses. When this seizes upon a gentle and virgin soul
it rouses it to inspired expression in lyric and other sorts of
poetry, and glorifies countless deeds of the heroes of old for
the instruction of posterity. But if a man comes to the door of
poetry untouched by the madness of the Muses, believing that
technique alone will make him a good poet, he and his sane
compositions never reach perfection, but are utterly eclipsed by
the performances of the inspired madman. These are but some
examples of the noble effect of heaven-sent madness."*

—Plato, *Phaedrus*

*"If you can find the trigger that kicks off the idea, the rest is
easy. It's just hitting the first spark. Where that comes from,
God knows."*

—Keith Richards

SPRING, 1985

EIGHT

THE FIRST THING you noticed upon stepping into the coffee house was that the sound seemed too big for the space. It was only an acoustic with an electric pick-up. Two amps, one for the guitar, one for the mic. But the music filled the house so completely that the people inside remained nearly motionless, as if compressed by water. They tried to make room for the sound that came from an unlikely source: an eighteen-year-old girl whose pained face bore the marks of an unbearable burden.

The second thing you noticed were the large black-and-white photographs, propped on easels, around the performer. The photographs depicted women in various public places—museums, libraries, shopping malls, city parks, crowded sidewalks, beach boardwalks, governmental buildings, train stations, bus stops. The women, all of whom appeared to be around twenty, looked like sprites. They wore white, loose-fitting garments that flowed down to their ankles. They were barefoot. All of them had black hair, which was pulled up with the exception of a few loose strands dangling around their foreheads. Some had small flowers adorning their curls. Others wore wreaths of ivy around their heads. Like the music in the coffee house, the women were out of place in their environment.

The performer played a dark song that made the coffee house, dimly lit with Dadaist art hanging on the walls, seem haunted. Those seated closest to her, mostly girls dressed in black, sang along. At the back of the coffee house stood a middle-aged man, lined shoulder to shoulder with the other latecomers. He looked out of place among the youth. He stared at the performer, trying to make eye contact. She knew he was there, even though she didn't look directly at him. Every now and then, he scratched his beard.

She concluded her final set with a cover of Patti Smith's version of "Gloria." "Jesus died for somebody's sins but not mine," Smith had intoned in the song's opening. The performer changed the last word. She sang, "Jesus died for somebody's sins but not yours." And for the first time Cali Sky looked directly into the eyes of the middle-aged bearded man standing at the back. The man met her stare with visible agony. When the performer looked away, he slipped out of the coffee house and into the California evening, where the song, though muffled, chased him.

"Great set, Cali Sky!" proclaimed a girl who pushed her way through the small crowd that gathered near the side stage, from which the performer descended. The girl's hair was shaved on the sides and back. A large tuft of bangs spread from one side of her head to the other, angled slightly downward toward her left eye. "Just want to give you these, and I hope you use them!" Cali Sky acknowledged the girl and took the piece of paper, folded into a tight square. Inside was a guitar pick. The paper, once unfolded, revealed a handwritten phone number.

Slowly, one by one, fans, admirers and know-it-alls said what they wanted or needed to say to Cali Sky. And Cali Sky listened, passively but attentively, saying little to nothing. The crowds thinned, revealing a girl seated in the center of the room, surrounded by now empty chairs, some of which were littered with empty coffee mugs and used napkins. Cali Sky noticed her and smiled. The girl smiled back, rose, stepped around the maze of chairs, and gave Cali Sky a hug. She had porcelain skin and, like her photography subjects, black hair, though short and spiked, pulled in various directions.

"Oh my God, Cali Sky," said Zoe, "You cast a total spell again."

"The fairies helped me," replied Cali Sky, looking back at the pantheon of photographed girls lining the stage.

"I think they are more like Sirens when they are on stage with you."

Cali Sky grinned. "We enchant only to destroy."

"Oh my God, I love it." Zoe looked back at her photographs. They looked eerie, alone on stage, washed in the echoes of Cali Sky's music. "But what, or who, do they destroy?"

Cali Sky shrugged. "Whoever they choose."

She sensed someone's approach. She braced herself for the adulations of a fan or the sermon of some crusader.

"Hi," said a small, thin girl who looked like she was about to cry. She had short blonde hair. No make up. She shuffled her feet until she stood close to Cali Sky, teetering momentarily, racked by two warring impulses. The first, rooted in shyness, was to run away. The second, fueled by the fuck-it-all species of desperation, compelled her to do the impossible. The girl looked young. Cali Sky looked around for her parents, judging that the girl was probably fourteen.

"Hi," Cali Sky replied.

"Hi." A long pause. "I just wanted to say," the girl began, "that I love your music." Fear and joy painted the approach of tears on her face. "It's so powerful." She hesitated.

"Thank you," said Cali Sky, thinking that was the end of the encounter.

"And," the girl continued, "your music really…connects with me. Like, it's about real life, you know?"

"Yeah. Thank you."

"But I just wanted to know. What do you think it's all about?"

Cali Sky paused. "What my music is all about? Or what life is all about?"

"Yeah," replied the girl.

Cali Sky laughed. The girl laughed. The tension and fear disappeared from her face.

"Well, my music is about passion. About casting emotional spells." Cali Sky looked at Zoe, who peered down at the girl like a mother watching her daughter grow up. "What is life about?" Cali Sky asked rhetorically. "There is no meaning to life. No larger meaning anyway. Or if there is, it can't be put into words. It's in those photos." Cali Sky pointed back at the fairies. "It's in the music."

The girl looked spellbound.

"Hold on," said Cali Sky on a whim as she walked back to the stage, picked up a piece of paper taped to the stage floor, returned to the girl, and handed her the paper. "Do you know what this is?"

The girl took the sheet and looked at it. She shook her head.

"This is my set list. If there is a meaning to life, it's buried somewhere in those songs."

The girl looked overwhelmed, tears trickling down her cheeks. "Thank you," she sobbed. She turned to shuffle away. Then stopped suddenly and turned back around. "Sometimes when I listen to your music," she said, now more confidently, "I feel like bad things have happened to you." The sobbing increased. "I only say that because some really bad things have happened to me. And when I watch you sing, you look like I feel." More sobbing. "Have really bad things happened to you?"

Cali Sky was shocked, but labored to conceal it. "Yeah," she whispered. She turned and walked to the stage, pretending to dismantle her equipment. When she looked back, amp cord in hand, she saw Zoe and the girl wrapped in a hug.

Cali Sky unplugged cords and rolled them into loops. She put her guitar into its case.

"Alright," said Ian, announcing his approach. He was the owner of the coffee house. He wore earrings in both ears. "As always, you receive half of all sales for the evening. That amounts to $87." He handed Cali Sky the money. "Not much. But then again, not bad for an hour's work. You drew another great crowd."

Cali Sky pocketed the cash. "Thanks, Ian. Just give Zoe and me fifteen minutes or so to take everything down."

"No worries." Ian turned to leave, then changed his mind and added, "Cali Sky, I've heard enough of your music to know that you are good. Really good. Have you ever thought of making a demo?"

"I've thought about it." Cali Sky knew the thought distressed her. Not because of any fear of failure, but because the idea of recording a few songs for a record company seemed tantamount to trapping them in a box, imprisoning them. Like turning a dynamic potential, explored with every gig she played, into a static reality. A song performed live had infinite possibilities, recording that song chained it to just one of them. "But I'm not ready to record anything yet," she answered.

"Well, I think you're good enough. No, I *know* you're good enough," Ian replied as he tidied up the coffee house for closing.

Zoe pulled a boom box from the corner of a room, plugged it in to the nearest outlet, and pressed play. She liked to listen to music when she set up and took down her photography displays. She usually listened to mix tapes. She made hundreds of them. For others and for herself. The watery opening chords of the Pretenders' "Back on the Chain Gang" poured through the speakers. Their album *Learning to Crawl* had been released just a few months earlier, their first since tragedy had befallen the band when the guitar player and bass player both died of drug overdoses. Zoe sang along as she carefully deposited her photographs into their cases. Cali Sky helped by folding up the easels. They exchanged no words. Just worked and listened to music. Always surrounded by music.

Once when they were walking across the leafy campus of the California Institute of Art Design, where Zoe studied photography, Cali Sky said, "I wish I could always listen to music. Without headphones. Even when I'm outside like now. The music would just come from the sky."

"It does," Zoe announced.

"What?"

"It does. Music does come from the sky. It's called the music of the spheres. People used to believe that beautiful music accompanied the movement of planets. The music echoed through the heavens."

Cali Sky loved Zoe's knowledge of such things, knowledge always limited to the mythological, fantastical, cultic, and strange. Ask her to explain Reaganomics and she'd give you a blank stare; mention the name Gaia and she'd give you a history of mother goddesses and fertility cults.

"I like that," Cali Sky replied. "The music of the spheres. Did these people actually claim to hear it?"

"No. By the time the music reached earth, where everything is so fucked up, no one could hear it. It's like the music was too good, too pure for this place."

"The most beautiful music you'll never hear."

"Exactly."

By the time "Back on the Chain Gang" faded out Cali Sky was folding up the final easel. The next song surprised her: the Runaways' "Cherry Bomb." The song surprised her because it was one of the few songs by a female band that Zoe hated. Cali Sky set down the easel and looked at her; Zoe looked at Cali Sky as the power chords thudded along. A smile slowly spread across Zoe's face, a contagious smile that spread to Cali Sky. They both laughed in spite of themselves. As the chorus approached, Zoe grabbed a sugar dispenser from one of the coffee house tables and lip synced, satirically capturing in her over-the-top movements the worst sort of rock-and-roll theatrics.

"Hello Daddy, hello Mom
I'm your ch ch ch ch ch cherry bomb!
Hello world, I'm your wild girl
I'm your ch ch ch ch ch cherry bomb!"

It was Zoe's impersonation of any given musician in any given hair band, which by 1985 made their hyperbolic presence felt on the airwaves and music charts. Zoe strutted around with male aggression, a female version of a cock-rock hero, widening her stance and thrusting her hips with each "ch ch ch ch ch cherry bomb."

Zoe performed her farce and Cali Sky laughed. But as the lampoon neared its end the laughter died away and the smile faded. Cali Sky tried to keep it plastered to her face for Zoe's sake. She faked a laugh now and then. But inside she felt a wave of sorrow. She tried to ignore it. Once it passed she tried to forget it. But then another came, this one longer and more acute. *What is this?* said a voice inside her head.

You know what this is, said another voice. *A desecration. Pollution. Like pouring dirty water into a white bathtub. But don't blame Zoe. You laughed too. At least at first. Enjoying a song not because it's good but because it's bad. Remember the night with the records spread across the living room floor? The holiness of it? What has happened to music, to rock and roll? Another false appearance. A lie. But I thought music was different.*

That night at her mom's apartment Cali Sky called Aunt Nancy at the nursing home.

"I'm not calling too late, am I?"

"No," answered Aunt Nancy, "You can call me anytime."

"Can I come visit you tomorrow? Mom said she'd give me a ride."

"Sure. Anything in particular you want to talk about?"

"I played at the coffee house again tonight."

"Great, how did it go?"

"Really well. I felt like I played every song the way I needed to play it. And Zoe displayed her photographs on the stage. A really cool effect."

"Terrific. I wish I could've been there."

Silence.

"Anything else happen? Cali Sky?"

"He was there again. Standing at the back."

"Your dad?"

"Yeah, my dad."

Cali Sky knew that within five minutes she would get used to the smell of urine and Lysol. She always did. It was the third nursing home for Aunt Nancy. Cali Sky felt they were all pretty much the same: polished white floors, overweight nurses, drooling old men in wheelchairs who wanted to shake her hand, and the smell of urine and Lysol.

Then she made her way to room 9. When Aunt Nancy first moved in she impressed Cali Sky with an arcane Beatles reference. In her best John Lennon voice Aunt Nancy intoned, "I reside in room numba 9, numba 9, numba 9." The look on the nurse's face resembled the expression of many Beatles fans when they spun on their turntables for the first time the White Album and got a load of Lennon's avant garde "Revolution 9."

Aunt Nancy sat in her wheelchair doing a crossword. Despite a body now ravaged by multiple sclerosis she still looked much younger than the other nursing-home residents. Cali Sky saw posted on Aunt Nancy's bulletin board various fliers advertising her gigs. She pinned one more to the board, a flier announcing an upcoming show at That's Entertainment.

"That's going to be a tough gig," Cali Sky said, handing Aunt Nancy a Dr. Pepper with the straw dangling from the opening.

"Why's that?"

"I'm opening for John's band. Remember him?"

Aunt Nancy's face turned sour. "The guy who kicked you out of his band?"

"That's the one."

"Well, you'll just have to show them up."

"That's my plan."

Cali Sky plugged in the boom box. She decided to play a Beach Boys tape. They talked about what the Beach Boys might have become, what Brian Wilson could have helped the Beach Boys become.

"His idea was to create a rock symphony," Cali Sky explained. She knew the story well; it had become rock and roll lore. "It was going to be called *Smile*, Brian Wilson's most complex creation. It would surpass anything the Beatles ever did. Really transform music, take a completely new direction. But the other Beach Boys didn't like it. Brian Wilson's drug and alcohol problem got worse. He actually went crazy, some sort of mad genius thing."

"So *Smile* remains unwritten," Aunt Nancy marveled. "We'll never know what it sounds like."

"Pretty much. All we have are a few songs, like 'Good Vibrations.'"

Cali Sky took a swig of Dr. Pepper. "But I kind of like the idea that it will never be written, that the album is unfinished. Because you can only *imagine* what it might have sounded like."

"'Heard melodies are sweet, but those unheard are sweeter,'"

Aunt Nancy quoted with a far-off look in her eye. Cali Sky knew that Aunt Nancy could drop a quote for nearly any occasion.

"Exactly."

The notion of unheard melodies hung in the air, danced about room number 9, and settled deep into Cali Sky's psyche. Immediately it ignited the desire, the longing, thrusting the imagination forward until it overreached itself. The experience flooded her soul, spilling over into the infinite. When she regained the ability to think clearly, to reason, two words appeared in her de-pressurized mind: Blue Flower.

Aunt Nancy, who was oblivious to Cali Sky's existential upheaval, said, "So is the University of San Francisco still your first choice?"

"Huh? Oh, yeah."

"What an opportunity. What an exciting prospect. I am proud of you. We are *all* proud of you. Even your dad."

The mention of her dad quickly dispelled Cali Sky's metaphysical reverie, sobering her mind and bringing her back to the universe of urine and Lysol.

"So how was school?" asked Joan the next day from the driver's side of the Celica.

Cali Sky hated this. Hated being picked up from school by her mom. Hated being asked by her mom how school was.

"Okay," she replied absent-mindedly, flipping on the car radio and dialing it to KROQ. R.E.M.'s "Talk about the Passion" came on. Cali Sky tried to listen to the song but something kept getting in the way. What was it? Static? Road noise? Michael Stipe sang about carrying the weight of the world when she realized that the distraction interrupting the song was her mom. She was saying something.

"What?" asked Cali Sky, annoyed that her mom had just ruined her listening experience.

"Cali Sky, is it too much to ask to have a conversation with me?"

"I just wanted to listen to the song, Mom. Is *that* too much to ask?"

Joan reached down and turned the radio off. Something snapped inside Cali Sky.

"Fine, mom," she roared. "You want to have a conversation? Fine. Let's have a conversation…. So… When are you gonna meet someone, huh? Find someone new."

"What are you talking about?"

"You know what I'm talking about. Meet a new man. Get back at Dad."

Joan turned her attention away from the road, looking at Cali Sky in shock. "I don't think I even know you anymore. You need to get rid of all your anger."

"That anger drives me, Mom. It's my inspiration." Then she continued without hesitation, "You didn't answer my question. When are you gonna meet someone new?"

"Yeah, well, I'm not going to answer that question."

"Oh come on, Mom. It's not that hard. It wasn't hard for you to meet guys when you were my age."

"That's enough, Cali Sky!"

"One of those guys was even my real dad."

"That's enough!" Joan pulled off to the side of the road and slammed on the brakes. "That's enough! Fuck you, Cali Sky! Fuck you!"

Cali Sky did not dare look at her. She stared straight ahead, remorse contending with her bitterness.

"Get out!" yelled Joan. "Get out!"

"Here?"

"Yes!"

Cali Sky opened the car door, stepped out and slammed the door shut. Joan peeled away. Cali Sky began walking, the warm air still beckoning Californians to the beach, the glorious spring sun shining in mockery of those who carry the weight of the world.

By the time she reached the apartment Cali Sky was fifteen minutes late for her 3 o'clock lesson. Vince was in middle school. Shy and easily intimidated Vince had nevertheless learned much from Cali Sky's instruction. He had learned to read some music, at least the notes up to the fifth fret, and could play just about any chord up and down the guitar neck.

What struck Cali Sky about Vince was his wholesomeness. He seemed too squeaky clean to play guitar, unless he wanted to join a Christian rock band, which may in fact have been the case. But whenever he asked Cali Sky to transcribe a song for him so that he could play it—something they generally did at the beginning of every lesson—he always brought in something hardly innocent. This time he brought in Billy Idol's "White Wedding."

"Sorry I'm late," Cali Sky said as she took the tape from Vince and popped it into the boom box. "I had a long walk to get here," she added loudly so that her mom, who disappeared into her bedroom once Cali Sky arrived, could overhear. She picked up an electric and pulled her chair close to Vince's.

"Alright," she said, trying to compose herself after her long walk, renewed anger for her mom now seeking a new expression. "'White Wedding' huh?" It struck her that maybe Vince via Billy Idol had found that expression for her.

"I basically want to learn the beginning part of the song," Vince said in his Theodore Cleaver voice. "I like that first guitar part."

Cali Sky pushed the play button. She cocked her head to the side, listening closely to the rising and falling guitar lick. Once it concluded, paving the way for the first verse, she pushed stop. She fingered the fret of her electric until she found the right notes, the same ones in the song. She played the lick herself. Then she penciled the notes onto a composition sheet. Vince's face glowed, though as usual he never looked Cali Sky in the face.

"That wasn't too hard," she said as she set the pencil down on the music stand. "Let me figure out the chords to the song so you can play the whole thing."

"Gee, that would be great!"

Cali Sky wondered if this kid might be a reincarnation of her grandpa, bringing back from the dead a pre-Elvis American Eden where teenagers are still called "youngsters" and have the good sense to conclude every address to their elders with the word "sir" or "ma'am." But why would her reincarnated grandpa want to learn guitar? *Could a kid this innocent play rock and roll?* she wondered. *This is supposed to be the devil's music. What would Billy Idol say if he knew I was teaching this kid his song?*

Cali Sky pressed play. Billy Idol sang about his sister's shotgun wedding. "Hey little sister what have you done?" *Hey mom and dad what have you done?* Cali Sky found the chords for the verse. She did the same for the chorus and let the track continue, remembering the bridge. "And there's nothing sure in this world." *Like your religion, dad.* "And there's nothing pure in this world." *A slut—that's what my own dad had called my mom.* Distracted by her wandering thoughts, anger filling her up again, she missed the chords and was forced to rewind the bridge. *Does this kid even hear the lyrics?*

"Okay," said Cali Sky, writing out the chords for the bridge, "that's pretty much the whole song. Why don't you try now? Start with the opening lick."

"Um, okay," Vince replied, "I'll try." He played it haltingly. He did better the second time through.

"Good. Now the chords."

Vince played the first verse and chorus. As he began the second verse Joan walked out of her bedroom and into the kitchen to grab a snack. Cali Sky glanced up at her. No eye contact, retriggering her anger. She stopped Vince.

"The bridge is coming up. Why don't you sing it?" she said.

"Sing it?" replied Vince incredulously, as if the idea never had occurred to him, like asking Grandpa in the 1950s about integrated drinking fountains.

"Yeah. Sing it," answered Cali Sky, now glancing up at her mom again. She continued in a flirtatious voice loud enough to be overheard, "You know, girls love that sort of thing. You can sing it to your girlfriend."

The blush that spread across Vince's face transformed his appearance: he looked scandalized, frightened, overwhelmed. If he was the reincarnation of the 1950s, he was now being introduced to the 1960s. But like all blushes Vince's blush was ambiguous, revealing what it intended to conceal: an awareness of something inappropriate and an acknowledgement of being embarrassed, flattered or otherwise stirred by that very inappropriateness. Eve's blush sealed her sin before she even held the fruit in her hand. In Vince's case the blush showed traces of pleasure, shocking, unexpected pleasure, like a first orgasm.

"Um," he stammered, awed by the pleasure and pain he was experiencing, "I don't have a girlfriend."

"Well," replied Cali Sky suggestively, "Once you start playing and singing songs you *will*."

More uncertain ecstasy. He dared not look at her, but could sense that she was looking at him. Cali Sky adjusted her guitar strap around her chest area. Their knees touched. She was singlehandedly orchestrating the undoing of Vince. And while he felt her presence overwhelm him in ways only his blush could suggest, Cali Sky felt only the presence of her mom in the form of a radiating anger.

"Come on, Vince," teased Cali Sky, speaking now as much to

her mom as to her over-stimulated pupil, "I'll sing it with you. Let's take it from the second chorus. Here we go."

"There is nothing fair in this world."

"Come on, Vince. Sing it louder," she encouraged while playing a run on guitar before the next line.

"There is nothing safe in this world."

"Okay, better." Vince had actually gotten quieter. Cali Sky was singing more loudly.

"And there's nothing sure in this world."

"You can do it Vince!"

"And there's nothing pure in this world."

"Louder!" shouted Cali Sky orgasmically.

"Look for something left in this world."

By the time they reached the end of the bridge Joan returned to her bedroom and Cali Sky's passionate singing rendered Vince mute. He looked spent. Had he been able to look at Cali Sky and had he been less naïve, he might have noted that her warmed and satisfied face showed traces of a post-coital contentment, the sort that might have appeared on the faces of Adam and Eve the first time they had sex after the Fall.

They were working on scales when Vince's mom knocked on the door. Vince jumped and missed the next note, completely losing his concentration. By the time Cali Sky finished the scale Vince had already stood up and placed his guitar in the case. As if he had been doing something shameful and was hiding the evidence.

"Hi Mrs. Sorenson," said Cali Sky cheerfully as she opened the front door. Vince stood behind her, guitar in hand, looking guilty.

"Hello Cali Sky. How'd it go today?"

"Fine, though we had a shorter lesson today. I was late. I apologize. I didn't know that I would have to walk home from school today," she replied, raising her voice once again. "So today's lesson is half price."

Vince moved awkwardly toward his mom, as if trying to prevent her from peering into a den of iniquity, the pleasures of which he had ashamedly just indulged. He looked disappointed in himself now in the presence of his mom, like a fully clothed Adam standing guiltily before a pissed-off Yahweh.

"Oh, okay," Mrs. Sorenson said as Vince made his way through the door. "See you next week!"

"Looking forward to it! Oh," she added suddenly, fetching Vince's Billy Idol tape from the boom box. "Don't forget *White Wedding*." She handed it to Vince. "And remember, Vince. Try singing along as you play."

Cali Sky shut the door with satisfaction and stared smugly at her mom.

"Well, that was quite a performance. Something to really be proud of."

"The apple doesn't fall far from the tree, mom."

"Why are you doing this? What's happened to you?"

Cali Sky saw in her mom that look of despair. The look that first appeared after Cami's death, creeping up from the hopelessness of an unhinged existence. Cali Sky last saw that look a few years ago at a restaurant when they ran in to a new acquaintance who innocently asked Joan how many children she had. Joan first said two, and then remembered. Cali Sky now felt the anger and smugness inside of her disappear.

"Mom," began Cali Sky. She thought about how her mom loves to play with her hair. She thought about how her mom used to love to joke around, play games, dance to Muzak in the aisles of grocery stores, cook an elaborate meal and enjoy watching her family eat it. She wanted to talk to her about these things. But she couldn't. It wouldn't come out. She couldn't get past the word "mom."

Joan waited. Then walked toward her bedroom.

"There's a microwaveable dinner in the freezer. Please lock the door when you go out tonight. Please be home by midnight. And your dad left you something. It's in that envelope on the counter."

Joan closed her door. Cali Sky stared at it. She knew every detail of its white-painted surface: the scratch near the doorknob, the discoloration in the shape of a comma at perfect eye level when she stood next to it, the broken and splintered bottom corner.

She picked up her dad's envelope. Something heavy was inside. Something metal. She tore it open. A set of keys fell to the floor.

"Hello?"

"Hey, it's me."

"What's up?"

"Guess what?"

"What?"

"I got a car."

"What?"

"A car. A Honda Civic. Only 29,000 miles."

"How'd you get it?"

"A present."

"From who?"

"Guess."

"Your dad."

"Yeah. My dad."

"Oh my God."

"Now you don't have to drive me everywhere. I can drive *you*. *And* your photographs, along with my guitar and amp."

Everything in her elementary-school playground looked smaller than she remembered, even in the dark. Around the sandbox stood the two-foot high wall upon which she and her third-grade friend Kim Watson used to sit and eat popsicles after lunch, watching the fifth graders play kickball. When Cali Sky was in the fourth grade

James Beller created a scandal when he sat atop the monkey bars on the other side of the sandbox and remembered too late that he forgot to put on underwear that morning. These recollections shot a pang of wistfulness into Cali Sky's heart, a wistfulness that became angst once it reached her gut. She felt nervous, then scared. The above-time sensation settled in. *What if when I was in the fourth grade I could look ahead to now, see myself now, and know what happened in between.*

Jeff and Christine sat side by side on the swings, smiling and talking, holding bottles in their hands, alcohol Jeff bought with his fake ID. They had decided to consume their drinks in the playground of their old elementary school. The swing chains squeaked and moaned, triggering a new set of recollections, intensifying the wistfulness, angst, nervousness and fear, all of which now knotted her gut and throttled her heart. Cali Sky saw herself pushing her sister on the swings during a lazy summer morning. Visions of the past buzzed around her head, impossible to swat away, a Promethean torture. She brought the wine cooler to her lips and emptied the bottle, trying to make herself forget.

"Take it easy, Cali Sky," remarked Ari, who put his arm around her, "You're gonna make yourself sick."

She felt an urge to shove Ari away but was distracted by the demons hovering around her head, darting in and out of her brain. She took another drink.

"Check out my sand graffiti."

They all turned to see what Stone was up to. Using his brown vintage Hush Puppy boots he had traced something in the sand. He stood marveling at his creation, tucking his black bangs behind an ear with one hand, holding a bottle of Miller Genuine Draft with the other. Everyone rose to behold Stone's creation. Cali Sky felt relief as she walked with the group, away from the swings, her now occupied mind keeping the swarming demons away.

Standing alongside Stone they read the two sand-carved words at their feet. "The End." Stone was forever channeling the spirit of Jim Morrison. Like the Lizard King himself Stone was a poet. But he inexplicably grew annoyed if anyone ever compared him to the Doors front man. At poetry readings the comments afterwards were predictable: "Jim Morrison would be proud, man." "You have the Morrison thing nailed, bud." And Stone would reply, "Thanks. But I'm trying to do my own thing." The problem for Stone was that Morrison was doing Stone's own thing before Stone was even born.

As they all stood in the quarter-moonlit night in the sandbox of an elementary school playground reading words written in sand, Stone began to sing,

"This is the End,

Beautiful friend, the End."

Then he began reciting, Stone once again became Jim Morrison.

"The killer awoke before dawn, he put his boots on.

He took a face from the ancient gallery

And he walked on down the hall…"

"I don't think a fifth grader will catch the Doors reference, Stone," replied Jeff.

"They don't have to," Stone answered. "They'll *still* freak out. And even if they don't know the reference, they'll remember. When they *do* hear the song for the first time, *then* they'll freak out."

Jeff smiled. Ari felt out of place, as he usually did when he was with Jeff and his friends, looking as though he longed for the familiarity of a tennis court with its intelligible straight lines. He was prepared to join everyone in an isn't-he-weird-let's-make-fun-of-him sort of laugh. But it never came.

Instead Jeff said, "Let's hear some poems, Stone."

Stone gingerly set his MGD on the wall, then slowly withdrew his outstretched arms from the bottle precariously perched on the uneven surface. He pulled from his back pocket a book that looked like it had been rescued from a fourth-century library in Constantinople or Alexandria before the barbarian hordes from the north brought down the curtain on Greco-Roman civilization.

He carefully opened the cover that might have been mistaken for calf vellum and solemnly turned the pages that might have passed for parchment. He read a Robinson Jeffers poem. The poem, in fact, from which he derived his own nickname:

"...the falcon's

Realist eyes and act

Married to the massive

Mysticism of stone,

Which failure cannot cast down

Nor success make proud."

He breathed the words with an oracular solemnity that straddled the line separating storm-and-stress artistry from unintentional self-parody. Ari waited for everyone else to heed the seemingly irresistible call to ridicule. But no one else seemed to hear it. Instead they retreated into an awed silence that set Ari longing for the crisp satisfaction of a well-struck forehand volley.

Stone began reading one of his own poems when Jeff interrupted.

"Oh shit!"

Everyone looked at Jeff, who stared into the distance toward the school parking lot. A police car crept furtively along, headlights off, and pulled to a slow stop.

"Everyone empty your bottles and hand them to me," commanded Jeff with the calm intensity of a field general.

As the sandbox soaked up the red liquid descending from her bottle, Cali Sky tried to steady herself. She was drunk. Very drunk. So were Christine and Ari. Jeff, Brodie and Stone were less drunk, but hardly sober. They huddled together. Jeff positioned himself on the other side of the circle from the police car, out of the officer's line of sight. He was using the huddle as a screen, blocking himself from view. He knelt down and buried the two brown bags beneath other garbage that had accumulated on the other side of the two-foot wall: popsicle wrappers, sandwich bags, used napkins, lunch sacks and a child's black sweater. He then re-joined the huddle and passed the Binaca around. He looked toward the parking lot, where the door of the police car was now open.

"Be cool," Jeff said. "Walk innocently. Casually. We did *nothing* wrong. Right?"

"Right," they murmured.

Cali Sky had trouble focusing. Fear sobered her a bit, but she still felt wobbly on her feet.

They made their way across the soccer field. They could just make out the cop, obscured by the dark night, strolling across the kickball diamond. They would meet somewhere in between. The distance slowly narrowed. For Cali Sky the anticipation, though dulled by alcohol, was sickening. For Jeff it sharpened concentration.

Twenty feet. They could see his badge. Fifteen feet. They saw him reach for his belt a second time. Ten feet. They could hear his footfalls. Five feet. They all stopped. He was young and intimidating. He stared at each teenager like a bully choosing a victim.

"Good evening," he said in a grim, monotone voice.

"Good evening," answered Jeff without hesitation.

He really does sound innocent, thought Cali Sky. *Maybe we can get out of this.*

"Whose vehicles are those in the parking lot?" the cop asked.

"One is mine, officer," Jeff replied. "The silver Honda Accord."

"How about the other one?"

Cali Sky wondered why no one answered. She felt the others glancing quickly at her. Then she remembered that the other car was hers. *Shit shit shit.*

"The other one is mine," she blurted. *Do I sound drunk? Shit shit shit.* "I just got it. My dad bought it for me. I just forgot that it was mine." *Shut up shut up shut up.*

The cop looked at her for an excruciating moment. "Okay, all of you follow me."

When they reached the parking lot everyone gathered around the police car. The cop collected IDs. He took Jeff's and Cali Sky's registration and proof of insurance, then ran checks inside his car. Jeff scattered looks of encouragement to the others. The ever-tanned Ari looked pale as he watched Pepperdine, or at the very least a year of eligibility, evaporate into the night. For some reason Brodie and Stone smiled at each other. Christine looked nervously (yet hopefully) at Jeff. Cali Sky stared at the oil-stained parking lot surface, too ashamed to meet anyone's eyes, certain that she had sealed their fate.

The cop got out of his seat with painstaking deliberation and walked slowly and confidently to the front of his car, where the teenagers stood waiting.

"Cali Sky Braithwaite."

The panic felt like an electric charge that spread through her nervous system and made her feel like she was melting. Her name sounded unfamiliar coming from the mouth of the cop, as if he had commandeered it and it was no longer hers.

"Yes." She half-whispered the word.

He stared at her, looking her up and down. Her legs were shaking. In her desperation she felt she had nothing more to lose. She resigned herself to the worst possible fate. She resolved that she would at least combat his intimidation, defiantly if necessary: a symbolic act to take back her name. Anger now strengthened her legs, the familiar buzz of rage grounded her, reconstituting her melting world.

But instead of dealing her the worst possible fate the cop merely returned her registration and proof of insurance. He did the same to Jeff.

"I'm gonna ask you this question once," he began, addressing them collectively. "Just once. You'll find that it is in your best interest to answer it truthfully."

"Yes sir," replied Jeff. The rest nodded their heads.

"Have you been drinking?"

"No," answered Jeff, again without hesitation. The word "no" echoed around the group.

The cop paused, letting the silence test their mettle.

"You haven't been drinking?"

"No."

"Are you sure?"

"Yes."

"So if I walk over to the sandbox there, I won't find any alcohol bottles or cans?"

"No." Jeff sounded sure of himself, like he really believed it.

"Then why don't you tell me what you are doing in the playground of an elementary school at 9 o'clock at night?"

Once again without hesitation, with the un-ironical face of a five-year old, Jeff gave an answer that the cop could never have anticipated: "We were reading poetry."

"Poetry? You were reading poetry?"

"That's right."

Before the cop could recover from his surprise and regain control of the situation, Stone produced from his back pocket his ancient-looking manuscript.

"See," said Stone as he sidled up to the cop, "these are the poems."

The cop looked at Stone as if he had leprosy. Cali Sky recognized that expression: It was the sort that the popular kids at school flung at the unpopular kids, the losers.

Stone leafed through the journal.

"Here," he pointed. "We were just reading this one. I actually wrote it."

Channeling Jim Morrison, Stone began to recite his poem for the cop. Jeff looked nervous, hoping the Binaca had successfully neutralized Stone's beer breath. Stone stood so close to the cop that, had he opened his arms, he could have wrapped him in a hug.

"Alright, alright," interrupted the cop. "That's enough."

He appeared both flabbergasted and uncomfortable. The tables had now turned. The cop had a harder time believing what was true than what was untrue. The teenagers were now emboldened because they were no longer defending a lie. The cop took a step back and said, "The next time you want to get together and read your *poetry*"—he made it sound like the silliest word in the English language—"don't do it at night in an elementary school playground. Or any other public place for that matter. It looks too suspicious. Just stay at home and do it behind closed doors. Got it?"

They all nodded.

He walked to his car door. And as he descended into his driver's seat, they all overheard him mutter, "Fucking weirdos." He began to drive away. Jeff chuckled. Stone wore the cop's epithet as a badge of honor. But Cali Sky's anger and defiance would not let it go. Before the cop's car exited the parking lot she yelled in its direction, "Well, fuck you too!"

"Cali Sky!" cried Brodie, as he physically restrained her. She felt warm and animated in his arms, but still drunk and unsteady. Jeff breathed a sigh of relief as the cop car continued down the road. Stone tucked his poetry book back into his back pocket, hurdled himself atop the wall surrounding the school's bicycle lot, and proclaimed, "I am the Lizard King, I can do anything!"

Back at Jeff's house they gathered around the TV.

"The movie came out in theaters just a few weeks ago," Jeff said with amazement. "How did you get a bootleg already?"

"I'm Brodie, bro. That's how."

Jeff's house was parentless for the evening. He pushed *This Is Spinal Tap* into the VHS player. He settled onto the couch next to Christine, remote in hand.

Cali Sky stumbled into the living room. "Do you have a guitar, Jeff? I need a fucking guitar!" She was drunker than they thought.

"For the fourth time, Cali Sky, no. I don't have a guitar," answered Jeff.

"I need a guitar!"

"Just sit down and watch the movie. You'll like it. It's about rock and roll. Sort of."

Ari took her by the hand and led her to the couch.

She had trouble focusing, distracted by her desire to play. "I need a guitar!" she proclaimed every few minutes. She eventually became aware that the others were laughing, occasionally at her but primarily at the movie. So she tried to focus on the film. Once she did she quickly caught on: a lampoon, making fun of heavy metal, a satiric take on the rock-and-roll industry.

She watched as the character of Nigel Tufnel, lead guitarist for Spinal Tap, explains to Rob Reiner that his amps have volume knobs that go up to eleven instead of ten.

"Why don't you just make ten louder and make ten be the top number and make that a little louder?" asks Reiner.

Tufnel stares blankly at his amp for a while before replying, "These go to eleven."

Cali Sky heard the laughter around her and joined in.

She watched as the band energetically prepares itself for a concert in Cleveland. "Rock and roll!" yells the character of David St. Hubbins. The enthusiasm wanes, however, when the band gets lost backstage, unable to find the entrance to the stage, despite being pointed in the right direction by the facility's janitor. St. Hubbins' "Rock and roll!" war cries become less convincing as he and his bandmates get more and more lost in the venue's backstage labyrinth.

Cali Sky once again heard laughter around her and joined in again, but this time half-heartedly. Eventually she could not laugh at all. She rose, steadied herself and rushed to the bathroom.

Ari followed. "I think she might be sick."

Thirty seconds later he returned and said to Brodie, "She wants to talk to you."

"Me?

Ari nodded. Attention shifted to Brodie; Ari was crestfallen.

"Is she sick?" Brodie asked.

"No, she's crying."

Brodie knocked on the door. "It's me."

He entered and closed the door behind him.

Cali Sky's eyes and cheeks were wet with tears. She leaned against the sink, looking into the mirror.

"What's wrong?" asked Brodie.

No answer. More tears. A convulsive sob. He hadn't seen Cali Sky like this for years. Like last time, the experience hit him viscerally, a tug inside his rib cage.

"Why are you sad, Cali Sky?"

Instead of answering she threw her arms around Brodie, weeping.

"What's wrong?" asked Brodie.

She released him, wiped her face and murmured, "The movie."

"The movie? The movie made you sad?"

She nodded.

"Why?"

She wiped her face again. "Because this is what's happened to rock and roll. It's like it has imploded. It's gotten too big, too commercial, too…fake. So people make fun of it."

"Are you serious?"

"Can *anyone* take it seriously anymore? It's all a farce now: novelty acts, hair bands, puppet pop stars."

"Cali Sky, you don't…"

"Maybe it started with Bowie, you know? All the personas. Ziggy Stardust. The Spiders from Mars."

"Cali Sky, I really don't think you need to worry about this. I mean, you and I both know there are some really good bands out there that aren't fake. The movie is just supposed to be funny, it's not…"

"I miss my sister!"

Cali Sky nearly collapsed. Brodie lifted her up and held her in his arms. The weight of her statement settled in his chest, tugging harder inside his ribcage. She wept the tears of a desperate mourner whose declaration of a hopeless agony paradoxically generates hope: the sensation of rebounding from the depths of an emotional abyss that seemed to have no bottom. Brodie felt her wet, warm cheek on his neck. He placed his hand on her head and stroked her back with the other. They could hear *This Is Spinal Tap* playing in the living room. The band was performing "Rock and Roll Creation."

Five minutes later they emerged from the bathroom arm in arm. Cali Sky leaned on Brodie to maintain balance.

"I'm going to take her home," he said as Jeff pushed pause.

"Are you sure? I can do it," Ari said.

"No, I'll do it."

"Are you okay, Cali Sky?" Ari asked, wondering why he wasn't driving her home.

Cali Sky didn't answer.

"She's okay," said Brodie. "It turns out she *was* sick. That's all."

Brodie guided her to her car. He helped her into the passenger side, put on her seatbelt.

"Is there a guitar in here?" she asked.

"No Cali Sky," Brodie answered as he started the car.

She fell in and out of consciousness during the drive to her apartment.

"Cali Sky, wake up. Cali Sky, we're here."

She struggled to open her eyes. The spinning made her sick. She clumsily rolled down her window as Brodie turned off the ignition. The cool night air felt refreshing.

"I'm dropping you off, Cali Sky. But I'll bring your car back tonight."

She managed to understand his words a few moments after she heard them.

"Okay," she slurred, "but you have to promise to bring the car back tonight. My dad bought me this car."

"I will. I promise."

"But you have to promise."

"I do."

"Because my dad promised me this car. Promise?"

Brodie laughed. "I promise."

He helped her up the stairs. He removed the apartment key from the key chain, then unlocked the door.

"Can you make it to your bedroom?"

She nodded and said, "You promised."

"I promise."

"Thank you, Brodie."

In the porch light Brodie studied the flush in her cheeks. Her eyes were a bit unfocused, but maintained their expressiveness. He felt another tug inside his rib cage when he deciphered their meaning: They conveyed desire. He thought she would lean over and kiss him. Instead, she laughed and mumbled, "I need a guitar in my hands."

The apartment was dark. She remembered the enchanted glow of nightlights. She stumbled into the couch and made it into the kitchen, where she drank a glass of water and took two aspirin. She then walked unsteadily across the apartment, past her room, past her guitars, and straight into her mom's bedroom. She removed her shorts and shirt, then climbed into bed. Joan stirred.

"Tell me a story," whispered Cali Sky.

"What?"

"Never mind."

"Cali Sky, have you been drinking?"

"Yes."

Cali Sky quickly fell asleep. But before she lost consciousness she felt the reassuring comfort of her mom's loving fingers gently stroking her hair.

She was chasing a ghost. It was leading her into hell. But then it was not really hell. It was Denmark Street in London, or at least what her imagination pictured as Denmark Street in London, based on what she had read in her dad's journal when he visited there. The ghost vanished into a building. She stopped and looked at the sign outside. The 12 Bar Club. Her dad had seen a gig there.

She walked inside. A band was playing. Her dad was singing and playing guitar. But it wasn't Philip. It was her real dad: the unknown rock and roll star. They were playing a song that took her breath away. It revealed everything that was roiling inside her: inspiration, anger, mystery, desire. She listened carefully to every chord and note, every drumbeat and bass line, every lyric. But she knew it was futile; she knew when she awoke from her dream she wouldn't remember.

She became aware that a wind was blowing through the room. It became stronger, until it blew everyone and everything away. When the blur of windswept objects and people disappeared, all was calm and quiet. It was nighttime and she knew where she was.

She walked to the window where the musical instrument hung. A now gentle zephyr brought it to life, sounding through its pipes a lilting melody. She stood at the window and looked around the meadow, saw the river, the rocks, and in the distance the waterfall. She saw the treetop leaves, rustling in the heavens, glistening in the soft moonlight. Then she saw someone dancing along the river, barefoot, wearing an ankle-length dress. It was a little girl, moving in rhythm to the golden notes of the wind's music.

NINE

POSTERS FESTOONED THE halls of Red Hill High: men's baseball vs. Capistrano; Students against Drunk Driving meeting next week; end-of-the-year Senior Trip to Magic Mountain theme park. Brodie looked at none of them. His eyes were irresistibly drawn to the girl walking his way. She wore a tight-fitting Sex Wax t-shirt. The sun had tanned her face and bleached her blonde hair. Brodie smiled, she smiled back. As she passed he hesitated, as if tethered to her smile. But then he saw Cali Sky standing at her locker. Compared to the surfer girl she looked pale.

"Hey," he said, casting a final look down the hall where he could still make out the Sex Wax t-shirt.

"Hey." Cali Sky saw that he was distracted and knew the reason why. "You're so predictable, Brodie."

He turned to face her and opened his mouth to defend himself. But when he looked into her blue eyes his intention tripped over itself.

"So," he began, changing the subject, "are you ready to start a band?"

Cali Sky flashed him her annoyed, angry look.

"You know," he said, "your scowl is prettier than most girls' smiles."

"Brodie, I leave for San Francisco in five months. Even if we did start a band it wouldn't last long."

"I don't get it. You are too good *not* to be in a band. You don't even plan to study music in college. How can you do that?"

"I don't know what I'm going to study...or what I'm going to do."

He saw a quiver of desperation spread across her face, but she fought it off and it dissipated, diluted by the fierce blueness of her eyes.

"Well," he said, "I know what you *should* do: Start a band and let me play bass."

He waited for a response. She put a final book into her backpack and then began to laugh, the same sort of laughter that, a few weeks earlier, paralyzed his impulse to kiss her outside her apartment door.

He tried to conceal his anger. "You laugh, but you know I'm right."

As he exited the school along with a river of other students heading home for the day, he avoided the hang-out spots and parking spaces where he customarily gathered together with friends. His stride was impatient and angry. Cali Sky's laughter echoed in his head.

He noticed a girl walking not far from him through the parking lot. It was Trish. She was in his history class, but the only words he had ever heard her speak were "here" and "present." She wore her dark-colored pants and long-sleeve shirt like she didn't want to call attention either to them or the small, thin frame around which they clung. Her meek gait could have been mistaken for fear. He avoided her in class, only because she looked like she wanted to be avoided. But now in the day-lit world, he saw that she looked different—no longer a classroom wallflower but an individualized human being. Though she rarely looked up as she walked, he could see her face and detected the inscrutable qualities of attractiveness.

"Hi," he said, now walking alongside her. "You're Trish, right?"

She nodded, now walking faster.

"Take it easy, I just want to talk."

She slowed, but only slightly.

"I don't think I've ever seen you outside class," he continued.

"That's because I spend most of my time outside class with my boyfriend." Her voice was soft, yet unexpectedly assertive.

"Who's your boyfriend?" asked Brodie. It was his stock response to the I-have-a-boyfriend line, an attempt to call a bluff.

Just then they reached the edge of the parking lot where a late-model Volvo was parked. Brodie saw a figure exit the driver's side and approach. He couldn't tell if it was a man or a woman. The person neared. Brodie saw an effeminate-looking boy about his own age. He looked vaguely familiar.

"What do you want?" He looked just like Trish; they could have been siblings. The only immediately noticeable difference was that he had short hair. But they shared the same Gothic face and slight frame.

"What do I want?" asked Brodie with a laugh. "Um, nothing. I was just talking to Trish." Brodie searched his memory, trying to remember where he saw him before.

"What about? I don't mean to pry. I'm just curious. What was the subject of your conversation?"

Brodie thought he detected irony in the boy's voice, but couldn't be sure. He aimed for the same ambiguous tone: "Nothing, really. Just small talk."

"Small talk as an end in itself? Or small talk as a prelude to a pick-up line?"

"What the fuck are you talking about?"

"If it's small talk as an end in itself then your conversation is now over. If it's small talk as a prelude to a pick-up line then your conversation is *likewise* over because Trish is my girlfriend."

"Jesus Christ. Don't get all aggro, man."

"Don't call me man."

Brodie watched Trish get into the Volvo. It had a Cocteau Twins sticker on the back window. Brodie saw a guitar case in the back seat. The music paraphernalia jogged Brodie's memory.

"You used to be the guitar player for Forest Murmurs!" Brodie exclaimed. "I saw you guys at That's a bunch of times!" Brodie recalled the ethereal music and the unique guitar sound. "Your lead singer—what was his name, Brian?—he split, right? Went to Argentina or some crazy shit?"

"His name is Brian, yeah. He moved to Ecuador—not Argentina. He went there to live a life of simplicity and enlightenment, and to get away from America and the sort of people who hit on other people's girlfriends."

"I have a copy of your demo at my house. You guys made some incredible music! 'Painted Universe'—that song blows my mind—Brian's keyboards and voice—he could hit that upper range! And your guitar work…incredible! "

"Yeah, well, thanks."

"You're Tam, right?"

"Yeah."

Tam began walking to the Volvo.

"Holy shit. Tam from Forest Murmurs. So what are you up to now?" asked Brodie.

"Nothing."

"Are you in a band?"

"No," answered Tam as he opened his car door.

"Why not?"

"Because I haven't found the right people."

"Where have you looked?"

"What is this? What do you care? Do you want to be my manager or something?" Tam reached over to pull his door shut.

"No, nothing like that."

"Move so we can be on our way."

"Have you ever been to the University Coffee House?"

"No."

"You'll find the right person there."

"Who?"

"Cali Sky Braithwaite."

"Never heard of her. Now get out of the way."

"Just wait a second. I'm telling you, she's just the person you've been looking for. She plays guitar and keyboards—as good as Brian. No…better than Brian. And she sings. She writes."

"Good for her."

"She knows who you are," Brodie lied. "I'm sure she'd love to meet up with you, discuss music, maybe jam, and see if you two could, you know, put a band together."

"No thanks."

"She's playing the University Coffeehouse this Saturday night at 7. Just drop by and listen. What do you have to lose?"

As Brodie stepped out of the way of the closing door Cali Sky walked apathetically toward her car parked on the other side of the school lot. In the distance she saw balloons tied to the radio antenna of a car. *Someone pulled a prank*, she thought. The balloons were silver and red, shimmering in the spring sun. *Wait a second. Shit. That's my car.* She walked faster, heart pounding. Two juniors stood nearby, watching Cali Sky's approach. She glared at them, then looked over her car, assessing the extent of the prank and the damage to her vehicle. But there was no damage, this was no prank. Just four silver and red balloons tied to her antenna, accompanied by an envelope pinned to her front windshield by the wiper blades.

She removed the envelope, opened it and read:

"People say 'beware!'

But I don't care

The words are just

Rules and regulations…"

At first Cali Sky thought it was from Ari. But Ari would never quote song lyrics, let alone lyrics to Patti Smith's version of "Gloria." The only song Cali Sky heard Ari listen to of his own volition was "Candy Girl" by New Edition, which he blasted across Beverly Hills through his high-end stereo the one time she visited him in his parents' postmodern mansion.

She continued reading,

"So,

Will you go to prom with me?

Ben"

Who is Ben? There was a Ben who was a part of Brodie's surfer/skater set, but he had a girlfriend and hardly ever spoke to her. There was another Ben who was her partner for a psychology class project but he did not seem remotely interested in her romantically and, based on his answers to the personality test, she strongly suspected that he was gay. Besides, neither one of these Bens was the type to quote Patti Smith lyrics. Then she recalled Ben from Spanish class—a quiet, forgettable sort of boy, neither jock nor nerd, skater/surfer nor stoner, social butterfly nor loner. She tried to remember what he looked like: tall and thin, short hair, not especially attractive, but not ugly either. Shy and reticent—a small presence. *Great—Ben from Spanish class has asked me to the Senior Prom. But how does a guy like that know the music of Patti Smith?*

"So are you going to go?" Joan asked, pulling a chip away from the mountain of nachos. She spread a dab of sour cream on the chip with her knife.

"No, I'm not going to go," answered Cali Sky.

"Why not?"

Cali Sky wiped guacamole off her hands and reached for another napkin. "Because I don't even know him. Plus, Senior Prom is not exactly something I'm interested in going to."

"You'll have one Senior Prom in your life. Why not experience it?"

Cali Sky ignored the question. She watched a fishing boat putter through the harbor, making its way out to sea.

"Besides," added Joan, "He'll pay for everything."

Cali Sky looked at her mom, saw the mischievous gleam in her eye, and laughed in spite of herself. They returned their attention to the nachos, mining the mountain for the perfect chip.

"It's nice to be back here, Mom. I'm glad we came."

"Me too, sweetheart. It's been too long."

They first came to Dana Point Harbor not long after the divorce. It became a mother/daughter ritual. They ate nachos on a restaurant patio from which they could watch the seals sunning themselves on the islanded gas-pump dock and occasionally hear the warning bell of the buoy bobbing on the other side of the breakwater. And they discovered that time slowed during this ritual, that the Lethean wind filling the sails of the passing boats caressed their bodies and the beatifying sunlight kissed their faces.

"Cali Sky, just so you know, I *would* like to find someone new."

"Mom, I didn't mean what I said that day. I'm sorry."

"I know, I know. I *don't* want to meet someone new just to get back at your dad. But I would like to meet someone. I just don't want to rush into anything."

Cali Sky reached for another chip.

Joan continued, "I don't need to tell you that I've made some huge mistakes in my life. It's like I got swept up into things before I even had a chance to think about what I was doing. You read your dad's journal; you already know what I mean."

"You rushed into marriage."

Joan nodded.

"But why?"

"Why? Because I wanted to raise you in a stable environment. Because I wanted you to have a father. Because…I couldn't do it on my own."

"So you convinced Dad to marry you."

"My instinct was to provide for you."

"If you could do it over, you wouldn't have married him?"

The despairing look, the one she shared with her daughter, spread around her eyes, which now welled with tears. "Probably not. But who knows for certain? How would I have provided for you?"

"What about before Dad?"

"What do you mean?"

"The guys you met on Sunset Strip. The rock stars? Did you rush into that too?"

"Yeah, I guess I did."

"But didn't you like it? Wasn't it fun?"

Joan sighed. "At the time, yeah, it was fun. But that doesn't mean it wasn't wrong…. Don't look at me that way, Cali Sky! You do realize that what I did was wrong, don't you?"

"If you say so."

"Besides, it's not so much that it was fun. It was more of a way to…"

"To what, Mom?"

"To get attention. To feel special, I guess. To feel loved."

"It sounds like you slept with rock stars for the same reason Dad became a Christian."

Joan looked at her daughter with uncertainty, almost like she was afraid of her. Then the tears of sorrow and shame blended with tears of laughter, which came over her suddenly. Cali Sky joined in.

"You have learned something from my mistakes, right?"

"Don't worry, Mom. I would much rather be a rock star than someone who sleeps with rock stars."

Joan smiled and watched a kayaker paddle past the restaurant, a fish jumped at his approach. The marine colors washed over Joan's face. Their waiter refilled their water glasses. He was young and focused his attention on Cali Sky.

"Can I get you anything else?"

"No thanks."

"Be careful!" said Joan, forcing the waiter to stop ignoring her, "She's a rock star. Rock stars are dangerous."

"Really!" the waiter exclaimed. "What band are you in?"

"No, she's joking," replied Cali Sky. "I'm not in a band. Ignore her, she's a troublemaker."

"Well, you *look* like you could be a rock star."

"Thanks… I guess."

The waiter walked away, looking both pleased and confused.

"You *are* a troublemaker, Mom. You're nothing like Philip."

"Don't call him that. He's your dad."

"Well, technically, he's not."

"He helped raise you, Cali Sky. He *is* your dad. Don't be so hard on him."

"Why not be hard on him? He's fake, mom. He's a hypocrite."

"No he's not. He's no more of a fake and hypocrite than you and me."

"What are you talking about? Aunt Nancy agrees with me. He hides behind all that religious bullshit."

"It's not bullshit. Watch your mouth, by the way. And he doesn't hide behind it any more than you hide behind music."

"It *is* bullshit. Music is real—no pretenses…" Her voice trailed away as she recalled *This Is Spinal Tap*.

"Cali Sky, I think we all hide behind something at some point. And there is probably some bullshit in whatever it is we choose to hide behind. Can we stop saying bullshit? You also need to understand where Aunt Nancy is coming from. She and your dad have had a strained relationship for years."

"Yeah, and Aunt Nancy finally brought it out into the open. Unlike Dad, who sweeps everything under the carpet."

"What does he sweep under the carpet?"

"A strained relationship! The reality of the past! The truth!"

"Maybe what you call the truth he thinks is bullshit. See what you've started…and maybe he thinks that bullshit is best kept under the rug. Look, I'm not saying I agree with him. I'm just asking you to try to understand where he's coming from."

"He cheated on you! He left you for another woman! And you defend him!"

"You're right. He did all those things. Terrible things. But I also know that he loves you so much…"

"If he loved me so much he wouldn't have cheated on you."

Joan paused, then said quietly and calmly, "Well maybe your dad and I are not so different after all. Maybe he did what he did without thinking, maybe he too acted on instinct, an instinct to feel special and loved."

From where she stood on the low stage tucked in the corner of the room, surrounded by Zoe's black-and-white photographs, Cali Sky stared at the faces. The grin began at the corners of her mouth and turned mischievous once it reached her eyes. All she could see were faces, heads and faces, some smiling and laughing. On one side she could see Brodie standing next to two people, a boy and girl, who might have been brother and sister, perhaps the gothic spawn of Peter Murphy or inky-cloaked Hamlet. Brodie spoke to them, they said nothing. Not far from Brodie, Jeff and Christine looked like they were bickering, until they suddenly began to laugh, hugging and kissing. She saw Stone resembling an Inca, gazing around the room as if the clues to the riddle of existence were written on the coffee-house walls. Zoe kneeled near the stage, fitting to her camera a lens she retrieved from her bag.

All of these faces she expected to see. They harmonized with the scene, resonating in their own ways with the coffee-house vibe. Three other faces brought their own vibes into the room. Scanning these faces, Cali Sky felt her mischievous grin grow, conveying now the confidence to accept the challenge. These three faces changed the dynamic in the room, creating a new context for her music.

The first face—unassertive and subdued, but more assertive and less subdued than she remembered—was Ben from Spanish class. He leaned against the wall at the back of the room. The second face exuded a strange combination of parental pride and exhilarated complicity. Joan stood at one end of the crowd, dressed in form-fitting jeans and blouse, looking like the sort of parent who might buy her kid beer. Philip's smiling yet thin and sallow face shone love—a desperate love—toward Cali Sky from the other side of the crowd.

"The most talented artist I know without a recording contract....Cali Sky!" proclaimed Ian, introducing Cali Sky to the stage. Applause from the crowd. She walked to the mic, adjusting her guitar strap.

She began with some original songs. The girls in the front row sang along. Stone danced. Cali Sky fed off of their reactions. Brodie smiled, glancing furtively at Tam, who remained stoical. During the second song Cali Sky noticed that her mom and dad both had the same expressions on their faces: expressions of pride. Unlike Philip however Joan danced, danced with a self-imposed restraint that just barely held her back from rushing the stage and surrendering her body to the music. By the conclusion of the third song, even stiff-looking Ben appeared to be moving.

As the applause died down Cali Sky spoke into the mic: "I'd like to dedicate this next song to my dad."

She strummed an overture, vague chords linked by wandering notes, all of which eventually resolved themselves into the opening four chords of Blind Faith's "In the Presence of the Lord." Philip recognized it at once, even though he hadn't heard it in fifteen years. Recognition registered on his face as gratitude. He wiped away a tear.

Cali Sky sang,

"I have finally found a way to live

Just like I never could before.

I know that I don't have much to give,

But I can open any door."

Cali Sky sang with closed eyes. She played with no embellishments, paring down the song to its irreducible essence, as if she were performing the archetype of the song that had existed before Eric Clapton had even written it. The anticipatory sevenths chord at the end of the verse sparked to life in Cali Sky's breast the infinite longing, opening the existential door about which she was singing at that very moment. The song then became more aggressive. She opened her eyes and jerked the guitar neck with each chord.

"Everybody knows the secret,

"Everybody knows the score.

I have finally found a way to live

In the color of the Lord."

The girls in the front row swayed. Stone looked like he had finally deciphered the Incan hieroglyphs on the coffee house walls. Brodie cast a didn't-I-tell-you? look at Tam, whose stoicism began to falter. His eyes darted back and forth from Cali Sky's face to her guitar, looking like he was contemplating possibilities. Ben had moved away from the wall, slowly making his way through the crowd toward the stage. He stopped and joined the others in applause after Cali Sky concluded the song.

She adjusted her ponytail, surveying the crowd again. "I have a lot of friends here tonight. And family." The smile faded. She scanned the back of the room until she spotted her mom. "You've been there for me. Despite what I've done." She looked down at her guitar, occasionally looking up, focusing now on no one in particular. The room became silent. "You see, some bad things have happened to me. Someone really perceptive once told me that those bad things are reflected in my music, which is probably true. But they're also reflected in the way I've treated other people." She paused, pretending to tune her A string. "I lashed out and...hurt some of them. Sometimes things just happen so quickly. And you want to slow everything down. Just stop the world...."

She backed away from the mic, unable to go on. She looked disoriented and confused, like she forgot how to play guitar. No one moved, unsure what to do. Suddenly a singing voice arose. It did not come from Cali Sky. It did not even come from the stage.

It came from the audience. Taking a cue from Cali Sky's last utterance one of the girls in the front row burst into song.

"I'll stop the world and melt with you.

You've seen the difference and it's getting better all the time."

Her off-key voice was quiet, but in the silence of the audience's panic, it carried into the distance. The voice bore no trace of self-consciousness. The girl was either insensitive, inspired or drunk. Those who heard it—nearly everyone near the front of the stage—looked uncomfortable. Whispered questions traveled between those beyond earshot: "What was that?" "She was singing?" "Who is she?" The audience turned expectantly toward Cali Sky, awaiting her reaction.

She laughed. Like the singing voice her laughter was spontaneous, unencumbered by forethought or fear of consequences.

"'Melt with You.'" Cali Sky focused her attention on the girls in the front row. "Do you all know that song?"

They looked at each other, now self-conscious, smiling and laughing. They nodded in unison.

"Will you come up here and sing it with me?"

With little hesitation they jumped onstage, standing side-by-side with Cali Sky. As they did so Cali Sky probed some chords, trying to remember the song. Zoe had put it on a mix tape, sandwiched between Depeche Mode's "Just Can't Get Enough" and Echo and the Bunnymen's "Gods Will Be Gods." Cali Sky and Brodie had played a rendition of the song—both on acoustic guitars—at a party at Zoe's house a few months before.

"Okay, I think that's it.... Ready?"

The front-row girls nodded and laughed. The song mostly makes use of only two chords. Cali Sky strummed them quickly, her right hand blurred in motion, slowing down occasionally to play the riff that gives texture to the song. The front-row girls crowded with Cali Sky around the mic.

"Moving forward using all my breath."

They laughed and danced. Cali Sky backed away and let them cover the vocals. They nearly shouted the next line, moving their bodies suggestively:

"Making love to you was never second best."

Catcalls from the male members of the audience. Brodie laughed and howled. Even Tam smiled, a smile replicated on the face of Trish. Zoe's eyes sparkled when she made eye contact with Cali Sky. Stone's body succumbed to a Native American tribal dance. By the time Cali Sky and the front-row girls reached the chorus, everyone in the coffee house was singing:

"I'll stop the world and melt with you."

Cali Sky helped the front-row girls through the bridge, where the song slows down:

"The future's open wide."

Then came a cappella humming. Cali Sky extended this part of the song an additional measure. The tune was easy to pick up, so that Philip and Joan, who were the only two in the room who did not know the song, could join along.

"Mmmmm mmmm mmmm

Mmmmm mmmm mmmm mmmm."

The sound of sixty-five people humming produced considerable noise. When Cali Sky brought them back into the chorus, enthusiastically strumming the chords with a frenetic right hand, delirium spread. The front-row girls were shouting again, too frenzied merely to sing. They gleefully butchered the song, transforming Modern English into middle American youth. Cali Sky gradually slowed the song down, pulling hard on the reins, until it finally halted.

The front-row girls hugged her as the audience applauded. She thanked everyone for coming out. She set her guitar on the stand and tucked a few sweaty strands of loose hair behind her ears. Before she had a chance to step down from the stage Brodie accosted her.

"Great set! Listen, I need to introduce you to someone, someone who really wants to start a band with us. He is an incredible musician. I'll be right back so you can meet him."

"Brodie, what are you..."

Brodie disappeared into the crowd before she could finish her sentence. She stepped down from the stage, took two steps and found herself standing face to face with Ben.

He spoke in a voice so nervous that his words were slurred: "Tha' 's 'credible."

"I'm sorry?"

A flash of embarrassment spread across his face, then he tried to laugh it off. "I said, That was incredible."

"Oh, thanks."

He awkwardly put his hands in the pockets of his rolled-up jeans. He wore a white Banana Republic t-shirt that had a world map printed on the front.

"Um," he stammered again. He forced himself to look into her eyes. "Did you get my note?"

"Yeah...yeah, I did."

"I took the words from the song you always play. 'Gloria.'"

"Yeah...that was cool."

Cali Sky noticed that her dad had approached. He was standing just beyond Ben, waiting to talk to her.

"I've..." Ben hesitated, noticing that Cali Sky was distracted. "I've been to most of your concerts here."

"Really?" Cali Sky now focused her attention back on Ben, appearing surprised and flattered. "I don't think I've ever seen you."

"Well, I usually stand in the back..." Ben began.

But Cali Sky was once again distracted by her dad's presence.

"Listen," she said, "I need to talk to my dad for a second. Okay?"

"Yeah sure..."

She stepped away from Ben before he could finish. She now stood face to face with her dad.

"Thanks for the song," he said.

"You're welcome."

"It sounded good, even better than I remembered it."

"A car doesn't make up for anything."

Cali Sky sounded angrier than she meant. But the expression of patient love on Philip's face was unperturbed.

He replied with no hesitation, "It wasn't intended to."

"But thank you," she added.

"You're welcome. It's hard to believe you're nearly finished with high school. Then college. You're right—it's all happened so fast. I also sometimes wish I could stop the world."

Ben finally walked away. Brodie reappeared with Tam and Trish at his side, standing just beyond Philip.

"Your music career seems to be going well," Philip continued.

"I wouldn't exactly call it a career."

"You could make it one if you chose."

"I don't know. Maybe. I suppose you could pray about it."

Philip once again seemed unfazed by Cali Sky's tone.

"I will," he replied. "I tell Desiree about you all the time."

Cali Sky could see that Brodie looked impatient. She nodded in his direction.

Philip turned around and said hello to Brodie. He then turned back to his daughter.

"Could we get together and talk sometime?"

She repositioned a few strands of hair behind her ear and answered after a moment's thoughtfulness, "Not yet."

Philip nodded, offered her a smile that appeared both pained and patient, and walked away. Brodie stepped forward into Philip's vacated space, ushering Tam and Trish along.

"Cali Sky," he began, "this is Tam."

Cali Sky and Tam nodded at each other stiffly.

"And this is Tam's girlfriend Trish."

Cali Sky and Trish smiled at each other suspiciously. No one else said a word.

Brodie intervened: "Yeah...well... I introduced you two because I think we have the next great California band right here." He addressed Cali Sky, "Tam here used to be in a group called Forest Murmurs. He's an awesome guitar play and keyboardist." He addressed Tam, "And Cali Sky not only plays guitar and sings, as you have just witnessed, she also plays keyboard."

No one else said a word.

"So...how about we set something up?" Brodie asked.

Still no one else said a word.

"*Cali Sky*," exclaimed Brodie, looking unusually flustered, "what do you think?"

"What do I think? I've only just met him. I've never even heard him play an instrument. What *should* I think?'"

"I'll play you one of Forest Murmurs' demos," Brodie replied, trying desperately to bring everyone together inside his net of intimacy. "Trust me, your mind will be blown!"

Cali Sky grew impatient with Brodie when she saw Zoe standing beyond Trish, waiting to talk.

Brodie looked with panic at Tam, then said to Cali Sky, "So when do you want to get together and jam?"

Tam intervened, "You said *she* wants to start a band with *me*."

"She does," Brodie lied. "Cali Sky?"

"I don't know, Brodie. We'll see." She smiled at Zoe, then addressed Brodie, Tam and Trish with aloof formality, "Excuse me, I need to talk with Zoe. Nice to meet you both."

As Cali Sky walked away Tam turned on his heels and headed swiftly toward the door. Trish seemed to read his mind; she mirrored his movements step by step. Brodie followed behind them both, pleading with desperate words drowned out by the coffeehouse chatter.

"What was that all about?" asked Zoe.

"I'm not sure," Cali Sky answered. "Brodie introduces me to this guy who supposedly wants to start a band with me. I don't even know him."

"Tam? Oh my God, Cali Sky, he used to be in this band, Forest Murmurs—they were amazing!"

"Yeah, that's what Brodie said."

"Their music was…enchanting. They actually influenced me as a photographer."

"Really?"

"Yeah. I went to high school with Tam…actually used to have a crush on him."

"You did?" Cali Sky's eyes grew big. "Well, he has a girlfriend now, some girl I've seen around school. It looks like she follows him around like a puppy."

"He bought some of my photographs."

"Really? How many?"

"Ten."

"No way."

"He paid full price."

"Oh my God. How much is that?"

"Five hundred bucks."

"No way!"

"Dinner is on me tonight."

Zoe began dismantling her photograph displays. Cali Sky unplugged her guitar and wound up the chord, looking distracted. She turned to Zoe: "So you heard this guy's band play before?"

"Yeah, they really were good."

"What's his name again?"

"Tam."

When she unlocked and opened the door of the apartment Cali Sky found her mom, wearing pajamas, talking on the phone.

"Okay. We'll see. We'll see. If you're lucky. Listen, my daughter just got home. Gotta go. Okay. Bye."

"Who was that?" asked Cali Sky.

Joan looked mischievous. "A guy."

"What guy?"

"*A* guy. Brodie called three times while you were gone. You better call him back."

Cali Sky looked suspiciously at her mom. She placed a brown paper bag on the kitchen counter. "Um, okay. I brought you home some leftovers. Zoe and I had Chinese for dinner."

She reentered the family room and sat on the couch next to her mom. "What guy?"

"A guy from work."

"Did he ask you out?"

"Yeah."

"What did you say?"

"We'll see."

"Why? I mean, why didn't you say yes?"

"I don't think he's my type—just like all the others."

"What others?"

"The others who have asked me out."

"Others have asked you out?"

Joan's smiled revealed arrogance and mischief. "Yeah."

"Why didn't you tell me?"

"Well, we haven't exactly had an open line of communication the past few months."

"So what are these guys like?"

"Shouldn't you call Brodie?" Joan now looked coy. She handed Cali Sky the phone. Cali Sky smiled and dialed Brodie's number. Joan remained seated, braiding and unbraiding Cali Sky's hair.

"Hey Brodie."

"Okay," he replied. "This won't sound great over the phone, but it will at least give you an idea."

Cali Sky could hear Brodie cueing up the demo tape.

"Are you ready?" he asked.

"Just play it, Brodie."

Cali Sky felt relaxed, eyelids half closed, as her mom undid a braid. She could hear Brodie fumbling on the other end of the line.

"Are you still ready?" he asked.

"Just play it, Brodie," she murmured.

She heard rich keyboard notes. They sounded spacey, otherworldly. A guitar entered. She detected the use of an echo unit, reverberating the guitar notes around the mesmerizing atmosphere generated by the keyboards. It was a soundscape unlike anything Cali Sky had heard. The intro sped up, drums entered and the vocals narrated the creation of an alternative universe, sky painted gold, oceans shimmering in the reflected light. The echoes of the ocean surf slowly disappear. The narrator reaches out for the reflected light but is cut short by the chorus, which tells of the universe being painted all over again. With each verse the narrator nearly reaches the light but is stopped by the chorus, which recreates painted universes that the narrator can never fully enter. The song concludes with evocative cries of the vocalist, whose longings remain unsatisfied.

"Well?" Brodie stopped the tape.

The combination of the song and her mom playing with her hair had a narcotic effect.

"Cali Sky?"

"I like the song. Very much."

"I knew you would."

Brodie waited futilely for a response.

"Cali Sky?"

"What?"

"What's wrong with you? Are you high or something?"

She laughed. "No, my mom is playing with my hair."

"Lucky her. So should I set something up? We could meet at Tam's house."

"I don't know, Brodie. We'll see."

"We'll see? Come on, Cali Sky. Please!"

"Are you begging?"

"Yeah, I'm begging."

"We'll see." She hung up the phone and set it on the floor. She lay down with her head in her mom's lap. The apartment was silent.

"What do you think, Mom? Should I meet up with Brodie's friend about maybe starting a band?"

"Why not? What do you have to lose?"

"Yeah, you're probably right. So how many guys have asked you out?"

"I don't know, three or four."

"Do you want to know what I think?"

"No." A tone of teenage defiance inflected Joan's voice. Cali Sky smiled with her eyes closed.

Cali Sky and Brodie were absorbed into a world of white nothingness. They lay on a bed that resembled an unpainted canvas. A universe of potential. She took his hand. He stroked hers. He fondled her forearm, then slid his hand up to her shoulder. She ran her fingers through his hair. Then they were naked. They drew close. As they did so the canvas upon which they lay burst into color.

But she was no longer herself. She was her mom. They kissed. Colors now leapt off the canvas and into the atmosphere around them. She felt his warmth through her mom's body. They rolled over so that she was on top. She sat up. His hands glided down her mom's body, from her shoulders, across her breasts, and to her hips. But she felt it and closed her eyes.

Then a phone rang. She picked it up.

"Hello?"

"This is Brodie."

"Brodie? But..."

"I can't believe you are doing this."

"Doing what?"

"You know what you're doing. You're doing it right now."

She looked at the Brodie lying between her legs. He had no connection to the Brodie on the phone, the Brodie who was now incensed and jealous.

"How could you do this?" he cried.

"But Brodie..."

"How could you do this?"

"But I'm..."

"How could you do this?"

The repeated question jarred her awake.

TEN

CALI SKY GOT off the Santa Ana Freeway at Red Hill Avenue. Brodie, who sat in the passenger seat, told her to follow it all the way to the top. The route brought back memories: she, Cami, and her dad, in the orange Ford Bronco, on their way to higher ground so that they could watch the Disneyland fireworks show. Brodie rolled down his window. The warm humid air filled the car, overwhelming the air conditioning. Cali Sky rolled down her window. Her unkempt hair intermittently whipped around her face. It was mid-morning but already the sun had scorched away most of the marine layer. Coming to a stop at a traffic light, they felt in the sudden stillness the warmth of the sun on their forearms. The Forest Murmurs demo played in the deck. Brodie glanced at Cali Sky nervously. He took a deep breath.

"So when we get there, just be cool, okay?"

Cali Sky's face brightened. She was pleased by Brodie's uneasiness. "Of course, Brodie. Why wouldn't I?"

"You know what I mean."

"No, I don't."

"Yes you do. When you get a guitar in your hands."

"What?"

"Or when you're behind a piano…or a keyboard."

"What?"

Brodie looked exasperated. "Just don't fuck this up, okay?"

"Wow, Brodie. I've never seen you like this. You're really taking this seriously. Imagine that: Brodie taking something seriously."

"Yeah, well, not all of us are going to college."

Cali Sky looked closely at Brodie, trying to read his expression before returning her eyes to the road.

"So what does Tam do?" she asked. "Does *he* go to college?"

"He goes to some art school."

Cali Sky laughed and said, "How cliché."

"What do you mean?"

"Clapton, Bowie, Pete Townshend, Keith Richards, Jeff Beck, pretty much all of Pink Floyd—they all went to art school. Every musician has to go to art school."

"See! That's what I mean!"

"What?"

"Please don't fuck this up."

Cali Sky laughed again. "So how'd you meet him?"

Brodie answered sheepishly, "I tried to pick up his girlfriend."

"Jesus, Brodie. Doesn't that get old?"

Brodie shrugged. "Why, are you jealous? Anyway, it's cool. Music comes first."

"Yeah."

"Why do you say it like that?"

Cali Sky flashed him an insincere expression of innocence.

"I'm better than you think, Cali Sky. You don't realize how much I practice the bass."

As the road became steeper the houses became more expensive, the neighborhoods safer, and the stores more upscale.

Brodie pointed Cali Sky down a narrow, even steeper lane. Mansions, no longer houses, lay sprawled on the either side of the hill, privacy protected by orange and avocado trees, security cameras and perimeter fences. They pulled into a driveway barricaded by a gate. Cali Sky eased up to the call box and pushed a button.

"Yes," spoke a strongly accented female voice through the intercom.

"We're here to see Tam. My name is Cali Sky. I'm with Brodie."

The call box beeped and the gates slowly swung open. She parked behind a late-model Volvo with a Cocteau Twins sticker on the back. A new-model Mercedes was parked on the other side of the driveway. Every door of the three-car garage was closed.

"The driveway is bigger than our apartment," remarked Cali Sky as she turned off the ignition.

Walking toward the mansion's ten-foot double doors she detected an unusual noise that she could not quite pinpoint. At first she thought it was the sound of birdsong, but then recalled she also heard chirping birds from her own bedroom down in the valley. Then she realized it was not a *sound* that was odd, it was the *absence* of a sound that seemed abnormal. She heard no traffic noise, the ubiquitous humming of southern California.

Near the front porch she peeked around a side gate. She could see a small patch of the backyard, consisting of an expanse of impeccably manicured lawn. Beyond the lawn was the view that quadrupled the value of every home in the neighborhood: Tustin, Irvine, Santa Ana, Orange. If it weren't for the California haze she might have caught a glimpse of the Pacific and even the LA skyline. She concluded that the far edges of the backyard descended precipitously, for the lawn seemed to hang in the sky.

Brodie placed his bass on the front step and pushed the doorbell. Chimes echoed inside the house. Cali Sky set her guitar and amp down. She had still not heard a car since they arrived. The fragrant smell of jasmine wafted in the spring breeze. Just then the door slowly swung open. A Mexican woman smiled at them.

"Come eeen."

The floors were marble. Cali Sky looked up at the twenty-feet-high ceiling. A grand piano stood in the center of the plush, white-carpeted living room.

"Follow me," said the Mexican woman.

Walking through the living room Cali Sky got a better look at the backyard. She saw a veritable canyon wall with a waterslide zig-zagging around rocks, winding toward the pool. A waterfall descended from the top of the rock formation, half concealing what appeared to be a cave or grotto.

"Theees way."

They followed the Mexican woman up the stairs. When they reached the top Cali Sky heard music. She and Brodie both recognized the song: the Cure's "Let's Go to Bed." They passed a grandfather clock. Cali Sky now had an eye-level view of the crystal chandelier cascading from the ceiling. The sunlight, filtered through high-hanging windows, cast a lazy warmth on the living room below. The music became louder. The Mexican woman knocked on a closed door.

"Enter!"

She swung it open, smiled at Cali Sky and Brodie, and walked quietly back down the hall. Stepping into Tam's room Cali Sky felt like she entered a different house. Black curtains blocked out the sun save for slivers of light at the edges of the windows. A single lamp provided what little light there was. Cali Sky waited for her eyes to adjust to the darkness. When they did she saw a Bauhaus poster in the center of the wall. It was flanked by two prints, one of Goya's *May 3 1808*, the other of Gericault's *The Raft of the Medusa*. At the top of the wall was an Echo and the Bunnymen poster upon which were written the words "Heaven Up Here," the band standing in silhouette on a beach at sunset. Cali Sky's eyes continued to acclimate.

Tam and Trish were seated on a black leather couch opposite the bed. They sat so close that, in the dusky light, Cali Sky could not see where he ended and she began. They remained motionless and mute as Cali Sky and Brodie settled into the room. The Cure song was building toward the climax of its eponymous title. Brodie began unfurling his net of intimacy. He danced whimsically, lip syncing the song.

"And I won't play it if you won't play it first."

He sang the next line to Cali Sky:

"Let's...go to bed."

Cali Sky rolled her eyes and pushed his beckoning finger out of her face. She had seen this sort of act before. It was one of Brodie's roles, the goofball charmer.

"Do you know why Robert Smith wrote this song?" asked Tam, still motionless with Trish at his side.

"To get laid?" offered Brodie.

Tam scowled. "He isn't a simpleton."

Brodie looked slightly embarrassed. "No, why?"

"After the band released their album *Pornography*, their producer wanted to make them into a pop band. Robert Smith hated the idea. So he decided to kill the band by writing the most ridiculous pop song he could. Take the premise of every pop song— you have a pretty face, you make my heart beat fast, I want to make you mine, I love you. He boiled that premise down to its essence, to what every pop-song artist is ultimately singing about: Let's fuck. He wrote 'Let's Go to Bed.' He wasn't just trying to destroy his band, he was trying to destroy a whole genre of music. Except it backfired. He failed...or succeeded, depending upon how you look at it. No one understood the irony of the song, and it became a hit."

"That's hilarious!" exclaimed Brodie.

Cali Sky suddenly felt disgusted and fought off an urge to pick up her guitar and amp and leave. "Hilarious...or tragic?"

Brodie once again looked slightly embarrassed, searching Cali Sky's face. Tam merely smiled. Trish sat silent.

Cali Sky looked more closely around the room. She saw keyboards in one corner of the room. On the other side was Tam's guitar and amp. She noticed the distortion and flanger pedals. But what held her attention was the Memory Man, an echo unit that U2's guitar player, the Edge, used. She thought about the U2 songs that created walls of sound with just one guitar—thanks to this device.

"You live in a mansion, Tam," Brodie said.

No reply. Cali Sky scanned the books on Tam's nightstand: Sartre and Camus volumes sat atop the Bible.

"What does your dad do?" Brodie asked.

"He's a businessman."

Pinned to the wall above the nightstand was what appeared to be a menu flier. Cali Sky folded back the front page to read the cover. It said, "How to get into hell." She turned the page. There was nothing inside—no words, no pictures.

"What *is* this?" asked Cali Sky.

"It's a Bible tract," Tam answered.

"Why do you have it pinned to your wall?"

"Because I find it to be...hilarious and tragic. Do you get it? Do nothing and you go to hell."

"Yeah I get it."

"How 'bout we play some music?" Brodie announced suddenly.

Tam rose from the couch, making Trish appear lost and pitiful.

Brodie pulled his bass from its case.

"So you play?" asked Tam.

"Yeah, I play."

Cali Sky brought out her guitar and other equipment. She set her wah-wah pedal off to the side. Tam noticed it.

"Yeah," he said derisively, "I don't really play Jimi Hendrix."

Cali Sky stopped and glared at him. "You don't, or you *can't.*"

Tam smiled. All three now had instruments hanging from their necks.

"What will it be?" asked Brodie.

Tam answered without hesitation: "'Bela Lugosi's Dead.'"

"Sounds good to me. Cali Sky, what do you think?"

"He's got the poster above his bed. We might as well play Bauhaus."

"Key of D, right?" asked Brodie.

Tam nodded. Cali Sky looked with surprise at Brodie, who began playing the descending bass line. Tam fiddled with his effects box and managed to get his guitar to produce ethereal, haunting sounds. Cali Sky, who lacked Tam's sophisticated equipment, had to be imaginative. She found notes and created riffs consonant with the Gothic music. After a few measures they loosened up and experimented. Tam walked to the keyboards, disentangling his amp chord along the way. He rotated his guitar around his body to free his arms and hands, which he brought down upon the keypad. He played a measure of atmospherics and sound effects. He then looped the measure so that it played continuously. He had created a sonic landscape underneath the jam. Noise whirled around the room. Slowly the song changed. It no longer resembled "Bela Lugosi's Dead." Tam's guitar no longer sounded like a guitar. Cali Sky coaxed preternatural whines and screams from her instrument. Brodie's bass pulled the bottom out of the jam, forcing it to reconstitute itself.

He watched as Cali Sky walked over to Tam, yelling something in his ear. Tam nodded and followed her to the keyboards.

He disengaged the loop. Cali Sky spun her guitar around and played the keyboards. The jam once again transformed.

The familiar sensation descended on Cali Sky: experience stripped of self-awareness. The room disappeared. There was only sound, as if all of her senses developed the capacity to hear. But these were unfamiliar sounds. She had never created music like this before.

Twenty minutes later Tam rejoined Trish on the couch, though she did nothing to acknowledge his presence. Brodie sat on the bed. Cali Sky found a seat on a stool near Tam's guitar equipment.

"So you obviously play keyboard too," Tam observed.

"Piano is my first instrument."

"You play all kinds of music, don't you?"

"I can, but I have my own style."

"And what's that?"

"You were at my gig. You heard it yourself."

"Okay. How would you describe it?"

Cali Sky paused. Her eye caught the Bible tract and then took in the Bauhaus poster. She shrugged.

Tam pressed her. "If you had to describe your style in one word, what would it be?"

"Aggression."

Tam nodded. "What about that song you dedicated to your dad?"

"That was an exception. You have no idea who originally wrote that song, do you?"

"No. None. It's not my style. But the other songs you played that night, they *are* my style. What we just played—*that's* my style."

"And what would you call it? In one word?"

Tam replied instantly. "Subversive."

"Aggression. Subversive. What do you get when you mix the two?"

Brodie butted in. "Our new band!"

Tam ignored him and spoke directly to Cali Sky: "I could make music with you."

Brodie butted in again. "You mean us."

"No, I mean her and me."

"What the hell?" shouted Brodie. "I set this whole thing up, man!"

"I told you before: Don't call me man," Tam replied.

This time Cali Sky did the interrupting. "If Brodie's not in, then neither am I."

"Fine. Then we're done here. Bye." Tam looked the other way.

Cali Sky began to pack up her things. Brodie stood in shock, staring at Tam.

Then for the first time Trish spoke. Her voice was soft, yet assertive. "You sounded good together...all three of you."

Tam turned to face her. Love and compassion lit his face. Cali Sky thought he was going to kiss her. Instead he smiled and said, "Okay. We need a drummer."

The tension fled Brodie's body. He said gleefully, "I know of someone."

"Who?" asked Tam and Cali Sky simultaneously.

"Nobody you know, trust me."

"Why?"

"He's in a band right now that doesn't exactly play the sort of music that either of you listens to. But he wants to change musical directions."

Tam and Cali Sky looked at each other uncertainly.

Brodie continued, "They're playing a gig this weekend in Hollywood. Let's check them out."

Cali Sky squeezed through the noisy hallway crowd. Friday afternoon in spring—she felt like school was irrelevant. Seniors had escalated their pranks and high jinx. The previous day two cars in the senior row of the parking lot were completely wrapped in toilet paper. The week before someone had vandalized the school sign, changing "Red Hill High School" into "Bed Thrill High School." *Two more months and I'll be out of here*, thought Cali Sky.

She entered Ms. Gibbon's Spanish class. Most of the students were already seated. Three student-council girls stood gossiping in the corner. Cali Sky took one of the few remaining desks not far from them. On the other side of the room she saw Ben, looking nervous. He was staring down at his desk. The conversation taking place nearby distracted her.

"What school does he go to?" asked Hilary.

"I don't know," replied one of the other student-council girls. Cali Sky could overhear the whole conversation.

"How do I find out?"

Cali Sky tried to tune out their discussion.

"She used to be in his band. She'd know."

Now Cali Sky knew they were talking about her. She could not make out the whispering that followed. She tried to ignore it but then their voices rose again.

"I heard he's an asshole."

"Really? But he's so hot," said Hilary.

"Ask her about him."

"Cali Sky," began Hilary. But just then the bell rang.

Ms. Gibbon closed her classroom door, looking miserable as always.

"Let's talk after class," Hilary said to Cali Sky, who ignored her.

Ms. Gibbon looked like she was about to cry. Cali Sky heard that she broke down during one class earlier in the year and ran out of the room weeping. They had a substitute for three days after the alleged event. The only time Ms. Gibbon did not look utterly miserable was when she played Spanish music, which was most of class. At first Cali Sky thought that Ms. Gibbon truly believed that English-speaking students could learn Spanish by listening to "La Bamba," "Don Gato" and "El Pipiripau" for fifty minutes every day. But then Cali Sky realized that Ms. Gibbon was doing it for herself, fending off depression by drowning in Latin music.

She walked to the tape player.

"Now sing along. Sing along!"

Ms. Gibbon's depression turned to fury if students did not join in the lyrics. She singled out the silent ones, standing directly in front of their desks, gesturing madly with pointed fingers, aiming them at her ears and then the lyrics sheet, until the dumb student joined in. In the end Ms. Gibbon's voice rose above the vague murmuring of the students, which may or may not have been singing and which may or may not have been Spanish.

Ms. Gibbon pressed play. But instead of a Spanish guitar or electric piano, the speakers produced at full volume Modern English. It was "Melt with You," cued at the beginning of the chorus.

"I'll stop the world and melt with you."

Cali Sky thought of her gig and her between-songs confession. The class erupted in laughter. Ms. Gibbon quickly pushed stop.

"Who did this?" she demanded.

Everyone looked at the likely suspects. But not Cali Sky. When she looked at Ben, she found that he was already staring back at her. He smiled faintly, mischievously. She laughed. Ms. Gibbon noticed.

"Was it you?"

"No."

Ms. Gibbon stared at her suspiciously.

Hilary whispered to one of the council girls.

"What? What did you say?" Ms. Gibbon pointed to Hilary.

"Nothing."

"Yes. Yes you did. What did you say?"

Although she was the interrogator Ms. Gibbon looked uncomfortable. Hilary appeared relaxed and defiant, in control of the situation.

"Do you really want to know?" asked Hilary.

"Yes. Tell me."

"Are you sure?"

"How dare you? Yes!" Ms. Gibbon had tears in her eyes.

"I said that I would much rather listen to that song then all the Spanish songs you play."

Ms. Gibbon's tears were angry. "I'm sending you to the office!" she screamed.

"For what? Because I don't like your music? You can't write me up for that!"

And Ms. Gibbon knew Hilary was right. She crushed the referral slip into a ball and threw it into the trash can. After the bell rang Ms. Gibbon collapsed into a heartbroken heap into her chair. Ben slowly gathered up his folders and made his way to the classroom door, glancing back shyly at Cali Sky. She joined him as they entered the hallway.

"Thank you. I can't believe you did that," she said.

"Did what?" he said with feigned ignorance.

She suddenly felt a twinge of nervousness.

"Yes," she said.

"Yes?"

"Yes I'll go to the prom with you."

He smiled with a blush, opened his mouth to say something, then blushed some more. He became skittish.

"That's great," he said finally, walking away. "That's great. Thank you!"

As he disappeared into the crowded hallway, Hilary approached.

"Cali Sky. Hey. Lame class, huh? Except for the little trick on Gibbon. Did you do that?"

Cali Sky turned and faced Hilary. "Yes. No. Maybe."

Hilary gave Cali Sky an expression that said, 'You're a weirdo.'

"Yeah, well, anyway. Do you know John Lanza?"

"Yeah, I know him. I mean, I used to know him. We don't really talk anymore."

"I saw his band play last weekend. I'd like to meet him. Do you think you could, like, introduce us?"

"Sorry, Hilary. Like I said, he and I don't really talk anymore."

Brodie approached with a swagger, a Pee Chee folder and never-opened textbook tucked behind his right hand.

"Ask him," Cali Sky gestured toward Brodie. "He'll hook you two up."

"Ask me what?"

"You know John Lanza?" Hilary looked like she was loving this: the thrill of pursuing a guy, the excitement of sharing her pursuit with others.

"Yeah, I know him," he said. "You wanna meet him?"

"Yeah."

"Add him to your collection?"

"Don't be an asshole, Brodie."

"You'll make a good groupie."

"Up yours, Brodie!" Hilary began to walk away.

"Take it easy, Hil. I'll call him. Tell him about you. See if he's interested. Then I'll get back to you."

"I forgot, what's the name of his band?"

"Nowhere."

Cali Sky butted in: "As in, his band is going nowhere."

Hilary now gave her a look that said, 'You're a loser.'

"You know," she said, "I overheard your conversation with Ben. Are you seriously going to prom with him?"

Before Cali Sky could respond Hilary began to walk away. "Thanks, Brodie!" she gushed flirtatiously over her shoulder. She blew him a kiss.

Brodie turned to Cali Sky and asked, "You're going to the prom with who?"

"Nobody you know.... God I hate her. She and John will make a perfect miserable match."

"No wait. *Who* are you going to the prom with?"

"I told you, nobody you know. So what time is Tam picking us up tonight?"

"Seven. Just tell me his name."

Cali Sky had already begun walking away. In mock Hilary fashion, she blew Brodie a kiss.

The late-model Volvo pulled onto the Santa Ana Freeway. It merged into Friday rush-hour traffic. Brake lights flashed off and on in the hazy twilight. Inside the car the post-industrial electronica of the German band Kraftwerk traveled through the speakers. Tam sat calmly in the driver's seat, keeping a patient distance between himself and the vehicle in front of him. He seemed unflustered by the cars darting in and out of the lane ahead.

"How late will we be?" Cali Sky asked.

"We might miss the beginning of the show, but that's alright. We'll see enough," replied Tam as he eased the Volvo to a crawl.

"In southern California," he announced apropos of nothing, "you're rarely more than thirty feet away from another human being, even inside your car. Just look at all these people around us."

Cali Sky observed the expressionless face of the driver next to them. "They look unhappy."

"Do you think they really are?" asked Tam.

"How should I know? They seem incapable of feeling any emotion."

"Look at her," Brodie interrupted. "She's feeling something."

The girl in the car to their left was singing along to the radio. Brodie smiled and she smiled back.

"The younger they are, the happier they are," said Tam. "Just watch the people for the next ten miles. The younger people have not yet given up. The older people look like they have seen too much."

"Hope I die before I get old," Cali Sky recited.

Tam glanced in his rearview mirror. "What is that, Led Zeppelin?"

Cali Sky scowled, then lied, "Yeah."

"It's the Who, Tam," Brodie interjected impatiently. "You two are depressing. *You* sound like old people."

Traffic thinned as they reached the outskirts of Orange County. They remained silent until they approached LA.

"A few years ago I locked myself in my room for a week." Tam turned down Kraftwerk slightly. "Only came down to eat now and then. You want to know why I did that?"

"Why?"

"Because I wanted to experience loneliness. Just get away from all these people." Tam waved his hand across the gridlock. "I needed to be away from Trish as well. I wanted to see if loneliness would bring clarity. At the end of that week I almost committed suicide."

The car became silent again as Kraftwerk droned on.

"You know why I didn't? Because I couldn't. Even though I felt like there was really no reason to live, I wanted to continue living anyway."

"What about Trish?" asked Cali Sky.

"What about her?"

"Isn't she a reason to live?"

"Yes and no. I both hate and love love. It deceives you. At first it's just this outrageously powerful emotion. But then it becomes a need for security, something you can't live without, not something you want but something you need, like an addiction."

Trish seemed unperturbed by her boyfriend's candor. She remain focused on the road ahead

"What about music?" Cali Sky asked.

"I don't know. Music is different. Like love, it takes us out of ourselves. But unlike love it never really puts us back. Love is an emotion or need that has an object, it becomes comfortable with that object. Music triggers an emotion that has nowhere to go, it just consumes itself."

"It's like a desire for something, but you don't know what it is," offered Cali Sky.

"Yeah, or like a desire for a desire."

Cali Sky was about to mention the Blue Flower but by then they had exited the Hollywood Freeway and merged onto Santa Monica Boulevard. Traffic increased as they made their way into the heart of Hollywood. By the time they found a parking spot they were a half hour late for the show. Cali Sky gazed up and down Sunset and imagined her mom strolling along the avenue from club to club twenty years ago. She pictured her dad and Lester in the VW bus.

"What is this?" asked Tam.

Outside the Whisky a Go Go they saw a loitering crowd consisting of long-haired males in torn jeans smoking cigarettes. The females in the crowd wore tight-fitting leather pants and heavy makeup. They too smoked cigarettes. Their hair was indistinguishable from that of the males in the crowd, from length down to the abundant use of hairspray. The music that poured from the club was pure power chords and falsetto screaming.

Tam stopped and repeated his question. "What is this?"

"Just come on," Brodie encouraged.

Inside was Tam's worst nightmare: a mob of stoners rocking out to the predictable machismo of a three-chord heavy metal song.

"What is this?" Tam repeated once again, this time with a yell that could be heard over the din.

Brodie gathered them together and screamed, "Forget the band. Don't even listen to the band. Just focus on the guy in the back. That's our drummer. His name is Chris."

Aunt Nancy sat in her wheelchair, sipping a can of Coke from a straw. Cali Sky pulled a pin from the cheap bulletin board hanging on the wall, removed a flyer, and replaced it with another.

"There," she said as she sat back down on Aunt Nancy's bed.

Aunt Nancy read aloud. "That's Entertainment Productions presents...Nowhere..." She grimaced, then continued, "Cali Sky with Special Guests ?????... April 8th...$5 cover...Doors open at 7...show at 8."

Outside room number 9, down the hall, a belligerent old man yelled incoherently. Cali Sky could never get used to the sounds of the nursing home: the Alzheimer rants, the dementia-induced non sequiturs and occasionally a haunting scream or moan that evoked an existential crisis or the approach of hell. Aunt Nancy seemed able to ignore it.

"So the only difference between the two flyers are the words 'with Special Guests,'" she said.

"That's right," answered Cali Sky.

"Why are there five question marks?"

Cali Sky smiled. "I don't know. It's a *mystery.*"

She pushed play on the boombox. The Replacements' "Left of the Dial" sounded through the cheap speakers.

"What's wrong, Cali Sky?" asked Aunt Nancy. "You look distracted."

"I'm just not sure if I want to play gigs anymore. Sometimes I'm not sure if I want to play music at all."

"What are you talking about?"

A streak of despair appeared in Cali Sky's eyes as she looked up at Aunt Nancy and said, "Before Cami died... Before Cami died my music was inspired by the Blue Flower. Remember?"

Aunt Nancy nodded.

Cali Sky continued, "Mr. Nussbaum said that it was the source of all passion. But I don't feel that anymore."

A nurse walked by the open door of room number 9, barking orders to one of the nursing-home residents.

"Aunt Nancy, will I *ever* feel that again?"

"I don't know, Cali Sky."

Three figures walked side by side on the sidewalk near the gym. When they reached the bus pick-up area they slowed, shuffling their way through the crowd of students waiting their turn to file into the bus. A sense of after-school liberation settled on the crowd, generating a spirit of recklessness and volatility. The air smelled like sweat and rotting bananas. The three figures emerged on the other side of the crowd and returned to their side-by-side formation.

They drew a few curious looks, for one of the three seemed out of place. He walked uncomfortably on the right-hand side. With each step he looked like he wanted to stop and go the other way. He was dressed in Levi jeans and a white collared shirt with gray stripes: an ensemble his mom purchased when she took him clothes shopping over the summer at JC Penney. This was Ben.

On the other side walked Ben's polar opposite, Brodie. He moved with a swagger that made his surfer shag bounce around his forehead and eyes. He occasionally dropped behind the tandem formation to joke around with a jock or flirt with a girl.

In the middle was the bridge between the two: Cali Sky. She wore plain, brand-nameless clothes, yet she walked confidently. She acknowledged no acquaintances or friends, yet she was known. And she knew how she was known: a weirdo, but also a guitar goddess.

"So tell me again why we are meeting him on the basketball courts," she said to Brodie.

"He said he had to take care of something there."

"Take care of something? On the basketball courts? Like a drug deal?"

"No, nothing like that."

"Then what?"

"You'll see."

Brodie looked over at Ben, who remained silent. They neared the courts. When he wasn't joking, flirting or evading Cali Sky's questions, Brodie wondered what Cali Sky saw in Ben. He had been teasing her for days.

"Ben?" he had asked her incredulously. "You mean Ben the wallflower?"

"What do you care?"

"I don't. It's just that, he's so ordinary, so…boring. Unlike you. Unlike *me*. Seriously, what do you see in him?"

Cali Sky could have told him about the episode in Ms. Gibbon's Spanish class, about Ben's prank. She could have told him that no wallflower would do something as audacious as that. She could have told him that the prank was not only audacious, it was thoughtful, romantic even. Instead, she had merely said, "You wouldn't understand, Brodie." Brodie shrugged, trying to look cool.

Up ahead in the distance a crowd formed a circle near center court. Those on the periphery of the circle craned their necks, standing on tiptoe to see inside. A few jocks dribbled and passed a basketball, moving back and forth from the circle, where they pushed their way to the center, to the chain-netted rim, where they fed each other alley-oops and hung on the rim. They never seemed to cease laughing.

"What's going on?" asked Cali Sky.

"You'll see. Let's hurry up," replied Brodie.

Ben looked more uncomfortable than ever. He fell slightly behind as Brodie and Cali Sky increased their pace toward the circle, which grew denser with adolescents spanning the social hierarchy of Red Hill High.

Three skaters giggled their way to Brodie and said, "Dude, you'll never believe this. He's *sick!*"

Hilary was there with three other student-council girls. "That's *so* nasty!" they repeated as they looked around for someone cool and popular with whom to express their revulsion.

Two lineman from the football team started a chant. Their voices were deep and belligerent, causing their faces to turn red and the veins in their necks to bulge: "Do it! Do it! Do it!"

The outer circle consisted of those from Ben's caste: borderline nerds, wallflowers and wanna-be's. Their disgust and fascination were no less intense than the others, but they kept their reactions muted, not wanting to draw attention to themselves.

"Come on!" Brodie called to Cali Sky. He grabbed her arm and led her into the circle. She gave a what-can-I-do look to Ben, who remained with his sort outside the circle. Everyone was willing to let Brodie inside as he led a reluctant Cali Sky to the center of attention, the hub of the circle.

The first thing she noticed was a scattered pile of cash. She saw ones, fives, tens, and even a few twenties. The second thing she saw was translucent green blob, about six inches in diameter. She could see strands of mucus and saliva fizz. She quickly looked away, disgusted. Someone dropped a five on the cash pile, which stood about four feet from the green blob. The same person then hawked a loogie and spit it onto the green blob. It grew slightly.

"That's seventy-two bucks!" someone shouted.

The linemen's chant started up again: "Do it! Do it! Do it!"

All eyes were on a barrel-chested, thick-armed senior. He wore a black Ozzy Osbourne shirt and blue-suede Vans high tops. He paced back and forth, between the money pile and the green blob. He gestured toward the circle surrounding him, egging them on to cheer some more, like a veteran showman.

"Oh Jesus. Is that Chris?" Cali Sky looked ill.

Brodie smiled. "Just watch."

Chris approached the green blob like a weightlifter stepping up to a clean-and-jerk bar. As he kneeled down into a push-up position, the shouting from the circle drowned out the linemen's chant. The nearest spectators got on their hands and knees to get a better look. Pale faced, Cali Sky glanced at Brodie, who wore an expression of both delight and disgust. Hilary and the student-council crew covered their mouths and noses with their hands, looking as if they were about to cry, but unable to look away.

What happened next could only be observed by the spectators whose heads lay close to the black top, at nearly eye level with the green blob. They in fact signaled the performance of the deed by the sounds of their collective "Ohhhs!" and "Ewwws!" Those standing in the circle saw only the slightest movement of Chris's head. The shouts and groans became deafening.

Chris rose to his feet, mouth open. Facing the circle he emitted a barbarian roar while violently shaking his head, his now green and yellow tongue flopping back and forth like a putrified fish. Those standing closest could see the reconstituted texture of the loogie, now spilling over Chris's tongue. The linemen laughed raucously as the sound of groans doubled in volume. Cali Sky stopped watching altogether and walked away from the inner circle, searching for Ben.

Theatrically terminating his caveman yelp, Chris closed his mouth, preparing himself for the final deed of the dare. Before he had a chance however he gagged, hurling his entire body into an involuntary convulsion. The inner circle leaped back to avoid what seemed to be inevitable: a spew of vomit combined with the community loogie created by at least fifteen different people. Somehow Chris fought it off, regained his composure and to the disbelief of the horrified and fascinated onlookers smiled. An expression of intense concentration suddenly covered Chris's face. He drew back his head, bringing his chin toward the base of his neck. The inner circle once again jumped back, expecting the next gag to come to full fruition as an upchuck. But the crowd was deceived, for Chris had merely set in motion the first step of the swallowing process. His chin suddenly sprang forward, his Adam's apple quickly rose and fell: the loogie slithered down Chris's throat.

He rose his hands in triumph. The crowd cheered and groaned some more. He picked up the wad of cash and shook it in the air, then deposited it in his front pocket. The linemen congratulated him with hand slaps. Then as quickly as it had assembled, the crowd dispersed in groups of twos, threes, and fours, spreading out in sundry directions across the basketball black top, conversing gleefully about the spectacle they had just beheld.

Ben was visibly shaken. Cali Sky had found him standing well beyond the outer edges of the circle before the completion of the dare.

"Are you okay?" asked Cali Sky.

"Yeah."

She barely heard him. "Are you sure?"

He looked up at her and nodded, smiling feebly.

Just then Brodie joined them. "Chris! Chris! Over here!"

Chris approached slowly, acknowledging the expressions of revulsion and admiration from the last of those leaving the scene.

Brodie made the introduction: "Chris, Cali Sky. Cali Sky, Chris."

"That was real impressive," Cali Sky said unenthusiastically. "I don't think I'm going to eat for a week."

Brodie quickly changed the direction of the dialogue. "Yeah, well, Cali Sky and I saw you play last week. We liked what we heard and want you to join our band."

"No," interrupted Cali Sky warmly, "we want you to *try out* to join our band."

Brodie looked embarrassed.

Chris replied, "I'm cool with that. I can tell you right now, though, you won't find a better drummer than me."

"We *do* agree that you are a good drummer," explained Cali Sky, "at least based on what we heard. We're just not sure if your style of drumming works with our band."

"I'm sick of heavy metal."

Cali Sky looked quizzically at Chris's Ozzy Osbourne shirt. "Why?"

"Because it's limiting. Loud and fast—that's pretty much it."

"So what kind of music do you want to play?"

"Brodie mentioned you guys are kind of Gothic and New Wave. I can do that. Just as long as we don't do any top 40 bullshit."

"Okay," Cali Sky pressed, "but what kind of music do you *want* to play?"

Chris hesitated and looked around. They were now pretty

much alone, with Ben waiting in the background. "I want to play stuff that allows me to express myself…at least more fully than heavy metal."

Cali Sky glanced at the remnants of the green blob. "Heavy metal doesn't cover it?"

Chris answered with a smile, "No, I'm a sensitive guy."

"Obviously," laughed Cali Sky. She looked at Ben. "Well, we gotta go. See you tomorrow."

"Where are you going?" asked Brodie.

"Ben and I are going to study for the AP government exam."

"Are you serious?" mocked Brodie. "You're going to study?"

"Yeah, Brodie. Some of us are going to college."

"Whatever."

As they walked away Cali Sky overheard Chris ribbing Brodie: "Yeah, you dumb ass. They're going to college." Cali Sky looked back to see Chris give Brodie a playful shove.

"Who's the dumb ass?" she heard Brodie respond. "You just swallowed a pint of other people's snot."

Cali Sky and Ben walked to the parking lot and got into their respective cars. Cali Sky followed Ben to his house, a two-story cookie cutter in a recently refurbished development with clean gutters. A crew of joyless Mexican landscapers, all wearing long-sleeved brown shirts and panama hats, was in the midst of trimming lawns and hedges. The whine and hum of lawnmowers and blowers assaulted Cali Sky's ears the moment she opened her car door. The din faded the moment they stepped inside the house and closed the door behind them.

"Ben?" It was a maternal voice coming from upstairs.

"Yeah!" shouted Ben. "I'm home. I'm here with a friend."

A moment later an overweight woman carefully descended the stairs. She had no inclination to speak again until she reached the bottom of the stairs. Ben waited awkwardly. Cali Sky was amused.

"Hi, I'm Ben's mom. Sylvia." She formally extended a hand to Cali Sky. Cali Sky wondered how often Ben brought a friend—let alone a girl—home with him from school. With glowing maternal pride Sylvia seemed to be savoring a parental first: Ben's first word, Ben's first footsteps, Ben's first crush and now, Ben's first time bringing a girl to the house.

Cali Sky shook Sylvia's hand. "I'm Cali Sky. Nice to meet you."

"We're going to study for the AP government exam," Ben announced sheepishly.

"Great! You can have the downstairs. I'll be up here, folding clothes and whatnot. Can I get you anything? Something to drink? Something to eat?"

"No, Mom. I'll take care of it. Thanks, though." Ben became more embarrassed. "We'll just go into the living room."

"Okay." But Sylvia remained stationary.

"Alright," mumbled Ben, whose embarrassment seemed to converge with irritation. He began to shuffle toward the living room. "Okay. Well. Bye."

"Have fun! Or I mean, study hard!" Sylvia finally began to make her slow way back up the stairs.

Cali Sky followed Ben into the living room.

"So," he said, now looking relieved, "do you want something to drink?"

"Sure. Do you have any alcohol?"

"Um…"

"I'm kidding. A glass of water would be fine."

Before Cali Sky had a chance to sit down a stocky boxer came bounding through a doggie door tucked in the corner of the room. It noticed Cali Sky and began barking.

"Pet. Pet!" yelled Ben. "Shut up."

Cali Sky rubbed the dog's head. "Your dog's name is Pet?"

"Well, it's short for Petrarch."

"Your dog's name is Petrarch?"

"Yeah, my dad's part Italian and wanted an Italian name for the dog...or something."

Ben sat down on the opposite couch with two glasses of water. Cali Sky saw that Ben had hazel eyes. At the moment they appeared timid.

"So tell me about that prank you pulled in Ms. Gibbons' class. When did you change the tapes?" asked Cali Sky.

"Before class. I pretended like I was getting something out of my backpack for Ms. Gibbon."

"Didn't anyone see you make the change?"

"No, no one noticed it at all."

A *wallflower*, thought Cali Sky, remembering her earlier conversation with Brodie. *No one notices a wallflower.*

Cali Sky said, "Everyone thinks you're quiet and shy. But actually you're this devious jokester."

Ben laughed but as always averted his eyes. "No. I've never done anything like that before."

"So why'd you do it?"

The question appeared to be too direct for Ben. He blushed. "Well, I...you know...I thought...a nice thing to do."

Cali Sky put him out of his misery. "So what kind of music do you like?"

"Well, I like the kind of music you play at your shows."

Cali Sky seemed bored and impatient with that answer. "What else? What do you really like to listen to when you're at home?"

"I listen to a lot of classic rock."

"Yeah? Like what? What's in your stereo right now?"

"Um. The Steve Miller Band."

"Yeah? Can we listen to that now?"

"Really?"

"Yeah. A little study music."

A few moments later Ben came down with a tape of the Steve Miller Band's greatest hits. He put it into the family stereo, stored neatly below the family television, and pressed play.

"Would you like anything to eat?" asked Ben as he sat back down on the couch, opposite Cali Sky.

"No thanks."

She observed that he could not look her in the eyes—at least not for more than a second.

"So what are you in to?" she asked.

"What?"

"What are you in to? What do you like to do?"

"I don't know. Nothing much."

"Come on, Ben. You've got to have some interest. Some passion."

"Not really. I'm...I'm not really good at anything."

Cali Sky looked frustrated. She wanted to defend Ben from Brodie's accusations. *Show me something, Ben. Don't be a wallflower.*

"That's not what I mean," she said, annoyance evident in her voice. "I'm just asking what you like."

Cali Sky realized she was glaring at Ben. She felt angry. Angry at Brodie for being right and angry at Ben for *letting* Brodie be right. Ben looked up at her, this time without fear or intimidation. To her surprise Ben looked angry as well.

"I'm not like you!" he exclaimed. "I'm just ordinary. I'm not talented. I'm not like your friends. Your friends make fun of me."

"*I* don't make fun of you. And I defend you to my friends."

Ben could no longer return her stare. He muttered, "Maybe this is not going to work out. Maybe you should go."

"Are you serious?" Cali Sky stopped masking her anger and frustration. She gathered her belongings and rose from the couch.

"All I was asking is what you have a passion for." She walked toward the front door. Pet followed her.

Before she reached the hallway leading to the front door however Ben rose and exclaimed desperately, "I like to hike. To be outdoors. On the weekends, I hike up Mt. Baldy. Sometimes, I get up early and drive all the way to Arrowhead. I like it best when there's no one around—to be in the mountains by myself. I want to be a forest ranger someday. I know that all sounds stupid. But that's my passion. That's what I'm passionate about."

Cali Sky had turned around halfway through Ben's speech. Now she smiled, slowly walking back toward the couch. Before she could reply Ben continued.

"Before we moved to California we lived in New Mexico. On some weekends my dad would take me hiking through the Gila National Forest. It is *so* beautiful there."

On her way to the couch Cali Sky passed within five feet of Ben. His hazel eyes looked lighter. The anger in his voice was now barely perceptible as he said, "New Mexico is called the land of enchantment. You would know why if you saw what I've seen. I could show you a place on a mountaintop where the sky is huge, and you can see for miles, and it's so quiet because you're miles from civilization, and...." He stopped suddenly. Cali Sky was now seated on the couch.

She finished his sentence: "...and you feel this strong desire to become a part of all that beauty, like your soul belongs in the mountains and in the sky, but it's stuck in your body."

"Yeah. Something like that," murmured Ben.

"My dad used to take me hiking. I felt what you felt. That feeling used to inspire my music."

"Used to? It doesn't anymore?"

"No. Not really."

"Why not? What happened?"

"My sister died."

"Oh, I…"

"I just can't seem to feel it anymore."

"I'm sorry."

Cali Sky laughed. "Nothing kills a conversation like saying that your sister is dead."

"I didn't mean to bring it up…"

"No, it's not your fault. Don't be sorry. Besides it was worth it. At least I've learned something about you."

"Maybe we could go hiking sometime."

"I'd like that."

Ben reached for his glass of water. His movements were now relaxed and confident. As he returned the glass to the coaster he said, "Maybe we should do some studying now."

"You're probably right."

They pulled xeroxed handouts from their folders and opened a textbook with an image of the Founding Fathers on the cover. As they set up the material Cali Sky asked, "Ben, have you ever heard of something called the Blue Flower?"

The next day Cali Sky and Brodie drove up Red Hill Avenue once again to Tam's parents' house. This time they were followed by Chris in his Suzuki Jimny, into which he had packed with well-practiced dexterity his drum kit. Once again Brodie looked nervous.

"Please don't fuck this up, Cali Sky."

"You said that last time, Brodie. Did I fuck it up? If anything *I'm* the one who *prevented* it from getting fucked. Remember? Tam didn't even want you in the band."

Brodie winced. "I know, I know. You're right. I just really want this band to work out."

"Brodie, I'm going away to college. Even if it did work out, it wouldn't last long."

"Maybe if it works out, you won't *want* to go away to college."

"Not likely. Besides, you think in the next three months we're going to sign a recording contract and go on a world tour or something? We haven't even started a band yet."

"We will. And yes, we *will* become big."

Cali Sky looked in her rearview mirror and laughed. "If you're worried about someone fucking it up, you better be worried about the drummer you picked out for our band."

Once again the Mexican maid answered the door and led them up to Tam's room. Once again when they entered, Tam and Trish were seated on the couch as one. When Chris entered the room, he announced, "Fuckin' a, man. This house is the shits!" He wore a tight-fitting t-shirt that revealed his muscular upper body. Cali Sky laughed. Brodie looked nervously at Tam, who remained seated next to Trish.

"Alright," said Brodie, "Chris and I will go downstairs and bring up his drums."

As they descended the stairs, Cali Sky overheard Chris say to Brodie, "I wanna swim in that pool. Check that out!" His laughter echoed through the museum-like house.

"What a boor," said Tam, "He makes me feel relieved that I'm no longer in high school. Sophomoric idiot."

Cali Sky shrugged, "You agreed to give him a tryout."

"I doubt it will last long."

"What about your last band? Forest Murmurs? How did it all come together?"

Tam leaned back on the couch, folding his hands in his lap. "Brian and I had been playing together for years. We always knew we'd be in a band. We were kindred spirits. We could just read each other's mind musically. We were that close."

"Do you still talk to him? By phone? Or send letters to Ecuador?"

"No."

Tam became silent. Trish didn't move. Cali Sky looked around the room. Eventually the silence was broken by Chris's unrestrained laughter. Cali Sky could hear him and Brodie lumber up the stairs.

"Seriously," Chris was saying, "I want to swim in that pool."

Brodie entered the room with a cymbal tucked underneath an arm, a tom drum in one hand, and a snare drum in the other. Chris carried the bass drum loaded with cymbals and hardware.

"Just got to go back down and get my stool and the rest of the stands. You know how it is. Everyone has to wait for the drummer to set up." He laughed and left the room again.

"What have I gotten myself into?" asked Tam as he slouched down in the couch.

"Come on, Tam," Brodie replied, "Give him a chance. You know he's a good drummer."

"He's annoying. He has the mind of a thirteen-year-old. And the emotional range of a goat."

"No he doesn't. He's a sensitive guy." The words came out before Brodie realized what he was saying.

"A *sensitive* guy?"

"That's what he told us yesterday," Cali Sky said with a smile. "He wants a different musical outlet for his sensitivity."

Brodie glared at Cali Sky. Tam appeared ready to ridicule when Chris walked back into the room.

"That's everything. Where should I set up?"

Tam said, "Let's move the couch. You can set up in this corner."

Trish rose from the couch and walked catlike to Tam's bed. She sat demurely. As Chris helped Tam push the couch Tam said, "So Brodie tells me you're a sensitive guy." Chris gave the couch one final heave until it nudged the opposite corner. He straightened back up. His eyes suddenly looked wild and his body language dangerous.

All eyes were now on Chris. Even Trish surmounted her apparent reticence to see what Chris would do. But as quickly as the anger came to a boil behind Chris's eyes, it softened and vanished. He composed himself, looked at Tam, Cali Sky and Brodie, then said, "Yeah, that's right. I'm a fucking sensitive guy." Tam smirked. The irony—was it irony?—of Chris's affirmation pushed him off-balance.

"Well," Cali Sky, "then you'll balance things out, because I'm an insensitive girl who doesn't care about what kind of guy you are. Let's just play some music."

Brodie walked awkwardly to his bass. Tam stepped leisurely to one of his guitars. Chris sat down confidently on his drum stool. They tuned the guitars and bass, then adjusted sound levels.

"Okay," began Tam. "Let's warm up. Follow my lead. We'll start with E minor to C."

The jam began tentatively, each musician settling in to their instrument. As they loosened up, however, they took it in different directions, Cali Sky weaving into their improvisation licks that suggested new chord progressions, which Tam quickly seized and developed. Brodie felt more comfortable and began to experiment. Chris played harder, more dynamically.

Cali Sky contributed the sound and structure of blues-based rock and roll. Tam's contribution was rooted in European atmospherics and expressionism. Chris added percussion that gravitated toward heavy-metal flourishes but was longing for something more nuanced. Brodie adapted. His bass playing was minimalist, but occasionally Cali Sky heard him produce a run of lush octaves or a descending line that gave the jam a sense of movement.

Ten minutes later they stopped playing. Tam brought it to a halt. Brodie smiled with satisfaction. He looked at Cali Sky, then Tam. "Tell me that wasn't awesome," he gushed. But Tam ignored him. He took two steps toward the drum set and said to Chris, "You don't have to play so loud. You don't have to add a fill-in after every measure. And you don't have to play your bass drum so spastically. We're not Black Sabbath, or Metallica, or...what are those shitty bands called...White Snake...or whatever."

For the second time that afternoon all eyes were once again on Chris. Cali Sky anticipated a screaming match. Brodie thought he might have to break up a fight—or at least pull an enraged Chris off of a bloodied Tam. Instead Chris looked up at Tam respectfully, like a student eager to learn, and said, "You're right. I've been in heavy metal bands for a long time. Bad habits. Just give me more time."

No one, including Tam, expected such a humble and placid response. No one expected Chris to be so tractable.

Tam continued, looking back and forth from Chris to Brodie. "If I'm going to be in a band with you, you need to understand my musical philosophy. For me, every note matters. Or in your case," he gestured toward Chris, "every time you strike your barbaric instrument with a stick, it should have a specific purpose. When we write songs, every note, every cymbal crash *has* to be where it is."

Chris's expression did not change. He appeared calm, receptive to Tam's lecture. Trish re-crossed her legs on the bed, a look of deference appeared on her face as she gazed up at Tam and then back down at the floor. Cali Sky turned her back on the others, fingering some notes on the guitar fret, notes that winded this way and that, somehow becoming the opening riff to Bowie's "Rebel Rebel." Tam heard it and interrupted his own lecture.

He turned round impulsively. "Yeah, let's play that. You two know it?" he asked Brodie and Chris.

"Of course," replied Brodie.

"Yeah," Chris answered.

Tam brought the mic stand forward, into the center of the room. He plugged the mic chord into an amp. "There you go," he said to Cali Sky, "It's all yours."

Despite playing together for the first time, the band sounded tight, tighter than Nowhere ever sounded even after a dozen rehearsals. She realized that much of that had to do with Chris, his timing was perfect. His mistake-free drumming gave the band confidence. Brodie played the bass line cleanly. Tam filled out the chords and riffs with unexpected, creative notes that gave the song a big, rich sound. She took all of this in. Then she looked around at the others and experienced a sharp tug inside her chest. She had felt this before: when she listened to Aunt Nancy combine sincerity and sarcasm; the first time she heard the first Led Zeppelin album on vinyl; when, as a little girl, she watched her dad hike through the mountains; when Ben's face lit up as he described his experiences in the forest; when Mr. Nussbaum talked about the Blue Flower. It was a feeling of love and respect precariously possessed. It felt like admiration was dangerously balanced on a tightrope stretched across her heart.

She felt tears in her eyes. She turned away from the others. The tears came from wellsprings she had forgotten. She widened her eyes to give the tears room. She felt Tam's presence and looked at him. She discovered strong emotion in his pale face, emotion not unlike hers. They recognized in each other a shared experience. Cali Sky realized that she, like Tam, was on the verge of tears for the simple reason that four people were creating something that sounded so good. A sound that goes all the way to the source of emotion itself. Thirty minutes later the song ended. It felt like thirty seconds to Cali Sky. Trish looked up at Tam, beaming.

"Well," said Tam to her, "What did you think?"

"It sounded powerful," she answered.

Tam put his guitar on the stand, slowly pacing around the room. Brodie kept his bass around his neck, apparently wanting to play more. As Cali Sky placed her guitar on its stand, Tam asked her, "Well, the gig is in two nights. What about a set list? What do you think we should play?"

Cali Sky answered with an arrogance that spread to the others, "I don't think it really matters."

Chris was standing behind his drums, raising his shirt to wipe the sweat dripping from his face. "Dude, I'd *really* like to jump in your pool."

Tam sighed. "Alright, go ahead."

Chris exited the room with pent-up excitement and devious pleasure on his face.

"Well?" Brodie asked.

"He *is* a good drummer," said Tam. "And he *is* annoying."

"Most drummers are, right?" Brodie answered hopefully.

Tam sat down next to Trish without answering.

"What about you, Cali Sky?" asked Brodie. "What do *you* think?"

She smiled. "*I'd* pay money to hear us play."

Brodie laughed and finally put his instrument down, resigning himself to the fact that they would play no more for now. But Cali Sky's reply put him at ease. From his position alongside— and nearly on top of—Trish, Tam glanced furtively at Cali Sky, searching her face for something.

"Guys, you gotta come here and check this out," announced Brodie. He was standing outside Tam's bedroom, looking out of one of the massive windows at the pool area below. They all rose and joined Brodie on the hallway balcony.

Chris, wearing only his boxer underwear, was climbing the rock formation alongside the pool. At its apex, it stood about ten feet above the water. The apex was Chris's apparent destination. He had a muscular build above his stomach paunch. He was climbing on all fours, placing his hands and feet gingerly on the reddish-brown rocks.

"What an idiot," commented Tam.

The apex consisted of a narrow rock above the entrance to the slide, which twisted underneath the rocks and jutted out over the deep-end of the pool. Chris scurried up the rock formation until his feet were firmly planted on the apex. Then, with careful balance, he rose to his feet, spreading his arms for balance.

"Oh no," said Cali Sky.

To reach the pool Chris would have to jump far enough to miss the jutting slide and the rocks that surrounded it.

"Oh no."

"Don't do it, you idiot," Tam said with a soft dread in his voice.

In seeming slow motion Chris crouched into a spring position, then launched himself through the air. The onlookers held their breath. He cannonballed into the water, the back of his head narrowly missing the slide.

"Jesus," breathed Brodie.

"What an idiot," repeated Tam.

Trish, meanwhile, stood behind the three of them, laughing quietly.

ELEVEN

ZOE FUMBLED IN her purse and pulled her camera from its case. It was the perfect shot and she knew it. The setting sun was at her back, one of the two golden moments, she realized, for photographers: dawn and dusk. The band stood outside of That's Entertainment, waiting to carry their instruments around the side of the building into the back entrance of the stage. Above the spot where they stood was the marquee. The outdoor light had faded just enough for the backlit letters of the marquee to cast an ethereal glow. At the top it read "Nowhere." And below that, "Cali Sky and Special Guests ?????" Zoe framed the shot to exclude the word Nowhere.

She took five shots before the band even realized what she was doing. When she later developed them she discovered that the first of the five was the best. In it Brodie stands at the far left. His body is turned slightly as he gazes into the distance with his hand resting on the top of his bass case, propped upright on the sidewalk. Next to Brodie stands Cali Sky. She alone looks into the camera, unsmiling. She holds her guitar case in her right hand and wears a sleeveless dress. Her bare arms look white and soft, off-set by black hair cascading around her shoulders. Tam is on her left. He is staring down, looking simultaneously peeved and preoccupied, the expression of a temperamental artiste. His guitar case lies on the sidewalk next to him. Chris stands behind them all. One of his arms is blurred, in motion. He is apparently flicking a cigarette into the gutter, smoke floats around his head. He wears sunglasses that make it impossible to see where he is looking.

As Zoe returned her camera to her black purse that was nearly as big as a duffle bag, the dark-glass front door of That's opened and a man who appeared to be in his thirties stuck his head out. It was Jerry, owner of the nightclub. He wore a short-sleeve Polo shirt and brown Sperry topsiders with no socks. Cali Sky had surmised when she first met him years before that he was one of those who belonged to a new demographic that media pundits and late-night talk show hosts alike referred to as "yuppies."

"Alright, guys," he said, "I unlocked the back entrance. You can bring your stuff around." He spoke curtly, all business.

Forty-five minutes later the band had finished the sound check and was waiting in the green room. Nowhere had still not shown up. Jerry peeked his head in, looking impatient and annoyed. He muttered some expletive under his breath. He shouted "Five minutes," then withdrew. From the couch in the green room Cali Sky could hear the crowd noise: an incessant droning with an occasional whistle, scream or shout. Tam sat in a chair with Trish on his lap. Chris stood near the door, twirling a drum stick in his fingers.

"Don't do that on stage," Tam warned. "*No* heavy metal antics."

"Relax!" replied Chris. "Don't worry, I won't."

"Um, guys," Brodie said, "We go on in five minutes and we don't even know what we're playing yet. Shouldn't we decide now?"

"I knew we were forgetting something," said Cali Sky.

"Cali Sky, you decide," said Tam.

"I don't think we have much of a choice," she said. "We'll play the three songs we played last week. We can stretch out 'Bela' and 'Marquee Moon' to fill up the hour. Other than that, we'll just see what happens."

The green room door opened. The crowd noise became louder.

"Alright guys, you're on." It was Joe, the sound guy. "Follow me."

He led them through the darkened passage way that led to the stage, the crowd noise becoming louder and louder. Joe carried a flashlight to light their way. Up ahead Cali Sky could see figures in the dark where the passage way opened up into a holding area. It was John. Cali Sky could see that he was being lectured by Jerry, whose angry voice now met Cali Sky's ears, above the din of the crowd. As she got closer, she could see the rest of Nowhere moving their instruments into position. Cali Sky walked past without looking. She heard John defending himself.

"But we have *plenty* of time, Jerry!"

"When I say to be here at 7:30, you be here at 7:30!"

After she passed she heard John exclaim, "What the fuck?"

Only Brodie, bringing up the rear, saw what happened. As Chris walked past, John took a step back, away from an advancing Jerry. Chris went by without moving, bumping John away with his shoulder.

Oblivious to these events Cali Sky heard two more voices. One was Jerry's: "He's the least of your worries right now, John!" The other voice Cali Sky recognized. Jocular and fun-loving, it had to be Jim, John's brother and Nowhere drummer. "He must be one of Cali Sky's *guests*." The last word evolved into Jim's cackling laughter.

As she climbed the stage stairs Cali Sky's heart beat fast. She knew this moment well, had experienced it many times before. But for the past three years she had always done it alone, as a solo act. All eyes would not be on just her. The success of the performance depended on others besides herself. She felt a sickening sensation as she walked past the side curtains, where she could be seen by the audience for the first time. At once a roar washed over her. She was now fully exposed. She knew this moment as well. It was always accompanied by feelings of vulnerability counterbalanced by confidence, power and—she had never spoken of this to anyone—vague sexuality.

She picked up the guitar and raised the strap over her head. The crowd noise continued unabated. The house lights were off; she could only hear the audience. To her right, she looked over at Tam, who was settling his guitar into position. She looked over at Brodie, who stood on her other side, to her left. He was already prepared. Chris tested his bass drum and gave his snare a light tap. The sound carried into the darkness in front of her. She looked back at Tam, who, guitar around his neck, was checking over the keyboard. Satisfied, he turned to Cali Sky and gave her the slightest of nods. She looked back at Chris, who nodded much more visibly.

She faced the darkness, took a breath and tore into the opening riff of "Rebel Rebel." By the end of the third measure, when the rest of the band joined in, she was barely aware of what was happening. She still could not see the audience, but she could sense its electricity, which to her pre-reflective consciousness seemed to be a part of the song.

"Hot tramp, I love you so." As she sang this lyric, during which the band paused momentarily, the crowd noise flooded the stage. She felt like she was singing the song for the first time, mainly because others joined her in playing it. Vocally, she found herself reacting to the band's fine touches, moved by their musical flourishes to emote more impulsively, unpredictably. The band was drawing her out of herself.

With the explosive last chord the house lights were raised. A chorus of yells and whistles caught Cali Sky's attention. It came from a smattering of people off to the side, all of whom stood out because they looked older than the general audience. Cali Sky had noticed them earlier, smiling bemusedly at their surroundings, talking to each other with an above-it-all haughtiness. Once she heard the yells and whistles directed toward Tam, she understood: They were old Forest Murmur fans.

Brodie heard and noticed as well. As the band prepared for the next song he played the first few notes of a bass line that only that agitated segment of the crowd would recognize: the unmistakable bass line to one of Forest Murmur's most popular songs. When they heard it they all became more attentive and lurched closer to the stage. Their yells and whistles doubled in volume. Their anticipation mounted when Brodie responded with a smile in their direction.

Suddenly a shocking noise blasted through the venue. The audience collectively flinched and grimaced. Many instinctively brought their hands to their ears. The noise shot a bolt of adrenalin through Cali Sky's body, evoking a fight-or-flight response, as if she, or the band, or even southern California were under attack. Two seconds later she thought it might be feedback from the amps. By now moans and expletives were raised from the floor. Then Cali Sky realized the noise came from the keyboards. Tam.

He had brought both hands down on the instrument like a two year-old throwing a tantrum. He glared at Brodie, neither moving nor blinking. Once Brodie recovered from the blast of noise, he too discovered its source. And turned pale. Tam looked like a maniac, still glaring. Brodie looked stunned, shell-shocked.

It occurred to Cali Sky that Tam might very well attack Brodie. Cali Sky sensed the tense atmosphere. The moment had become combustible. And the band had only played one song.

She turned her back on the stand-off, walked to her amp and turned up the gain. She violently strummed a chord in the key of "Bella Lugosi's Dead" and let the feedback become almost unbearable. The crowd was now distracted by another shocking noise. She backed away from the amp. As the feedback died down she played a run of distorted, haunting notes. At that very moment Tam seamlessly surrounded the notes with keyboard atmospherics. Chris gave the song shape with his high hat and rim shots. Once Brodie was liberated from Tam's death stare he regained his color and made the song instantly recognizable with his bass line. Cali Sky saw that the band had restored the crowd's composure. They thought it was part of the show. The audience mistook near disaster—a band on the verge of implosion—for showmanship. For them it was all part of the act: subversion and aggression.

Forty-five minutes later the band exited the stage to a thunderous ovation. Tam ignored the crowd as he walked off. Cali Sky, Brodie and Chris thanked them with quick waves. With the assistance of Joe the sound guy they had ten minutes to remove their instruments from the stage. Chris complained the whole time.

Halfway down the backstage corridor they met Nowhere. John looked nervous. Jim turned away as they approached.

"Good luck, guys," remarked Chris with a smirk and a wink. He had been playing shows long enough to know that any band would have trouble going on after what they had just done on stage. "Break a fucking leg!" he added over his shoulder.

They entered the green room, ears ringing. Immediately Tam rounded on Brodie.

"Don't ever, ever play a Forest Murmurs song again!" he

screamed. "If you do, I swear to God I'll rip that bass out of your hands and walk right off the stage!"

Instead of defending himself, which Cali Sky expected, Brodie simply looked hurt and defeated. She didn't wait for him to try to reply. She stepped up to Tam and said, "You need to relax! What is wrong with you? He was just playing to the crowd."

"He," exclaimed Tam, pointing at Brodie, "was never in Forest Murmurs. He has no right to play that song."

"Alright, alright," said Cali Sky, "He won't play the song. Just cool out."

Finally Brodie spoke: "I'm sorry, Tam. I just saw some of your old fans and thought I'd give them something."

At that moment Trish entered the green room and walked to Tam's side. He took a deep breath. His anger subsided and he said, "Yeah, alright. Just don't ever do that again, okay?"

"Obviously he won't," said Cali Sky.

Chris sat down on the couch, put his feet on the table and said, "You guys are worse than a heavy-metal band."

Cali Sky pulled some cans of soda from the refrigerator and offered them to the others. All were now seated. They talked about their performance, though they had little to say. They knew it was good. And gradually Brodie became less rattled and insecure as Tam became more sociable.

Chris pulled his feet off the table and leaned forward. "So here's the thing. If you ask me I'd say we killed it out there. I'd like to try to make this band work. But if you all don't think so then you need to tell me. Carnage doesn't even know I'm doing this. I'm still officially their drummer. But I'll quit if you three want to give it a shot with this band."

"Hell yeah we want to give it a shot!" Brodie exclaimed.

Cali Sky and Tam said nothing.

"Right, guys?" pressed Brodie. Cali Sky leaned back

and sighed. She looked like she was about to speak, but still said nothing.

"Well?" Chris sounded calm yet insistent.

Nowhere began their second song, a Social Distortion cover.

"Come on, Cali Sky," interrupted a desperate Brodie, "Say something."

Cali Sky felt the weight of their stares, Tam's included.

"I'm going away to college in August, I'm moving to northern California," she said irritably. She added with disappointment, "I can't be in a band if I'm not here." Her voice trailed off.

The door opened again and Zoe walked in.

Cali Sky look relieved. "Hey sister!"

"Oh my God, that set blew everyone away. I'm serious, I've never seen That's so packed before."

Brodie gave Cali Sky a look that screamed, "See!"

Zoe continued, "The place emptied out after your set. There's a group of people waiting near the backstage entrance. I think they're waiting for you, Tam. Forest Murmurs fans."

Tam looked uncomfortable. Trish pressed her body against his in a gesture of reassurance.

"Look, Cali Sky," said Chris, "I need to know. You too, Tam. Are we a band or not?"

The direct question yanked Tam out of his distractedness. "I'll do it...if Cali Sky's in." Trish's face brightened. Brodie looked hopeful, until he peered at Cali Sky.

"I'd love to be in a band with you, I really would. But like I said I'm going to college in the fall. Everything is set. I'm sorry." She couldn't look at Brodie. Zoe placed her hand on Cali Sky's shoulder.

"Well, we played one hell of a gig," said Chris. "Might as well ride it out to the end. Where's the after party?"

"The Strand," replied Zoe.

They rose from the couches and chairs. Chris, Tam and Trish filed out of the green room, followed more slowly by Cali Sky and Zoe, who spoke softly and confidentially to each other. At the door Cali Sky turned around to see Brodie still seated on a chair, staring at the floor.

The caravan wound out of the That's parking lot, merged on the 5 and leveled off at eighty miles per hour. Cali Sky had her radio tuned to KROQ, but as they neared the coast that station faded in and out. She spun the tuner to the other side of the FM dial, trying to get 91X, but it too was staticky. Halfway between LA and San Diego she couldn't get radio stations from either city. Zoe sat in the passenger seat, describing the earlier scene in That's from her vantage point where she took photos of the band. In the backseat Stone nestled closer to some girl he met at the show.

"Do you have a cigarette?" she had asked him outside of That's.

"Should I?" he had replied. Stone often answered a question with another question. Five minutes later she appeared to have a crush on Stone but still no cigarette.

Cali Sky followed close behind Chris in his Suzuki, loaded down with drums and three more concert-goers. In front of him, leading the caravan, was Tam, driving his late-model Volvo, with Trish in the passenger seat and in the back two of Tam's close friends, people Cali Sky never met before who were from Tam's Forest Murmurs days. Behind Cali Sky followed about five more cars, all piled full of mostly teenagers.

The caravan exited at Crown Valley Parkway and wound up and down the hilly road to Golden Lantern. Here they stopped at an In-N-Out Burger and continued to PCH. The parking lot of the Strand was empty. A good sign. Police broke up their beach parties here but not very often.

Cali Sky began the slow descent with Zoe at her side. She had a Diet Coke in one hand and bag full of In-N-Out cheeseburgers and fries in another. The air smelled of brine and skunk. Stone walked arm-in-arm with the cigarette girl. Zoe looked back and saw over thirty people making their way down the beach. Among them she saw "Tram," as Tam and Trish were now called behind their backs, with the two Forest Murmurs fans close by. They both dressed like Tam: tight-fitting black trousers and dark-colored shirts. Chris swaggered with a beer already in hand.

"Didn't Brodie come?" asked Zoe, now focusing on the first step of stairs.

"No," Cali Sky replied.

"The guy is heartbroken. I could see it in his eyes."

"He'll find another band," offered Cali Sky, fending off a rising sense of guilt.

"But he won't find another you."

"Zoe, I can't even think about this right now."

As they neared the footpath the sound of the surf became audible. The trees cleared and Cali Sky gazed out at the ocean. Instantly she felt a tightening in her chest and a tugging at her soul. Aside from a few lonely boat lights offshore she saw only darkness stretching into the horizonless distance. Somewhere to the north was Catalina Island, now obscured by night and fog. She heard music in her head, somber and chilling, immortal notes of sadness suggested by the waves breaking in the distance. That distance now beckoned to her. She longed to dissolve into the darkness.

They trudged through the deep sand toward the water until they reached ground hardened by the receding tide. They then walked south along the shoreline, occasionally scampering inland at the encroachment of an ambitious wave. Sea cliffs, thick with overgrowth, stoically facing the sea, towered above them on the left. Cali Sky opened the bag of In-N-Out. She and Zoe shared some fries. Up ahead she saw something large lying among the flotsam and jetsam on the beach. At first she thought it was a piece of driftwood. Fifteen feet away, she saw that it was in fact a fish, newly dead—a California Corbina. Its scales glittered in the foggy moonlight. Zoe voiced a groan of sympathy for the dead creature. Cali Sky stared briefly at its bulging eyes, then passed on.

They walked until there was no more beach, until they reached the spot where the cliffs of Dana Point meet the sea. Here they sat down, thirty teenagers scattered around the beach, eating In-N-Out Burger, talking and drinking.

"Does anyone have a Goddamned cigarette?" asked the Cigarette Girl.

"I got something for you to smoke," answered Chris, now downing his fourth beer.

"Chris," said an exasperated Tam, "try to say something we *don't* expect you to say."

Tam was flanked by the tight-trousered Forest Murmurs fans. Chris finished off another beer.

Sitting away from the others, sharing a meal, Zoe whispered to Cali Sky, "How does he get away with that?"

"Who? Tam? I don't know. But if anyone else said something like that to Chris, Chris would pummel him."

Cali Sky closed her eyes and listened deeply to the waves.

"So Tam," exclaimed Chris, "why don't you introduce me to your friends?"

Cali Sky opened her eyes and looked at Zoe. She braced herself for a confrontation…again.

Instead Tam answered congenially, "This is Marc. And this guy goes by the name of Synth."

Chris shook their hands and sat down, opening another can of beer.

"You play a mean set of drums," said Synth to Chris. Chris searched his face for signs of irony, saw none, and nodded thanks.

"Yeah," said Marc, who wore wire-framed glasses, "you guys sounded really tight."

Tam addressed Chris, but spoke loudly enough for Cali Sky to overhear: "I was just telling Marc and Synth that our band is finished. One and done. One of us wants to go get educated."

"Just like you, Tam," replied Cali Sky, remembering that Tam was a student at an art college.

"Yeah," said Tam, "it's probably for the best. Besides, the demise of Cali Sky and Special Guests"—he enunciated that latter two words with ironic significance—"reminds us of the transience of all things. It's like preparation for death, you know?" Synth smiled with admiration at Tam, who looked wistfully into the dark night. "Just look out there," he continued, nodding toward the ocean, "doesn't that look like death?"

Chris looked out at the waves, then back at Tam. "Not really," he said.

"Are you afraid to die, Chris?" asked Tam.

"Haven't really thought about it, Tam," Chris answered. "Are you?"

"Terrified," said Tam.

Cali Sky set her Diet Coke down on the sand. She wrapped her arms around her knees and steadied herself, closing her eyes, listening to the eternal notes of the surf.

"Think about the concept of forever," Tam said. "Forever. Forever. Now imagine non-existence forever. How can that not terrify you?"

"It will be no different than before you were born," called out Zoe, whose raised voice startled Cali Sky. She opened her eyes. Zoe continued, "Before you were born you were unconscious, you had no awareness. You die and you return to that state of oblivion."

"No, it's not the same!" Tam replied. He rose, agitated. "Before I was born, as far as I know, I was always oblivious." He stepped toward the ocean, then turned to face Zoe and the rest. "The difference is that now, at this very moment, I am aware of the approaching oblivion. I am conscious now, but I *know* I won't be when I die. That's just...cruel." He looked like he was about to cry. Trish was antsy. She wanted to go to him. She positioned herself to rise, but then knew that she could not comfort him in this state of dread, or perhaps she knew that he did not *want* to be comforted at this moment. She moved into a cross-legged position, staring at him helplessly.

"What about God?" asked Cali Sky. Her voice sounded strange to her. "What about an afterlife?"

"Who knows? Maybe," said Tam. "But an afterlife on what conditions? Confessing my sins to God? Asking Jesus into my heart? Bullshit. I don't find myself believing any of that. Except when I'm terrified, like I am now, so maybe it *is* true. But then my own fear is coercing me to believe. I can't believe in a God like that, like an object of terror."

"Maybe the Christian view of God is wrong," Zoe offered. "Maybe God is totally different than that. Maybe God is a she. Fear and terror are male characteristics."

"*That's* what I believe," declared Chris in an inebriated voice. "A female god. Just as long as I'm allowed to have a boner in heaven."

"Jesus, Chris," Tam said indignantly, "Are you really that shallow?"

"Lay off, Tam!" interrupted Cali Sky. "Some poets actually compare death and sex. Like they're similar sorts of experiences."

"Orgasm as death," added Zoe.

"Right," Cali Sky replied. "Led Zeppelin even has a song about it: 'In My Time of Dying.' As Robert Plant sings about death, like he's about to die, he simulates an orgasm."

"Bernini's *St. Teresa in Ecstasy*," murmured Marc. "St. Teresa receives the stigmata. The Holy Spirit descends on her. And she seems to experience it sexually, like God is penetrating her. St. Teresa is in ecstasy."

"So maybe there *are* boners in heaven!' cried Chris triumphantly.

"Yeah, maybe there are," Tam dejectedly replied. "All I know is that when I'm on my deathbed, I want to be surrounded by music. To ease my passage into Godforsaken oblivion or God-damned hell." He slowly turned away and walked along the beach in the direction from which they had come. Trish rose and chased after him, followed closely by Synth.

"He's a fascinating guy, I have to admit," Zoe said to Cali Sky, reentering their private conversation space.

Cali Sky shivered. "He bears a heavy burden of some kind. I recognize the marks of his pain. I know them well. He's tortured inside. That's why we play good music together."

"You share the same muse," said Zoe. She rose to her feet. "Are you sure you don't want to defer your enrollment at USF?"

"I'm sure. Where are you going?"

"Gotta pee. I'll be back in a few."

"Be careful." Cali Sky watched Zoe advance along the beach with quick steps. In the distance, a hundred yards beyond Zoe, she could still make out the small, silhouetted figures of Tam, Trish and Synth.

"We're gonna go look for a cigarette," announced Stone.

"You think you'll find one somewhere along the beach?" asked one of the teenagers sprawled out on the sand.

"You never know," Stone answered with a devilish grin as he and Cigarette Girl also headed into the darkness, veering a bit inland, however, to locate a secluded spot. Stone had started a movement. Gradually three other couples paired off and disappeared into the darkness.

Many of those remaining in the group became self-conscious as the mysterious phenomenon of hooking-up passed them by. But not Chris, who was now too drunk to be self-conscious of just about anything. And not Marc, whose maturity seemed incompatible with the phenomenon. And not Cali Sky, who had more profound mysteries to contend with. These three formed their own conversation space, separate from the others.

"What's it like, Chris?" asked Cali Sky, "being in Carnage?"

Chris finished off another can of beer. "Carnage? Fuuuuck. It's like...fuuuuck. It's like being on speed. Sometimes we actually are on speed." He laughed. "But even when we aren't, it's like we are... Fuuuuck. Just pure adrenalin."

Cali Sky smiled and nodded.

Chris opened another can and continued, "We played this gig in LA once. Some private club. I don't even remember. These two girls come on the stage, completely naked. Bouncers don't even kick them off. The whole band did them after the show."

Cali Sky tried to fend off the associative thread of ideas conjured by Chris's story. But once she sensed its presence on the periphery of her awareness, she knew it would not pass until she confronted it. So she flashed her mental spotlight on the dark deeds of her mom's past. Her mom the groupie, prostituting herself to rock stars for the simple fact that they were rock stars. The spotlight seared her brain, but in her mind's eye she did not blink. She gave it due observance, allowing the shame to sink in once again, as if she were performing a ritual, a sacrifice she must periodically offer.

Chris continued, "But after a while the music just.... I got tired of...."

Cali Sky and Marc turned their attention from the ocean to Chris at the same time. Drunks, Cali Sky knew, rarely struggled for words, especially drunks like Chris.

"Fuck it," he said, apparently mustering up resolve, "When I was a kid my dad wanted me to play football, right. Which was alright. I liked playing football, beating people's heads in and all that shit. But I really wanted to play drums, right. Or at least play football *and* drums. But my dad...my fucking dad told me to focus on football. He used to beat the fucking shit out of me...if I was playing drums instead of football."

"So what does that have to do with being the drummer for Carnage?"

"Because... Fuuuuck. I forgot. Oh yeah, because...being the drummer for Carnage now kind of makes me feel like I did when I was a kid and my dad made me play football. I just wanna do something else."

Cali Sky had heard drunks wax philosophic before, but not like this. Being drunk actually made Chris more articulate. Or perhaps...the epiphany struck Cali Sky as a jolt: Perhaps Chris was fake, a fraud. Maybe the bad-ass drummer thing was mere appearance. So who was the real Chris? Cali Sky was now fascinated.

"So how does your dad feel about your drumming now?" asked Cali Sky.

The smile on his face had been gradually flattening out. Now it all but vanished, its presence feebly visible though a dying effort of will. The smile now looked pathetically artificial.

"He still hates it...except when I bring money home..." He suddenly stood up. "You dare me to swim out there?" he nodded toward the waves. But before they had a chance to answer Chris had already set out, shedding articles of clothing.

"Chris! Don't!" shouted Cali Sky, rising to her feet.

"It'll help me sober up!" Chris returned. He was now ankle-deep in water, wearing only boxers.

"Idiot," exclaimed Cali Sky, sitting back down next to Marc.

"Yeah, it's amazing that any of us survive past the age of twenty," Marc replied.

Cali Sky looked at him quizzically as Chris suddenly bolted full speed and dived into a wave. Marc said, "It's like everything happening out here is either survival or self-destruction."

"How so?"

"Well, the people lying somewhere along this beach right now having sex or being intimate—that's survival, coping with all the hurt and pain they experience. And self-destruction is unfolding somewhere out in those waves right now."

He sounded like a teacher to Cali Sky, authoritative and wise. But his effeminate voice made him seem young, returning him to Cali Sky's social orbit.

"So which one are you?" she asked "Surviving or self-destructing?"

"At the moment? Neither. Tonight I'm just an observer. But I've done my share of both. And you?"

"Me too: neither. I'm a musician. I create. Or at least I used to."

"You create so that others can either survive or self-destruct."

"Why is it either/or? Why aren't there other options?"

"No, you're right," Marc confirmed. "There are other options. The concept of either/or is so western."

"Oh yeah?" Cali Sky felt like she could trust Marc. He seemed intelligent but not arrogant.

"Sorry, I'm a philosophy major. I like to talk about this sort of thing."

"Well, what are the other options?"

"A reconciliation of those opposites. Like the eastern notion of ying and yang."

Cali Sky strained her eyes, peering into the dark distance, trying to spot Chris, but eager for Marc to elaborate.

He added, "That's why Chris and Tam were made to be in a band together: the reconciliation of opposites. Chris is obviously hard on the outside but soft on the inside. Well, in a way, Tam is soft on the outside but hard on the inside. It's ying and yang twice over."

"Well, maybe they'll stick together. Start a different band."

"Not without you."

"Why?"

"Tam told me so. Please don't tell him I said this, but he told me the only way he'd play in a band again is if you're in it. Obviously he sees something in you."

"Like what?"

"Probably the same thing he saw in Brian."

"What happened there? Why did Forest Murmurs break up?"

"That's a long story." Marc looked like he didn't want to say anymore. "I think we better see if we can find Chris."

They removed their shoes and walked toward the sea. A wave rolled over Cali Sky's feet. It felt icy cold and took her breath away as she emitted an involuntary scream.

"How did he do it?" she called out to Marc above the roar of the surf.

"I don't know. It's freezing!" Marc expressed the shock of the cold water with effeminate gestures.

Cali Sky's feet became numb. She and Marc called out Chris's name, but the pounding waves seemed to buffet the sound of their voices. Just then Cali Sky saw a lone figure walking toward them along the sand. She soon realized it couldn't be Chris; the figure was much too small. It was a girl, but one Cali Sky did not recognize. She walked out of the water and toward the girl, whose short, rapid steps and tiny frame suggested the approach of a frightened child. A painful longing spread through Cali Sky's body, as breathtaking as the frigid water that had washed over her feet. She longed with a sickening need to protect this frightened child. She looked helpless, surrounded on all sides by dark elements: cliff, sea and sky. The child became Cami, and Cali Sky could hear in the waves and wind the heart-wrenching sound of weeping, retching and drowning. The elements seemed to collapse on her. She found herself hurrying toward the child, nearly falling to her knees, mouthing the words of her sister.

The darkness yielded the child as the dull moonlight now illuminated her face. Before Cali Sky could embrace the relief for which she had searched for the past three years, the relief that seemed now so tantalizingly close, a cold and cruel realization of betrayal and deception came crushing down upon her. This was no child. It was Trish. Cali Sky did not recognize her because she was alone, detached from her accustomed place at Tam's side. Once Cali Sky had a dream in which the disembodied voice of God spoke to her from a stormy mountaintop. The voice, in the form of music, was on the verge of explaining unfathomable mysteries before she woke up. She felt a similar sense of crushing disappointment now. She stared as Trish, expressionless, walked by.

"Where's Tam?" she heard Marc ask behind her.

No answer.

"Trish, where's Tam?"

"He'll be right back."

"Okay, great. But where *is* he?"

"He'll be right back," Trish repeated.

"Trish…" A gust of ocean wind bore Marc's voice away. Cali Sky could hear no more of their exchange. She turned around to see Marc following behind Trish toward the southern point where cliff meets sea.

Then everything became still. The central group of teenagers had thinned some more, a few last-minute, desperate hook-ups sent them two-by-two to farther reaches of the beach. Cali Sky still saw no sign of Chris. With dawning certainty she knew that Chris was dead. She pictured what would happen next: She and Zoe would hike back up the stairs and drive her car to the gas station on PCH. They would call the police. Police cars and ambulances would descend upon the Strand. They would recover Chris's body. It would be pale and bloated. She would have to admit that Chris had been drinking. And through it all, the couples scamming on the beach would remain hidden behind her. They were surviving. In front of her, Chris had self-destructed. She herself was the dividing line, the boundary between the two, the unification of opposites. She both survived and self-destructed.

The scenario played out in her mind like a script. She had already adapted her outlook to its reality. Just then she became aware of a small group of people approaching from the footpath. She hoped to see Zoe among its members. But she was more than disappointed. At the front of the group she saw a boy and girl holding hands. These were John and Hilary. Thirty feet away she heard Jim's cackling laughter. It was Nowhere. After finishing their set they must have decided to join Cali Sky and Special Guests????? for an after-party on the Strand. She could hear Hilary speaking loudly to John. Evidently she had successfully hooked up with him, despite Cali Sky's unwillingness to help. Jim, shorter than his brother, appeared from behind the new Nowhere guitarist. *Where is Zoe?* thought Cali Sky. *Where is Tam?* It was way too late to hide. She would have to face them alone.

"Hey," said John.

"Hey."

"Where *is* everybody?"

Before Cali Sky could answer, Hilary interjected, "Where's *Ben?*"

The uncoupled teenagers remaining in the attenuated group

began to make their way over to the newcomers, relieved by the presence of a new social dynamic that might recharge their sagging morale.

"Seriously, Cali Sky, is he out here somewhere?"

Cali Sky wondered how many questions she could ignore at once before she would have to say something. *Where are Tam and Zoe?*

"I mean," Hilary continued, "he is such a loser. You could do a lot better."

John still held Hilary's hand, looking at Cali Sky with a subtle expression of superiority and lust. Cali Sky knew she had to tell them now: Chris was dead. Drowned somewhere out there. They had to go back and call the police.

"What is that?" shouted Jim, pointing toward the waves. He and two other guys were standing near the water, away from Cali Sky's face-off with John and Hilary, whose three questions remained unanswered. Their attention was now focused on a figure waist deep in the water coming toward the shore. It walked slowly but with a powerful gait. It paused and turned as a wave approached. Cali Sky was shocked that Chris was alive. How could he have survived the cold and the currents? But she also felt strangely proud, proud that this crazy idiot was her drummer... or at least used to be her drummer. Or perhaps she was simply relieved by the distraction, which made everyone forget Hilary's three questions. The wave broke right across Chris's chest, he remained standing, then turned and continued to trudge toward shore.

"Who the hell is that?" John asked, another question for Cali Sky to ignore.

She looked more closely. Chris appeared to have something in his mouth. Or maybe something attached to his chin. Obscured by the dark and the distance, it looked to Cali Sky like he had been harpooned in the head, in one side and out the other. But then she saw that the object curved downwardly on either side of his face. Closer still, she could see that the object was in fact in his mouth. By the time he was ankle deep Chris was fully visible in every detail. The spectacle no longer left anything to the imagination, the mystery was revealed. His dripping hair gathered in three points around his face, his brawny chest was goosepimpled, his boxers clung to his hips and private parts. And in his mouth was a fish, over which Chris's jaws were locked tightly, teeth bared. Stepping out of the last wave he growled menacingly. He stopped just five feet short of the crowd now gathered on the beach. Cali Sky knew that the fish in his mouth was the dead California Corbina that washed ashore, the fish with the bulging eyes that they had spotted earlier.

"What the fuck are you doing?" asked John incredulously.

Chris looked at John, then at Hilary and spat the Corbina at her feet and said, "Fishing." The fish landed with a splat on the wet sand. Teeth marks and ruptured fish skin were visible along the belly. Hilary screamed and walked off. Jim's cackle erupted at full volume.

"Shut the fuck up, Jim!" yelled John, following Hilary into the darkness.

Jim watched his brother disappear, then approached Chris laughing. He slapped his hand, laughing quietly this time, and said confidentially, "That was awesome." Chris smiled and nodded.

"What is *wrong* with you?" said Cali Sky as Chris pulled his shorts over his boxers. "I thought you were dead. I was about to call the police."

"I told you, I needed to sober up. What are they doing here?" he asked, motioning toward Nowhere.

"I don't know. Let's just go."

Chris picked up his clothes and got dressed.

"Was Nowhere your first band?" he asked once they were side by side.

"Yeah. How did you know?"

"Because most musicians don't choose their first band. It just forms and you don't want to miss out. I didn't think you would choose to be in a band like that."

"You're right. I would never want to be in a band with John again. I mean, Tam can be a real asshole, but at least he knows what he's doing."

"But that doesn't matter now, right? You're going off to college."

Cali Sky paused, as if remembering, "Yeah...right."

"Just between you and me, Carnage is my first band."

"Seriously?"

"Yeah. That's probably why I don't want to be in it anymore."

They walked in silence for a while until Chris said, "Look who's coming."

Cali Sky had been staring down as she walked. Chris's announcement halted her wandering mind and drew her attention outwardly. Tam and Zoe were walking toward them.

"I wonder what *they* were doing?" asked Chris.

Cali Sky tried to ignore the insinuation. Still, the circumstances were suspicious. Cali Sky had never seen Tam and Trish apart. And now when she did, Tam was with Zoe.

"Where have you guys been?" asked Cali Sky.

They both hesitated. "In the bathroom," Zoe blurted. "I mean, *I* was in the bathroom. I ran across Tam on the beach."

"Why are you all wet?" Tam asked Chris.

"Went for a swim."

"Scared me to death," said Cali Sky. "I thought for sure he drowned."

"Well, Chris," reflected Tam, "maybe you answered the question I asked earlier. Maybe you *aren't* afraid to die."

"I guess not," grinned Chris.

"Where's Trish?" Tam asked.

"Oh, shit," exclaimed Cali Sky, "we forgot about Trish. She's down there somewhere. And Nowhere is here. Did you see them?"

But Tam had already begun walking away in search of Trish.

"Maybe we should go help him?" offered Cali Sky.

"I can't," Zoe replied.

"You can't? Why not?"

"Because I don't want to see John again. He gives me the creeps."

"He gives all of us the creeps, Zoe. Don't worry, we'll stick together."

"No! No, Cali Sky, I can't." She looked agitated, flustered, and a bit embarrassed.

"It's alright," interrupted Chris. "I'll help Tam. You two can leave."

"Um, okay," answered Cali Sky, trying to read Zoe's face. "Just don't start anything if you see John. Alright, Chris?"

Chris nodded and disappeared down the stairs.

The sound of the waves vanished as they reached the top of the bluff. The smell of skunk became more pungent. The parking lot remained mostly empty.

"So what happened?" asked Cali Sky.

"He hit on me," Zoe replied.

"Tam?"

"No, John."

"He did? Where was Hilary?"

"She was walking into the bathroom, I was walking out. He came up to me and dished out all these lines. He tried to put his arm around me. So I pushed him away."

"Oh my God! Are you alright? I hope Chris *does* bump into him..."

But Zoe had no chance to reply. Someone emerged from one of the seemingly empty cars parked in the dark lot. It was a tall male. Standing next to the vehicle, unaware of the presence of Cali Sky and Zoe, he zipped up his pants. It was Synth. He walked unselfconsciously toward the beach stairs. As he neared Cali Sky and Zoe he waved hello and asked about Tam and Trish. The yellow light from the public restroom made his gentle face appear pale. Cali Sky answered pleasantly and tried to avert her eyes, not from his benevolent face, but from his half-tucked shirt.

When Cali Sky pulled into the apartment complex parking lot it was nearly one in the morning. She eased the car into a space, put it in park, turned off the ignition and brushed a strand of hair from her face. The salt breeze from the beach had weighed it down so that it immediately gravitated back toward its wayward place on her cheek. Opening the car door she felt chilled by the cool, humid night air. Her ears rang with the echoes of amplified music and pounding surf. Guitar in hand she wearily made her way to the apartment, anticipating the warmth of her bed.

She unlocked the apartment door and entered. She didn't get far before she nearly slipped on a piece of paper lying on the floor. She turned on a light and saw that her mom left her a note.

"Cali Sky,

Call Brodie. He said it doesn't matter how late it is.

And please tell him not to call anymore past 11 p.m.

Love,

Mom

P.S.—Also tell him I'm sorry for yelling and swearing at him for calling so late."

Cali Sky entered her room, closed the door quietly and picked up the phone.

Brodie answered the phone not with the word "hello" but with a question: "Guess who called me about an hour ago?"

"Uh, Flea?" It was the first bass player that came to her head.

"Jerry."

"Garcia?"

"Jerry the owner of That's."

"Jerry? Why did he call you? How did he even get your number?"

"I don't know. But he called because he wants to pay for us to make a demo."

"What? A demo? Why?"

"Why? Because he thinks we're *that* good."

"He wants to pay for us to make a demo?"

"That's what I said."

"But why? I mean, what does he get out of it?"

"Well, he wants us to commit to play a certain number of gigs at That's."

"Wow. He must really think we're good."

"Hell yeah he does! Everyone does!"

"Wow."

"There's also one more thing he wants."

"Yeah? What's that?"

"He wants us to sign some sort of contract guaranteeing him a certain percentage of our royalties."

"Royalties? Royalties from what?"

"From our first album."

"Our first album?"

"That's what I said."

There was silence on the line. Cali Sky's head was swimming.

"Don't you see?" asked Brodie. "He thinks we're going to be big."

Cali Sky once again made no reply. She was making plans for the next day, wondering how, in between guitar lessons, she would find time to fill out the necessary forms to defer her enrollment to the University of San Francisco.

"It's all Stone's fault," said Cali Sky from Tam's walk-in closet. She looked over his music collection and counted eight full-size, wooden cassette tape cases. She had seen them in the Wherehouse Record Store and knew that each one held one hundred tapes. "He was the first one to call us Quest."

"Stone's nicknames always stick," Brodie said.

It was the second time the band got together since learning of Jerry's offer. The first time they met, they proposed names for the band, even though most people had taken to calling them Quest. Stone had adapted it from their name as it appeared on the That's marquee: "Cali Sky and Special Guests?????". The five question marks had caught his attention. He had first called the band the Question Marks. Then the Questions. Then just Quest. Cali Sky and Tam hated it. Brodie didn't care; he was just happy to be in a band that was going to make it big.

But no one could think of another name. So Tam proposed that they revisit the problem after their next band practice, but with this difference: The second time they gathered together to brainstorm names, they would all be drunk. "It was a practice of the ancient Persians," Tam had offered. "Whenever they had to make some important decision, they debated the matter twice: once when they were sober, and once when they were drunk." The problem was that in between their first (sober) and second (drunken) meeting the name Quest caught on. A name change seemed hopeless, so the debate became meaningless. But they decided to get drunk anyway.

"You know," Cali Sky called out from the closet, wine cooler in hand, "most band names sound stupid, until they make it big. Then all of a sudden, the name sounds cool. Take the Beatles.

Before they made it big, they were the Beatles. *After* they made it big, they were *the Beatles*."

Brodie and Chris stared at her, then erupted in laughter.

Brode recovered, took a sip of Guinness and said…"We're on a quest then, I guess. But for what?"

"To make good music," Chris answered. Everyone waited for a punch line from the seldomly serious Chris. They looked at him expectantly, Tam and Cali Sky bracing themselves for some wise-crack. But none came. Chris added, "To make really good music." He wiped the remaining sweat from his brow. His exuberant drum playing, even during practice, always left him soaked.

"Well, *obviously*," said Brodie. "I have no doubt we'll do that."

"Where do you get all this confidence?" challenged Tam. "Why are you so sure that we're going to be this great band?" Trish sat quietly at Tam's side as he continued, "All we've done so far is play other people's songs. Yeah, we do that pretty well. Do you have any idea how hard it is to write music? Have you ever even written a song, Brodie?"

"Yeah, I have," Brodie answered defensively. "But, I mean, you and Cali Sky as main songwriters? With me helping out some? Come on, Tam. You know we can make great music."

"No, I don't know. We *might*, but I don't know. Songwriting is a mysterious process."

"To be honest," said Cali Sky, "I don't have a single original song inside of me right now."

Brodie looked deflated. He turned to Tam, who said, "Me neither. I haven't felt inspired to write a song in a long time…ever since Forest Murmurs broke up."

"Well," said Brodie, "what inspires you?"

Tam shrugged. Trish blushed, looking uneasy.

"What about you, Cali Sky?" asked Brodie, frustrated. "What *does* inspire you?"

She walked to the closet doorway. She felt the effects of the alcohol: the heightened sense of perspective and significance, the willingness to speak truth. Her eyes seemed to glitter with emotion and a far-off vision.

"Once upon a time," she began, "there was this girl who lived in a beautiful valley surrounded on all sides by tall mountains. The grass was soft on her bare feet. The trees towered above her head, their leaves rustled faintly. A river ran through the middle of the valley, trickling down small waterfalls, and swelling where the ground was flat." She paused to take a sip of her wine cooler. They were initially baffled. But as the story continued they became transfixed. All eyes were now fastened on her; they listened like children. "In the middle of the valley, alongside the river, stood a cabin. It belonged to the girl. From a window the girl saw the moonlight sparkling on the water. It danced on the treetop leaves and made the distance mountains glow. Beautiful music filled the valley, golden notes so beautiful that it made the girl's heart break. She fell to her knees, her elbows placed upon the window sill. She realized that the music came from an instrument hanging from the window frame above her. It was the wind that made it play, filling its pipes and reeds. The wind was gentle but insistent."

The room remained silent. Cali Sky came out of the trance and smiled self-consciously. Chris then blurted out, "That was fucking beautiful! Where did it come from?" She did not answer and returned to Tam's collection.

Brodie asked, "Great story, Cali Sky, but how does that help us find…"

"Brodie!" interrupted Tam. "That's enough. Just let it go for now."

She arrived home later that night tired and numb. When she opened the apartment door she found her mom talking to a man she had never seen before. He was middle aged. When Cali Sky entered he broke off conversation with Joan and stood up. He looked thin and athletic. His hair was short and kinky: a white-man's afro. His eyes were narrowly placed in his head, giving the impression that he looked upon everything with penetrating insight.

"Cali Sky," said Joan, "this is Lester."

They shook hands.

"I'm an old friend of your dad's."

"Nice to meet you," Cali Sky said with stiff politeness. Intrigued as she was with her mom's male visitor—especially one who knew her dad—she nevertheless wanted only to lie down in her bed and listen to music. She had already begun thinking of possibilities to suit her mood: Harold Budd, Pink Floyd, Brian Eno. But the name "Lester" intruded upon her musical brain-storm. Why did that name sound familiar?

"I recently re-connected with him," Lester was saying, "and thought..."

"Oh my God!" interrupted Cali Sky. "Lester! You saw Bob Dylan in London with my dad! The van! The conversation piece! Oh my God!"

"So I guess your dad has told you about me," laughed Lester.

Cali Sky did not dare mention her dad's diary.

"So what are you doing here?" asked Cali Sky.

"Well, like I was saying, I recently re-connected with your dad. I thought I would also say hello to Joan here...and meet you!"

Cali Sky's mind was racing. She did not respond.

"Lester is actually a talent agent in L.A.," said Joan.

Cali Sky was trying to re-trace the narrative of her dad's diary, to remember Lester's place in her dad's life.

"You disappeared after my mom and dad got married... before I was born," Cali Sky said, now thinking aloud.

"Well, I don't know if I *disappeared*. Actually I finished college with an accounting degree. Spent five miserable years working at an accounting firm when I decided to shift careers. I had a friend who worked at a talent agency in Hollywood and he helped me get a job. Some of my clients became successful so I…"

Cali Sky's mind wandered. She was still trying to remember, to connect the flesh and blood man standing before her with the events that seemed as faded as the diary itself. *This is the man who cruised Hollywood Boulevard with my dad in a VW bus, who took acid with my dad, who hiked the Alps with my dad, who knew my mom when she….*

"…and that brought me back into contact with Philip," Lester concluded.

"Cali Sky?" asked Joan hesitantly. She guessed what her daughter was thinking.

"Wow," said Cali Sky.

"Your dad," began Lester, filling the space of the prolonged silence, "tells me you are a fantastic musician and that you recently joined a band that shows great promise."

"Yeah…yeah. We actually just had band practice."

"That brings me to another reason why I stopped by. While I represent some pretty big-name actors I don't represent any musical acts. Nevertheless, if you want I could represent your band. At least for a while. As a favor to your dad. I could be your band's agent."

TWELVE

T HE MIND TRICK unsettled her as always. She posed the dizzying question: What if five years ago she could look into the future and see only this discrete moment, nothing before, nothing after? What would she think? Here was the moment:

She sat in a recording studio with a guitar in her lap. Brodie sat nearby with a bass guitar. On her other side sat Tam, a grimace clouding his clean-shaven face. Across from her sat Chris behind a drum kit, confident and patient. She wouldn't have known two of these musicians five years ago, but the moment would seem promising: recording music in a studio. But a menacing presence bore down on her. It originated from an image taped to the wall. The image was gruesome: It depicted a wild-eyed, crazed monster eating a decapitated corpse. The monster gnawed on an arm as blood oozed down the supple flesh of the dead body. Five years ago she would not know that the monster was actually a god, the god Saturn, and that the corpse was his own offspring. She would not know that the image was a reprint of Goya's *Saturn Devouring His Son*.

As it turned out the fully present Cali Sky—the one actually experiencing the moment—knew that Tam taped the poster there because it reflected his interest in Dark Romanticism and thus inspired him. But Cali Sky's command of the answers to these questions simply made her ignorance of the significance question more ominous.

"Tam," she asked, "What is the significance of that image?"

"Just think about it, Cali Sky," he replied petulantly. "You're smart. You'll figure it out."

Before she could snap at him for his condescension, Chris exclaimed, "I think I saw that picture once on an Iron Maiden shirt. Yeah, some stoner was wearing it in my shop class."

Tam looked at Chris with a disgust so intense that it rendered him speechless. Cali Sky did not try to disguise her laughter. But it was quickly extinguished. Not because of Tam's anger, but because of her realization that their studio time was turning into a failure.

Jerry had paid the $500 for three hours of recording time at a small, dingy studio equipped with eight-track equipment. In exchange the band agreed to give Jerry exclusive rights to their shows for one year. They refused him however a percentage cut of any royalties they might earn, should they happen to produce a successful record. The contract was written up by their new manager, Lester, who after schooling the band on the head-spinning science of performance-rights royalties, mechanical royalties and recoups informed them that Jerry was a shyster. Tam thought they were both crooks.

"I've worked with Jerry for years," Tam had said. "Believe me, he exploits every band that plays at That's. And I don't trust Lester. He's an ex-hippie."

"How is that relevant?" Cali Sky demanded.

Tam glared at her as if the answer to her question was obvious.

She added, "He's paying the sound engineer out of his own pocket. He's doing us a huge favor."

So they had agreed to bring on Lester as their manager and had signed the contract he negotiated with Jerry. Cali Sky now wondered what would happen to the contract if they never even cut a demo. Their studio time was half spent. The sound engineer was cranky.

"Anytime you're ready guys," he said with sarcastic patience. "We can try another take."

"Alright, alright," Tam replied. "Brodie, you're missing your entry point. You come in *after* Chris's first snare beat. Okay?"

It doesn't really matter, thought Cali Sky as Brodie nodded.

"Begin whenever you want," said the weary sound engineer.

They played the song proficiently, with as much enthusiasm as they could muster. Cali Sky and Tam had co-written it one night at Tam's house while Chris and Brodie were swimming in the pool. At the time Cali Sky was elated. Theoretically the song should have been outstanding: an interesting chord progression, an aggressive melody, some nice hooks. But the next morning she discovered that it had sounded better the night before.

"Got it!" announced the sound engineer at the song's conclusion. "That was a good take. Just give me a moment and we can record the second song."

Brodie looked pleased and Chris ever-patient. Tam avoided eye contact with anyone. Cali Sky appeared pale.

"Ready guys?" the sound engineer asked a few minutes later. "Okay, we're rolling."

The band began the second song. Cali Sky had written this one in the apartment one Thursday afternoon after school. When she first played it for Tam, he thought it sounded too much like a "rock song. It's too obvious."

"What the hell does that mean?" she had asked.

Instead of answering he had picked up a guitar and made some small changes to the song's structure, scaling back its blues-based context. She sensed the direction he was taking it, made some alterations of her own, and was pleased. She felt it was the perfect combination of their styles. But once again with each passing day she felt less satisfied.

"Great! Great!" the sound engineer enthused. "A great take! Give me another moment. Then you can come in and give it a listen."

Cali Sky rushed out of the studio, followed closely by Tam.

"It's all wrong," she said as she leaned against the parking lot light pole.

Tam stared down at an oil stain. "I know." The parking lot was quiet and still, the heat rising from the pavement.

"The songs are not really me, you know?" she said. "They just lack something."

They heard the studio door open and saw Trish step tentatively onto the sidewalk. The blazing late spring sun made her figure look more diminutive. She spotted Tam talking closely to Cali Sky and decided to keep her distance. She walked with small steps to Tam's Volvo and sat on the hood.

"Forest Murmurs consumed me," said Tam. "That band...was everything to me. When we broke up I didn't think I'd ever find anyone...any band to replace it. But I knew that if I did it would have to be a completely different sort of band. I'd have to forget the music we made. I knew I'd have to consume Forest Murmurs. That's what I taped that poster in the studio. But now I'm not sure. Who's Saturn and who's the child?"

"So I was supposed to figure all that out?" Cali Sky laughed.

Tam smiled. "No, I guess not."

"That's strong language, Tam. Your old band *consumed* you?"

Tam nodded.

"What afflicts you Cali Sky?"

She saw that he was looking in her eyes. Her instinct was to become defensive, to ask, 'Why ask such a strange question? Why do you supposed that I am *afflicted*?' But then she realized that he knew her better than that.

"My sister died five years ago. She was only five. After that, everything pretty much fell apart."

He looked down and nodded.

"We need different muses, Tam. The anger, the aggression, the subversion. I'm tired of all that."

"If you lose it, what do you have left? You feed off of it. Maybe *you're* Saturn. Maybe you consume *everyone*."

"Don't say that." She turned away and then said, "What inspired you when you were in Forest Murmurs?"

"Strong emotions, curiosity, I don't know. I was in love at the time. I don't know. We just discovered some new musical universe and we were the only ones there."

Cali Sky wiped some beads of sweat from her brow. "Do you wanna go in and listen to the demo?"

"No."

"Me neither."

"I wanna destroy it."

"Me too."

Ten minutes later they stood outside the studio holding their cased instruments. Brodie was helping Chris load his drums, back and forth they walked from the studio to the parking lot. Tam held in his left hand the original recording of the demo, they had made no copies. Brodie heaved a tom drum into the back of Chris's Suzuki.

"Be careful, Brodie!" Chris warned. "Or I'll break your bass over your Goddamned head."

"I just can't believe this," exclaimed Brodie, turning toward

Tam and Cali Sky. "Jerry pays for our studio time, we record our songs, and now you just want to throw the demo away."

"I gotta go," muttered Cali Sky, sounding exhausted.

"Are we at least going to practice tomorrow?" asked Brodie.

Tam ignored him. Cali Sky replied in a crestfallen voice, "No."

"What do you mean no?" demanded Brodie.

Cali Sky ignored him.

"What? Are you going out with Ben?"

She continued to ignore him.

"Don't you think our band is more important than a date... with Ben?"

"Shut up, Brodie." She began to walk away.

"The songs we recorded don't suck, Cali Sky!" Brodie yelled. "They're *good* songs. And they might be our ticket to a record contract."

Cali Sky froze and set down her guitar. She turned suddenly around and marched with focused purpose to Tam. She snatched the tape from his hand and threw it with all her strength. It sailed over the studio where they lost sight of it in the sun. Brodie nearly succumbed to the instinct to scale the building's front facade and retrieve the tape, his body already angled toward the endpoint of the flying tape's trajectory.

Instead he yelled, "What is wrong with you?"

"Brodie, those songs *do* suck."

As she turned to leave Tam spoke to her softly, "The goddess consuming her children."

"Tam," she replied, "don't ever put that poster on a studio wall again."

A week later on a Saturday night, Cali Sky set her guitar case next to the apartment front door and ran through her checklist. *Brodie has the amps, I have my guitar, cords, and pedals. Picks in my back pocket.*

"Mom!" she called out. "Gotta go. I'm late!"

The phone rang. *Shit.* She picked up the phone.

"Hello." She said the word hurriedly and coldly, hoping her tone would discourage the person on the other end of the line.

"Cali Sky?"

"Yeah."

"This is Lester."

Shit. "Hey Lester."

"What happened?"

Cali Sky sighed and sat down on the edge of the couch.

"It...didn't work out."

"It didn't work out? What do you mean? The sound engineer said you cut a demo. Where is it?"

"I...destroyed it."

"Destroyed it? Why?"

"I just didn't like it. I hated it actually. So did Tam."

"But it's *your* music. Did you not play it well?"

"No, no. We played fine, played it just like we wrote it. But that's just the thing. It *wasn't* our music. Not really. I mean, we *wrote* it. But it's just not me...or Tam. We can do better."

"Okay, here's the thing," Lester now spoke sharply. "As you know, Jerry paid a lot of money for you and your band to cut this demo. When you destroyed the demo, you threw all that money away."

"I know, I know. I'm sorry."

"I'm pretty new to this myself. But I'm pretty sure that one rule of recording is the musician doesn't destroy his own music."

"I know, I'm sorry."

"Well, I managed to work some wiggle room into the contract. It won't be easy, but I'll see if I can get Jerry to terminate it."

"Um, okay."

"But I can't guarantee anything. I'm sure Jerry will demand

his $500 back. Your parents are my good friends. And as *another* favor to them, if that happens, I'll reimburse him myself...no strings attached, no hard feelings."

"Really?"

"I'll try."

"Okay. Thanks." Cali Sky's voice broke.

"You okay?"

"Yeah."

"And I'll still see you around, I'm sure."

At that moment Cali Sky saw an image of Brodie. He was seated in his messy room in his parents' ramshackle house playing bass, practicing hour after hour. Listening to songs, playing along. Composing bass lines for Quest songs, eager to ask her what she thought.

"Wait! Lester. Are you still there?"

"Yeah."

"Could you give us one more chance?"

"Cali Sky, I..."

"Just give us two weeks to write two songs. I promise you we'll record them and send the demo out this time."

"How do I know you won't destroy it again?"

"I won't, I promise."

"You realize that if you were any other client I would have dropped you already."

"I know. But we'll make it work this time."

"Okay. I'll talk to Jerry and see what I can do. No promises. If I can't get him to agree to pay for *some* of the studio time, then I'm afraid I'll have to pull the plug."

"Yeah, I understand. Thank you, Lester."

"One more thing, Cali Sky..."

She looked at the digital clock on the microwave. *Shit I'm going to be late.* "Yeah?"

"I think I have the right to know more about why you destroyed the demo."

"I guess because it wasn't honest."

"What do you mean?"

"I felt like we we're just...playing a role, going through the motions, like it was an act."

"But Cali Sky, *that's* what rock and roll is."

"No, it doesn't have to be."

"Cali Sky, rock and roll hasn't been honest in twenty years."

The words were like punches to her solar plexus. "What are you talking about?"

"It must've been '67 or '68. The Mothers of Invention—you know, Frank Zappa's band—came out with this album called *We're Only in It for the Money*. It was merciless satire, it made fun of hippies and hippie music, it made fun of the Beatles. Actually, the cover of the album was a lampoon of *Sgt. Pepper's*. But the thing about it was, Zappa was actually *really* good—I mean, as a musician and a lyricist. I remember listening to that album and thinking I could never go back. And I just feel like rock and roll changed after that. Of course, then the Stones got really big, then came Altamont, the death of Brian Jones, the Beatles broke up, Lennon started singing about how the dream is over."

Cali Sky felt her mouth becoming dry. She didn't want to hear any more but Lester continued, "Rock and roll became a pose, an image revolving around sex...well, I suppose it was always revolving around that, but now in a more self-conscious way. But who's to say that's bad, you just have to play the game..."

"No! No, I don't. See, that's what I *don't* want my band to do. That's what was wrong with our demo."

"Obviously you feel strongly about this, Cali Sky," said Lester reassuringly. "And that's great. I'm willing to pay studio time for you and your band to record some songs that shoot for honesty."

"Thanks, Lester." She felt tears in her eyes.

Cali Sky picked up her guitar case and scurried down the stairs. She started the car, turned on the AC and studied the directions scrawled on a wrinkled scratch piece of paper. Someone's house. A kid who went to a different school, someone Brodie knew. And Brodie was the only one in favor of playing the gig. They wouldn't be paid; they probably wouldn't know anyone there, and few would even know their music, with the exception of their small following, to whom the band distributed fliers. Cali Sky and Tam agreed to do the gig because they felt they owed it to Brodie after what happened to the demo. For his part Brodie said it would be good practice. At the moment Cali Sky was in no mood to play a gig.

The directions led her to the right neighborhood. From there she simply followed a train of cars filled with teenagers. She parked behind a lowered mini-truck and followed two boys, who noticed her and carried her equipment for her. *A promising start,* she thought. They walked three blocks and entered an enormous backyard through a side gate. The first thing she noticed was a boxing ring, makeshift, constructed of plywood with tan-colored rope stretched around its perimeter. Stools were placed in opposite corners of the ring. Someone was jumping up and down in the center, laughing. The second thing she noticed were the people standing on the balcony, connected to the second floor of the huge house, which yawned over the backyard. She could see that they were adults, non-teenagers. The third thing she noticed was the sound of George Thoroughgood's song, "Bad to the Bone."

"You're late!" shouted Brodie, red cup in hand.

"What the hell is this?" she asked.

"What?"

"Why is there a boxing ring in the backyard?"

"For the boxing matches. Lake Park vs. Washington High.

You missed the middleweight fights. They'll do one heavyweight fight and then we'll go on."

"Where do we play?"

"Over there." Brodie pointed to a dark corner of the yard.

"Brodie. This is not good."

"Why?"

She ignored the question. "Who are those people on the balcony?"

"Pat's parents. They live here. Pretty cool parents, huh?"

"Where's Tam?"

"He's over on the stage, tuning his guitar."

"Where's Chris?"

"He's over there." Brodie pointed in the direction of a crowd gathered in a circle near the house, the direction from which "Bad to the Bone" blasted from a cheap boom box.

Cali Sky walked into the darkness toward the "stage," where Tam sat alone, cross-legged on a turned-off amp strumming his guitar, oblivious to his surroundings. A few stray party-goers wandered around the area. Cali Sky set her guitar next to Tam.

"I have left my body," he said without looking up. "I am not here because I do not want to partake in this disaster."

"Come on, Tam!" Brodie said as he stepped onto the darkened stage. "It won't be a disaster."

"What is Chris doing?" asked Cali Sky.

Still focusing on his guitar Tam answered, "I don't care and you don't want to know."

"Brodie?"

Brodie scratched an imaginary itch on his back shoulder. "A drinking contest," he murmured.

"He's in a drinking contest?" shouted Cali Sky. "Right before we go on?"

"Don't worry," Brodie said, "I've seen Chris so drunk that

he could hardly walk, but once he got behind his drums he played perfectly."

"Like any heavy-metal musician worth his skin-tight leather pants," mocked Tam, still ignoring them and strumming his guitar.

Cali Sky rolled her eyes and headed toward the crowd, followed by Brodie. They winnowed between people until they could go no further, the audience was too tightly packed together. "Bad to the Bone" was winding down, suddenly drowned out by an eruption of cheers and applause.

"I can't see, Brodie," yelled Cali Sky. "What's happening?"

"Chris just downed a cup of beer. They've been at it for over an hour and a half. One cup every five minutes. The first person who pukes loses."

"Great."

"The other guy is about to take a drink," continued Brodie. "His name is Shawn. A football player."

Cali Sky tried to peer through the throng. She caught a glimpse of a brightly lit table. On one side she could make out Chris's burly figure. On the other side sat a blonde-haired kid whose tank top displayed massive biceps.

Cali Sky was suddenly startled by a massive groan, collectively emitted by the drinking-contest spectators. To her ears the groan—a sustained monosyllabic exclamation of "Ohhhh!"—was singular in its harmonized pitch, as if the assembled had rehearsed it beforehand. It started low, conveying anticipation, and throttled suddenly to a higher range, then broke apart into a hubbub of elation and disgust.

"What happened?" Cali Sky asked.

"Chris won. Shawn was taking a sip and threw up into the cup...and all over the table."

People turned away with sour looks on their faces. The crowd quickly thinned. Cali Sky could hear Chris before she could see him clearly on the other side of the dispersing crowd.

"You had Taco Bell for dinner, didn't you?" he shouted.

Cali Sky could now see Shawn, who smiled sheepishly and nodded. She watched Chris inspect the vomit more carefully.

"What is that? A burrito supreme?"

Shawn's goofy smile never faded. He nodded again. The crowd that remained became hysterical, not knowing whether to marvel more at Chris's drinking prowess or his ability to identify the remains of partially digested fast food. A puddle of vomit on the table encroached on a pile of cash, which Chris quickly scooped up.

"Everyone watch out!" shouted some kid holding a garden hose crazily spraying water in every direction. Cali Sky and Brodie sprang back as the kid used the high-pressure hose to wash away the vomit and the spilled beer. Chris approached them triumphantly.

"At least one of us is getting paid for this gig!"

Cali Sky frowned, Brodie laughed and slapped Chris's hand.

"He may have been big," bragged Chris, "but he knows nothing about drinking contests. Hey Shawn!" he shouted, looking over Brodie's shoulder and holding up the wad of money, "You wanna go back to Taco Bell? I'll buy!"

Shawn smiled drunkenly.

"So what did *you* eat, Chris?" asked Brodie confidentially.

"A loaf of bread."

"An entire loaf of bread?"

"Yeah. It soaks up all the beer.... I think I might really go to Taco Bell, though, I'm starving."

"No, don't. Wait till after we play a set," Brodie said.

Cali Sky glanced back at the stage. She could see Tam in the darkness, still playing. Trish was now seated on Brodie's amp.

Cali Sky turned angrily toward Brodie and said, "We have a drunk drummer, a guitar player who has mentally checked out, a dark stage in the corner, and a violent crowd. Do you still really expect us to play this gig?"

Before Brodie could answer Chris exclaimed, "Hell yeah! These are the best kinds of gigs…as long as no one touches my drums. They touch my drums and we have a problem." In his drunken fog Chris addressed his response to Brodie. Then he seemed to remember that Cali Sky asked the question, so he said to her, "Don't worry, Cali Sky. I'll protect you. Just stand close to me. I can play drums and kick someone's ass at the same time."

Cali Sky stared at Brodie. He put his arm around Chris and said, "See? There's nothing to fear when you have a drummer like this."

Cali Sky began walking away. Brodie tried to slow her progress, walking alongside her.

"So did you talk to Lester?" asked Brodie.

"Yeah."

"And?"

"He's going to give us another chance."

"Yes!"

"I'm only doing this for you," she said, stopping. "You realize that, right?"

"Really? Why?"

"Because we've known each other a long time. Because we've been through a lot together."

"It's all going to work out, Cali Sky. We're going to be big."

"I don't think so," she said as a burden of fear and regret materialized in her mind and settled over all of her thoughts. "I feel like I made a huge mistake, like I should be going to college this summer."

"Don't worry. We're going to make it. We're going to be huge.".

"Ladies and gentlemen," announced someone standing inside the boxing ring. His voice caught about half of the party-goers' attention. "Ladies and gentlemen," he repeated. Conversations ceased. Someone pushed the stop button on the boom box, which was now blasting Run-D.M.C.'s "King of Rock." "It's time for the main event, the heavyweight fight. Let's get ready to rumble!"

"Come on," said Brodie, "Let's watch the fight."

"No Brodie. Not interested."

"Come on!" He grabbed her hand and led her, half-resisting, to the ring. Along the way she spotted Ben, standing beside a tree planted at the back of the yard, supported by two wooden poles.

"Brodie, let go," she said. "I don't want to stand close to the ring. Besides, I want to go say hi to someone."

"Who?" He followed her line of vision to the place where Ben stood. "Oh. Go to your boyfriend," he said. The tenderness evaporated from his voice and body language. As Cali Sky reached Ben the fighters were standing in their corners, moving nervously from side to side.

"This is horrible, don't you think?" she asked Ben.

"Yeah."

"I am *not* looking forward to playing a set afterwards."

"I think Brodie likes you."

She looked at him and smiled. "I know. He's liked me since we were thirteen years old."

"You never liked him?"

"No, not in that way."

"Why?"

"Well…it's complicated."

"Listen. I've got something I need to tell you."

He was interrupted by the sound of a bell. The fight began. Untrained and undisciplined the two fighters went after each other furiously. Their wild roundhouse punches and frenetic uppercuts did not seem to connect, or if they did, they had little effect. Adrenalin transformed them into madmen, endowing them with the capability to afflict and withstand punishment of which their bodies would be otherwise incapable. Cali Sky felt the same sensations she experienced when a fight broke out at school: a stirring in her gut that betokened an existential despair, as if the two combatants symbolized the dark reality of the human condition, and that what really lies at the center of it all are violence and chaos.

The fighters' movement began to slow. For the first time Cali Sky became aware of the screams and whistles from the spectators. They were expressing their disapproval of the slackened pace of the fight. She could see blood on the face of both boxers. Apparently they *had* landed some punches. She also saw that as their chemical-induced rage waned, their fear waxed. They almost looked like they wanted to quit, like they realized that everyone had had their fun but it turned out that it was all a big mistake. Their punches seemed half-hearted; they were just going through the motions. Cali Sky felt sorry for them as the catcalls from the spectators grew louder.

Then without warning one boxer, re-adrenalized by threats from the onlookers and the shame that they engendered, threw a punch like he really meant it. It was an obvious punch with a big, elaborate windup, like the kind Cali Sky watched on TV shows like *Magnum P.I.* and *Knight Rider* where the bad guys seem to wait to get hit. In fact Cali Sky initially thought the fighter was joking, making fun of himself and the whole abysmal spectacle. Certainly everyone saw the punch coming...everyone except the other boxer. Was it a mental lapse? Was he distracted? Or did he want it to end so badly that he submitted to the punch? Whatever the case when the blow landed on his chin a splash of blood sprayed out over the crowd. Cali Sky drew close to Ben in the ensuing pandemonium. He put his arm around her as the existential despair spread throughout her body, so visceral as to be nearly sexual, experienced as a throbbing pain that bordered on an unexpected pleasure.

The boxing match had lasted barely two minutes. Brodie emerged from the pandemonium. He had blood on his shirt near his chest. More blood was smudged on his shirt sleeve, which he had used to wipe his face.

"That was disgusting!" he said. "Look at this." Blood had also splattered on his shoes.

The fallen boxer was now on his feet and had already removed his gloves. He pressed a towel to his mouth. Cali Sky glanced up at the balcony. She saw two men laughing, beer bottles in hand. Next to them she saw two women, perhaps their wives. They were drinking from wine glasses.

"This is a bad scene, Brodie," Cali Sky.

Brodie looked around. The triumphant boxer had exited the ring, but he kept his boxing gloves on, as if he wanted to fight some more. He yelled challenges and struck poses of bravado.

"I think you're right," Brodie replied. "We'll just play one set, then get out of here."

Cali Sky nodded.

On their way to the stage they collected Chris, who was standing in a circle of people whom Cali Sky did not recognize. Only as she approached the stage did she spot some familiar faces: Stone and Cigarette Girl, some of the girls who went to her solo gigs, and Tam's friends Marc and Synth. Tam still sat on the amp, implacable, playing guitar.

"Tam," said Cali Sky as she pulled the guitar strap over her head. "Tam. Tam!"

"What?" he responded calmly, finally looking up at her, as if awakened from a deep slumber.

"We're just going to play one set, okay? Then we leave."

"Sure."

Trish, Marc and Synth walked off the stage. Without introduction or fanfare Quest began playing its first song. At first not many seemed to notice. Cali Sky's friends and followers moved to the music. A minute into the song, however, others began to gather around the stage. They looked up at the band with lingering violence in their eyes and pent-up aggression seeking a release. They had been incited by the fight. Cali Sky barely heard the music she was playing; she just wanted to get through it.

"Show us your tits!"

So that's how it's going to begin, thought Cali Sky. She had heard it before, but not very often and not in an explosive environment like this. But like the few other times it happened she ignored it. *Focus on your guitar. Ignore them.*

"Come on! Show us your tits!"

The voice was reckless and giddy; she did not dare look in its direction. She played like a robot until the song mercifully came to an end. But now in the absence of music, shrill and ugly words from the audience were more audible.

"Tits, tits, tits, tits!" The reckless and giddy voice had begun a chant. Cali Sky turned her back on the crowd. Chris motioned for her to stay close to him.

Suddenly a different and new voice rose up above the chant.

"Hey man! No more pussy music!"

Back still turned to the audience, Cali Sky focused her attention on Chris. She knew that he would warn her if she needed to protect herself. She was even prepared to run around the drum kit and hide behind him if necessary.

"Don't call me 'man.'" Tam sounded ostentatiously defiant. Amplified through the microphone his voice was exponentially louder than those from the throng.

The response from the second voice in the crowd sounded feeble, almost trivial: "Fuck you, faggot!"

Tam walked calmly to his amp and unplugged his guitar. He carefully placed it in the case and nonchalantly walked off the stage, guitar in hand, staying clear of the crowd along the outer reaches of the backyard. He executed his exit with Zen-like detachment.

"Did Tam just walk off stage?" asked Cali Sky, back still turned to the unfolding drama.

"Yep," answered Chris.

Following Tam's tactic Cali Sky packed her guitar into the case and unceremoniously walked off the stage, following his circuitous path away from the crowd. Ten strides later she entered the darkest part of the yard and felt afraid. She could feel the grass, taller and untrampled at the back of the lawn, graze her shoes with each step. Up ahead she saw three figures near her escape route; she did not look directly at them. She pondered the possibility of using her guitar as a weapon. Closer now she saw that one of the three figures was shirtless and wore boxing gloves: the victorious boxer. As she approached he turned to face her and said something she could not comprehend. His smile was unhinged.

An amplified voice rose from the stage: "This show is over!" It was Chris. The announcement distracted the boxer. Cali Sky capitalized on the moment and pressed on. The boxer called out to her but was distracted again, this time by a cacophony of boos. Cali Sky did not look back. As she reached the gate leading to the street she heard from afar raised angry voices. "Shut the fuck up!" Chris shouted into the microphone, sounding irritated but mostly amused. Still Cali Sky did not look back. As she turned the corner and began walking down the street the sounds she heard from the backyard were ambivalent: The din might have been the start of a bloody riot or a call to renewed celebration. She wondered where Tam was. *All those amps are his. What if they're destroyed?* she thought. *At least I have my guitar.* She felt more at ease. *As long as Brodie sticks with Chris he'll be alright. I think.*

She suddenly heard someone running up behind her. She swung around, startled.

"Shit!"

"Sorry!"

"Ben, you scared the hell out of me."

"Sorry, I just wanted to make sure you're alright."

"Yeah, I'm okay." She paused for a moment to calm her nerves. "What's going on back there now?"

"A lot of people seem pretty angry. Chris kept them off the stage. But I left right after you, so I don't know what's going on now."

They walked together toward Cali Sky's car.

"I'm going to kill Brodie," she said. "I can't believe he signed us up for this gig."

"Are you sure you're alright?"

"Yeah."

He carried her guitar for her. She looked back. The street was quiet and peaceful. Compared to the backyard it looked almost Edenic, as if the Fall of humankind were confined to the half acre fenced around the party house.

"Like I said," Ben said, "There's something I need to tell you."

"What?" she whispered.

"I'm moving away."

"What? When?"

"Next week. My parents and I. We're moving back to New Mexico. I can't go to prom."

"But... but there's only a couple more weeks of school. What about your finals?"

"I'll take them early. My dad is being transferred back to his old job and has to start on Wednesday. We looked into ways for me to stay, at least for a few more weeks, but it wouldn't work out. I'm leaving on Monday. I'm so sorry I can't take you to prom."

"That's alright."

"I feel really bad."

"No really. It's alright."

"Are you sure?"

They reached Cali Sky's car. She opened her trunk. Ben put the guitar inside. They stood there silently for a moment, a few feet apart.

"It's just that this is so sudden," said Cali Sky.

"I know. I don't want to go," said Ben.

"I don't want you to go either."

"You're shaking."

"Yeah, sometimes that happens to me after gigs when…"

Ben interrupted her with a hug, sudden and unexpected. It was so unexpected that Cali Sky stood frozen for a while, arms still at her side. But Ben maintained his fervid embrace. Finally she relaxed and wrapped her arms around him. She was surprised by how soothed she suddenly felt, how comforted and safe.

"I'm not shaking anymore," she said.

Ben released her and took a step back. "I have something for you. Something I want you to have before I leave."

"I actually have something for you too," she said. "But we have to go inside my car."

"Okay."

Cali Sky unlocked the doors and sat down in the driver's seat, Ben settled into the passenger side. She reached over and opened the glove box. She pulled out a cassette and said, "I made you a mix tape."

Ben smiled. "Let's listen to it."

"Of course."

She turned the key and all the dashboard warning lights flashed momentarily. Then she pushed the tape into the stereo. A woman's voice spoke softly, "He's here, he's here." Then the voice began to sing, accompanied by a lush piano.

They both listened silently.

"Do you know who this is?" asked Cali Sky.

"No."

"Kate Bush. It's a song called 'The Man with the Child in His Eyes.'"

"I love it." He straightened his legs, pushing himself up on the seat, and pulled a small box from his pocket.

"Here," he said, "This is for you."

The box was square with faded blue vertical stripes on all sides. She pulled off the lid. Inside was a ring. The band was silver. Its crown was glass, encasing a blue flower.

"I remembered the story you told me. About passion, symbolized by the Blue Flower."

She pulled it from the box and studied it carefully.

"I hope it fits," he said, "If not you can get it sized."

She slipped it on, then leaned over and kissed him warmly. One of the fingers that cradled his face wore the ring. She leaned in closer, deepening the kiss, her hand now caressing his neck.

"Ben," she whispered, "you're shaking."

"I know. I'm going to miss you."

When the cops descended on the party house later that night and the teenagers fled in predictable fashion, breaking willy nilly out of the backyard and bringing the Fall with them, Eden was squeezed into the small space of Cali Sky's car, cloaked from view by fogged windows, which on this night offered protection as secure as any flaming sword.

PART THREE

*"In like manner the Muse first of all inspires men herself;
and from these inspired persons a chain of other persons
is suspended, who take the inspiration. For all good poets,
epic as well as lyric, compose their beautiful poems not by
art, but because they are inspired and possessed."*
—Plato, *Ion*

*"The best song will never get sung
The best life never leaves your lungs
So good you won't ever know."*
Wilco, *"The Late Greats"*

1985-1987

THIRTEEN

Summer 1985

CALI SKY SAT at a large table made of thick glass. Tam sat directly opposite, with Brodie and Chris on either side, each band member to a side. Trish slouched on a barstool in the corner of the room, within listening distance in the vast quiet emptiness of Tam's parents' house. Fading sunlight filtered through the windows, stretching two stories to the ceiling, washing the marble-floored room in a slowly dimming half-light.

"Are your parents *ever* home?" asked Brodie.

"Can I live in one of the guest bedrooms?" asked Chris. "I swear no one would ever know."

"Can we start this meeting?" asked Tam.

"Yeah," said Brodie, "I think Cali Sky should go first. This was her idea."

"Actually," Cali Sky replied, "it wasn't. This was Tam's idea."

"I still don't get it," said Chris. "You say we need a new direction. Why? We're playing gigs at That's, the place is packed, and Lester said that some labels are interested in our demo, right?"

Cali Sky glancd at Tam, who still didn't trust Lester.

Anticipating her thoughts Tam said, "Whether or not we can trust Lester is irrelevant right now. Chris, to answer your question, we need to change musical directions because Cali Sky and I *do* agree that we're not happy with the music we are currently making."

"But people like it," said Chris.

"So what!" answered Cali Sky. "It's not really coming from *us*. Tam and I feel like we're playing variations of the same old thing."

"We need a new muse," added Tam. "The old one is a whore, like the groupies you used to screw in your old band. They're not exactly discriminating."

Chris stared at Tam blankly.

"Did everyone bring something?" asked Tam.

Nods around the table.

"So who wants to go first?" Tam continued.

"It was your idea," Cali Sky said, "why don't you go first?"

"Yeah, but you have that huge book in front of you," answered Tam, "we're curious to know what's in it. Why don't you go first?"

"Fine." When she opened the well-worn book the binding creaked and groaned. She flipped through the pages, most of which contained reprints of old photos. Just as Zoe had done five years earlier, she opened the volume to the photos of pixies frolicking around adolescent girls. She had in fact borrowed the book from Zoe for this occasion.

"These," she began, "are the Cottingley Fairies." She passed the book around, explaining the sensation they created in England.

When the book came into Chris's hands he said, "This girl here, the one looking down at the fairy, she kind of looks like you."

"She's not surprised or alarmed," Cali Sky commented.

Tam stared at the photos, much longer than anyone else. Trish watched him from a distance. Tam said, "You're right. No surprise or fear. She's at home in a world where fairies live. In fact she looks almost as magical as the fairies."

Brodie turned to Cali Sky and asked, "So how does this translate into our new musical direction? What's your idea?"

"What do you think, Brodie?" Tam asked.

"I have no fucking idea," answered Brodie.

"Come on," replied Tam, "Don't be so simple minded."

"Fine, uh, it's mysterious," answered Brodie.

"And mythological," added Tam.

They sat quiet for a moment. Tam studied the pictures some more.

"So," said Brodie, suddenly appearing frustrated, "if you translate what we've said to music, you get, what, 'Stairway to Heaven'?"

"Don't be so quick to make such a specific connection," Tam said disapprovingly. "Just let the images percolate in your mind."

"Desire," said Cali Sky suddenly. The dying light made her face radiant and her hair appear auburn. "When I look at that photo I *want* it to be true, so badly that it almost seems like it is. But it's more than that." She looked agitated. "I mean, the desire is bigger than that. It's a desire to see the reality behind appearances. A supernatural reality, but because it's reality it's not even supernatural anymore. It's just the way things are but we can't see it…" She trailed off.

Brodie suddenly experienced deja vu, but then realized it wasn't deja vu but a memory, a memory of a recurring event. He felt now as he often did when he watched Cali Sky play guitar or piano. He felt like she was beyond his reach.

"Brodie," said Tam, "Why don't you go next?"

Brodie shook off his overreaching thoughts and returned to the moment. "Okay," he replied, taking a deep breath and pulling a tape from his back pocket. He set it on the glass table and pushed it over to Tam. "Play this."

Tam rose from his seat and carried the tape to his parents' stereo. Trish watched him the whole way with the settled apathy of an unflappable cat. The unmistakable rhythm and simplicity of a punk song began playing as Tam returned to his seat. It was "Bloodstains," by Agent Orange. No one spoke through the first verse and chorus.

Then Chris said, "So you want to make our band more punk?"

"No, of course not," answered Brodie. "Do you remember this song, Cali Sky?"

She nodded.

"This is the first song I ever learned to play on guitar," Brodie said. "Cali Sky tabbed it out for me. Do you remember that?" Cali Sky nodded again. He continued, "It was, like, one of the coolest moments of my life. I was actually playing a song."

"Anyway," interrupted Brodie, "I'll never forget that moment, that feeling. And if I can have that feeling in this band, in whatever new direction we take, then I'll be happy. " He looked at Cali Sky, searching her eyes, but instead was distracted by the strong emotion in Tam's. They listened to the song in full. As Tam retrieved the tape Brodie and Cali Sky exchanged brief smiles that bore the marks of nostalgia and affection, which Chris pretended not to notice.

"Your turn, Tam," said Cali Sky.

Tam looked one by one at each person seated at the table. The sun had nearly set. The room was now illuminated primarily by artificial light as darkness pressed in from the outside. Tam adjusted his weight, reached into his back pocket and set a card onto the glass table. Cali Sky, Brodie and Chris strained to see. The card depicted an ornately armored man, powerfully built, wearing a crown and holding a staff in his right hand. He had the appearance of a Roman centurion or an Egyptian pharaoh. A walled city rose behind him. He stares majestically into the distance, just over the viewer's right shoulder, where one might imagine an enemy army nervously closes ranks, or plebian masses await their deified leader, or a beautifully tragic future approaches with unavoidable certainty. He stands in what resembles a columned booth with short curtains draped at the top, just above and beside his crown. The words at the bottom of the card identify this structure: "THE CHARIOT." Two sphinxes, one white and one black, sit directly in front of the chariot, poised to pull the man toward one of these imagined destinies.

Cali Sky, Brodie and Chris studied the details of the card, then looked expectantly at Tam, who stared at the window in a pose not unlike that of the man depicted on the card. Cali Sky turned around to see what he was staring at, but by now the darkness outside was solid, transforming the window into a mirror. She tried to see beyond the reflection but all she could see was herself and her bandmates.

"Last week," Tam began, "Trish and I were in Hollywood. We walked past a soothsayer and I felt like I was being inexplicably beckoned..."

"What the hell is a soothsayer?" interrupted Chris.

"A fortune teller," said Cali Sky.

Tam continued, "So I sit down at this table in this dark room and I start to freak out. The whole experience was uncanny. It was like a panic attack, I can't calm down, I can't concentrate. But I can't move either. Then I hear the soothsayer say, 'Look at me.' Actually she whispered it, but it was like it wasn't her voice. But I still can't move so I can't look at her. Then suddenly she stands up and reaches over the table. She grabs my face and lifts my head up. 'Look at me,' she whispers again. So now we're face to face, eye to eye, just inches from each other. Without looking down she pulls a Tarot Card from the pile. *This* card."

During the pause that followed Cali Sky half expected the card to begin levitating.

"And then she used it to look into my future," Tam said. "But I actually think it was *our* future."

"Well?" asked Cali Sky.

"She said that the chariot will soar. It will soar to 'undreamt of heights,' that's how she put it, if the steeds work in unison."

"So the chariot is our band?" asked Brodie.

"Maybe," answered Tam.

"By steeds," Cali Sky clarified, "she means these two sphinxes."

"Yes. You see how one is black and the other white. They have a natural tendency to work at cross purposes. I…*we* need to coordinate them."

"My musical style and your musical style," mused Cali Sky.

"Maybe," Tam repeated.

"This is freaking me out guys," said Brodie.

"So how do we bring about this balance?" asked Cali Sky.

Tam shrugged. "She made it seem like that would not be hard. She mentioned a different problem…"

Tam trailed off, gazing at his doubled bandmates in the reflection of the window.

"Well?" pressed Cali Sky. "What's that?"

"She said the danger was not in getting off the ground. She said the danger was in soaring too high. She grabbed my face again, stared hard at me and said, 'They would be offended…and would have their revenge.'"

"Who's 'they'?"

Tam shrugged.

"Why would they—whoever they are—be offended in the first place?" asked Cali Sky.

Tam shrugged again.

"Is that all she said?" asked Cali Sky.

"No," answered Tam. "But the rest is personal."

"How do you know?" asked Cali Sky. "Maybe it all fits together."

"It doesn't."

"How do you know?"

"Because everything else she had to say pertained to another card she drew."

"What card was that?"

"'The Lovers. No offense, but I'm not in love with any of you."

Cali Sky was finally silenced. She, Brodie and Chris peered at Trish, who averted her eyes.

"It's your turn, Chris," Cali Sky said. "Why don't you go?"

Chris answered sheepishly, "I didn't bring anything."

"Why not?" she shot back, "We all were supposed to bring something."

"I'm just the drummer. You write the music, I'll lay down the drums."

"You're not just the drummer. You're *our* drummer and you're part of this band."

Cali Sky's mood turned visibly sour. Chris remained motionless. Cali Sky stood up and said, "Come on, Brodie. I guess we're done."

She took two steps when Chris suddenly exclaimed, "Wait! You want me to show you something? I'll show you something!" His shouts froze Cali Sky in her tracks.

He rose suddenly. He took off his shirt, pulling it over his head. He turned around. Across his lower back, from one side to the other, horizontal to the floor, ran a continuous yellow and black bruise. Chris turned back around, hurriedly putting his shirt back on. Everyone, including Trish, stared at him.

"My dad," he said, "my dad hit me with a baseball bat. My back was turned. So you want to know what I think about new directions for the band? I need to make more money so that I can move out of the house. Whatever direction that will take us there is fine with me."

"Jesus, Chris!" exclaimed Brodie. "Why'd he hit you?"

"He was drunk, and he's an asshole."

"What about your job? Don't you make enough to rent an apartment or something?" asked Brodie.

"Not yet. I'm saving up. I've got car payments. And my dad charges rent now that I graduated from high school."

"Jesus, Chris!" Brodie exclaimed again.

"You can live with me," said Tam unexpectedly. "You can live with me. I'll have to hide you from my parents. But I think I can pull it off."

"Seriously?" asked Chris.

"Yeah. They never go into the guest bedroom. You'll have to keep quiet and leave on the days the maid comes. It will be tricky but I think we can do it." Cali Sky directed her stare to Tam. He continued, "You can't live at home anymore. Besides," he continued, "if you live with me it'll make band practice more convenient."

Cali Sky sat back down and smiled. "The sphinxes are working in harmony."

Brodie looked relieved and said light-heartedly, "Chris doesn't believe that bullshit."

"He doesn't have to," replied Tam.

They settled into a brief silence. It was now pitch black outside. Their reflections in the window were vivid.

Brodie cleared his throat and said, "So what did this meeting accomplish? I mean, besides Chris scoring a rent-free room in a Tam's mansion. I mean, what is our new direction?"

Tam answered, "I don't think there is a straightforward answer to that question. Not yet anyway. But this meeting accomplished a lot. Everything we said tonight helps to form our new muse. It just takes time. And it will eventually come through in our music."

"I have one more thing to share," announced Cali Sky. She hadn't planned on this, but she decided to risk it.

She pulled a photo out of her back pocket and set it alongside the Chariot card. Tam picked it up and examined it. He saw a dirt road meandering through the heart of a desert plain beneath a big blue sky. The low-lying green vegetation lining the road suggested high country. The ground looked moist from a recent rainfall. The road stretched into the distance toward a chain of snow-covered mountains, sparkling in the wide-open sunlight.

"Ben sent me this photo," she said. "He took it somewhere in New Mexico."

Tam studied the photo for a few seconds and passed it on to Chris.

"Why can't something like that be our inspiration?" she asked, then held her breath.

Chris looked at it for a moment and passed it to Brodie.

Cali Sky continued, "The mountains, the sky, the trees."

Brodie handed it back to Tam, who studied it some more.

Cali Sky asked, "Have you all ever been in the mountains? Have you ever walked up a trail miles from anywhere?"

"Never," said Tam.

"It's a spiritual place," she said. "It has a mystery about it. Being there is a powerful experience."

Tam returned the photo to its place alongside the Chariot card.

"Why can't we write songs based on that mystery and experience?" asked Cali Sky. "Why can't that be our new direction?"

Tam said, "Plenty of art over the centuries has focused on nature. Mostly visual art. Some classical music."

As Cali Sky spoke she noticed how animated her face

appeared in the reflection, "Some modern music has captured the spirit of the desert and mountains, of nature…in its own way. Like the Eagles, or the Grateful Dead, or an album like Traffic's *The Low Spark of High Heeled Boys*. But nothing more recent."

Tam felt himself being tugged toward Cali Sky's enthusiasm. He said, "There's already the New Romantics. We could be a return to the Old Romantics, the nature poets from centuries ago."

"And our music would be real, you know?" added Cali Sky. "No posing, nothing contrived, nothing fake."

"Yeah, nothing formulaic."

Cali Sky leaned back, content. She turned to the others and asked, "What do the rest of you think?"

"It's worth a try," replied Brodie.

"Whatever," Chris answered, "I just play drums."

It was nearly 10 p.m. when two cars pulled into the empty parking lot of Cornerstone Community Church. The Thursday night Bible study had long since adjourned. Nevertheless Cali Sky killed the lights of the first vehicle so as not to attract attention. She turned off the engine and scanned the area.

"I don't see anyone around," she said.

Zoe opened the passenger-side door and exited, followed by Brodie behind her. Chris brought the second vehicle—his Suzuki, loaded with drums and amps—to a stop next to Cali Sky's car. He rolled down his window.

"Look alright?"

Cali Sky nodded. She could hear Tam's voice from the backseat, barking orders to Chris to park the vehicle and let him and Trish out.

"Let's see if we can get in," said Cali Sky, "before we unload all our stuff."

They walked vigilantly to the church's side door, watching for any sign of life. The last time Cali Sky had been there was for Cami's funeral. She tried unsuccessfully to block out the memories: her mom's uncontrollable weeping, her dad's pious self-control, the empty words of would-be comforters, the small size of the casket.

"I've never broken into a church before," said Chris.

"Have you ever *been* to church before?" asked Brodie.

"No, I think this is the first time." Chris smiled.

"The door's over here," said Cali Sky.

They followed her to a set of glass doors that led to the church offices. Chris tried to open them, knowing they were locked, but testing their strength: they rattled and shook. Cali Sky peered into the darkened offices. *Inside one of those rooms,* she thought, *is where it happened—my dad and Michelle. God I hate this place.* Chris pulled his driver's license from his wallet. He slid it into the millimeter-sized gap between the door and the silver aluminum door frame, trying to catch the lock. The door remained fast.

"Tam," he said, "Let me have one of your credit cards."

Tam handed him a Visa. Chris slid it into the gap, jiggling it back and forth and pulling on the door handle. With a clicking sound the door swung open, releasing an invisible cloud of stale, conditioned air. More than anything else that smell triggered Cali Sky's memory, but this time not of the funeral, but of the countless hours she spent in the church as a kid: holding her dad's hand as they walked into the sanctuary; kicking the pew in front of her during a long sermon; tugging at her mom's dress as the small talk droned on after the service, begging her mom to let her have another doughnut. Inside Cali Sky saw that little had changed. Pastor Kevin's office looked the same. Something was different, though, something she could not pinpoint.

She led them to the organ, the same organ she had played on countless Sunday mornings. She turned on the music-stand light.

"Let's not turn on any other lights. Just to be safe," she said.

"Alright. Let's get our stuff," said Brodie. "I'll help Chris with his drums. You guys get the amps and guitars."

Cali Sky looked around. The memories were so thick that she could barely breathe. In the darkness they were like ghosts.

It took three trips but they finally managed to haul all of their equipment to the area surrounding the organ. During the second trip Cali Sky realized what was different: the color of the carpet. Tam directed Brodie and Chris where to place the amps. Then Chris set up his drums while Tam and Cali Sky tuned their guitars and Brodie his bass. Trish and Zoe sat in the front pew. So far their plan was falling into place.

The day before the band had gone hiking in the San Gabriel Mountains. They had followed the trail Cali Sky, Cami and her dad used to hike, the trail that led to Cucamonga Peak. They had ascended the rocky switchback, fighting off the bugs, just as Cali Sky remembered them, blemishing Cami's young skin with their grotesqueness. When they had reached the green valley at the switchback's summit she pointed out the dilapidated cabin. The hike was hot and dusty but Tam, and to a lesser extent Brodie, and to an even lesser extent Chris got a sense of what Cali Sky meant by the band's new direction. They sat with their backs against some sugar-pine trees. Tam said the mountainside "felt sacred." Brodie said it was "cool." And a sweaty Chris said he was "hot as fuck."

As the silence enveloped them and the gentle breeze dried their sweat Tam commented dreamily, "We need a bigger sound. Not louder. Bigger." Cali Sky nodded, staring into the distance.

Tam continued, "How about an organ? Not a keyboard. An organ. In a large space, where the sound can spread out."

Cali Sky replied, "I know just the place."

Chris's first snare shot was shockingly loud. Cali Sky was sure someone outside would hear it. But then she remembered how relatively isolated the church was, surrounded by parking lots, business complexes and a stretch of road rarely traveled at this time of night. She tested out the organ. The feel of the keys on her fingers and the pedals on her feet were familiar. She shook off more memories, this time of accompanying Michelle as she sang some old-time gospel number or another lilting contemporary Christian song.

Tam and Brodie tuned their instruments to the organ. Chris joined in as they then adjusted volume levels. After that they broke into their first song, a warm-up, one they had prepared for this occasion: Simple Minds' "Up on the Catwalk." Chris counted it off and the song exploded from their instruments. Cali Sky used the organ's great manual for the piano part, one she adjusted for maximum resonance. She used the swell manual for the run during the lyric, using a synth effect. But before Tam began singing Zoe rose from the pew, grinning from ear to ear, and danced. Trish remained seated, staring fervently at Tam. Goose bumps spread over Cali Sky's body. Chris played with power and precision, looking down, his whole body moving, arms and legs each doing something different, each one following its own rhythm. Brodie stood near the altar, his bass swinging from side to side. In the dim light Cali Sky could see the outline of the bass, his thin frame and shag hair.

Chris brought both sticks down on the snare, ushering in the chorus. The goose bumps spread over Cali Sky's body again. The edges of the sanctuary were pitch black. Cali Sky looked around, at the baptismal font, the communion railing and the cross above the altar. The song filled every inch of the church, pushing away the oppressive memories with every pulsating measure until Cali Sky could breathe deep, filling her lungs with the joy of the music. Zoe continued to dance, Chris played frenetically, Tam sang with closed eyes and Cali Sky fed off of all of them: every one of their movements and notes became critical to this moment. And at the conclusion of the song all they could do was smile.

Then they tried out some directions for new songs. Cali Sky explored the whole range of the organ. Tam searched out echo effects on his guitar. Together they drew closer and closer to the bigger sound they both had imagined, a sound that gave expression to a spirit of mystery, holiness and, most importantly for Cali Sky, desire and longing. Explorations went awry only when they fell back on the expected song intro, structure or chord.

"Try to forget what you know," advised Tam. "Play what you feel."

They offered each other vague advice, aiming at abstraction rather than detail.

By midnight they had not written a single complete song. Instead they had written enough bits, pieces and parts for about ten songs: an intro here, a chord progression there, riffs, melodies and moods. All of them comprised of golden notes. They recorded the entire session on a device Tam had bought the day before. They rose from their instruments, sat on the floor and pews around Zoe and Trish, and played some of it back. Chris was drenched in sweat. Brodie seemed unable to sit still, energized by the session. As they listened to the recording Cali Sky and Tam smiled at each other, nodded now and then, and suggested ways of piecing parts together. Tam pushed stop.

"This is good, Tam," said Cali Sky. "Really good."

Tam smiled.

"Oh my God," added Zoe, "Not good. Great!"

"Right on!" Brodie gushed lamely.

Tam removed the tape. "This," he said proudly, "is a gold-mine." He carefully inserted the tape into its case. "I've heard a lot of music," he said, looking at Cali Sky, then Chris, then Brodie, "but nothing like this."

"We need to go back to the studio," announced Cali Sky. "In a couple of weeks. That's all we need."

"Do you think Lester will pay for it?" asked Tam.

"I don't know," Cali Sky answered. "I think so. I'm still trying to convince him."

"I hope so," said Tam. "My parents definitely will not foot over any more money."

Cali Sky nodded toward the tape, "Once we turn that into a couple of songs we'll make some rough recordings. And once Lester hears them he'll pay for the studio."

"You think so?" said Tam doubtfully.

"I think so," she answered. "Maybe then you'll trust him… And maybe then we can destroy the other demo."

"Don't worry about that," Tam remarked, "You're good at destroying demos."

They loaded their equipment back into the two vehicles in a mood of triumph. Zoe snapped some photos.

"I've never shot in a church before," she said, her flash momentarily illuminating the altar. She sought angles that put the cross and stained-glass windows in the background.

"So what did you think, Chris?" said Brodie, lifting the floor tom, "your first time in church."

"Hallelujah."

Cali Sky had planned to spend the night at Zoe's. That's what she had told her mom. But the night's events changed her plans. She wanted nothing more now than to work on the songs: to sit in her room with a guitar in her lap, probably all night. So while Chris followed Tam to his new living arrangement, Cali Sky took Brodie and Zoe home. The streets were empty.

"You understand, right Zoe?" asked Cali Sky.

"Totally," answered Zoe from the passenger seat. "Go home and work on the songs. Now is the time…when you're inspired."

Cali Sky smiled at her.

Zoe continued, "I swear, Cali Sky. It's like I can see the inspiration in your eyes."

"Really?"

"Oh my God, yeah. Like it's coming from your soul and spreading through your body."

"Maybe I should go home with you," offered Brodie from the backseat. "I mean, it's spreading through my body too."

Cali Sky and Zoe laughed.

"Seriously," he said, "why can't we do some writing together? I feel inspired too."

Cali Sky peered into her rearview mirror but didn't respond.

Brodie continued, "We could write some songs for a few hours. Or at least start writing some songs. Then I could just crash on the couch. You know Joan wouldn't mind. Then you could just take me home sometime in the morning."

Zoe looked sidelong at Cali Sky.

"Alright," Cali Sky finally answered.

Cali Sky and Zoe shared the same ambivalent expression, wondering what the other was thinking. When Cali Sky dropped her off Zoe said bye and gave her an ambiguous wink.

"Call me tomorrow!" said Zoe.

"I always do!"

Brodie got out of the backseat and moved into the front.

"It'll be just like old times," he said.

Cali Sky pulled out of Zoe's driveway and eased onto a main drag.

"That night at Tam's" she said, "when you played the Agent Orange song…"

"Yeah."

"That really meant a lot to me."

The streets were empty. Cali Sky felt like she and Brodie had Orange County to themselves.

"You taught me pretty much everything I know about playing music," said Brodie.

"The first time is special. When you first learn to play a song."

"Yeah."

"So when we get to my room here's what we'll do. There's one guitar part Tam played that I want to fiddle with. We'll play it, riff off of each other, and just see where it leads us."

"Okay."

"But you gotta stop playing if I tell you to stop playing, okay?"

"Why?"

"Because if we stumble upon something promising I have to work it out myself."

"Whatever you say."

"Explore all you want," she added quickly. "Just stop when I say stop."

Brodie laughed. "Okay…. Are we still talking about music?"

Cali Sky was straight-faced. "What else would we be talking about?"

Brodie looked away and said, "Nothing…. Just like old times."

"Except this time," Cali Sky said, "Don't try to kiss me."

"Why not?" he asked without hesitation.

"Because I don't get involved with musicians."

Brodie laughed and they spent the rest of the ride reminiscing about those early days, when Brodie nearly lived at the Braithwaite house over the summer playing guitar.

Cali Sky pulled into the apartment complex. She spotted her mom's Honda.

"We'll have to be real quiet," she said as they got out of the car. "Once we get into my room we'll turn on the fan. That will drown out some of the noise."

Brodie helped Cali Sky with the music equipment. They both struggled up the stairs and paused at the front door. Cali Sky fumbled in her pockets for the door key. She inserted it into the lock, turned to Brodie and brought her finger to her lips in a shushing motion. She then slowly opened the door. Light from the guest bathroom alerted her that her mom must be awake. This realization struck her simultaneously with the awareness of presences in the room. The light illuminated a bottle of wine on the coffee table with two empty glasses on either side. Articles of clothing were draped over the couch. But what more specifically created in Cali Sky the awareness of presences in the room was the sound of her mom moaning. When Brodie stepped into the room he saw immediately what Cali Sky's faltering senses perceived more gradually: Joan, naked, head tilted back, eyes closed, black hair cascading toward her hips, lying on top of a man with curly hair that, when grown to full length twenty years ago, resembled an afro.

FOURTEEN

Winter 1985

CALI SKY PULLED into an apartment complex called the Village Green. She and Zoe rented a two bedroom, walls adorned with Zoe's photos, concert flyers, Andy Warhol reprints and a large image of the Royal Air Force roundel, which only a few of their visitors recognized, remembering the image from pictures of WW I British aircraft in their history textbooks. In spite of everything Cali Sky put the geode that belonged to Lester and Philip on the dressing table in her bedroom, alongside pictures and postcards from Ben, all of which depicted images of mountains, rivers, rocks and trees.

As she expected Cali Sky found Zoe to be an ideal roommate, with one exception: Zoe's obsession with the Smiths. Every time Cali Sky came home from anywhere one of the Smiths' two albums—the eponymous first album and *Meat Is Murder*—was playing from the stereo.

"You over-play those two albums," Cali Sky had warned, "You're going to grow to hate them." As soon as she said it she realized she was talking more about herself than Zoe.

Of course Zoe had replied, "No way! Oh my God, how can I hate music that speaks to me so personally?"

In her room Zoe had posters of the Smiths posing around different locations in Manchester. She had a poster of Morrissey swinging a noose on stage, a poster of Morrissey holding a flower, a poster of Morrissey swinging his hips on *Top of the Pops*. She even took up reading Oscar Wilde. *The Picture of Dorian Gray* was a permanent fixture on their coffee table, *Lady Windermere's Fan* and *The Importance of Being Earnest* stood prominently on their only bookshelf. Cali Sky liked the music of the Smiths. She certainly did not want to hate them, but Zoe was not making it easy.

When she turned the key and stepped inside her heart dropped and she froze. Sitting primly on the couch, just below the giant image of the roundel, was her mom. Cali Sky could tell from the knee-length skirt and collared blouse that she had come straight from work. She had been talking with Zoe, who sat on a green-upholstered chair directly across the coffee table from her. But as soon as Cali Sky entered she looked at her daughter intently, defiance and a bit of pride written on her face. The expression reminded her of something she saw in Brodie a long time ago when they were fourteen or fifteen. She was being cruel to Brodie—cruel, she knew, for no real reason. With no motive she had told Brodie coldly to get out of her house. But he refused. He looked at her and said no. His face conveyed a fiery self-dignity.

Zoe rose from her chair. "I'll be in my room."

Cali Sky filled the seat that Zoe left occupied. She and her mom waited for Zoe to close the door. A large object rested against the couch, an object Cali Sky had not noticed before. Joan rested her left hand on it. Cali Sky saw the slender fingers whose touch she knew so well, especially as they had run through her own hair countless times over the years. The muffled sound of the Smith's "Still Ill" came from Zoe's bedroom.

"Cali Sky," said Joan, "I have some bad news. About Mr. Nussbaum."

"Oh no." The words escaped spontaneously from Cali Sky's mouth.

"I'm afraid so. I'm sorry. In his will he left you a few things."

She raised the large object and awkwardly handed it across the coffee table to Cali Sky, who now saw that it was a framed poster. She took a quick glance at it and saw the image to be some sort of pastoral landscape with two figures in the middle, one an old man and the other an animal. But she was too mentally preoccupied to give it much attention.

"He also left you this," said Joan.

She picked up a book off the couch next to her and set it on the coffee table alongside *The Picture of Dorian Gray*. It was a slim volume, leather-bound and ancient looking. She saw no title. She decided not to inspect it, not now, not in front of her mom.

"And here," continued Joan, "is a letter from Ben. Didn't you give him your new address?"

"Yeah, he must've sent this off before he got it."

Cali Sky took the letter and tossed it on the old book. She glanced again at the poster frame and then at the dark leather book.

She said, "I hadn't seen Mr. Nussbaum in...I don't know how long."

"He was a fascinating person, wasn't he?" said Joan.

Cali Sky nodded somberly. "His birds. Remember his birds?"

Joan smiled. "And the thick accent."

Cali Sky felt once again the warm imprint on her heart. This time she tried to resist its manifestation as tears. But she couldn't stop them. Joan got up and walked around the coffee table. She rested a hand on Cali Sky's head and began lifting the other one toward her face. But Cali Sky pulled away, leaving Joan's arms dangling pathetically at her sides. Joan dropped to her knees.

"Cali Sky, look at me."

She didn't move.

"Cali Sky, look at me."

Still motionless.

"Look at me, Cali Sky."

Cali Sky jerked her head angrily toward her mom. Tears streamed down her flushed cheeks. The white of her eyes was shot through with red, but the blue irises blazed fiercely.

"Listen to me carefully, Cali Sky," said Joan in a tone at once tender and firm, "I am your mom. And I am not going to let you shut me out the way you shut out your dad."

"He's *not* my dad. I don't know who my real dad is. And neither do you," Cali Sky sobbed like a child.

"We've been through this…"

"Why, Mom? Why Lester?" she was now shouting. "Of all people why him? Is it a music thing? You couldn't get any rock stars so you had to fuck the manager of one? Is that it?"

The defiance and pride remained on Joan's face, but she let escape a sigh. "That's unfair and mean."

"Is it, Mom?"

"You know it is."

"You just can't control yourself, can you?"

"You sound just like your father."

"Don't say that! I do not! I have *nothing* in common with him!"

"You're making me feel the way your father used to make me feel. I got rid of all that guilt when he and I divorced."

Joan took a deep breath and continued: "Lester and I are in a relationship. What we do is our business."

"But he is…or was our manager. It's my business too."

"How is Lester's private life your business? He can still be your manager. Trust me, he *wants* to be your manager. He thinks you guys are going to be huge. He's been trying to contact you for the last week and a half."

"I don't want to talk to him."

"Do you know why he's been trying to contact you?"

"I don't care."

Joan ignored her. "Because in the last two weeks he's received two offers from record companies."

Inside Zoe's bedroom the Smith's "What Difference Does It Make" was now playing. The pause in the argument drew Cali Sky's attention to the song. She couldn't speak again until she had listened—listened at least until she could catch up with Morrissey's lyrics and Johnny Marr's guitar line. It was a compulsion that overwhelmed her, to stay on top of the song, to know where it was going so that when it came she would be ready.

"Cali Sky," continued Joan. "Don't you at least want to hear the details of some of the offers? I mean, we're talking about possible record contracts here."

"Tell Lester he can pass them on to our new manager…once we get one."

"Fine. I'll tell him."

Joan rose from her knees. "I want you to succeed. Whether that's with Lester as your manager or not I don't care. What's more important to me is our relationship. We've been through too much together, Cali Sky. I love you too much. *Listen* to me. I'm *not* going to let you shut me out."

Joan adjusted the strap on her purse and walked toward the door. She looked around and said, "Your apartment looks great." She opened the door and walked out.

"What Difference Does It Make" was reaching the end. *Damn it, Zoe.* Cali Sky leaned forward and picked up the book Mr.

Nussbaum left her. There was no title on the cover. She opened it to the flyleaf, upon which were handwritten words:

"May 1980

To Cali Sky, meine liebslinge Studentin

Chase the Blue Flower

Mr. Nussbaum."

She turned the page and read the title: *Henry von Ofterdingen*. She surmised that the author's name was Novalis. She couldn't tell for sure because the entire thing was written in German. She opened it to a random page and saw absurdly long words and umlauts. She flipped the pages from right to left, searching for a note or a clue to explain why Mr. Nussbaum had left her this book. She found nothing so she turned back to the flyleaf. *1980. Five years ago. About the time when I had my last lesson. Typical Mr. Nussbaum.*

She then picked up the framed poster and studied it. A red-cloaked man wearing a wide-brimmed hat and a long gray beard sat on a stone. A lithe deer, unafraid, stood directly in front of him, apparently eating something out of his cupped hands. A creek ran directly down the center of the painting, cutting through a rolling landscape of grass, flowers, trees and rocks. Mountains and cliffs towered in the background. Immediately Cali Sky thought of the valley. The valley from her story. Her memory of its first telling played vividly in her imagination. She could picture herself kneeling at Cami's bed. *Did I see this painting in Mr. Nussbaum's condo? Is that where my story came from? But what about the cabin? The girl? The wind instrument?*

She turned the poster over and looked at the back of the frame. Here too she found handwritten words: "Der Berggeist." She studied the painting some more. This time she noticed a squirrel poised vertically on a tree and a bird perched on a limb.

She now became more attentive to the ways in which the painting differed from her vision.

The Smiths album suddenly stopped playing. The apartment was silent for a moment. Then a bedroom door slowly opened and Zoe peeked her head out.

"Zoe," asked Cali Sky, "Do you speak German?"

"Um, no." Zoe sounded like she was dreaming. "Why?"

"Just need to know what some of this means."

Zoe entered the living room and sat down on the couch. "What is all of this? What happened? Are you alright?"

"Yeah. How much did you hear?"

"Nothing. I swear to God. I couldn't hear over the music."

There were only two people who knew what Cali Sky saw on the floor of Joan's apartment on that fateful early morning six months earlier. One was Brodie, who knew what Cali Sky saw because he had seen it himself. The other was Zoe, to whom Cali Sky described what she saw.

Cali Sky asked, "What did she say to you?"

Zoe adjusted a wayward strand of her hair. "That she misses you. That she loves you. She's heartbroken. I saw emptiness in her eyes."

"Yeah, I saw it too."

"She's miserable. She really is."

"Remember my...vision? The one with the cabin and the girl?"

Zoe nodded as if the occurrence of visions were periodic facts of everyday life.

"That girl," continued Cali Sky, "was always alone. As if she liked to be alone. As if she had to be alone."

"An image of the solitary artist. That's you, right?"

Cali Sky shrugged.

"Like Morrissey!"

"One more thing, Zoe."

"Yeah?"

"No more Smiths tonight, okay?"

"Oh my God, whatever," Zoe replied.

Cali Sky noticed that she had neglected Ben's letter. When she opened it a picture fell from the envelope. It showed Ben and his dog in front of their house in New Mexico. She unfolded the paper and read,

"Dear Cali Sky,

Great to hear the band is doing well. Can't wait to hear the new name (when you come up with one). I'm not surprised that your gigs are sold out. I'll listen to your demo (for the thousandth time) on Jan. 9 when you play The Roxy. I know you don't play those songs anymore but it's the closest I can come to being at the show.

I have bad news. Pet died. I had only been home a few days for Christmas break when it happened. My mom says he waited until I came home so that he could see me once more. He was really old and his time had come. But it was still hard. He was a good dog. Remember when you first met him? You thought it was weird that we named our dog Petrarch. Remember how he barked at you? I never told you this but he really didn't like you. He was jealous. Even after we moved I'd tell him about you and he would growl (I swear!).

He was in a way a connection between us. When I first got home a few days ago I saw him and could think about how he was a part of my memories of you. Now that he's gone I feel like you are even farther away from me. I still love you and I always will.

I finished my first semester of college. The homesickness really never went away. I'm not sure I want to go back but I have to (my parents already paid for it). I want to tell you more about it but I have to go. I wish you were here so that I could tell you in person. I'll write again soon.

Love always,

Ben

p.s. I also think that Zoe and Stone make a great couple. They're both weird in the same way (a good way)

"Why does cold air make my eyes water?" asked Chris.

For a half mile they had hiked up a dirt road. Now they funneled into a single file line as they followed a trail diverging to the right. Each footfall on the sand and gravel produced a crisp crunching sound. When they stopped the silence was enormous.

"It's not the air, Chris. It's the wind," Brodie said.

"What's the difference, dumbass?" replied Chris. "The wind blows the air."

"Actually," Brodie mused, now correcting himself, "I think the wind *is* the air."

"Either way I'm right."

Cali Sky laughed as she looked back at her drummer and bass player. Half the time she couldn't decide if their banter was moronic or profound. She stood on a rise overlooking a sand wash that ran along the base of a chain of hills dotted with sandstone, yucca and blackbrush. On the other side of those hills, some twenty miles in the distance, was the city of Las Vegas, where they had spent the previous night watching Synth's new band play opening act at a small venue in some seedy area near downtown.

Cali Sky untucked her chin and mouth from the warm air inside her zipped-up jacket. Her cheeks were red. She asked, "You sure you guys want to follow this trail?" It felt weird to speak. Her face and mouth muscles were cold.

"Where does it go?" said Chris.

"How the hell should I know?" Cali Sky replied. "I've never been here before."

The foliage was denser and the ground less rocky than the area surrounding the trailhead where they began their hike. They hadn't realized how much elevation they had gained until they looked back in the direction from which they came. They could see a small stretch of the road they had ascended earlier, veering around a canyon wall.

"Check it out," exclaimed Brodie, pointing up to the top of one of the hills on the other side of the sand wash. "That rock looks like a movie camera."

The others gazed in the direction to which Brodie pointed.

"Oh yeah," said Chris. "like a Flintstones camera."

Above the rock a lone vapor trail streaked across the pale blue winter sky. Cali Sky pulled off her right mitten with her teeth, reached into her back pocket and awkwardly unfolded a trail map. She nodded toward the Flintstones camera and said, "The map says those are the White Rock Hills. We can take this trail to La Madre Springs."

"That's where we're going," announced Tam, as if he already knew that the trail terminated at a place called La Madre Springs and he had planned on going there all along.

Cali Sky led the way, followed by Brodie, Chris, Tam and Trish. This was their usual formation on what Tam had come to call "inspiration pilgrimages." They had hiked Mt. Baldy, Big Bear and even Mt. Zion in Utah. Tam's idea of morally supporting Synth's band in Las Vegas gave them the opportunity to explore Red Rock. Chris was hung over. Brodie carried a backpack full of snacks and drinks. Trish was silent and invisible. Cali Sky and Tam kept their eyes and ears open. These pilgrimages challenged them to create soundscapes modeled after natural landscapes: the search for a big sound evoking mystery and desire.

They pressed on, gaining more elevation. The trail now wound through an area forested with high desert and mountain flora, a transition in frame of reference, from panoramic distances and wide-open sky to a limited visual range in which all sensory details—the angle of sunlight, the stateliness of a Joshua tree—assume heightened significance. The trail veered around a boulder, fifteen-feet high. As she passed Cali Sky extended a mittened hand to feel its solidity. The coldness of its surface passed through the synthetic wool and into her palms. The branch of a juniper tree overhung the trail. She sensed its importance, that it should be right there and that it should look just like that.

She heard Brodie's voice behind her. "I can't see the Flintstones camera anymore."

Cali Sky searched the White Rock Hills. Brodie was right. No trace of the camera now from their vantage point. She felt that that too was somehow important, connected in some way to the inscrutable quiddity of these hills. She thought about the music, the eleven songs she had written with Tam, the eleven songs that tried to capture some of this. She stopped suddenly.

"What?" asked Brodie, who nearly ran into her.

She used her teeth once more to remove the mitten from her right hand. This time she reached into her other back pocket and pulled out a small notebook with a small pencil inserted into the cylindrical wire binding.

"Turn around, Brodie. Let me use your back."

Brodie obeyed and Cali Sky recorded some notes into the little book. No one commented or complained. They all knew what she was doing. Tam often did the same thing. These notes, consisting of ideas, moods, notes, descriptions, chord progressions, lyrics and even sketches, shaped and re-shaped every song they had written over the past six months—the eleven songs that defined their new sound.

They continued on until the trail eventually flattened. The rigor of the climb had warmed their bodies. They hiked in a group across open ground, abandoning their single-file formation. Ahead they saw a trough with water dripping over the sides. Cali Sky approached with a sense of satisfaction.

"La Madre Spring," she said as they stood silently around the trough. The silence was once again profound. It didn't seem to be the absence of sound—more like the presence of something unnameable. But moments later they became aware of a veritable sound: the thin ripple of water on stones.

"Look," said Brodie.

A clear rivulet trickled down a ravine and emptied into the trough.

"Let's follow it," said Tam. "Find the source of the spring."

They began climbing the ravine. There was no established trail to follow, though Cali Sky could see footprints on either side of the brook. When the ravine quickly became rocky, with no more footsteps to follow, Cali Sky had to guess which direction to lead the others. The brush scraped against their clothes. Occasionally they had to hold back branches to clear their way. Chris had the misfortune of following Brodie, whose well-timed release of one branch left him with bark in his mouth. Brodie laughed uproariously. Tam assisted Trish up some of the rock climbs. She took each step with trepidation, but never once vocalized her uneasiness.

After a half hour of hiking, climbing and scrambling, Cali Sky reached a break in the terrain. The ravine widened into a small arbor where meadow grass grew around the swelling brook. A majestic ponderosa pine grew near the center of the arbor. Cali Sky joyfully entered the space. The others were still struggling up the last rock climb. She stood beneath the tree, hands on either side of the trunk, gazing up at the branches and needles.

The longing stirred in her heart. She desired to experience this moment more fully than her senses were capable. The moment was like a song, ahead of time's cusp, neither past nor future.

"Wow!"

Brodie's exclamation startled her. She released her clasp of the tree and faced him.

"It's incredible here, isn't it?" she said.

"Here," he said, slipping the backpack off his shoulder and pulling out of it a thermos of water. "Have a drink."

She tilted back her head and drank deeply from the thermos, a motion that drew Brodie's attention away from the ponderosa pine. He studied the gradual variation of her chin and neck. She returned the thermos. He took a swig and realized the others had fallen well behind.

"Are you tired?" he asked as he sat near her beneath the pine.

"Yeah," she replied cheerfully, "but in a good way. Are you?"

"Yeah. In a good way." He smiled. "Want something to eat?"

"Yeah, but let's wait till the others get here."

"Yeah." He rubbed the remnants of a dirt clod from his jeans. "Chris nailed me right there."

Cali Sky smiled. "You two are funny."

Brodie took a deep breath and admired the grove. "This is beautiful," he remarked.

"*Beautiful*? I don't think I've ever heard you use that word."

"Yes I have."

"Unless you are describing a girl... Well, even then I don't think beautiful is the word you use."

Brodie leaned back on his hands. He appeared indignant. "I'm not like that anymore, Cali Sky."

"No?" she replied.

"It's like you don't believe that people can change."

Cali Sky turned away, staring at the mountains towering above the ponderosa.

Brodie added, "I have changed."

"I know, I know you have."

"I take this band seriously. It's my priority."

"I know. I see that."

"I'm a good bass player. A *really* good bass player."

"You are. I agree."

Brodie moved into a cross-legged position. "I don't hook up with random girls anymore."

Cali Sky laughed. "Too bad for them."

"I'm trying to be serious."

"Okay, Brodie. You don't scam with a different girl every night. You're committed to the band. I know all this. Great. What else do you want me to say?"

He picked a blade of meadow grass. "You also know that I have strong feelings for you."

He tried unsuccessfully to read her reaction. She looked into his eyes for a moment, then returned her stare in the direction of the ponderosa.

"I know," she finally said.

"And what about you?"

She tried to brush a strand of hair from her eyes, remembered she was wearing mittens and returned her hands to her lap. "No."

"No?"

"I don't know."

"You don't know?"

"No."

"No, you don't know?"

"Brodie, stop."

"Just tell me."

"Stop, Brodie!"

"Why?"

"Because I said!"

"Is it because of Ben?"

"No."

"Okay," Brodie said calmly. "But can you answer one question? Why after all these years have we never …you know… gotten together…I mean, a relationship?"

She laughed at his clumsiness. "Because it's never felt right."

"Why?"

"When we were younger, I guess because you were so arrogant. After that, I guess because you were with different girls all the time."

Brodie heard the others nearing the grove. He spoke quickly. "So what about now? You agree I've changed. I'm not arrogant… at least not as arrogant. I'm not with different girls all the time. Actually with *any* girls lately. So what about now?"

Cali Sky heard the others approaching as well. She answered, "Because I don't want to get involved with anyone who is a musician."

Brodie stared at her incredulously. "Are you serious? You really mean that?"

She gave him a meaningful glance, the sort of glance that only Brodie could understand.

"Because of your mom?" he asked, already knowing the answer. "And everything else?"

Cali Sky could now see Chris's face. He was nearly within earshot. She said softly to Brodie, "So maybe if our band doesn't work out we have a chance."

The succession of emotions—hope, despair, perplexity and relief—spread so rapidly across Brodie's face that they appeared simultaneous.

"What took you so long?" Cali Sky called out to Chris as

Brodie sat there flummoxed, fumbling with the Gordian knot that she had thrown into his lap.

"You led us up a damn cliff," exaggerated Chris, winded and spent. Tam and Trish followed close behind. All three sat next to Cali Sky and Brodie, forming a circle. Cali Sky passed around the thermos of water. Brodie distributed granola bars. The White Rock Hills were no longer even visible, obstructed by the steep rises surrounding the arbor. They had reached the source of La Madre Springs, where the numbingly cold water surfaced from the earth. They exchanged casual remarks about the climb, the ponderosa, the spring and the cold.

Then Tam turned the conversation toward band matters, the subject they all knew was inevitable.

"So," he began, "I found us a possible new manager. A guy I knew when I was in Forest Murmurs. He's managed a couple bands that have done pretty well."

"I think we should stick with Lester," said Cali Sky.

Everyone but Brodie looked at her with disbelief. Tam said, "Why? *You're* the one who said we should drop him."

"I know. I changed my mind."

"Why?"

"Because he found us some record companies that are interested in us."

"He did? Why didn't you tell us?"

"I just found out myself," Cali Sky lied. "I wanted to wait till now to tell you."

Tam looked confused as well as a bit suspicious. Cali Sky cast Brodie another glance that only he could understand.

"So who are the companies?" he asked before Tam could respond.

"He said they were small, independent labels," answered Cali Sky, "I had never heard of them before."

"That's not a good sign," Tam said.

"We should still look at their offers," said Chris. "Can we meet with Lester?"

"Yeah," answered Cali Sky. "We will. But I agree with Tam. I don't think we should sign anything now." Confidence blazed in her eyes. "Once we make a new demo, *everything* will change."

"You don't know that," warned Chris. "You sound like you've already rejected the offers we do have. And you haven't even seen them yet. Trust me, I've been through this with Carnage..."

"Have you talked to Lester about a new demo?" asked Tam, ignoring Chris.

"Yeah," Cali Sky lied again. "He'll hook us up."

"We need to get into the studio right away," said Tam, "so that we can distribute the demo right after the Roxy show."

"You're getting ahead of yourself," Chris admonished again. "Let's not make any decisions till we look at the offers. When I was in Carnage..."

"We don't want to hear about your experiences in that God-awful band," interrupted Tam again. "This is different."

Ever since Chris began living secretly at Tam's house, Tam was even harder on him than he was before. Chris bit his tongue as usual. And as usual Cali Sky stepped in to warm things over.

"Don't worry, Chris," she placated. "We'll look at the offers. But Tam and I both agree that a new demo really will change everything."

"What about a new name?" asked Brodie.

A pained look appeared on Tam's face. Over the past weeks they had proposed hundreds of names. Chris's were either too dark or, conversely, too frivolous. Brodie's ideas were cliché. Cali Sky and Tam brainstormed names the same way they wrote music. Tam might begin with a guitar part, then Cali Sky might come in with keyboards. Tam might initially think that it sounded all wrong, that she was taking it in a direction he had not intended. He would push more forcefully in his direction, she in hers, until they both felt dissatisfied. But then when they later listened to it together, they discovered possibilities that neither one had fathomed. But in the case of coming up with band names, this sort of collaborative method had failed them.

"It's too hard," said Tam dejectedly. "It's just too hard to come up with a name."

They sat silent for a while.

"You know why?" Tam continued. "Because there's too much pressure. Our name is too important. A word is not the thing it refers to. But a name… a name is closer to the thing it refers to than any other kind of word. You know what I mean?"

They looked at him blankly, Chris and Brodie because they didn't understand, Cali Sky because she wasn't listening to Tam. She was listening to her own internal voice repeating a name in her mind.

Tam continued, "Take the word 'rock.' If I say the word 'rock,' it doesn't refer to any one rock. The word might mean a big rock, a small rock or any of the millions of rocks in this canyon. But if I pick up just one rock," he picked up a rock, "and give it a name, then it has something that none of the other millions of rocks have. Its name becomes the word that is only associated with this one rock."

"That's deep, Tam," Brodie remarked.

"What the hell does it mean?" asked Chris. His face looked blanker than it had before.

"Blue Flower," Cali Sky said. She had never mentioned it before because it seemed too personal to vocalize. But its repetition in her mind emboldened her to bring it out into the open. She explained the word's origin. She told them about Mr. Nussbaum.

But her explanation was more like a story, and because it

happened so long ago—at least it felt so long ago to her—and because so much tragedy intervened between then and now, she felt like she was narrating a myth, and because the subject of the myth was something so important to her, she felt like the myth was also a theogony, the story of a god's birth.

"Blue Flower," said Tam after Cali Sky had concluded.

"Blue Flower," said Brodie.

They turned to Chris, who shrugged and said, "I just play drums."

"I like it." The wind seemed to carry the words. It took Cali Sky a half second—an uncanny half second—to realize that the voice was Trish's. "I like it," she repeated. "I think it's the perfect name."

The following Sunday morning Cali Sky awoke in her bed and found herself thinking about Sunday mornings from the past. The ritual of preparation: donning her dress clothes, helping Cami with hers, hearing her dad shut the front door, a box of donuts in his hands, the drive down abandoned streets to the church with its plastic smiles and choreographed sentiments of piety.

She looked at her clock. 9:27 a.m. She picked up the phone and dialed a number.

"Hi mom.

"Yeah, everything's fine.

"You were right… again. I'm sorry…again.

"I promise I won't shut you out…again.

"I love you too.

"Yeah we're excited. Definitely ready.

"She's fine. You know, Zoe is Zoe. How are you?

"I miss you too. Maybe we can go to Dana Point this week. Have nachos in the harbor.

"Yeah that would be great.

"Listen, Mom. Is Lester there?

"Just a hunch.

"Can I speak to him?

"Hi Lester.

"I'm fine. Listen, the band and I would like to meet with you to discuss those offers.

"Yeah, anytime this week.

"But there's something else…something else we need to discuss.

"We found our sound. The sound we were looking for. Truthfully the sound I've been looking for ever since I started playing guitar.

"Yeah, it's serious…and sincere. But I don't want to try to explain it. You just have to hear it. We wrote eleven new songs.

"Can you come to our show at the Roxy?

"Well, that's just the thing. That old demo is no longer us.

"Yeah, we *really* need to make a new one. What do you say?

"I know, but the band is really gelling. Tam and I are on the same wavelength. Well, actually we're not exactly on the same wavelength—we've *never* been on the same wavelength. But we've managed to get our wavelengths to intersect.

"This will be the one, I swear.

"Great.

"Yeah.

"We could do it tomorrow. Whenever you want to schedule it.

"Thanks.

"You won't regret it."

Exhilarated she sprung from her bed and burst into the living room, half dancing. She stopped in her tracks when she noticed someone sitting on the couch. She was prepared to feel embarrassed until she saw that it was Stone, who was busily scribbling in a journal, writing poetry, Cali Sky guessed. He wore last night's clothes, now wrinkled and rumpled. Cali Sky stretched her night shirt more fully over her panties.

"Hey Cali Sky," he said distractedly but not unpleasantly without looking up from his book. "I made some coffee."

"Oh. Thanks, Stone."

She poured herself a cup and leaned against the kitchen counter.

"Have you seen the sky yet?" asked Stone, now looking up from his book.

"No."

"Take a look."

Cali Sky walked to the small kitchen window, leaned over and beheld an atmosphere made golden by the morning sun.

"Do you sense the rebirth?" asked Stone.

"The rebirth of what?"

"The sun."

"The sun?"

"Yeah."

"Yeah, I guess so."

"Today is the winter solstice. We're going to celebrate tonight. Want to join us?"

"Sure."

She looked at her watch. 10:12 a.m. She finished off her coffee, dumped the remainder of her cereal in the sink and ran the garbage disposal. She hurried to her room and threw on some clothes.

"Gotta go," she called out to Stone and Zoe, who had emerged from her room.

"Where are you going?" Zoe asked.

"To celebrate winter solstice. I'll be back in a little bit."

She sped down side streets until she reached the route she used to know so well. The sharper red and orange colors of the morning sky had faded into the attenuated sunlight of a cool California winter day. She rolled down her window so that she could let it soak into her skin. She shivered, from both the cold and her excitement. Stores whizzed by. She remembered them all, remembered how she sounded out their names from the backseat of the orange Ford Bronco when she first learned to read: the Carpet Barn, Hanson's Bread and Bakery, the Ski Chalet, Herda's TV and Appliances. The Jesus and Mary Chain blared from her car speakers. She stopped at red traffic signals, waiting impatiently as the green light signaled go to a road emptied of cross traffic. She made the final left-hand turn and spotted her destination: Cornerstone Community Church.

Casually dressed couples herded their young children through the parking lot. It was 10:41. The last of the post-church crowd was making their way toward their vehicles. Cali Sky hoped she was not too late. She squeezed into a small space and headed toward the church. As she neared the entrance the old associations sprung to life from the recesses of her memory. One painting in particular, hanging in the breezeway, mined from the past a specific event that momentarily reduced her to the emotional fragility of her child self. It depicted a Caucasian Jesus with a drooping face, each hand extended from a furrowed robe and resting gently and protectively on the head of two small children, apparently guiding them down a darkened path lit only by antique oil lanterns that always reminded Cali Sky of the Pirates of the Caribbean ride at Disneyland. She associated the painting with Mr. Kraft, a stern disciplinarian who taught kids Sunday school. But why would that painting be associated with him? She concluded that she must have gazed at the painting after being told one Sunday morning after church that Mr. Kraft would be her Sunday school teacher the following year.

She began to wish she hadn't come. But then her eyes fell on the sanctuary, with its pews, altar, cross and, most of all, organ.

These recalled another memory, one from only a few months ago. Chris set up his drums just there. Brodie stood over there. And *Tam* was here (Tam of all people). Zoe and Trish sat in the pew over there. She and Tam wrote *songs* here, or at least the beginnings of songs. They played "Up on the Catwalk" at the altar for God's sake. She discovered that this memory—the memory of the late-night break-in—transformed her perception of the church. It baptized her thoughts so that she now beheld the church with her own sort of post-conversion assurance.

"Cali Sky? Is that you?" Someone was talking to her. "It is! So good to see you again!"

It was some lady whose name escaped her. Mrs. Peterson or Parson or something like that.

"Oh, hi," said Cali Sky, "Good to see you too."

"Are you looking for your dad?" asked the lady.

"Yeah."

"He's down there by the altar, helping with the communion ware."

"Thanks."

Cali Sky began to make her way to the altar.

"Oh," said the lady suddenly, "Merry Christmas to you!"

"Yeah, merry Christmas... And happy winter solstice!"

Cali Sky turned back toward the altar and thus missed the lady's reaction to her pagan well wishing. *I played Simple Minds in your church, lady*, thought Cali Sky with a laugh.

When she was fifteen feet from the altar Philip turned and saw her. A smile spread across his bearded face. She drew closer. Michelle was there, and when she asked him some question or gave him some instruction, he remained motionless, still smiling at Cali Sky. A little girl was swinging on the altar rail.

"Cali Sky," said Philip.

"Hi Dad."

He moved forward as if to hug her, then checked himself and held back, awkward and unsure. Cali Sky stepped forward and embraced him.

Philip said, "We were just cleaning up. What are you doing here?"

"Just came to say hi. I figured today would be a good day to start again. Hi Michelle."

"Hi Cali Sky. It's good to see you. I…uh…just need to take this empty tray into the foyer."

"Cali Sky," said Philip, "This is Desiree."

The little girl was now standing at Philip's side, her little fingers clasping his pant legs.

"Desiree, this is Cali Sky," continued Philip. "She's your half-sister."

Desiree peeked her head around Philip's knee, then looked up at her father.

"Daddy," she spoke, barely audible.

Philip leaned down so that Desiree could whisper something in his ear. She covered her mouth with her hand to keep it secret.

Philip smiled and whispered back, "Well why don't you ask her?"

Desiree stepped doubtfully toward Cali Sky, released her grasp of his pant leg and said, "Are you the one who plays piano?"

Cali Sky kneeled down and replied, "Yes, I'm the one."

"Show me," said Desiree.

Cali Sky took Desiree's hand and led her to the piano. She sat on the bench.

"Here," she said, patting the empty space next to her, "you sit next to me."

Desiree climbed awkwardly yet determinedly onto the bench.

And with a dramatic flourish Cali Sky played a beautiful song that began with the unmistakable power of an E chord.

FIFTEEN

W HEN CHRIS SAID, "Shut the fuck up, Brodie," it triggered a memory. John, from Nowhere. *He used to tell Jim to shut the fuck up all the time.* Cali Sky thought back. She remembered the sensation of being in a band. *I'm in a band.* Just saying it had changed everything. Saying it had given her a sense of identity. She used to repeat it like a mantra.

And what about now? She looked around the apartment. Chris sat on the couch next to Brodie, sunglasses raised atop his head, buried in his shag hair. He looked like some movie star. Trish was conjoined on the love seat to Tam, appearing distracted, even slightly paranoid, when he wasn't conversing with Zoe, whose eyes grew big as she made some point. Stone stood next to her near the kitchen and suddenly doubled over in laughter as he exchanged ripostes with Chris and Brodie. His hair swung in front of his face as he gesticulated with exaggerated movements, impersonating someone—maybe an actor, a rock star or even someone in the room.

I'm in a band. It was no longer enough. She wanted more.

They all did. They were all confident, at least on the surface. Chris was all bravado, but had become more violent. After their last gig a bodyguard separated him from a fan who had propositioned Cali Sky. Brodie acted like a rock star, but behind closed doors asked Cali Sky the same questions like a naïve boy craving assurance. Cali Sky and Tam fine-tuned the songs, hearing new possibilities with each live performance and making subsequent changes.

"The song's nearly perfect," Tam would say.

"Nearly," Cali Sky would respond. "But how will we know when it is?"

"We will."

"How?"

"When it's beyond our reach."

Cali Sky listened to the sounds in the apartment. The phone rang.

When she returned a minute later she announced, "That was Lester. We're not meeting at the coffee shop. Not at first. He wants to meet us somewhere else."

"Where?"

"At an underpass in Tustin. He wants to show us something."

"At an underpass in Tustin?"

"Zoe, he wants you to come as well. To take some shots."

"Of what?"

"No idea."

"Is this some sort of hippie thing?" asked Tam as he and Trish rose from the love seat as one.

"We'll see."

As she re-read the directions from the passenger side of Tam's Volvo she realized how close Lester was leading them to Cornerstone Church. This seemed odd. Her first thought was paranoid: she worried that the police had notified Lester that the band he managed broke into the church and that a squad car was waiting at the underpass with a police officer ready to point out some incriminating evidence linking her to the break-in. "We found a guitar pick at this location," she imagined the officer interrogating her, "Does it belong to you, Ms. Braithwaite?"

"He better have some good news for us," said Tam, pulling onto a side street.

"He will."

"I still don't trust him."

"I know you don't."

Up ahead they saw Lester standing beneath the underpass. As Tam pulled behind Lester's car Cali Sky watched her mom get out of the passenger seat, smiling.

"Hi mom," said Cali Sky uncertainly. "Hey Lester. What's this all about?"

"Let's wait till the others arrive. I want you all to see it at the same time," he answered cagily.

Tam stood uncomfortably next to Trish. He looked from Lester, to Joan, to Cali Sky. Lester's faint smile did little to lessen the intensity of his expression. Cali Sky remembered her dad's description of him in his diary. Eyes close together. That's what made him look intense. She recalled her dad's mention of his afro. That was long gone, but his hair, cut short, was coarse and curly. The above-time speculations lit her imagination: What if, twenty years ago, he could somehow know that in twenty years he, not Philip, would end up with Joan and that he would be managing a band led by her daughter whom she conceived with some unknown rock star?

Joan drew close and said privately, "This is exciting."

"What is?" Cali Sky whispered.

"You'll see."

Like Tam Cali Sky felt uncomfortable. And the anger welling

up inside her was gravitating toward her mom. Why did she have to come? No one in the band knew except for Brodie. *It's like she can't resist.* By now the others had joined them, looking puzzled and intrigued. Brodie's net of intimacy compelled him to say hello to Joan. But Cali Sky could tell that he was thinking the same thing as her.

"Okay, everyone," Lester announced. "Follow me."

He walked further into the underpass. Shards of broken green glass littered the sidewalk. Every time a car passed by, the sound of wind noise and muffled engine was amplified by the concrete and steel that surrounded them. Occasionally Lester looked back. Cali Sky noticed that when he wasn't smiling he looked extremely serious. They followed him out from the shadows of the underpass into the hot June sun. Then he stopped, turned and pointed in the direction from which they came. There, on the wall of the underpass, spray-painted in large black letters impossible to miss for any passers-by, were written the words,

"SIGN BLUE FLOWER"

For a moment no one spoke. A car passed. Cali Sky could sense her mom looking at her.

"Oh my God!" Zoe uttered.

"Hell yeah!" exclaimed Brodie.

Cali Sky stared at the graffiti. Just above it she could make out a slight discoloration in the concrete, as if someone had applied to the surface a now-faded blob of industrial-strength White Out. She knew its origins. Long ago, from the backseat of the orange Bronco on the way to church she used to gaze upon a different spray-painted message, but whose message was also in the imperative mood. It read,

"LET IT BE."

She smiled at her mom, who said, "This is the beginning. You're going to be famous."

Zoe was already snapping pictures.

"So this is what you wanted to show us?" Tam, unimpressed, asked Lester. "So what? Talk is cheap."

Lester gave Tam a penetrating stare. Tam didn't flinch. Cali Sky felt a strong temptation to say something, anything to relieve a brewing stand-off. As her mind began to spin, searching for words, the intensity etched on Lester's face suddenly broke, replaced by an encouraging smile.

"Talk *is* cheap, Tam," Lester said. "But these words are not mere talk. More like prophecy. Blue Flower *will* in fact be signed."

Brodie asked impatiently, his dark glasses hiding his ebullience, "Signed by who? For how much?"

Lester looked at each member of the band, smiling.

"You won't believe it," he said.

"Is it good?" asked Brodie, struggling to contain himself.

"Let's just say," Lester answered, "that I'm prepared to drop 90% of my clients. My focus could now be on this band. There's a coffee shop down the road. Let's discuss the offers in proper fashion there."

Back in the Volvo, now following Lester, Tam brooded. The car was silent, no music played. Tam and Cali Sky did not want to be influenced by anything they heard. The only music they listened to was their own.

"You know what's coming, Tam," Cali Sky said. "We're going to break through."

"Someone else once told me something similar."

"Who?"

Tam didn't answer.

"Someone from Forest Murmurs?" asked Cali Sky.

Tam didn't answer.

"Trish," said Cali Sky heatedly, now giving up on Tam, "Does

Tam ever allow himself to be happy? Does he ever allow himself to be successful?"

She didn't look back, knowing Trish would not answer. Tam drove the Volvo into the coffee shop parking lot and quickly exited without replying. Cali Sky walked past the two video games and cheap toy-dispensing machine to a sign that read, "Please wait to be seated." She and the rest were led to a large booth. Joan sat next to Lester. A waitress handed each of them a menu.

"Lunch is on me," said Lester.

"One of each!" Chris barked at the waitress.

Lester looked at Chris with his narrow eyes and laughed. "Pace yourself, Chris. This is the first of many celebratory occasions, I'm sure."

After drink orders Lester pulled a collection of papers from his briefcase. His smile was gone. Cali Sky got the sense that he adopted this demeanor when discussing business with his clients. He spoke carefully and confidently, and broached items on his agenda meticulously.

"So all the feedback I've received is positive. Execs, A & R men, the music critics I've talked to, down to the dweebs who write for fanzines—they all love your demo. When Cali Sky told me awhile back that you were going for an honest, pure sound— something direct and earnest—I was dubious. But you pulled it off. People think your music is poetry. Not just the lyrics, you understand. The *music*. You have something fresh and impor- tant here."

He took a sip of coffee. Chris flashed his smug smile. Cali Sky was shaking. Brodie gave up on trying to appear calm and kept grinning at Joan only because her overflowing excitement matched his own. Even Tam listened raptly.

Lester continued in his stoic mode of business-speak, "Record companies also know you have a significant underground following. And in southern California, that counts for a lot. They hear your songs on college radio stations in the area. They know your name is getting out. The graffiti we just saw on the underpass is evidence of that. As we say in my line of work they see that your star is rising and they want to hitch a ride."

He took another sip of coffee, letting the suspense build. He pulled a pair of reading glasses from his dress-shirt pocket and perched them on the end of his nose. Then he drew a single sheet from his stack of papers and held it up so they all could see, moving it slowly from his left to right.

"On this paper," he continued, "is a list of the so-called Big Six, the six major recording companies, the biggest labels in the world. Of the Big Six, four have offered you contracts. Four."

Cali Sky heard a gasp and wondered if it came from her.

"Now when I received the four I pitted them against each other. In essence I forced them into a bidding war. Quite successfully, I must say. Their war worked in your favor. The offers and terms got even better. Now *this* one..." He raised his head and peered through the reading lenses until he spotted from the list the name of the highest-bidding company. He pointed at it. "*This* one came through with the best offer."

He smiled, lowering his head, looking at each one above his reading glasses. "Are you ready for this? Here's the offer." He glanced at his notes. "A guarantee of three albums. A $100,000 signing advance. A royalty rate of 28%, which is much higher than normal. And last but not least—a sign of how much they respect you—complete creative control over music, recording and album art."

Brodie rose to his feet and stood on the booth. He bounced once or twice as if it were a trampoline. Then he jumped over Chris onto the floor below and ran around the coffee shop screaming "Yes!" and "Hell yeah!" Chris soon followed. Tam watched them and smiled in spite of himself. Cali Sky couldn't tell if she was laughing or crying. An elderly couple seated near the window looked afraid.

"Congratulations," said Lester. But no one heard him. He was drowned out by Brodie and Chris, as well as Joan, who exclaimed, "You did it! You did it! You made it! You made it!"

When Cali Sky rose from the booth she found that her knees were weak. Brodie raced toward her and they hugged. Chris followed and did the same. All three looked at Tam, who remained seated next to Trish. He stood up slowly. Cali Sky saw tears welling in his eyes too.

"We deserve this," he said softly. "We deserve this," he repeated more loudly. Then Cali Sky, Brodie and Chris, all laughing, hugged Tam together. Cali Sky heard the unmistakable sound of Zoe's camera.

Brodie asked, "The hundred grand. When do we get that?"

Lester laughed. "Well, it's not that simple. We'll have to discuss the details of the distribution of that money and expenditures. We'll have to discuss recoupable costs. We'll have to discuss performance-rights royalties and mechanical royalties. It's all pretty complicated. But don't worry. I can help you take care of all that. When the time comes I'll present you with all options as clearly as possible."

"How many bands have you managed?" asked Tam icily.

"Tam," replied Lester patiently, "I've already told you that I represent actors and actresses. I've never managed a band. But I've also explained that I will drop most of my clients to focus on you guys now." From the way he answered Tam's question it was apparent that Lester was accustomed to rebuffing attempts to put him on the defensive. "But as you know," he concluded, "the answer to your question is zero."

"He's done pretty well so far, hasn't he?" said Chris.

Cali Sky, who sat next to Tam, saw out of the corner of her eye how Tam wringed his hands under the table.

"What you need to do now," continued Lester, "is cut a record. Soon. As I said and as you know you guys have a veritable cult following. Fans have recorded your shows and pirated cassettes. They're making money off of you. You might as well get paid for what you're doing. You said you had eleven songs, right? Which is enough for an album. Are they ready to record?"

Brodie nodded.

"Not quite," Cali Sky said. "They still need a little work."

"Okay, but don't take too long. Your timing is critical at this point. You need to make an album as soon as possible. Any more questions?"

Still wringing his hands Tam asked, "What about tours?"

"What about them?"

Tam opened his mouth to speak but nothing came out.

Lester rushed to anticipate his thoughts. "Negotiations haven't gotten that far yet. But I'm sure you'll start off with a U.S. tour. The venues might be small, at least initially. College campuses, that sort of thing. But if all goes well they'll become bigger. I'm sure you'll have a tour manager. I'll do what I can to help…"

"Will we be an opening act?" asked Tam.

"Maybe at some shows. Maybe not at others. Again I just don't know yet."

"I want Isolation to tour with us."

"Who?"

"Isolation. They're a local band."

"Tam," interrupted Cali Sky, "Synth's band is getting better, but they still have a long way to go."

"They're working on their songs. They're writing new ones. In three months they'll be ready. Trust me."

"Guys," Lester said, "we're getting ahead of ourselves. We don't need to worry about that right now."

"Yes we do!" exclaimed Tam. "I owe it to Synth."

"What do you owe Synth?" asked Cali Sky.

"Nothing," answered Chris. "Tam doesn't owe him anything. We do *not* want to tour with Isolation."

"Guys, please," intervened Lester, now as peacemaker, "Let's not argue about it. See reason, Tam. At the moment this issue *is* minor. But don't worry. I'll look into it. I'll get more information about tours."

The waitress had returned, ready to take orders. The prospect of eating buoyed Chris's mood. He ordered last, a cheeseburger and fries.

"I'll put these in right now," said the waitress. "Oh, one more thing, if you don't mind. I overheard the news. Since you're all going to be famous soon, would you mind giving me your autographs?"

A knock on the door and it opened slightly. "One hour to show time," the theater manager called out. Lester had scored them a gig at the Orpheum Theater. For the first time in the band's career— sixteen gigs under their belt by Chris's count, fifteen by Brodie's— they didn't have to set up their instruments and do their own sound checks. Their new label arranged all of that for them.

Another knock on the door and in walked a short man wearing a black leather jacket and faded black jeans. His black hair was short and spiky on top and longer in the back. His dark eyes surveyed the room. They recognized him at once: the bass player for the Smithsonians, the headliners of the show.

"Hey everyone. How's it going?" he said. His wandering eyes halted on Cali Sky, who at that moment became the sole object of his attention. "Just want to thank you for opening for us tonight. And if there's anything at all you need just let me know and I'll take care of it." Cali Sky glared at him. "Oh," he now scattered his attention to the others, "be sure you don't put anything on my monitor. You know, like a drink...or your feet. The last opening act we played with shorted mine out."

"Yeah, sure thing," Chris replied.

The moment the door closed, Chris exclaimed, "Douche bag."

"What a dick," said Brodie.

"Yeah," Chris commented, "It's always the bass players."

"I hate opening for them," said Tam. "They suck."

Cali Sky picked up an acoustic guitar and began strumming it, warming up her fingers.

"Clear your minds," she said. "Just focus on our music. Remember where it comes from. Ignore everything else."

Another knock on the door. "Two visitors here to see you. Oh, and forty-five minutes to show time."

The door remained open as Philip carefully pushed Aunt Nancy in her wheelchair into the green room. Cali Sky embraced them both wordlessly. Brodie unfurled his net of intimacy and hugged Nancy, who looked weak and tired, struggling even to keep her head up. Brodie then shook Philip's hand.

"Everyone," announced Cali Sky, "This is my dad. And this is my Aunt Nancy."

"Your first Blue Flower show, right?" asked Brodie.

"Yes," Aunt Nancy replied slowly. "Actually this will be the first time I've ever watched Cali Sky perform."

"Not exactly," corrected Brodie, "What about all those songs we used to play in the old house? You were the only person in the audience, but still..."

As Brodie reminisced with Aunt Nancy, Cali Sky sidled up to her dad. She lifted the laminated backstage pass from his chest, where it hung from his neck, and said softly, "Into the lion's den, huh?"

"What? No. Not at all. I'm proud of you."

Cali Sky could picture her dad talking with some Cornerstoner later in the week, describing his experience at the Orpheum. "Yes, I'm proud of her," he would say, "but there's just so much Godlessness in a place like that."

"How's Desiree?" she asked.

The discomfort in Philip's face and voice vanished. "She's great. She still plays the chords and scales you taught her. She's even taking lessons now."

"Tell her I'll teach her more the next time I see her."

"I will, Cali Sky. She'd love that."

"Have you been hiking much?" she asked.

"No, not really. Have you?"

"Yes. Listen for it in our set."

"What do you mean?"

Just then Cali Sky heard her name mentioned in another conversation.

"What?"

"Nancy asked when our album is gonna come out," shouted Brodie across the room. "Tam doesn't know. I thought maybe you could answer the question."

She frowned. "We're working on it."

"You see," said Brodie, sarcastically rehearsing the arguments repeated during band discussions over the past few weeks, "*I* think our songs are ready for recording. They sound great. Tam and *Cali Sky* think that they aren't yet *perfect*. So they're not ready to record yet. Even though Lester tells us we need to record the album yesterday."

"The songs will be ready once they are beyond our reach," said Tam.

"The songs *are* great, Brodie," added Cali Sky, rounding out her and Tam's side of the argument. "The thing is, Aunt Nancy, they could be better. They don't yet realize our idea of them. What we hear coming out of our amps doesn't match up what with what we hear in our imaginations."

"'Ah, but a man's reach should exceed his grasp, Or what's a heaven for?'" quoted Aunt Nancy with characteristic oracular inflections.

"Just like old times," laughed Brodie.

"Five minutes," called a woman from the ajar door. "You two can follow me," she said to Philip and Aunt Nancy. "I'll escort you to the side stage. The best seat in the house."

Philip offered an encouraging wave to the band. "Good luck!"

"Break a leg!" called out Aunt Nancy as Philip pushed her out the door.

Once on stage Cali Sky's anxiety subsided the very moment her fingers met the Wurlitzer organ's keys. The exhilaration however remained. She felt energy pass from her body to the organ, from the organ to the pipes, and from the pipes to the darkness of the theatre, behind which mulled over a thousand people who were brought to attention by the sudden disappearance of the house lights and the wall of sound that broke over them. Their opening song began with a vague structure. To the audience's ears it could become a fast song or a slow song. Then it slowly took shape, becoming more definite, creating a sense of anticipation. But it stopped short of clarity, creating a soundscape that transformed the anticipation into the desire suggested by the band's name. The lyrics gave the song more shape, but they too remained vague, evocative of infinite longing. Some images were concrete—a mountaintop, a dust cloud—but then gave way to expressions of ecstasy and limitation, representations of beauty and decay, eternity and transience. Cali Sky emoted the lyrics, casting spells of various kinds on the now rapt audience.

She spotted Zoe in the photographer's area. She was on

assignment for an alternative-rock magazine. She saw Stone bouncing and swaying with a dreamy gaze on his face. She noticed Synth and the rest of Isolation, huddled together around Trish, who was expressionless. Cali Sky played guitar on the next three songs, standing between Brodie and Tam. She exchanged glances with Brodie every now and then, as she did during every show—mainly expressions of encouragement but occasionally signals to prolong a song or adjust volume. Tam on the other hand remained to himself, as he did during every show. He could pick up Cali Sky's cues musically.

The final song began with Chris playing a slow beat on drums. Then Cali Sky entered on the organ with a single note that doubled at the beginning of the next four measures, at which point Tam and Brodie joined in, to create a melancholy song that occasionally sounded desperate when Cali Sky began singing. Toward the end Cali Sky got Brodie's attention and beckoned him to come to the organ. She signaled to him to play four notes that corresponded to the four chords of the outro, in the key of E. Cali Sky could hear the crowd cheering above the song. And when he placed a finger on a key and Cali Sky rose from the bench, the cheering climaxed into a roar. She walked to the front mic smiling and said, "Thanks again…good night." She then walked off the stage, leaving the rest of the band to conclude the song.

She followed the path illuminated by the roadie's flashlight back to the green room. She shut the door and took a deep breath. She heard the final note of the song and grabbed a can of soda from the huge assortment of drinks on ice. She sat down on a couch, listening to the applause. A moment later the rest of the band entered the room, along with an entourage of reporters, industry reps and people she had never seen before.

"Great set!" said one, sitting down next to her. "Can I ask you a few questions about you and your band?"

"Congratulations on your recording contract," said another before Cali Sky had time to answer the first question. "Can you give me some of the details?"

Someone toward the back asked, "Is it true you learned to play organ in church?"

Cali Sky rose to escape the bombardment of questions. At that moment she saw Philip wheel Aunt Nancy into the green room. She looked paler and weaker. Philip looked around uncertainly.

"Excuse me," said Cali Sky as she pushed her way through the friendly mob.

Aunt Nancy's face turned from fatigue to elation when she saw Cali Sky. Philip simply looked relieved.

"Are you alright?" asked Cali Sky.

"Fine. Fine. Just tired. I don't think I've stayed up this late in ten years." Her voice was barely audible. Cali Sky had to crouch down to hear. A tear ran down Aunt Nancy's left cheek. "That was...fantastic," she said weakly. "Great showmanship. You displayed a really strong stage presence. And those first couple songs had such...gravitas. I'm proud of you. Thank you. You were great, whatever your Dad may say or think."

The noise level in the green room increased—people laughing, talking and partying. Chris was already on his second beer. Cali Sky had to bring her ear nearly to Aunt Nancy's mouth to hear the last sentence. She took hold of her aunt's hand, squeezed it and stood back up.

"I better take her back to the nursing home," shouted Philip.

Just then the Smithsonians' bass player approached from behind and put his arm around Cali Sky. "Great set!" he said into her ear. "I'd really like to talk to you about your music. Could we meet up after the show?" He handed her a piece of paper and slipped out the door. She tore the paper in two and threw it to the floor.

Philip watched him exit and said meekly, "Be careful, okay." He wore an expression she knew well, one of parental concern. The expression made her feel like a child. As he turned the wheelchair toward the door Aunt Nancy tried to give her a thumbs-up sign. But the gesture was so weak and uncoordinated that it simply looked pathetic.

Cali Sky turned to find Brodie smiling, holding a beer in his hand. He saw that Cali Sky looked nervous, an expression that reminded him of the day he told her that Nowhere kicked her out of the band or the time she told him about reading her dad's diary.

"What's wrong?" he asked, smile evaporating.

She was startled by the assurance she suddenly felt when she looked at his familiar features. "Nothing."

"You sure?"

She nodded.

"There's a party at Hermosa Beach."

"Let's get out of here." She handed him her soda. "But first will you mix this with Bacardi for me?"

Chris started on his ninth beer the moment he sat on the sand, just out of the reach of the boardwalk lights. Stone and Zoe joined them, along with a few hangers-on whom no one really knew.

"You killed it," one of them said. "I love your voice, Cali Sky."

"Thanks," replied Cali Sky without looking at her admirer. She dumped the rest of her Bacardi and coke out and watched it soak into the sand.

"We're getting closer, Tam," she said.

"You're right." Tam watched a wave break in the dark distance. "Closer and closer."

"I saw two people there with tape recorders," said Zoe.

"Don't say that," Chris said. "That just puts more pressure on them."

"Maybe we ought to put out a live album," proposed Brodie, half-joking. "Has anyone ever done that? A live album as your first record?"

"The Grateful Dead maybe," suggested Cali Sky. She considered the idea and immediately experienced a release of pressure, the unloading of a burden. A live album would consist of the *possibilities* for their songs. Not exactly the songs themselves, not the essence of the songs.

She was startled by the sudden presence of three men standing just outside their circle: Synth and two members of Isolation. They all exchanged greetings.

"Great show," said Synth. "Very moving."

"Why don't you get lost, you fucking faggot," threatened Chris.

Cali Sky wanted to believe that it was some sort of joke, that Chris and Synth had one of those strange, distinctly male sorts of friendships involving insults and ridicule. But she couldn't recall Chris and Synth ever exchanging *any* words, let alone insulting ones. The ensuing silence suggested the others shared Cali Sky's bewilderment.

"What the hell is wrong with you, Chris?" exclaimed Tam. "Don't talk to my friend like that."

"Why do you want these faggots to tour with us, Tam? Why don't you explain that to everyone?"

"Why don't you shut your mouth, Chris?"

"No, take it easy, Tam," interrupted Synth coolly, "Let Chris explain himself."

"I don't need to explain myself to you, ass wipe."

"Yes, I really think you should."

"There's nothing to explain," Tam said. "Chris is drunk and stupid."

"Come on, Chris," continued Synth. "Spit it out. What's your problem with me?"

Trish exclaimed, "He doesn't have a problem with you!"

"I think he does, Trish," responded Synth calmly. "I just think he's too dense to articulate it."

Chris threw his nearly full tenth can of beer at Synth. In the same motion, initiating a surreal sequence of events that Cali Sky experienced as a dream, he rose from his feet and attacked him in a rage. Before Cali Sky had time to process this terrible vision, Chris sat on Synth's chest, hurling down blow upon blow. Somehow, the punches were missing their mark. Chris's calloused and dirty knuckles were two steps behind the intentions of his alcohol-saturated brain. As Chris punched the sand that he mistook for Synth's face, Synth let escape from his mouth a monosyllabic scream. Before Chris had a chance to regain his balance and aim his punches more carefully, Brodie tackled him.

"Calm down, Chris!"

"Get the fuck off me!"

"Calm down!"

"Fuck you!"

The hangers-on moved to help Brodie, grabbing arms and legs until Chris's fury waned.

"Get off him!" Cali Sky yelled. "And you, Synth. You need to leave now."

Cali Sky kneeled near Chris's head. The hangers-on slowly got up and left. Synth and the rest of Isolation walked away, fearful for their own safety. Cali Sky stared into Chris's eyes, which looked impossibly dilated. He seemed like he was not fully present, the detached expression of a drunk or a maniac.

"Chris," she said. "Look at me."

His movements grew less violent.

"Look at me."

He slowly grew still until he was motionless, with the exception of his heaving chest. His lungs were still gasping for air.

She smiled. "It's okay. Breathe. Relax."

"What the *hell* is wrong with you?" shouted Tam. Trish was sobbing.

"Easy, Tam," Cali Sky said. "He just freaked out a little. He's alright now."

Chris sat up, staring vacantly at the sand near his feet.

"What was that all about, Chris?" asked Brodie with compassion in his voice.

Chris's eyes slowly came into focus. He said unsteadily, "I hate that guy."

"Why?" Brodie asked.

"Nooo," moaned Trish. She began to sob.

"Zoe," Cali Sky said, "Maybe you and Stone should take Trish for a walk."

Trish tried to resist, shaking her head as Zoe and Stone helped her to her feet. But her will was easily overcome. She meekly allowed Zoe and Stone to lead her up the beach, but not before she cast a last desperate look at Tam. When she turned back around she began to bawl uncontrollably, now leaning hard against Zoe. Cali Sky was thus distracted when she overheard Chris mutter a string of incoherent words. She wasn't sure if he said, "My fucked up dad's in Chino Prison" or "I'll fuck up Synth the next time I see him."

"What?" asked Cali Sky.

"I said," Chris began, but his drunken mind lost its train of thought. He suddenly looked at them all with zany affection. "I love you guys. Seriously." A dumb, drunken grin spread across his reddened face. "You saved me from that fucking band...Holy shit! What are they called? I can't even remember their name!...Oh yeah. Carnage. Carnage! Carnage! They are terrible, huh Tam?... Hey, did you guys know that Tam let me live at his house?... Oh yeah, you were there!" His laughter was sloppy and loud, terminating peremptorily in unconsciousness.

Cali Sky said, "Turn his head to the side. We don't want him to pull a Jimi Hendrix."

"Don't worry," said Brodie, "I've never seen Chris get sick when he's drunk." But he seemed to think better of Cali Sky's suggestion; he adjusted Chris's head anyway.

"How are we going to get him back to the car?" asked Cali Sky.

"We won't. We can just leave his drunk ass here."

Cali Sky flashed him a look of reproach.

"We'll have to stay with him," said Tam. "Until he sleeps some of it off."

Cali Sky laid back on the sand. It was a clear night, but this close to LA, she saw few stars. Her head spun as she listened to the surf. She heard Tam say, "He drinks too much. I notice alcohol missing from the fridge."

"Does he ever talk to his parents?"

"I don't know. He doesn't say much about them. But I can read between the lines."

"And?"

"You saw the bruises on his back that one night. That's just the tip of the iceberg."

"He's never said anything about it to me," said Brodie.

"He hides it. And puts everything into music. He's the best drummer I've ever known."

Cali Sky sat up and stared at Tam. "Have you ever told him that?" Cali Sky waited for Tam's ambiguous expression to resolve itself into something definite, like remorse or empathy. She waited in vain.

"Tam?"

He shook his head. He watched the sand run through the fingers of his left hand and into the palm of his right. "Remember the words of the soothsayer?" he said. "That we need to work together? I fear that Chris will be our downfall. He will divide us. All that rage—it will overflow, just like it did tonight. And something disastrous will happen."

"Come on, Tam," said Brodie. "Don't talk like that. Besides, the only thing that will cause our downfall is not recording an album."

"We will, Brodie," Cali Sky encouraged. "I heard some new possibilities tonight."

"*Possibilities?*" he rejoined. "We don't need possibilities. We need final cuts.'

"There is one other danger," announced Tam.

"Oh, no," Brodie moaned. "More gloom and doom from Tam. So what is it now?"

"Sex."

Brodie erupted in laughter. "Sex! Between who? What the hell are you talking about?"

Cali Sky meanwhile experienced a surge of panic, a surge of unwanted adrenalin. What could she say? Yes, her mom was having a fling with their manager? Sorry, but my mom just can't help herself? It's a problem she has: she likes to get really close with those involved in music?

Tam looked steadily at Brodie, then at Cali Sky. She felt like he was reading her mind. Aggressive, defensive words flashed in her mind, marshalling themselves in syntactical order, prepared to counter-attack Tam's too true accusation.

Tam said, "Romantic relationships within a band never work out. That's all I'll say."

Cali Sky and Brodie stared at Tam. Then they stared at each other. Brodie's eyes narrowed in disbelief. "Wait," he exclaimed. "You think Cali Sky and I have something going on?"

"I don't think," replied Tam. "I know."

While Brodie worked himself up into a disingenuous state of phony indignation, Cali Sky settled effortlessly into the calm of spontaneous relief. "Don't worry, Tam," she explained. "Brodie and I have an agreement. We won't get involved as long as this band stays together and as long as both of us are in it."

Cali Sky's bold admission rendered Brodie speechless.

Tam looked unconvinced. "An agreement? An agreement isn't strong enough to stifle feelings...and urges."

Brodie now looked embarrassed, as if Tam and Cali Sky were looking at his baby pictures or reviewing his medical history.

Cali Sky replied, "This one is. Brodie and I made a decision to choose either music or each other." She glanced at Brodie unemotionally. "We chose music."

The band spent that night on Hermosa Beach, along with Zoe, Stone and Trish, whose anxiety caused her to sink further into herself, though once she returned to Tam's side, she never left it. Chris had no memory of his assault on Synth. The band never mentioned it again. They spent most of their time over the next week at Tam's house, playing and re-playing their songs, making changes, none of which seemed to satisfy Cali Sky and Tam. Their label's A & R man ceased badgering them about recording their overdue album long enough to arrange various interviews, one of which brought the band to a university in San Diego. Because it was a summer Saturday night, the campus was sparsely populated. Palm trees lined the quad. Sidewalks stretched across and around it, forming geometrical shapes. Cali Sky imagined the place during September, students throwing a Frisbee, kicking around a hacky sack, heading to classes with names she remembered from the USF course schedule: Finite Math, Abnormal Psychology, Readings in Romanticism, The Age of Reason and Revolt.

They entered through the glass doors of the student union, which stood at one end of the quad. They followed a flight of stairs to the second level, from which they could see on the first floor a dining hall, now abandoned, chairs resting legs-up on the tables. They walked down a corridor that seemed to get darker and more narrow the further they went. There, on the right, protected by sound-proof walls, was the university radio studio. Inside was a reception area. The walls were festooned with posters, mainly of alternative bands. Cali Sky read some of them: Sonic Youth, And Also the Trees, The Ocean Blue, Happy Mondays. Her eye was drawn to the most conspicuous poster, framed behind glass, positioned on the wall at eye level above the reception desk. It depicted U2, a close-up of their faces, but Cali Sky could tell from the blurry background that the black-and-white image was captured during their *Unforgettable Fire* photo shoot. At the bottom of the poster she saw four autographs, one from each member of the band.

A man entered the reception area from the studio.

"Hi," he said. "You must be Blue Flower. I'm Teddy Matthews. Some people just call me T Matt."

He noticed Cali Sky staring at the U2 poster.

"Pretty cool, huh?" he said. "I actually interviewed the band a few months ago. It ran in the *San Diego Tribune* and the *LA Times*. Did you catch it?"

Cali Sky shook her head.

"Best interview I ever did. Bono was hilarious. I had the band sign that poster after the interview."

T Matt was short and wore an oversized, starchy blue shirt that covered his paunch. Though in his early twenties, his hair was thinning on the top but long in the back. He wore a beard and glasses, making him look a bit like a Quaker. He had a toothy grin.

"Anyway," he continued. "thanks so much for coming down. You're from LA, right?" He shook each band member's hand.

"Orange County," Cali Sky corrected.

"Right, Orange County. Can I get you something to drink?"

"Do you have any beer?" asked Chris.

"I wish!" replied T Matt. "All we have is water. Water anyone?" They all nodded.

"Water all the way around," he announced cheerfully. He filled four Styrofoam cups from the Sparklett's water bottle in the corner of the room while explaining the process of the interview. "Just relax," he said, "Be yourself. Have fun. I'll ask some basic questions: how long the band has been together, influences, goals, that sort of thing. Just take it from there. Sound good?"

Before anyone had a chance to respond T Matt said, "When I interviewed U2 we talked about much more than music. It was surreal. You gotta picture the band with Guineses in their hands, drinking like fish, and Bono, with that Irish accent, saying, 'We may be rock stars, but we can also change the world.'"

"So you *do* have beer," said Chris hopefully.

T Matt guffawed. "No. Interviewing U2 was kind of a special occasion. Anyway in a couple of minutes we'll go into the studio and begin the program. We'll do some interview, then play a song from your demo. More interview, and then finish by playing the other song from your demo. Sound good?" But he had already turned his back on them, apparently organizing interview materials. When he turned back around his toothy grin was on display.

"Anyone need more water?"

A few minutes later they were in the studio. T Matt introduced the band to his radio audience, "though they need little introduction," he spoke into his mic winsomely, "if you've been listening to my program. Blue Flower has become a popular part of my rotation." He mentioned their names as if they were long-time friends. He referred to Cali Sky as just Cali. He spoke of their music like he helped them write it.

"So, Tam," he said, "you play guitar and keyboards. Gotta ask you about your name. Is that a nickname? Or is that your birth certificate name? It's really unusual and interesting."

"Thanks," replied Tam. He rounded off the word with authoritative finality, leaving no doubt that he had nothing more to say about the matter. After a pause the rest of the band laughed. T Matt joined in, merely to side-step embarrassment.

"Okay," chuckled T Matt, as if he had feet on both sides of some inside joke. "How about you, Cali? You also…"

"Actually, I go by Cali Sky."

"Oh, so sorry. Cali Sky. Can you tell us a little bit about your name?"

"Yeah. When I was born, my dad was a hippie. Need I say more?"

"It *is* sort of a hippie name."

"It actually came to him during an acid trip… Am I allowed to say that on the air?"

Another guffaw. "This is college radio. You can say just about anything you want."

Cali Sky said nothing.

T Matt picked up the lost thread. "So growing up did you listen to much of your dad's music? Did his hippie-ness wear off on you?"

"No, not at all. I listened to his old record collection when I was a kid. But like my dad, I moved on. At the time, though, I loved that music."

"What about you, Tam. Did you also love that music?"

"No, I hated it. My musical roots are much different than Cali Sky's. When I was a kid I listened to Television, Roxy Music, Bowie. I was interested in completely different musical frameworks."

"Well that's interesting. Two contrasting styles. And now Chris, you play drums. But I understand that you were previously in a heavy-metal band?"

"Yeah."

"Blue Flower is a long way from heavy metal. How did you end up in the band?"

"Well, I think they saw me play a gig at the Whisky in Hollywood, when I was in...my old band. They knew I was looking for something new..."

"We heard about him from Brodie." Tam stole the question. "So we all went and checked him out. We saw that he was a great drummer. We just had to see past the kind of music he was playing at that time."

Cali Sky added, "Chris told us he wanted to be in a completely different kind of band. One with more substance."

"Interesting," said T Matt. "And how about you, Brodie? You play bass. What's your musical background?"

"I grew up listening to punk, especially southern California punk bands."

"So, wow. This is really unusual. How do you all make these eclectic influences work together?"

"We all share the same vision," said Cali Sky. She decided to pull a word from Aunt Nancy's stock of vocabulary. "We try to create music that has gravitas, that can change people."

"Some of your lyrics are pretty deep, pretty spiritual even."

"Yeah," she replied. "That is our vision."

"Kind of like the vision of U2? Are they an influence?"

"Who?" asked Tam.

"U2," said T Matt.

"Never heard of them," said Tam.

Brodie started the chain of laughter, which spread to everyone in the room except for Tam himself.

"So how about the future? I understand you just signed a *very* lucrative contract with a major label. And is it true that you've already begun shooting a video?"

"Not exactly. We've met with a director to brainstorm ideas."

"Any you like? What can we expect your first video to look like?"

"Nature imagery. Mountains. Canyons. Oceans. Deserts."

"Really? How unusual!"

"It's all reflected in our music."

"So when can we expect the debut album? Have you been in the studio yet?"

"No. Not yet." The subject had been raised so often that Cali Sky felt herself becoming defensive. "You know how before you go on a vacation you get really excited? You imagine how great it will be? Inevitably, the real vacation never lives up to the imagined vacation. Our album is somewhere between the imagined and the real right now. It's getting closer and closer to the real. But we need to be sure that it doesn't lose anything as it makes that transition."

"Yeah, I know what you mean. That's a great analogy."

"We are trying to turn the ideal into the real."

"Wow, that's a daunting task. Sounds like your album is going to be something special. What are your expectations?"

"It's going to be huge," said Tam.

"Could you elaborate?"

"Fucking huge," elaborated Tam. "Bigger than Jesus huge. Bigger than U2 huge."

For the first time T Matt was speechless. Brodie and Chris snickered. Tam casually raised his Styrofoam cup to his lips.

"Yeah, T Matt," Cali Sky finally filled the dead air space, "we have a lot of confidence in ourselves and in our music."

That confidence seemed to humble T Matt for the rest of

the interview. He played their two demo songs and asked them straightforward questions. Tam explained that as a song evolved it took on a life of its own until it reached the point where he and Cali Sky submitted to it rather than the other way around. Cali Sky fielded a question about being a woman and testily insisted that an inspired musician transcends gender, except when "some ignorant asshole in the audience yells, 'Show us your tits.'" And by the time they left the university, grabbed dinner at a fast-food joint, and drove the sixty miles north on I-5 back to Orange County it was 1 a.m.

Zoe was already asleep in her room. Cali Sky fell into her bed feeling exhausted. Her sleep was unrestful. She dreamed that she went back in time and was in a studio with U2. The band was writing songs for a new album. She sat next to Bono and the Edge, each of whom occasionally took large sips of Guinness from pint glasses. She watched them as they struggled to compose. Song after song they tried different combinations of chords, experimenting with riffs, arrangements and moods. Each song showed promise but ultimately eluded their grasp. Cali Sky decided to help. She picked up a nearby guitar. She began to show them the songs. But because she was from the future, they were songs she had already heard. She was helping them write songs that she already knew. She already knew them because they had already written them. She gave them the chords, licks, solos and even the lyrics. The dream faded away as Cali Sky fought off the troubling sense that something was not right.

SIXTEEN

Spring 1987

March 3

Dear Ben,

Thanks for the birthday present. It's a great shot and I'm sure Zoe will also appreciate it. It will help get her mind off Stone. We still can't believe that he converted to Mormonism. That just came out of the blue. He goes from Jim Morrison and winter solstices to Joseph Smith and secret underwear.

Supposedly he's in Utah somewhere studying for the priesthood or something crazy like that.

Anyway, we'll hang the photo somewhere in the living room. It looks apocalyptic with the stormy weather and the eerie light glowing from the stage onto the surrounding rocks. They really did play under a blood red sky. Sometime soon I'll listen to the album and stare at the photograph and imagine what it would have been like to be there.

Someday Blue Flower will play Red Rocks too.

We've recorded about half the album now. Tam and I are pleased, for the most part. But sometimes I feel that recording a song is like caging an animal. Or it's like finally seeing something you've dreamed about since you were a child—all the possibilities are condensed into one hardened reality. Maybe I feel this way because I just turned 20. Maybe growing up means the gradual narrowing of possibilities.

Our label is not happy. They expected the album months ago. They said that we're running out of last chances. They haven't shut down our band room yet. We go there just about every night. It's kind of creepy though. There's a front office where one of the A & R men works by day. Sometimes he's just leaving as we're just arriving. We call him Bundy (behind his back) because he looks like a mass murderer. He leaves behind all this hard-core porn on his desk. Of course Chris looks at every page.

We still worry about him. Every now and then he'll just lose it. He tried to attack Synth again. I told Synth to stop coming to our shows, but I always see him in the crowd.

Zoe's doing well, despite the breakup with Stone. Her photos are published in more and more books and magazines. Which is a good thing. She's been covering my share of the rent recently. We haven't seen any of the 100 grand..."

Cali Sky looked at the oven clock and dropped the pen. *Shit.* The band was supposed to meet in five minutes at Brodie's apartment, since it stood in the shadows of the 405, up which they would carpool to Hollywood for another show at the Roxy. They crammed into Tam's Volvo; Trish squeezed into the backseat between Cali Sky and Brodie, and sped up the California coastline.

They made it with thirty minutes to spare. Lester was waiting for them backstage, but not displeased. A team of roadies and technicians did the setting up and sound checking. Nevertheless Lester wore his stern expression, narrow eyes zeroed in on no-bullshit business efficiency.

"I called a post-gig press conference," he announced.

"What for?" Cali Sky asked.

"Announce a few upcoming shows. Give assurances that the album is progressing nicely and will be out soon."

To Cali Sky his tone sounded primarily benevolent and grandfatherly, but also a bit threatening. She asked for no elaboration. Lester had choreographed their concerts, conferences and appearances like a bard chronicling the remote adventures of a shadowy hero: the legend of Blue Flower grew. He encouraged, circulated, amplified and maybe even himself posed questions like, "Are they the best band you've never heard?" "Have they created a radically new style of music?" "Will they cut a record that will change the course of rock and roll?" "Do *you* change when *you* hear their music?" "Will they live up to the hype?"

They played their set and one encore—never more than one encore—and collapsed onto the couch backstage. Cali Sky wiped the sweat from her brow and drank some water from a plastic bottle. She watched a cadre of pen-and-pad wielding hipsters walk into the room and then remembered that Lester had called a press conference. The photographers snapped their shots. The reporters readied their pens and cued their recording devices.

"Thank you all for coming," began Lester, who stood next to the couch, which had just enough room for all four members of the band to sit comfortably and appear unified. In such a setting, manager speaking on their behalf, faces and cameras staring at them, they could not help but lounge with the unmistakable panache of introverted rock stars.

"The band is happy to answer questions," continued Lester, "but first a major announcement." Cali Sky and Tam simultaneously looked up at Lester, now pausing for effect. Then they furtively looked at each other, not wanting to betray the fact that this major announcement would probably be news to them as well.

"We have a release date for the album," Lester proclaimed. "April 22nd."

The shock registered in Cali Sky's eyes, so she rubbed her temple, hand concealing most of her face. Her mouth felt locked into a frown, as if she couldn't smile if she had to. Tam swallowed his anger and stared into the distance, over the heads of the reporters, like some modern-day Job glowering at God, knowing that it would come to this but who gives a shit anyway.

"And as you know," continued Lester, "the album will be self-titled. That hasn't changed."

Cali Sky could sense Tam's nervous energy. She knew by his agitated movements that he wanted to speak. But Lester spoke first, soliciting questions from the press. In the very back of the room a young man quickly raised his hand. Cali Sky couldn't see him through the crowd, but she thought she recognized his voice.

"Yeah, um, what's been the reaction to the announcement that a member of the band is gay?"

"Pardon me?" asked Lester.

The shock of the question was compounded by the jolt of recognition: She now remembered that voice, its lazy insolence and capacity for recklessness. John, the lead singer and guitar player for Nowhere.

"A person in your band is gay," answered John. "Don't you even know?"

"I'm not sure what you're talking about," Lester stammered.

All eyes were now turned to John, who wore no press credentials and in fact looked nothing like a journalist.

"There is a homosexual in the band." John emphasized the syllables "homo." "How do you think your fans will react?"

Cali Sky's first reaction was befuddlement. *Who is John talking about?* she thought. *What announcement? Wait, is he talking about me? Am I gay?* The other members of the band looked equally shocked and disturbed.

John seemed to revel in his command of the room. "My source is Chris. He himself told me that Tam is gay."

Cali Sky suddenly felt like she was in a room filled with strangers, all of whom were examining the reactions of the stranger called Tam, who unlike the Tam she knew was blushing, and the stranger called Chris, who unlike the Chris she knew actually looked guilty. Only one person in the room looked relatively unsurprised: Lester, who no longer seemed off-balance and now donned a politician's unflappable face. Cali Sky expected him to deny the charge, to explain that there was no announcement and that John was no reporter.

"Tam's sexuality is his private business," he replied calmly. "I'm sure Blue Flower fans will respect his privacy. And continue to appreciate Blue Flower's music."

The rest of the press conference mainly concerned the band's sexuality. "Who is Tam's lover?" "Is anyone else in the band gay?" "Has Cali Sky dated anyone in the band?" Lester intercepted these questions. The band remained speechless. When he didn't appeal to privacy he muttered equivocations. The conference ground to an awkward halt with Lester announcing, "No more questions for now." Gradually the reporters shuffled out of the room. John was long gone. After Lester closed and locked the door he turned and sighed. Tam's head was buried in his hands.

"Is it true, Tam?" asked Brodie. "Are you gay?"

Tam slowly raised his head. His eyes were red and watery. "Why, Chris?" he pleaded. "Why did you do it?"

"I'm sorry. I was drunk," answered Chris.

"And why John? Why would you tell *him* of all people?" Tam moaned.

Chris said nothing, head down.

"But what about Trish?" Brodie asked Tam. "Are you *sure* you're gay?"

Tam did not answer. The expression that came over his face was, to Cali Sky 's astonishment, the spitting image of Chris's.

"Look," Lester interrupted with take-charge efficiency, "it'll be alright. Look at Elton John. His record sales took a hit after he came out of the closet, but he survived. Or maybe we can play this like Morrissey. I never confirmed that Tam was gay. We can be cagey about it. I mean, everyone knows that Morrissey is gay, but he's smart enough to conceal it. And with Trish in the picture people will speculate that Tam is bisexual. He'll be like the second coming of Bowie. All of this may boost our publicity."

It's all about sex, Cali Sky thought. *Always has been and always will be.* For some reason the image of her mom, naked, straddling Lester on the apartment floor intruded on her thoughts.

Suddenly Tam shouted, "You ruined my life! Do you realize that? You ruined my life!"

Chris initially submitted to Tam's accusation with customary deference. Cali Sky adopted her usual role as peacemaker. "Take it easy, Tam. He didn't ruin your life…"

But then Chris spoke up. "Maybe I've just had enough, Tam. You always treat me like shit. Just like my dad!" He paused and shouted it again, "Just like my dad!"

"Is that why I gave you a place to live?" screamed Tam. "I opened my house to you. And this is what you do?"

He marched to the door. When he unlocked and opened it he nearly ran into Trish, who stood there weeping. He hugged her roughly, then the two of them disappeared.

Chris rose from the couch and walked toward the door.

"Fuck!" he thundered. Then threw a punch at the wall that bloodied his knuckles. He stormed out.

"Wait for me here, please," said Lester calmly as he followed. "I need to cool him down."

Cali Sky and Brodie remained seated on the couch.

"Is this the end?" Brodie asked her.

"No."

Another sexual image flashed across Cali Sky's mind's eye. This one of Chris and Hilary. Chris said they had hooked up. *How did that happen? Hilary dated John.*

"Why not?"

Brodie's voice transported him into her roaming thoughts. Why did her imagination suddenly turn pornographic, like the glossy images scattered luridly across Bundy's desk? She pictured herself straddling Brodie, all of his attention, all of his movements focused on her. She watched him look at her naked body and felt his hands on her breasts. She felt the comfort warm her body, comfort she so badly needed. And she saw the pleasure on his face—all because of her—pleasure rising and rising until it expended itself in an exquisite death. Her mind went blank.

The band did not get together once during the next week. Cali Sky and Brodie went to the band room at the usual time, but the only person they saw was Bundy, who was on his way out, leaving his porn scattered across his desk as usual. Cali Sky averted her eyes. Brodie pretended it wasn't there, which he wouldn't have done had Chris been there. The two of them played some songs, but only half-heartedly. Tam and Chris did not return their phone calls.

"Are you sure this is not the end?" asked Brodie.

"Yes," Cali Sky answered.

But she was not being honest. She knew Brodie's question would be answered the following Saturday night at Irvine Meadows Amphitheater. Blue Flower was part of the lineup for an all-day "Alternative Rock" Festival. They were slotted to play toward the end of the day, which Cali Sky realized was an honor. The closer in the lineup you are to the headliners the more respected is your band.

But when the day came and she stood backstage with Brodie and Lester, she felt more horror than honor. From where she stood she could see the sloped lawn, where some people were sprawled out on blankets. Those closest to the stage were standing, only a few dancing to music that sounded muffled and far off from her position on the wrong side of the speakers. The band playing was in the heart of the lineup, which may have explained the festival-goers' sapped energy. A mid-afternoon lethargy seemed to hang above the amphitheater. Lester looked at his watch.

"Where are they?"

"We don't go on for another three hours," said Cali Sky.

"Yeah, but they were supposed to be here an hour ago. You know how this works. Forty-five minutes per set. They want every band to be here early and ready to go."

The sun blazed down on the lawn from directly overhead. But Cali Sky could see dark clouds at the edge of the horizon.

"Lester," began Cali Sky, "you knew that Tam was gay all along, didn't you?"

"I didn't know, but I had my suspicions. It wasn't too hard to see the truth."

Two bands and two hours later, Tam and Chris had still not arrived.

"If they don't show up," warned Lester, "then we have a big problem. A *very* big problem."

He paced back and forth. The late afternoon sunshine was still warm. But Cali Sky could see a wall of dark clouds coming from the north. A gust of wind blew fitfully across the lawn and through the stage scaffolding, rippling the side curtains.

"Do they realize what will happen if we have to cancel this gig?" Lester asked, not expecting an answer.

"They'll be here," said Cali Sky.

Lester looked toward the north. "Maybe if it storms they'll cancel our set."

The band onstage finished a song. Then another and another.

"God*damn* it," snarled Lester as he walked away.

"Not the end, huh?" said a crestfallen Brodie.

"No."

Lester returned, furious. "We're fucked," he raged. "I just talked to the promoter. If we fail on our contractual obligations, then..."

Chris approached tentatively.

"Where the hell have you been?" Lester yelled.

Chris shrugged. "I'm here now."

Cali Sky noticed that Chris had a new black eye. She could also tell that he was drunk.

"Where the hell is Tam?" asked Lester.

"How the hell should I know," Chris replied.

"Jesus. You can't go on without Tam."

The band on stage finished the final song of their set. The crowd applauded. The house lights came on. Cali Sky felt a tingle of dread in her belly as she watched roadies carry their equipment onto the stage. Another fitful gust of wind swept suddenly over the lawn and across the stage. One of the long-haired roadies squinted into the gale, smiling in surprise and wonder, as his hair whipped around his face. A bank of dark clouds now comprised the entire northern horizon, which rolled toward them.

Chris wobbled a bit on his feet. Brodie moved forward to support him.

"Are you alright?"

Chris mumbled some words that Brodie took to mean yeah.

"Are you sure?"

"I may be too drunk to stand, but I can still play drums. Trust me, I've done it a lot. I just need something to eat."

Cali Sky motioned toward Lester, who at that moment spotted the promoter hurrying in the other direction. She overheard Lester shout, "Hey! Are we still going on? In this weather?" The promoter motioned to Lester for a private discussion.

"I need to eat something," Chris repeated. "If I don't I'll be sick halfway through our set."

"Alright," said Cali Sky. "Brodie, you stay with him. I'll find something for him to eat."

For the next five minutes she searched nearly every square inch of the backstage area, with the exception of the rooms reserved for the headliners. The sky grew dark, but she heard no thunder. She knew she was running out of time. *Will they go on without me? No. Tam's not even here yet.* She decided to run to the public concession stand. She ensured that she had her backstage pass, then crossed the security checkpoint and joined the throngs of festival goers. She stopped at the first food stand she encountered, one that sold pretzels and beer.

"Excuse me," she said to the two men ahead of her in line, "My band is supposed to go on in ten minutes. Do you think I could go ahead of you?"

The one closest to hear looked suspicious. *"You're* in Blue Flower?"

But the other recognized her. "Cali Sky!" he proclaimed. "Yeah," he said to the other man, "she really *is* in Blue Flower."

They stepped aside and she moved to the front. She ordered three pretzels.

"Shouldn't you be backstage, getting ready or something?" asked the man behind her in line.

"Probably. My drummer is hungry."

She handed the vendor a twenty.

"So," continued the man behind her, "when will your album come out?"

"April 22nd."

"Can't wait to hear it!"

She collected her change.

The man asked, "Is it true that Tam is gay?"

But she didn't respond. She stuffed the bills into her pocket and ran toward the security checkpoint, awkwardly clutching three salted pretzels wrapped in wax paper. She heard the resonant tap of Chris's snare drum. The techs were running sound checks on stage. She darted in and around the crowds. She noticed that some were slipping rain ponchos over their heads. As she neared the checkpoint she nearly ran into the back of someone who had the short black hair and pale white neck of Tam. She glanced back after she had nimbly slipped past and discovered that it was in fact Tam.

"What the hell are you doing?" she asked as she came to an abrupt halt, readjusting her grip on the pretzels.

"I'm going to play a gig."

"You're about four hours late."

"I'll be on stage when it counts."

"Well can you at least hurry?"

"Why? They can't start without us."

They flashed their backstage passes and continued at Tam's pace. As they walked Cali Sky caught a glimpse of the lawn. She could see people's hair and clothes fluttering in the wind. The stadium lights had come on. No, she remembered that they were on when she left to find Chris something to eat. While she was gone darker storm clouds had hidden the sun, accentuating the lights' illumination.

"Chris is drunk, isn't he?" asked Tam, gesturing toward the pretzels.

"Yeah. Totally wasted."

"Once he gets those in his stomach he'll be alright."

"What about you? Will you be alright?"

Cali Sky saw tragedy and despair in his face. His eyes were red, just as they had been on the day of the press conference.

"Jesus, Tam," shouted Lester, who spotted Tam in the distance, "You get here five minutes before show time. What is wrong with you?"

Tam ignored him. The wind rose and buffeted their faces. Cali Sky handed Chris the three pretzels, which he immediately began to scarf.

Lester added in a conciliatory tone, "But why you're going on in this weather is beyond me."

Briefly the dark clouds parted. The fading sunlight broke through the opening and transfigured the atmosphere into an apocalyptic red glow. Everything in sight now reflected a radiating otherworldliness. A roadie ran out onto the stage, making final checks of all the equipment. When he returned Cali Sky could see he was older. Gray stubble peppered his wizened cheeks, now painted red by the streaks of light. He stopped near her, looked to the heavens and said, "It's the Goddamned harrowing of hell!"

"Okay," said Lester, out of breath, "The promoter gave us the green light. He says they need to stay on-schedule. He says the clouds are breaking."

The promoter walked on stage and took ahold of the mic. He introduced the band. As usual Cali Sky could feel her heartbeat accelerate. Her palms became sweaty. *Just get out there and start playing. Then you'll feel better.* As she walked toward her guitar the crowd cheered. Her adrenalin pulsated. But what she primarily noticed was that out of nowhere the wind seemed to blow from all directions at once. It tossed her hair this way and that. No matter which direction she faced she could not prevent her hair from blowing in her face. *Fuck it*, she thought. So she let her hair be and began playing.

Zoe captured the moment on camera. At the front of the stage stands Cali Sky, looking down at her guitar, hair tossed wildly by the wind. Brodie stands to her left, bass slung low from his neck, staring at Cali Sky as if mesmerized. Tam stands to her right, looking wistfully at the approaching storm clouds. Chris sits head down at the drums, focusing on his beat.

Thirty seconds later a bolt of jagged lightning split the sky and struck a tree in the amphitheater parking lot. Cali Sky heard the startling crack as well as the screams from the crowd above the music. A torrent of rain burst from the clouds. She looked to her left. Lester, the concert promoter, and six roadies were gesticulating like madmen, beckoning them to get off the stage. Cali Sky promptly stopped playing and put down her guitar, laying it flat on the stage, not even bothering to return it to its stand. The music immediately sounded thinner. A panic spread across the lawn as people evacuated the open area. Brodie set his bass next to Cali Sky's guitar, removing the anchor from the song. When Chris dropped his sticks, the song lost shape. They rushed to shelter. Chris, still drunk, tripped over his own stool and fell, but quickly returned to his feet and joined the others next to Lester. Weighted down by the rain, Cali Sky's hair now stayed tucked behind her ears. Brodie swayed from side to side like a boxer, the unspent adrenalin preventing him from remaining still. Chris took his shirt off for some unknown, inebriated reason.

As they received towels from a roadie, they realized that their song was still playing. It sounded attenuated and anemic, but it continued on. Tam remained on stage, still playing his guitar.

"What is he doing?" asked Brodie.

The lawn was now almost completely abandoned as the rain fell hard. Only a handful of fans stood in front of the stage. The atmosphere was electric. Another lightning strike was imminent.

"Get off the stage!" yelled Lester.

"Tam!" Chris shouted.

But Tam continued to play. Cali Sky saw that he was crying. She also saw that he had abandoned himself to the music he was making. The atmosphere suddenly became even darker, no trace of color. Each individual rain drop, pelting Tam and his guitar, was starkly visible in the stage lights. He looked up from his guitar as he played, then stared unflinchingly at a person standing below.

"Someone cut the Goddamned power!" shouted Lester.

Cali Sky took five steps toward Tam where he stood onstage. The driving rain stung her legs. From this vantage point she looked out at the front of the stage and saw Synth, returning Tam's stare. He stood on top of a third row chair. Suddenly Cali Sky experienced a shock, the surprise of a sudden transition. The music stopped. Someone had cut the power. But Tam continued to play, though he was now the only one who could hear the song pouring from his powerless guitar strings.

Another bolt of lightning hurtled toward earth.

"Get off the stage, Tam!" yelled Brodie.

He saw Cali Sky move toward Tam, this time walking determinedly, but poised to break into a run. Brodie and Lester sprang forward and restrained her.

"It's too dangerous!" shouted Lester.

As they dragged her back to safety she caught sight of Tam's face. His expression looked familiar to her. She had seen it before. She had seen it on her dad's face when he prayed in church, asking forgiveness for the sins she knew about and the darker sins that she didn't: a look of penitence, of contrition, the remorse of a sinner/saint. But Tam's expression had an acutely desperate edge, as if his sin were so deep seated that only self-sacrifice was sufficient for atonement. She also saw anger on his face, not unlike that visible on her aunt's gaunt face at those moments when she shook her metaphorical fist at God for creating a universe plagued with blemishes like multiple sclerosis and exploding appendixes.

As Brodie and Lester clutched Cali Sky, Chris ran past, heaving his way toward Tam. His gait was heavy and plodding. His rescue attempt came up fifteen feet short. The bolt of lightning struck the amp at Tam's back, firing it with an explosion of sparks of electricity, which then surged from the cord to the guitar. The spasm that contorted Tam's agonized body brought Cali Sky to her knees. He fell in a heap. When Chris touched him he felt a jolt, for the electricity was still alive in Tam's body. He pried the guitar from Tam's fingers, then, struggling to his knees and grimacing in pain and terror, he dragged Tam off the stage.

Tam's face was white. A rivulet of blood, smudged by rain and Chris's touch, flowed from his mouth or nose, Cali Sky couldn't tell which.

"Tam," Lester cried. "Tam, can you hear me?"

His head rolled. His body was limp. He groggily opened and closed his eyes.

"Tam!" shouted Cali Sky.

She touched his arm hesitantly, then stroked it. The rain water felt cool, but his flesh warm. She tried to hold his hand, but it was clenched into a fist. She noticed that his guitar pick was locked between his thumb and forefinger.

All attention was fixed on Tam. That is why no one noticed Chris pass out behind them. One moment he was kneeling beside the others. The next his torso went limp. He briefly propped himself up on his elbows, then tried to steady himself on all fours. But he slowly succumbed to a heavy oblivion.

"Chris! Chris!" Brodie exclaimed.

At that moment a team of paramedics descended upon them in a whirlwind of lumpy medical bags, black boots and disciplined urgency. They nudged the onlookers aside but seemed unsure which victim to attend to first.

"Who was struck by the lightning?" asked a mustachioed paramedic.

"Him," answered Lester, pointing to Tam. "But I don't think it struck him directly."

"What happened to *him*?" The paramedic nodded toward Chris.

"He...rescued Tam," Lester replied.

"Okay, give us some room."

Cali Sky, Brodie and Lester rose to their feet and stood a few feet off. Brodie put his arm around Cali Sky. Lester paced. A second team of paramedics arrived with two stretchers. By now a small crowd of roadies, sound techs, VIPs and miscellaneous backstage hangers-on had gathered on the stage.

"Everyone needs to back off," barked a paramedic peevishly.

They lifted Tam and Chris onto the stretchers and began wheeling them away.

"Will they be okay?" asked Cali Sky.

"We don't know, miss," answered the mustachioed paramedic.

Finding out what hospital they would be taken to, Lester

escorted Cali Sky and Brodie to the parking lot. The rain had stopped, the storm had blown to the south, the sun was now shining. A few festival goers asked for their autographs, not knowing what happened. Those who did gazed morbidly at them—the sort of stares Cali Sky received when she was called out of class all those years ago to learn that her sister had died, the stares of fascination and horror. When they reached the parking lot they heard the sirens. She heard sirens every day. They were part of the sonic furniture of everyday life. But how different they sounded now—how personal and traumatic.

The waiting room at the hospital ER was lined with fellow sufferers, those wrestling with tragedies of varying degrees. Some seemed accustomed to it, the Aunt Nancy types who become habituated to nightmare. Others looked dazed. As for Cali Sky victimization stirred in her a sense of loss and anger. She had an urge to cry and scream.

They had not waited long before they were told they could see Chris. He had suffered minor burns and some residual electrocution. His main problems, they were told confidentially by a compassionate ER nurse, were trauma, exhaustion and—in a hushed voice—alcohol.

"He needs to take better care of himself," she warned. Her face then relaxed. "But he'll be okay. We'll discharge him soon."

"What about Tam?" asked Lester.

"I'll find out."

Twenty excruciating minutes later she returned. "He should be fine. His burns are more extensive. And we want to run some neurological tests. He'll stay overnight for evaluation. If he is stable tomorrow we'll discharge him then. The doctor will be out to see you shortly. He'll have more information."

Chris said few words when they visited him in his room. He looked tired and weak. Lester tried to cheer him up.

"You big hero, you!"

"Tam?" said Chris wearily.

"He's gonna be okay," assured Lester.

"You feel okay, Chris?" asked Brodie.

Chris didn't respond.

"Can we get you anything?" Cali Sky asked.

He shook his head.

Zoe and Synth were in the waiting room when they returned. Zoe's makeup was slightly smeared. Synth's clothes, still wet, clung to his body. A nurse had already updated them on Tam's and Chris's conditions. Zoe looked relieved. Synth was still agitated and restless. He spoke to no one.

Cali Sky sat next to Zoe and Brodie drinking stale coffee. Lester read some tattered magazine. Synth stood at a distance. An hour later he exited the waiting room without a word.

"He loves Tam," Zoe said softly. Cali Sky and Brodie nodded, both looking toward the door, out of which Synth had just exited.

"I know," replied Cali Sky.

"But he's not the first."

Brodie leaned forward, elbows resting on his knees, attention now centered on Zoe and her revelation. Lester lowered his magazine and peered at them. They waited until he returned to the article that he pretended to read.

"Who was?" asked Cali Sky.

"Well, I'm not sure, but I think Brian. From Forest Murmurs."

She paused. Lester turned a page.

Zoe continued, "I think they were lovers when they were in the band together. But then Brian freaked out or something. Maybe he stopped loving Tam. Maybe he couldn't admit he was gay. He left and the band broke up."

"What about..."

Just then Synth returned to the waiting room.

436

"What could be taking so long?" he demanded. "The nurse said a doctor would come out to give us an update."

"I don't know, Synth," answered Zoe. "He'll be alright."

Another hour later and Synth's restlessness turned into angry impatience. He leaned against a wall, face forward and pounded it three times with his fist.

"Come on!" he whisper screamed. "Please!"

A few minutes later he repeated the desperate act.

"Excuse me!" called out the receptionist from the other side of the room. "Excuse me! Please don't do that! Or I will have to ask you to leave!"

He stormed out of the room.

"What about Trish?" Cali Sky finally returned to her question.

Zoe pondered. "I don't know. I think he loves her in his own way."

"She wasn't at the gig today," Brodie said. "I've never seen them apart like that."

"Maybe now that everything's out in the open..."

Just then they heard Chris's voice. "I said I can walk!"

They watched him rise from a wheelchair near the receptionist's desk and add peevishly, "I'm okay!"

"Sir," exclaimed the nurse, "Please sit back down!"

Lester rushed to the rescue. "It's okay. I'll take it from here. Chris, go ahead and sit down. It's alright now."

"He needs to take it easy," explained the exasperated nurse. "He's still weak and experiencing some dizziness."

"Okay," said Lester. "We'll watch over him."

"You wanna get something to eat, Chris?" offered Brodie.

"No, I'm not hungry. And I'm okay. Where's Tam?"

"He has to stay here overnight for some tests, but he's gonna be okay."

Lester coaxed Chris back into the wheelchair.

"He just needs to sign some release papers," began the nurse, who suddenly went silent.

Cali Sky saw the nurse's attention drawn to something behind her and then felt herself being pushed violently. In the second before she hit the floor, her mind racing to process the event, Cali Sky thought she was being struck by lightning, lightning that had followed her from the amphitheater to the emergency room. She half expected to hear the boom of thunder and feel the pain of electrocution. But as she rose to her knees, hearing only screams and feeling only the unmistakable presence of violence, awareness dawned quickly.

Synth had returned to the waiting room, pushed everyone between him and Chris out of the way, and attacked. She saw Brodie and Lester holding him back. Chris sat passively in the wheelchair, making little effort to protect himself. The nurse screamed hysterically, "Call security!" Synth realized he couldn't overcome Brodie and Lester, but anger sustained his vain attempt. "Call security!" the nurse repeated. From somewhere behind the desk Cali Sky heard someone say, "I'm on it."

"No, Synth," said Brodie, trying to calm him down.

"Take it easy," Lester added.

Synth took a step back. His enraged voice then rose above the din of screams, gasps and coaxings. He pointed menacingly at Chris, who looked defeated in the wheelchair. Synth yelled with the doom of an unbreakable curse, "You are to blame! You are to blame!"

Tam was released from the hospital the following day. Cali Sky and Brodie were waiting for him. But so was Synth. In the week that followed he and Tam were inseparable. Trish meanwhile disappeared. Zoe told Cali Sky about a rumor that she had decamped to Ecuador. A rival strain of gossip held that she had become religious and ditched her dark-wave appearance for a wholesome mainstream look, a transformation so complete that you wouldn't recognize her if she walked right past. Tam wouldn't say one way or the other.

He didn't say much about the band during the week that followed. Whenever Cali Sky called, he said that he needed some time away. This continued for another week. When Brodie now asked, "Is this the end?" Cali Sky had to admit that she didn't know. Lester issued an ultimatum with a tactful mix of compassion and bluntness: a one month extension on the album deadline, to May 22nd, but no later. The record company, he explained, could not afford to wait any longer.

Tam wasn't the only member of the band disinclined to talk about their last chance to finish the album. After the incident Chris moved out of Tam's house and into Brodie's. Four days later Brodie awoke one morning to find that Chris was gone. He left no note, though Brodie discovered that he had stolen an unopened bottle of wine and a half-empty bottle of gin from the kitchen before he left. The day after Brodie informed her of this, Cali Sky drove directly to Orange Coast Community College and filled out an application for the fall semester. Her deferment to the University of San Francisco had lapsed but at least she could get her schooling started somewhere next term. In short Cali Sky, Brodie and Lester all realized that Blue Flower's prospects were dim.

This unexpectedly changed over the course of two consecutive days. On the first Chris called Brodie to ask—with absurd nonchalance, as if Tam had never been electrocuted—when the next band practice was.

"Band practice?" muttered Brodie.

"Yeah, isn't that tonight?" Chris slurred.

"Chris, we haven't had band practice in two weeks."

"We haven't?"

"Where are you?"

"At the studio."

On the second day Tam called Cali Sky to schedule a band meeting.

"Why?" asked Cali Sky.

"What do you mean why? To talk."

"About what?" She braced herself against all of the anticipated responses: to call it quits, to announce he's leaving the band, to deliver an ultimatum—either he goes or Chris goes.

But instead, in a voice far too optimistic for the Tam she knew, he replied, "About second chances. About getting back into the studio and finishing our album."

After this serendipitous second day Brodie stopped asking Cali Sky, "Is this the end?" She wished she hadn't applied to college and lost her $50 non-refundable application fee. Zoe told them both, "Bad things come in threes. First Tam was hurt. Then Chris was hurt. Then Synth attacked Chris. You've paid your dues. Now expect success!"

Cali Sky and Brodie carried these expectations with them to the studio on the appointed night of the meeting. Cali Sky was relieved to see that Bundy's car—a Datsun pickup with a camper shell fitted over the flatbed—was not there. The only vehicle in the lot was Chris's Suzuki, jutted diagonally across two spaces. Cali Sky noticed that the windows were rolled down. She peeked inside: cassette tape holders and one badly chipped and splintered drumstick lay on the passenger seat. Empty beer bottles were scattered on the floorboard.

"He probably has been living here," commented Brodie.

Cali Sky fumbled through her keys. Brodie tried the door and found it unlocked.

"Just like Chris," joked Cali Sky, returning her keys to her purse.

Inside the familiar sights and smells put Cali Sky at ease. The spartan office, containing only a desk, filing cabinets, telephone, a few reference books, and of course Bundy's porn collection, hadn't changed much. It triggered memories of late-night songwriting under the throes of inspiration. It struck Cali Sky how long it had been since they had written those songs. She felt determined to finish recording the album.

"It's good to be back here," she admitted.

"Let's just hope all our instruments are still in the band room," said Brodie.

"Where else would they be?"

"It's been weeks. Maybe the record company cleared them out."

"No way, Brodie."

His fear made her nervous. She walked ahead of him anxiously, as if roadies were at that very moment disassembling and removing their equipment. She knew her misgivings were unfounded, but she hurried anyway, anticipating the relief of finding the guitars, keyboard, drum kit and amps just as they left them.

She rounded the corner and froze. The light from the office dimly lit the band room. She never saw whether the equipment was there. Her eyes were instead drawn to a large mass hanging from the ceiling. In the half light she could see tattered sneakers. Untied shoelaces dangled from the right shoe. The socks were neither pulled up nor down. Around the girthy waist hung a loosely worn pair of short pants. Chris—for now there was no mistaking what she saw—Chris wore no shirt. His back was muscular and bruised. His head, or what she saw of his head before she averted her eyes, was impossibly angled. Her first reaction was anger. She nearly found herself saying, "Chris, get down from there." But then she spotted the overturned drum stool beneath his lifeless body. Stark reality, cold and hardened, flooded her consciousness with a settled inevitability. She felt like she had seen this spectacle before or like she knew it was coming, like it was awaiting its appointed time along the unwinding thread of her days.

She took two backward steps and bumped into Brodie.

"Jesus! Oh, Jesus! Chris!" He ran forward and grasped Chris by the legs. Cali Sky staggered back into the office and leaned against Bundy's desk. She felt dizzy. Her hands slipped on the porno mags. Women's breasts swirled in her vision. The overwrought sexuality in their seductive faces leered at her.

"Cali Sky!" they screamed. "Cali Sky, help us!"

She looked closer. *How do they make their voices come from the other room?* she wondered. Then she thought she saw Tam enter the office and look at her strangely. He tried to get her attention, calling her name over and over but she couldn't focus. When he turned the corner the naked women began to call his name too. She heard yelling and commotion in the adjacent room but she didn't dare return.

"Cali Sky!" screamed the porno girls. "Cali Sky, help us!"

Then Brodie reached over her and grabbed the phone. He spoke frantically, tears in his eyes. Cali Sky heard only fragments: "He hung himself... I think he's dead.... An office... in a large industrial complex.... on Red Hill... I don't know the address... Yeah, the one just down the road from the movie theater..." He hung up the phone.

The porno girls were talking to her again. "Help us!" But Brodie grabbed her by the shoulders and was shouting at her so she couldn't hear.

"Cali Sky! Cali Sky! Cali Sky! Listen to me!"

She looked into his eyes and felt the sensation of waking from a dream.

"Cali Sky, you need to go outside and wait. When the

ambulance comes you need to get their attention. Okay? Cali Sky? Can you do that?"

She nodded. Brodie returned to the band room. Ignoring the screams of the porno girls, she picked up the phone and dialed the first number that came into her head, not sure who would answer.

"Hello?" It was her dad's voice.

"Dad."

"Cali Sky?"

"Is Desiree okay?"

"Yes, she's fine. Where are you? Are you alright?"

"Um."

"Cali Sky?"

"Could you pick me up?"

"Where are you?"

"At the band room."

"Where is that?"

"I don't know. In a large industrial complex... On Red Hill... Just down the street from a movie theater."

It was quiet outside, even peaceful. Three cars were now in the lot. The voices of the porno girls had disappeared. Tam's Volvo was parked alongside Chris's Suzuki. *He's dead.* She looked up at the night sky, allowing the weight of those words to settle in her mind. She saw the dark haze of a marine layer. "He's dead," she whispered, now looking across the parking lot.

For the second time in three weeks she heard sirens as if the sound were novel or foreign. She knew they were coming to her, that the tragedy they announced to people who did not know Chris—to the old man comfortably eating his dinner in front of the TV and to the family waiting eagerly in line at the movie theater—was *her* tragedy. She watched the ambulance pull into the parking lot in the foggy distance. It steered in her general direction, moving tentatively. Then, the driver apparently spotting her outstretched arms, it sped forward directly toward her.

"In there," she pointed as the team of paramedics, with their bustle of urgency and cold efficiency, emerged from the vehicle. While they were inside the police arrived. The questions they asked made her feel like she was on a TV show: When did you arrive on the premises? What exactly happened once you entered? What is your relationship with the victim? When did you last see him? The police questioned Brodie, and while they were questioning Tam, Cali Sky spotted the orange Bronco pull alongside the ambulance.

Philip seemed to open the door before the truck came to a full stop. Cali Sky watched him approach. His movements were comforting, putting her in mind of hiking behind him up Cucamonga Peak. But the flash of red across his body from the spinning ambulance lights disoriented her.

"What happened?" he asked breathlessly.

She now found it difficult to speak. She willed herself to repeat the sentence. "He's dead."

"Who?"

"Philip," interrupted Brodie, wiping his eyes and standing alongside Cali Sky.

"Cali Sky," pressed Philip, ignoring Brodie, "Who died?"

She lowered her head and sobbed.

"Chris..." began Brodie, "committed suicide."

"Oh no."

The sense of deja vu struck her hard again. *This too has happened before.* Philip and Brodie helped her to the Bronco. As it pulled away she remembered the conversation from long ago, into which Philip had intruded, about the haunting name of the band Joy Division and the suicide of its lead singer, Ian Curtis.

When they arrived at Philip's house Cali Sky walked right around Michelle and her gestures of empathy, and made straight for Desiree's bedroom. She tiptoed around stuffed animals left on the floor and knelt at the bed, waiting for her eyes to adjust to the darkness so that she could study the sleeping child. After a few moments she made out Desiree's closed eyes, the soft skin of her forehead and, to Cali Sky's relief, the rise and fall of her chest, the delicate and precarious sound of breathing. Philip quietly entered the bedroom and gently tried to raise Cali Sky to her feet, but she resisted. She wanted to whisper a story before she left. She remembered it was a sacred story, for she felt like those who heard it would discover that they already knew it somehow. But only disconnected images came to her: a girl, moonlit lawn, a valley, a cabin, the wind, golden notes. She searched her memory and found that the images receded into a fog.

The fog hung across her consciousness for the next day. She fell in and out of sleep. She was fed soup by her dad. In one half-waking moment the nurturing presence of her mom hung above the bed, lovingly running her fingers through her hair. In another she thought she heard Aunt Nancy, level with the bed from the well-worn seat of the wheelchair, reciting poetry in her ear. She had a vision of Brodie standing over her, touching her cheek. She saw Zoe's mussed black hair. Once she became aware that Desiree was in the room, hoping to find her awake so that they could play. The familiar sound of Philip's gentle rebuke followed, reminding Desiree that Cali Sky needed to rest.

The next morning she awoke to the sound of a ringing telephone and discovered that the fog had dissipated. She heard the stilted friendliness of her dad's unnecessarily loud telephone voice. The morning sun filtered through the chalky, water-stained bedroom window. Then she heard other voices: her mom's short and rapid speech; her aunt's belabored words; her dad's soothing monotone; Brodie's casual intimacy; Zoe's "Oh-my-God" refrain, and the unpredictable chirpings of Desiree. The sounds, along with the sight of sunlight on the carpet, reminded her of sleeping-in summer days and exultant Christmas-break mornings of her past.

Sitting up in bed Cali Sky sighed, then grimaced. She knew the ways of tragedy. You have to confront it head-on, acknowledge its existence, admit that it had murdered, ransacked, irritated, gutted, inconvenienced, shocked and pretty much fucked you up. At which point a hint of light in your benighted mental universe suggests the paradoxical hope of hitting rock bottom.

Entering the kitchen felt a bit like walking onstage. All eyes focused on her. Two boxes of a dozen doughnuts sat on the center of the kitchen table. Desiree stacked blocks on the floor. Philip, Joan, Brodie, Zoe and Aunt Nancy sat around the table. Still they stared at her. Cali Sky smiled, at which point their expressions unanimously relayed to her, in their own irreconcilably divergent ways, the rock bottom truth: "Welcome home."

Later that afternoon Cali Sky awoke from a nap to find Brodie sitting by her side in Philip's spare bedroom. Through the closed door Cali Sky could hear Desiree laugh at some children's program on TV. Cali Sky did not look surprised to see Brodie at her bedside. She stretched and moaned softly.

"How long have you been here? she asked.

"About forty-five minutes."

He was holding a folded-up piece of paper. She saw that he had brought a boom box, which he set on the dresser. Visions of the past returned.

"What's that all about?" she asked, nodding toward the portable stereo. "Do you want me to figure out a song for you?"

He smiled feebly. Cali Sky saw in his eyes that what he wanted to share or say was painful. She saw that he was near tears. She sat up and brushed her hair out of her face. He ran his finger along the folds of the paper.

"They found this," he said, "in Chris's pocket...on the night when he...died."

Cali Sky stared at the paper for a moment, looked up at Brodie then took it from his hands. She unfolded it. In Tam's handwriting it read,

"Hyacinthus,

My love forever.

Thamyrsis"

She looked up at Brodie. "Hyacinthus?" Then it dawned on her. In unison they said, "Synth."

"There's more," said Brodie.

Below Tam's profession of love Cali Sky saw someone else's handwriting. The fourth-grade scrawl had to be Chris's. She read the sloppy words:

"I'm sorry. Please forgive me."

Cali Sky dropped her hands to her lap, still holding the letter.

"So how did Chris get this?" she asked.

"I think he found it...or stole it. Back when he was living at Tam's house."

"And so he found out that Tam was gay."

"If he didn't know already."

She returned the letter to Brodie. Tears blurred her vision. She wiped her eyes with her oversized pajama shirt. Her attention settled on the closet where she half expected to see a guitar. Then she remembered where she was. Turning to Brodie she saw that his eyes were also tear stained.

"Has Tam seen this?" she asked.

Brodie shook his head. "I haven't seen or talked to Tam since...it happened."

Silence followed. The boombox now caught her eye again. The promise of music challenged the silence.

"Push play," Cali Sky said, not knowing what Brodie had in store. He looked from her to the stereo and hesitated.

"Go ahead," she encouraged. "What's the matter?"

He wiped his eyes and said, "This is the new U2 album."

"*The Joshua Tree*?"

He nodded.

A tense organ slowly brought the first song to life, building anticipation, intensified by the entrance of an echoing guitar lick. Brodie adjusted the volume. Cali Sky laid down on the bed. Brodie laid down beside her. For the next fifty minutes and eleven seconds they listened wordlessly. Halfway through the first song Cali Sky understood Brodie's hesitation. What she heard stirred in her awe and disbelief, appreciation and disappointment. She felt like she had heard the album before.

At its conclusion they sat on the edge of the bed. Cali Sky was speechless. Brodie smiled ruefully, then looked at her hesitantly. They read each other's thoughts. "So is this the end?" he asked, already knowing the answer. She looked at him with a restless sorrow seeking new expression. She nodded and, yielding to an impulse for catharsis, leaned over and kissed him lightly and slowly on the lips.

"Let's listen to it again," she whispered.

"Cali Sky, how old were you when you played piano for the first time?" asked Desiree.

"About your age."

"Did you like it?"

Cali Sky nodded. "How about you? Do *you* like it?"

Desiree nodded, just like Cali Sky. She fitfully re-positioned a pillow under her head. Cali Sky re-tucked her in.

"Were you good when you first played?" asked Desiree.

Cali Sky nodded again.

"As good as me?"

"Probably not." She smiled.

"Do you think I'll be as good as you someday?"

"I don't know," began Cali Sky playfully. "Let me see your hands."

Desiree pulled her hands out from underneath the covers. Cali Sky took them into hers and studied them with careful scrutiny, first one side and then the other.

"Well," she concluded. "You have the hands for it. Those are musician's fingers."

Desiree put her hands back under the blankets, looking satisfied and proud. Cali Sky tucked her in yet again.

"But what's most important," she said, placing her hand on Desiree's heart, "is what's in here. What do you feel here when you play?"

Desiree look confused. "I don't know."

"That's okay. When you get older something magical might happen there while you're playing. If it does, then maybe you'll be better than me."

Desiree yawned. "Daddy said he's going to buy me a piano if I keep practicing."

Cali Sky reached toward the lamp on Desiree's dresser and turned it off. She sat back down on the edge of the bed. The nightlight near the doorway faintly illuminated the room.

"Well you know, I have this old piano that I used to play when I was a kid. It's called a Clarendon, and it's like a hundred years old…"

"Whoa."

"If you keep playing maybe I'll give it to you."

"Then what will you play?"

"I don't know. Maybe I'll just listen to you."

"And you can teach me."

Cali Sky nodded. Desiree yawned again.

"Are you sleepy?" asked Cali Sky.

"No."

"Why don't you say your prayer anyway."

"Okay." She folded her hands, just as Cali Sky used to do, and prayed the words Cali Sky prayed for the first thirteen years of her life. Desiree yawned again.

Then she looked concerned and thoughtful. "How old will I be when I feel something in my heart?"

"It's tough to say. Maybe in five years or so."

"How old will I be then?"

"Eleven."

"Will it hurt?"

"Sort of. But a different kind of hurt. It hurts only because the music is so beautiful."

"That's weird."

"I'll tell you a story that might explain."

"Okay."

"Once upon a time," began Cali Sky, "there was this girl who lived in this beautiful valley..."

"Was the girl you?"

"Yes, she's me, but she's also you. Huge mountains surrounded the valley, which was filled with soft grass and tall trees. And right down the center of the valley ran a meandering river of clear water. It bubbled over the rocks and splashed down waterfalls. Near the center of the valley the river moved slowly and swelled along the grassy banks. Sometimes the girl liked to sit on a boulder near one waterfall and listen to the sounds of her valley and watch the moonlight reflect off the leaves way up high on the tallest trees. That's when she began to understand that something so beautiful can also be painful."

Cali Sky saw that Desiree's eyelids were becoming heavy.

"And in the heart of the valley there was a cabin, the girl's cabin. From one of its opened windows she could see the river, the rocks, and the rise and fall of the green meadow stretching all the way to the distant mountains."

Desiree was now asleep.

"One night the girl returned to her cabin after a day of exploring her valley. When she opened the door she saw something hanging from the opened window. She stepped closer. It was a musical instrument with pipes and reeds like an organ. She stepped closer still until it was almost directly above her head. The instrument looked like it yearned to play music. It needed only a breath of wind. The girl kneeled, resting her elbows on the window sill, looking expectantly toward the mountains. The instrument remained silent, for the air was still."

Desiree had fallen into a deeper sleep. She breathed slowly and heavily.

"The girl waited. But the instrument, along with the entire valley, was quiet. She looked toward the windless mountains again and held her breath, listening for the golden notes."